BLACKBERRY HILL

A Novel

By

Rupert Pratt

Blackberry Hill: A Novel

I dedicate this book to the memory of my wife, Millie Pratt, and my other family members, Greg, Jon, Bobbi, Purvesh, Lizzie, Nathan, and Andy, and also to Audrey Meyer and Robert VanBuren, two deceased members of my "Monday Lunch Bunch."

Contents

Part One

1952–1969

A Tangled Morass

Part Two

1969–1970

Return to Blackberry Hill

Part One

1952–1969

A Tangled Morass

CHAPTER ONE

May 1952

Obie Gainsworthy was hot and perspiring after his brisk walk from the Duke University campus. As he approached the brick building where he shared a first-floor apartment with three other seminary students, he was surprised to see his father sitting on the front steps. Had it not been for the rolled-up sleeves of his white dress shirt and a failed Windsor knot in his ancient gray-striped tie, Ken Gainsworthy would have seemed very much out of character.

Trim, with firm muscles showing through his sweat-dampened shirt, Ken appeared younger than sixty-five years. The blistering North Carolina sun on his thinning hair seemed not to concern him.

A fleeting sense of guilt caused Obie to avoid his father's eyes as he shook a calloused hand. "It's good to see you, Dad."

Their last meeting had been at his Grandfather Petitucci's funeral in Albany two years previously, and there had been little time for conversation before Obie returned to North Carolina. That was the only time he'd seen his father over the previous six years. *Was he a neglectful son?* He pushed the thought aside; communication went both ways.

"You wouldn't come to see me, so I've come to you," Ken said in his matter-of-fact manner.

"Why didn't you go in out of the sun? The other guys wouldn't have minded."

"How many in your apartment?"

"There's four of us. There were five, but one joined the army. He's been in Korea for several months. We have room."

"I'll sit out here. It's a nice day."

"Dad, this is unexpected," Obie said as he sat on the steps beside his father. "You hardly ever write . . . only a half-dozen letters during the war, and no more than that while I was at Berkeley, and even less here. Can you see why I'm surprised?"

Ken shuffled his feet and cleared his throat. "Obie, there's something I need to say."

3

"I'm listening."

Ken spoke softly. "I've made a lot of mistakes in my life, Obie, and one of the worst was not appreciating you enough."

"It's okay, Dad, really."

"I had in my head what I wanted you to be, and I couldn't let go of that. But I've finally come to terms with who you are."

The admission was unexpected. During Obie's youth in the Adirondack Mountains, Ken diligently taught self-sufficiency skills but was often indifferent to his son's emotional needs. It was a harsh but accurate truth.

"And who do you think I am, Dad?"

"You're a preacher . . . or you soon will be."

"No, I'm certainly not that, nor will I be. There are many ways to serve God. Have you forgotten that I have a degree in journalism? That's my strength."

"So, will you work for a newspaper or magazine?"

"That's a possibility. But because of this new war, plans can be interrupted. I could be called back into service."

"I sure hope that don't happen. You've served your time." Ken had been sitting with his head down but now looked up, his voice rising. "I'm real proud of you, Son, for that Silver Star medal. I told everybody about it."

"I didn't do anything more to earn it than most of the other men I served with."

"Stafford Rest had a parade for all our boys. If you'd come home, there would've been something in your honor."

Talk of Stafford Rest was something Obie wished to avoid. "You have a medal too, don't you, Dad? Why didn't you tell me that while I was growing up?"

"What good would that have done?"

"It would have made *me* proud of *you.*" He was instantly sorry for the caustic words.

Ken looked down again. "I never liked to talk about the war, my war. Too many bad memories. Maybe that's something you can understand now."

Matt Burroughs' face flashed before him. His friend's death in the closing days of the Italian campaign had been a bitter pill. Hardly a day passed that he didn't think of Matt and of the other men who'd died there. "Yes, Dad, I do understand."

Ken, with his forefinger making imaginary circles on the steps by his feet, hadn't finished his apologies. "I failed you and your mother in many ways. I could've spent more time with her. I'm sorry about that, and I wish I could do it over. And after Vi died, I left you to fend for yourself far too much."

Memories of his mother always brought sadness. Violetta Gainsworthy, the youngest daughter of the emigrant Italian Petitucci family, died of cancer when Obie was thirteen. Obie had realized, even then, that Ken's heavy drinking after her death was to dull the edge of his grief.

"Dad, it's okay. I understand."

Ken was silent for several seconds before saying, "Obie, I've come here to tell you something. Three things, really, and I've come to tell you in person."

"Three things?"

"I've already told you the first . . . that I'm proud of you, proud of everything you've accomplished, and proud of what you'll go on to accomplish."

"That's not much to brag about."

"The second thing is that I've changed. I haven't had a drink in three years, five if you don't count a couple of minor setbacks. Of course, I'll always fight the booze battle, but I'm winning the war. I have steady work at the factory. I'm foreman of the chair section now."

"Dad, I'm happy about that. I really am."

"I hope you'll come back to Stafford Rest."

Those were the annoying words he'd anticipated. Maybe his father had turned his life around. Nevertheless, it had been for Ken's well-being that Obie, at seventeen, had made a hurried exit from Stafford Rest. Abigail Hunt had threatened to murder Obie and his father if he didn't leave. He'd never told anyone the real reason for that hurried departure, nor would he.

Although he no longer feared Abigail, he didn't intend to return to the Adirondacks. He needed his father to understand that. "No, Dad, I won't go back!"

Ken rubbed his chin. "It's because of the Hunt sisters, isn't it?"

"No, I've put all that behind me . . . but I don't need reminders."

Obie had never talked so freely with his father. Maybe that was because of the difference between the ages of seventeen and twenty-six.

"I see Laura sometimes when she comes home, but at a good distance. She has her little boy. He's eight. Danny, I think his name is."

Her little boy! She'd once promised Obie a son. She had given her "little boy" to another man. It had been wrong, the things he and Laura did, reaching the apex of sensuality too soon. Nevertheless, they'd been in love—or so he'd believed. They had sworn eternal devotion, even as Abigail tore them apart.

He'd never learned why Laura married Doctor Benjamin Williamson, a fact revealed just as he was finishing Army basic training. Nor had he seen or talked to Laura since the day he left to enter the service. Anger and bitterness were burdens he endured during two years of the Italian Campaign. The anger softened while at Berkeley, but the need to forgive came only with his decision to attend seminary.

Forgiveness, he'd been told, was what God required. Although she'd cruelly betrayed him, the passage of time would likely have led to conciliation, at least in his own mind; it was her later despicable act that made forgiveness so difficult. She had willfully destroyed his chance for happiness with her sister, Cassie, wrecking Cassie's happiness as well. The memory, when it let it in, galled.

Ken's timely words jerked him back to reality. "I see Cassie real often, too. She still teaches at the grade school."

"How is she?"

"As well as could be expected, I guess."

Obie's sorrow descended every time he heard Cassie's name. His love for her wasn't even in the same galaxy as his youthful lust for Laura. Awareness of Cassie's true feelings for him, and his for her, had grown slowly over their early years, like oaks emerging from acorns but coming to full growth at last.

Then, Laura had managed to uproot their courtship. Vindictive without basis, she was the culprit, the reason for his and Cassie's four years of silence. He'd written several times during his senior year at Berkeley, trying to patch things up, but the letters went unanswered.

"Is she dating anyone?" He couldn't help asking that question, even at the risk of embarrassment.

"I don't think so."

"Cassie deserves to be happy."

Ken studied his face. "It's you she loves," he said. "When she went to you in California, you shouldn't have let her leave. You should've married her then."

"You know about *that?*"

"She told me she was going. After your friend Adam came to visit, she made a special trip up Blackberry Hill. Said she was going to tell you how she felt about you. She was nervous about it because she feared it might endanger your friendship. Might scare you off, she said. I told her that was crazy thinking."

"She said Adam talked her into going out there."

"When she came back, I've never seen anyone happier. Said you were engaged, but not to tell anybody, yet. A month later I saw her in Mercer's General Store. She looked like she'd been crying her eyes out. I don't think I've seen her smile since. I've asked her about it a few times, thinking it might help her to talk, but she wouldn't tell me anything. Said I should ask you."

"You didn't, though."

"You'd of taken it for meddling."

"I don't think so, Dad." *He probably would have.*

"Well, you can tell me now. What *did* happen?"

"Yes, we did become engaged. I loved Cassie very much." He wanted to say, "I still do," but stopped short.

"And she loved you. Still does, I think." After a moment Ken asked, "So what happened?"

"She broke it off three weeks after she went home."

"*She* broke it off?" Ken waited with an expectant look.

"I guess I did my part too." The conversation had become painful. "Dad, I don't want to talk about this."

"So much for your inviting me to meddle."

It was Obie's turn to stare at the steps. Ken meant well.

"It still hurts! We quarreled. We said things we shouldn't have. We reached an impasse. She let it stay that way even with my attempts to make up. I finally gave up on it. I *do* love her, but I have to move on. She should, too."

"I suspect it had something to do with her sister. Am I right?"

Obie wouldn't let himself be roped into explaining details about unpleasantness four years past. "It's all over, Dad. There's no going back. There are issues we couldn't resolve."

"You can't even be friends?"

"It isn't my doing. I'll be her friend again any time she

wants."

If he were anything but blasé about his relationship with Cassie it would invite more questions, so Obie was silent and, to his relief, Ken turned his attention to a floral garden on the other side of the driveway. Obie tried, unsuccessfully, to listen as Ken rattled off the names of flowers and plants.

His thoughts still dwelled on Cassie, however. Her faithful letters throughout the war had carried him through the mental anguish of her sister's betrayal. He and Cassie had been friends all their lives. His mother had been the Hunts' housekeeper, and the three children had grown up seeing one another nearly every day. Nevertheless, it had been the older Laura to whom he was most attracted.

Obie and Cassie continued to write while he was at Berkeley, and she at Syracuse University. Adam Silverman, his wartime squad leader, friend, and later classmate at Berkeley, convinced Obie that Cassie was in love with him. Adam, playing the matchmaker, had also persuaded Cassie that Obie felt the same about her. She flew to California to see him.

Their two days together in Berkeley before the start of his senior year, were joy-filled ones. Their love for each other, built on the foundation of a solid friendship, was finally expressed in words, and Obie asked Cassie to marry him.

After she went home, his expectation was that they would set a wedding date for the following summer. By then, Obie would have graduated from Berkeley and enrolled in seminary; Cassie would have fulfilled her one-year teaching contract in Stafford Rest. They were going to keep their engagement secret so her mother couldn't interfere. Three weeks later, it all blew up.

He became aware that Ken was looking at him, waiting. Obviously, his father's attention had shifted from the flowerbeds and he had asked a question. "I'm sorry, Dad. I didn't hear."

Ken smiled. "I asked you what you're going to do about Cassie. I've told you today that I'm proud of you . . . and I am, but you've also been damned foolish in this instance."

Obie was defensive. "I told you that it wasn't my doing."

"The Hunt girls are nothing alike. Laura's like her bitch of a mother." His father's smirk, as well as his words, revealed long-held feelings. "Thing is, you fell for Laura. She was the wrong one, and it's brought you a heap of misery."

"I'm long over that."

"I think it's what this four-year dispute's all about. It's all about Laura."

"No!" It hurt to lie. Anyway, it was not *about* her. It was *because* of her—what she did.

Ken wasn't fooled, nor was he deterred. "You were foolish back when you were younger. Cassie was right under your nose all along. She loved you. She still loves you. And you're still acting foolishly. Whatever happened between you is something *you* need to fix."

"I've given up on it, Dad. On all romance, really. I don't expect I'll ever marry."

"Then maybe you should have been a priest instead of a preacher. That would probably have pleased your mother and your Aunt Angie."

"That kind of ministry doesn't interest me."

Ken's words had been pointed, but now there came the beginning of a smile. "Maybe we're talking too seriously. I came to tell you something, and I also came to celebrate with you. Unfortunately, I didn't attend your graduation at Berkeley, but I'm not missing this one."

"I'm glad you came, Dad."

"If you're not coming home, where will you go?"

"I like California. But I also have an alternative. We'll see." He wanted to stay away from specifics.

"I'm sure you'll do well wherever you go. How are you doing financially? I can help out."

"I'm okay, Dad. I was appointed assistant pastor of a little church near Blenden Hill two years ago. Didn't pay much, but it helped. It was a one-year appointment because it was closing due to loss of membership. Then they delayed the closure another year and kept me on."

"I thought you didn't want to be a pastor?"

"It was just a part of my training. Being an assistant didn't amount to much more than working with the kids. But I did fill in for the pastor a few times. That helped convince me that being a pastor wasn't for me."

"Well, if you ever need money, you can get a loan against your land."

"What land? What do you mean?"

"Maybe I forgot to mail you the papers about it. Your

grandpa left you the house and ten acres on Blackberry Hill."

"No, I didn't know. And I don't want it. It's your home. You can have it."

"Oh, I'm doing okay. I don't blame Papa for not deeding the land to me. I wasn't very responsible."

"I still don't want it. I'll not go back."

"You can sell it after I die. Just don't sell it to Abigail Hunt. She's been buying up other parcels on the hill. She's asked me several times about our place. I told her it belonged to you. She'll be after you about it as soon as I die."

"I wouldn't sell to her. But, anyway, that would be a long way off."

"I'll keep paying the taxes on it since I'm the one using it."

"As you wish, but I want no part of it." He wanted to leave the subject. "You had *three* things to tell me. You never got to the third."

"Oh yeah! Angie and I are getting married."

There was a moment of surprise but not shock. When Obie returned from Italy nearly eight years earlier, he had met his family members in New York City. His mother's two sisters, Izzie and Angie, had been there with Ken, his brother Abner, and Abner's wife, Claire. Ken and Angie were together a great deal during those three days.

There was nothing inappropriate about it. Angie's husband had died in the war and Obie's mother had been dead for many years. Even Cassie had noticed their continued visits with each other and mentioned it while she was in California. Angie was still dynamic and pretty.

Obie felt good about it. "Congratulations, Dad. You couldn't do better. But why has it taken so long?"

"I guess we're both kind of slow to make decisions."

That night, he gave up his bed for Ken and slept on the porch. More than rough boards delayed sleep. His father's presence, the eve of graduation, and the prospects of following a career his mother had predicted and encouraged were all happenings that should bring joy. But, instead, he could think of little else than his estrangement from Cassie. The conversation with his father had aroused old feelings. The events of four years ago had been resurrected in all ranges of emotion.

CHAPTER TWO

June 1952

Cassie Hunt took a final look around her classroom. The school year had ended the previous day; her student folders were all up to date, and her attendance register had been turned in to the principal's office. Closedown had been easier than in past years because she would take her students to second grade in the fall and occupy the same room. Except for furniture, all the essentials for her students' education were packed away in closets so custodian Hansford Gibbons could clean, wax, and buff the wooden floor.

She stopped by a high window near the door. An added benefit of not changing rooms was keeping the same familiar view. The fifteen-room elementary school sat a block southwest of the Baptist church, whose wooden steeple was visible through the window. Beyond the church was Blackberry Hill, with Cedar Creek flowing down its steep incline. Her eyes searched the area where Obie had lived—where he had grown up.

The one-story frame house, highest on the hill, was small with only two rooms, three if you counted the tiny kitchen. Forty yards from the house was a small Dutch-style barn. Obie had slept there in his "barnroom." He'd also used the room as a painting studio, utilizing the light through a tall window that Vi had added before her death.

Cassie had gone up there to visit Ken two years before and had been drawn to the unlocked barnroom. A familiar musty barn smell of old hay seemed never to dissipate. A kerosene lantern, covered by years of dust accumulation, sat on a battered oak table. Near a wood stove was Obie's bunk, with the mattress rolled and covered with a yellowed sheet. In a corner, under a layer of burlap bags, were his paintings, many unfinished. His wooden palette, scraped clean but still stained with residue of oil pigments, lay on the windowsill. She'd cried and made up her mind never to go back. Nevertheless, she remained powerless to stop watching the hill.

11

Cedar Creek Road, more of a pathway in its upper section, ended by the house. The road was too steep for vehicles to overcome the snows of winter and spring mud. But today was a dry June day, and she could see Ken's truck parked by the house. He'd returned two weeks previously from North Carolina. She'd hoped to learn details about Obie's graduation from seminary, but she wouldn't go up there. Instead, she would catch Ken in town.

How different it might have been had Ken gone to North Carolina to see Obie *and* Cassie. *They should have been together, married.* That had been their plan, and the weeks after her trip to California had been the happiest of her life. Finally, after years of frustration, of hoping he'd forget her sister and come to love her, it had happened—or it seemed so.

She'd accepted Adam Silverman's words of certainty about Obie loving her and had gone to California to hear it from him. That act of faith paid off; Obie asked her to marry him. She'd returned to Stafford Rest expecting to set a marriage date for the following summer. She'd wanted to shout the news out to everyone in Stafford Rest, to carry a giant banner declaring her love for Obie Gainsworthy. But then, Laura came to town.

She wasn't going to think about it. Turning from the window, she picked up a bag holding items from her desk that she'd need during the summer. With nothing more to do in the building, she walked three blocks to her apartment on Main Street.

She had lived over Hoovers Hardware for three years. Small, with a miniature parlor and one bedroom, the apartment was easy to care for. A window by a breakfast nook in the back afforded a splendid view of the park and Diamond Lake across the low roofs of two other buildings.

For a year after graduation from Syracuse University, she'd lived with her parents—a bad experience. Her amiable father let her live her own life; he was at the factory all day supervising his growing furniture manufacturing business. However, with flexible time, Abigail's real estate enterprise allowed her to show up at unpredictable hours. Cassie had little privacy, so when Hattie Bradford left her apartment to live with her son in Johnstown, she moved in.

Her mother was mortified that she chose to live in such a "tiny, noisy place." Abigail did respect Cassie's privacy after the move, except for a daily phone call; it was a small concession for

12

the privilege of having her own living space. She walked up to Garnet Point on Saturdays, where Abigail served a meal. At other times all three ate at Beth's Café. Beth Clarington still served the best food in town.

On this day, Cassie put together a simple evening meal. "Simple" had become a habit. "Boring fare," Laura said the last time she visited Cassie.

What Cassie ate mattered little to her; there wasn't much interest in food nowadays. Teaching was what lifted her from her moods. She wasn't looking forward to the long summer and might look for a job. Maybe the new church camp at the upper end of the lake would need another counselor.

After finishing her meal, she sat at the window sipping herbal tea and watching the sunset over the higher hills beyond the lake. She stayed there through dusk until the room was dark. Only then did she move away from the window to sit on her couch and try to read a novel started three weeks previously. She finally put it aside and surrendered to her terrible obsession with replaying the sequence of events that had destroyed her happiness.

Two days with Obie in Berkeley had been both joyous and frustrating. They had declared their love; his intensity had thrilled her and wiped away years of frustration from wanting to hear those words. They decided they would marry in a year, during the summer before Obie started seminary. They lay in each other's arms all through their two nights together. She would gladly have given herself to him, but he had made "a covenant with God" and felt such intimacy would violate it. He'd wanted her, though, she was sure.

On the second day, they toured the university campus. Obie introduced her to some of his professors. Hershel Silverman, Adam's uncle, made the most significant impression.

"Is this your young lady?" Silverman asked.

"Yes, Doctor Silverman, she is. We've been friends as long as either of us can remember."

"Obie and I were born the same day," Cassie said. Obie had grinned at that; she was trying to annoy him as she had when they were children. As a child, he'd been embarrassed to have that fact advertised, assuring that she announced it at every opportunity.

Hershel gave his full attention to Cassie. His fuzzy-haired

head jerked up and down as he talked, giving her the impression of a rag doll on a string. "Obadiah is living his dream here at Berkeley, and forming his future," he said. "Your friend has promise, Cassie. And I have a question, my dear. Will *you* have a prominent part in his future?"

Cassie wasn't sure how to answer. They'd agreed to keep their engagement a secret, so she was unsure whether their silence on the matter extended to those beyond Stafford Rest.

Obie came to her aid. "Doctor Silverman, Cassie and I will always be friends if that's what you mean."

"I'm sorry, I guess I spoke out of turn. My nephew, Adam, said you two were . . . entangled. It seems he, too, spoke out of turn."

Obie had laughed, she'd believed, to save her embarrassment. But, then, he'd said, "Adam's forever saying something like that."

She had found herself staring at the floor of Doctor Silverman's office. That was the moment she should have recognized warning signs that things may not be as they seemed.

She said, "Yes, Obie does have a bright future, and I hope to be a part of it."

She had expected him to validate that, but he'd said nothing.

They spent that afternoon in a park on the Bay. Once, they removed their shoes and waded in the water. Later, they dined at an outdoor cafe off University Avenue. Parting had been difficult, but the promise of their future together had made it easier.

Cassie had started that school year, her first teaching position, adjusting and getting settled, but it was hard to keep her mind on her duties. So when Laura and Danny came from Boston for a short visit the following weekend, Cassie found it difficult not to give her the good news. If Laura and Obie had been strangers, she would not have hesitated, but given their history, she vacillated about whether to even tell her.

A chance came for the sisters to talk privately. The morning was cool, so they sat in the enclosed portion of the flagstone-floored patio on the lake side of the Hunt home. They sat side by side on a metal glider.

"You were here only a month ago," Cassie said.

"I came back because I worry about Dad. He complained

of chest pains while we were last here."

Laura sipped coffee and set her cup on the table in front of the glider, a move that looked deliberately slow. Laura was familiar with fabrication but was never good at it.

"Dad's all right."

"I know that now."

Cassie waited, for she believed that Laura's real reason for coming to Stafford Rest was to hear about Cassie's trip to California; She would suspect that Cassie had gone there to see Obie. Keeping the engagement secret from Abigail was one thing, but the sisters were always honest with each other—to a point. Laura would want to know everything.

She got right to it. "Cassie, how was your trip?"

"Good. Very good."

There was an awkward silence. It was apparent Laura had more to say.

"Okay, sister. What is it?" Cassie asked.

"You saw Obie, didn't you?" Laura stared at her, waiting.

"Yes, I spent two nights with him." She was, at once, sorry to have given that information for how it might be interpreted. Cassie waited for some emotional reaction, but Laura's expression hardly changed, except for an uncharacteristic hardness around her eyes.

Laura said, "You always wanted that. I hope that will be the end of it."

"Oh, we didn't do anything! Obie, as usual, was a gentleman."

"You're still in love with him, aren't you, Cassie?"

"That's never been a secret from you, has it?"

Laura was biting her lip. "Does Mom know?"

"Only that I went to California. So far, she hasn't asked for details."

"She will."

"Laura, why does Mom hate Obie so much?" She'd asked the question before but had never received a satisfactory answer. She didn't expect one now.

"She has her reasons."

"You said something to me once that bothered me. You said I could do better than Obie. That was after I asked you to tell me what happened between you and why you married Ben."

"And I still don't want to talk about it."

15

Cassie had felt her anger growing. "I get so tired of hearing that! Always the insinuation of something behind your careful words, some secret about Obie making him, as Mom used to say, 'beneath' us."

Through a frozen frown, Laura said, "I'm assuming that since nothing happened between you and Obie, nothing is going to happen. If that's the case, then it's best to let it rest."

"Damn it, Laura, sometimes you're impossible to talk to! If you know a reason I shouldn't marry Obie, you should tell me."

"*Marry?* Laura touched Cassie's arm. Her expression was one of compassion. "Dear, dear, Cassie! Please don't speak of marriage to Obie."

"That needs some explanation."

"Not an explanation. Just a warning! Obie's not what you believe him to be. You should listen to Mom."

"What did he do, Laura? *Tell me!*"

"I can't. You can ask him, but I'm sure he won't tell you."

"You can't leave me hanging like this. I love Obie. He's asked me to marry him. We're engaged." The words came before she could stop them, but she was too upset to care.

Laura grabbed her shoulder and squeezed. "You must not, Cassie! It would disgrace our family. You must not!"

Cassie felt tears forming. Her words tumbled out. "And why not? He's the only man I've ever loved, or ever will. I've saved myself for him since we were little. I hated it when he fell in love with you . . . hated *you*, even. And I was overjoyed when you gave him up for Ben."

"Cassie, I didn't *give him up*. It was the other way around. He gave *me* up!"

Cassie studied Laura's face for evidence that she was lying. Maybe she still wanted Obie for herself. For love, her sister might be capable of that.

"That's nonsense!" Cassie said. "Obie wouldn't do such a thing."

"He would, and he did."

"Tell me what happened. *Please.*"

Laura relaxed her grip on Cassie's shoulder and sat back on the glider. She sighed. "I can't go into more detail. I promised Mom."

"So, Mom knows something, too?"

"Yes, and I'm not going to say anymore." She faced Cassie.

"Do you love me, sister?"

"You know that I do."

"Do you trust me to tell you the truth?"

Cassie was unsure but said, "I do trust you. However, you're not really telling me anything?"

"You only need to know that you must have nothing more to do with Obie. I love you and want to save you from heartbreak . . . the kind I had."

Cassie's frustration had reached a tipping point. "You're lying, Laura! Why are you saying these things about Obie?"

"Because they're true."

"You still love him, don't you? You want him back. You're trying to keep us apart."

Laura had a horrified look. "Don't be ridiculous. I'm married. Happily married!"

"No, you're not. I've watched you and Ben together." Cassie was sorry the conversation had taken such a dreadful turn. She tried bringing her emotions under control. "I'm sorry, Laura." she said, "I'm just trying to sort out what you're saying from what I know of Obie. I think you're wrong. There's been an awful mistake somewhere."

"No, no mistake. You can do as you wish, but I've told you. I've done my duty."

Cassie had left the patio, upset. She decided, rather than brood, she would call Obie. Wanting privacy, she walked to the new grocery store at the foot of the hill where there was a pay phone.

Their conversation began badly. "Obie, this is not going to be a pleasant call."

"Why? What's wrong, Cassie?"

She told him about her conversation with Laura and made no effort to assuage what had passed between the sisters or to hide her uncertainty. Obie listened quietly. Cassie finally asked, "What *did* you do to her, Obie?"

"That sounds like an accusation."

"I'm only trying to get to the bottom of an upsetting situation."

She could feel his anger. "What difference does it make, anyway? She's married and living happily in a big house in Boston with her four-year-old son. That's what she wanted. And, incidentally, she's lying to you."

"Why would she do that, Obie?"

"You tell me! She's your sister. You know more about what makes her tick than I do."

"Laura's told some white lies in her time, but I've never known her to tell a lie serious enough to hurt anyone."

"It seems this might be the first, then."

"Obie, damn it, don't get angry at me. I'm confused and trying to find the truth."

"Cassie, what else but truth do you expect from me? When I tell you I've done nothing to hurt your sister, that *is* the truth."

"Not according to her."

"Then, who are you going to believe?"

That may have been the moment her doubts overcame her better judgment and caused her to say things that would doom their future together. "You've never said anything to me about what happened between you. You've been silent on the subject in all the years we've written to each other. I've often wondered why. Have you been hiding something?"

"You think I'd do that?"

"Well, you have kept things from me."

"Like what?"

"You and Laura, what you did back then . . . you know."

"Back then, as you say, was none of your business. It was between Laura and me."

"After that, you never said anything."

"You never asked, not in so many words, anyway."

She hesitated but said, "Well, if you're so honest, you can tell me now."

"What do you want to know, Cassie?"

"Were you and Laura having sex?"

"Of course we were. I doubt that it surprises you."

It had bothered her that he answered the question so quickly without some preamble. It was unlike him. "Yes, I suspected, but that doesn't matter now. What matters is that you tell me the truth about your breakup. This matters a great deal to me. Tell me what happened."

She could hear him breathing. She waited. When words did come, they were measured, detached. "I did nothing wrong. She stopped writing to me before I finished basic training in South Carolina and never told me why. So it was a bombshell when I received your letter telling me of her marriage to Ben

Williamson."

"And why do you think she stopped writing?"

"The only answer making any sense is that your mother filled her head with the idea that her place in the world was privileged. Ben Williamson came along and was the answer to that delusion. She grabbed at the chance to have what your mother wanted for her and what I couldn't give her. She didn't love me enough . . . or maybe not at all. Maybe she's disillusioned with her life now. I don't know why she's blaming me. She is, though, and it won't work."

"She's miserable. She may still be in love with you."

Cassie thought she heard him utter a vulgarity. Then he said, "Goodbye, Cassie. Call me again when you've come to your senses." He had hung up.

After two worry-filled days, and after Laura returned to Boston, Cassie called him again. "Obie, I'm sorry. I shouldn't have doubted you. I love you. Please forgive me."

"Cassie, of course, you're forgiven. I love you, too. I shouldn't have hung up on you. It was childish. What's changed your mind?"

"I realized you and Laura believe what you're saying is true. Anger can do that sometimes. It's forgivable." From his intake of breath, she knew at once that she'd said the wrong thing."

"Cassie, you said you loved me. Yet, you still doubt my word. Love and trust go together."

"Obie, I do love you, but I think you've convinced yourself that Laura coldheartedly turned away from you to another man. I believe she made a mistake in marrying Ben, but don't you think she would have let you know if she had changed her mind about you? She must have written . . . and something must have happened to her letter."

"Are you saying she wrote a letter to me about her change of mind?"

"Well, no, I'm not saying that. She's told me very little."

"Doesn't that say something?" There was a pause. "Okay, let's say she did write, and the letter was lost. It's possible, but I wrote several letters asking if she was ill or upset. She never answered those. I even called your house. Don't you remember? I talked to you. You said she was all right."

"Yes, I do remember that. You didn't want me to tell her

about your call."

"Doesn't it convince you I wasn't ditching her? I was trying to get in touch."

His logic had given Cassie pause. Their relationship might still have been salvageable had she not said, "Mom dislikes you for some reason. You must know why. Are you going to tell me?" He was silent. "Did you and Mom have words over Laura?" Did she discover what the two of you were doing in your barnroom?"

"You're jumping to conclusions, Cassie."

"Mom found out, didn't she? That's why she dislikes you so much."

"I'm not going to talk about it . . . or about your mother."

"Why not?"

"Because it serves no purpose. You've made up your mind that I've done something terrible. And it's been my experience that when *you* make up your mind about something, there's little chance of anyone changing it. You're too stubborn! Cassie. The fact is, I'm getting tired of this whole conversation. I'm not going to keep making denials about something I have no knowledge of. Can we leave this topic?"

For four years, the words she should have said played in her head like a ghost recording. *"Yes, Obie, let's forget it and get back to loving each other and setting a date for our wedding."* But instead, she said, "No, I want to learn the truth about this, or it will be an obstacle between us."

He hadn't hesitated. "Then we'd better take a break from each other until you come to your senses."

"What about our wedding plans?"

"Do what you want. *You* make the decisions."

"Do you even want to marry me? You couldn't tell Doctor Silverman that we were engaged. You just said we'd always be friends. It hurt me."

"We said we would keep it secret until the right time. That's why I said what I did."

"I think Laura may have been right."

"What do you mean?"

"You're not what you seem. You're doing it again, aren't you? You're running out on the one who loves you?"

"No, Cassie, I'm not running out. I'll be waiting for you when you get your head straightened out. I love you."

"I'll probably never see you again!"

"You're angry. Take a few days and call me again."

"No, I won't call." She had wanted to hurt. "I don't love you. I've loved someone who never was. It's over with us!"

"You don't mean that, sweetheart. Call me when you calm down."

"I'll not call!"

"I'll call you then."

"Don't. Don't write, either," she said as she hung up.

He had written that first year. She'd burned his letters without opening them. *Why had she done that?* Now, she agonized, and life was empty. It was ironic that the reason for their disagreement no longer had a feeling of importance. Laura had moved on to her Bostonian lifestyle and childrearing. When she came back to Stafford Rest, she never mentioned Obie.

Cassie had, several times, considered swallowing her pride and calling him in North Carolina. But, as time passed, she believed he'd lost interest. Why else would he stop writing? He wouldn't have given up so quickly if he loved her.

Her girlish dream about being meant for each other had gone on too long. Anyway, there was that ember of doubt that had been fanned to life, an ember the winds of cynicism sometimes fanned into blue flame—causing her to agonize over her conflicting feelings. Cassie had dug a hole for herself, one from which she seemed unable to escape. She still loved Obie and probably always would, but she must take measures to move on.

A visitor was coming the next day. She'd met Edward Jackson in California. After leaving Obie, she'd gone across the Bay for a brief visit with an old classmate, Judy Ramos. Judy had introduced them. Cassie had hardly given Ed any attention.

He'd called from Albany, having gone to the trouble of finding her phone number. He had another day's work in the Capitol District but was willing to travel extra miles to see her, so she invited him to visit. She was flattered that he remembered her after four years.

Her humdrum life allowed few social contacts. Most teachers at the school lived in Tupper Lake, Evergreen, Saranac Lake, or even farther away. She'd been asked out frequently by local men and by one single male teacher. She had consistently declined.

Maybe it was time to get Obie out of her head. Being an

old maid was not an appealing prospect. Seeing Edward Jackson from San Francisco would be interesting.

CHAPTER THREE

July 1952–April 1953

Three days after graduation from seminary, Obie enrolled in the Army Chaplain School at Fort Slocum. The "alternate idea," hinted to his father, had become a reality. Entry of the United States into the Korean War had concerned him, as it did many seminary students. During "his war," issues had been clear. He'd emerged from that conflict with the idealistic belief that they were about to enter a world without war, where humankind had finally learned better ways of solving disputes. Therefore, rushing to aid a people so far away and so removed from the American way of life, humane as it might be, was a solution hard to fathom.

Along with other classmates, he'd watched President Truman's nationally televised speech about the war. Reactions to the address were varied. One fellow seminary student argued that American involvement was justified because North Korea, the Democratic People's Republic of Korea, was anything but democratic and, with the support of godless Soviets, had attacked South Korea across the 38th Parallel. Therefore, the South must be protected, he insisted. Obie was sure there was more to it.

There were many nights following Truman's speech when images of battle came in dreams, sometimes intruding into the reality of daylight hours—and they persisted. Thoughts about serving as a military chaplain were random initially but gradually edged into his consciousness. Two years into his seminary training, he decided to reenlist after graduation.

During his father's visit on graduation weekend, Obie had implied a desire to follow a career in journalism. He felt guilty at the deception because his plans were already firmly in place. But journalism was in his blood, and he was sure it could be used in the military. And there would be time for it when he returned to civilian life. Being an Army chaplain was what he felt called to do at this time.

He considered the United States' presence in the war questionable, but fighting men deserved support. For him, there would be no more killing; his pledge to God was that he would never again pick up a rifle for battle. During his youth, a time of innocence, he'd declared his intention of becoming a conscientious objector. But Laura's betrayal, and his anger over it, had derailed that plan. Then, the death of his friend Matthew Burroughs and the "incident at the wall" renewed his resolve to lay down arms.

The wall incident had occurred near the war's end. Right after Matt's death, a young German prisoner standing near an Italian farmer's stone wall had pulled what Obie believed was a pistol from his pocket. Obie had killed him. The "pistol" turned out to be a Bible in which he discovered a marked passage that nearly matched one he'd underlined in his Bible. His impulsive act haunted him for three years but eased after he reclaimed his youthful dream of living a life of service. But, even now, guilt and other painful memories surfaced without warning.

Obie had laid the groundwork required for entering the Chaplains Corps, and two years of service in the soon-to-be-torn-down little church helped him meet the requirements of civilian ministry. That, and his seminary education, should have been enough, but he asked for and received a letter of recommendation from the Reverent Charles Lansing for insurance. Charles had been the minister at Stafford Rest Methodist Church when Obie, at age thirteen, lost his mother. He became Obie's friend and mentor, and their correspondence continued over the years.

The Slocum mail system delivered a short and unexpected letter to Obie one day. It had a Boston postmark.

Dear Obie,   *July 14, 1952*

Finally, after months (years, really) of trying to catch up with you, I did the smart thing and wrote to your father. I will be in New York City next Saturday, the 19th. There is an Italian restaurant at Mulberry and Broom. If you can, meet me there for dinner at 1800 hours.

Yours truly, Adam

The note was a pleasant surprise. His friend, Adam Silverman, had graduated from Berkeley two years ahead of Obie with a degree in economics and had gone to work for his father at Silverman Financial in New York City.

They hadn't seen each other for four years, nor had they exchanged letters. While at Duke, and failing to reach Adam by phone, Obie wrote to his last New York address, but the letter was returned unopened. Once he reached New York, he'd planned to visit Silverman Financial in hopes of learning something from Adam's father. But unfortunately, his busy training schedule had made that impossible.

Their friendship spanned two distinct phases. In the first, Adam was his squad leader, already a seasoned combat soldier by the time Obie reached Italy. Adam called himself a "tough taskmaster," but his genteel side surfaced in quiet moments. Nevertheless, he was obsessed with killing Germans because of how they were treating "his people."

Obie had gone with him to the Jewish ghetto of Rome to look for his uncle's family. There, Adam learned that the Nazis had taken his uncle, wife, and teenage daughter to Germany. The disturbing news had sent him on a killing rampage.

At Berkeley, after the war, Adam cast off his hate and readied himself for a career in the financial field. Nevertheless, he exhibited dissatisfaction on a visit back to Berkeley during Obie's senior year; Obie was anxious to learn what had transpired in recent years. He managed to get a pass to meet his friend.

Adam, already seated at the restaurant when Obie arrived, had a positive aura about him, something not apparent at their last meeting. "So, you've become a preacher man after all?" were his first words as he arose from the candlelit corner table.

"Hardly," Obie said as they shook hands. Adam's hand was callused, which seemed odd.

They ordered wine. "We should not have been out of touch for so long," Adam said.

"Let's not let it happen again. So, what have you been doing?"

"I could make a long story of it, but the shorter version is that I split from Silverman Financial a few months after the last time I last saw you. Father has practically disowned me."

"What happened?"

"Do you remember me telling you that what I was doing didn't feel right, that there was something else for me that I couldn't put my finger on?"

"I remember."

"I finally got a finger on it."

"Wonderful! *What?*"

"It got to the point that I couldn't stand it anymore. I might have gotten through it and stayed with the firm if I hadn't had something else on my mind. But I did. I'd discovered a cause that wouldn't let me go."

Obie leaned forward. "Tell me."

"It's my people and their welfare. I've been in Israel, near Tel Aviv, for the last two years."

"But, how . . .?"

"It'd been gnawing at me since forty-eight when Israel became a nation. As soon as the Knesset passed the Law of Return, I couldn't wait any longer. I told Father I wanted to make a prolonged visit, hoping for his approval. After all, he'd applauded the formation of the Jewish state. But Father has his own agendas, and my going to Israel wasn't one of them. We had a serious breakup. We're speaking again now, but just barely."

"What's this Law of Return?"

"All Jews, and anyone with Jewish ancestry, along with their spouses, have a right to settle in Israel and become Israeli citizens."

"And you did that?"

"I did. And you won't believe what I've been doing there. I'm a farmer."

Obie had to laugh because of the improbability. "Isn't that a waste of your education?"

"Not at all. You and I once discussed the importance of connections, something you said you learned from your mother. Working in the soil connects me to something basic, feeding people. We're forging an agricultural system where little or none existed. It gives me a sense of helping, in this case helping a young nation and its people. I imagine it must feel like the years following the American Revolution felt here."

"What's it like?"

"Lots of problems. Jews from all over, two hundred thousand or more speaking different languages. Common Yiddish helps, but it's not something most of us have ever relied on in our daily contacts. And housing is impossible. There are temporary shelters all over the country. The government is doing what it can, but it's tough."

"But I see that you love it."

"Absolutely."

"Are you back here just to visit?"

"That's part of it. I've missed my sister. I also came to raise money. It's what I was doing in Boston. It's taken a vast amount of money to make Israel work. American Jews have contributed much. I've raised several million from Bostonians alone."

"So, you're not *just* a farmer?"

"That's right; I have other responsibilities. I'm also an officer in the Army reserves."

"Adam, I'm sure your skills will put you at the forefront in your new country."

Adam ignored the compliment. "I'm going to hit Father up for money, as well. He's already made substantial contributions, but I'm going to ask him for an amount that will stagger even him."

"Despite your being on the outs?"

"Naomi has been working to soften him up. I'll get the money. But what about you, Obie? Of course, I've known about your career change, but you never gave me details."

"Do you remember me talking about my friend Charles Lancing?

"I do. The minister. You had letters from him in Italy."

"We've always kept in touch. Before my senior year at Berkeley, Charles suggested I 'go into the wilderness for prayer and meditation.' I did . . . to please him. I fasted and meditated for three days and three nights. Adam, it changed my life."

Adam laughed. "That must have been hard at Berkeley. It's not much of a wilderness."

"It was in a Russian River Valley vineyard. I'd been working there all summer."

"And was this a religious experience?"

"It was more like a dream, only more vivid."

"A vision?"

"Maybe. I prefer to think of it as a dream. Visions come to prophets and saints. I'm neither."

"Yes, we certainly agree about that." The candlelight

revealed Adam's impish smile.

"I believe that God does speak to us, but in gentle ways, with nudges and insights."

"And in dreams?"

"Our Bible, and yours too, have many examples of dreams that have meaning."

"And you believe that your dream has meaning?"

"I can't say with certainty that God was telling me something, but it felt that way."

"Tell me about it?"

"You'll think it's crazy."

"Obie, you changed your career because of a dream. I want to hear more about it."

He could see that Adam's interest was genuine, but he hesitated and gave a condensed version. Adam listened intensely. When Obie finished the narrative and sat back, Adam said, "That's very interesting, Gainsworthy, but give me a few more details."

Obie had never shared his deeper feelings about the experience with anyone before. Adam, the sergeant in Italy, and Adam, the roommate at Berkeley, had always been able to draw him out. It seemed that hadn't changed.

"She was so real, my mother. I could smell her perfume and feel the warmth of her hands. She led me out of the vineyard and to the steps of Stafford Rest Methodist. I saw deceased people there."

"Who?" Obie was pleased that Adam wasn't laughing. He did seem caught up in the details.

"Family members and soldiers we knew. They all seemed at peace."

"I'll bet Burke wasn't there."

Burke had been the "tough guy" of their platoon. "You're wrong. He was. He asked me for spiritual water."

"Spiritual water?"

"In my dream, it seemed I was a dispenser of spiritual blessings . . . in the form of water. People on the church steps asked me to throw water on them."

Adam sat forward in his chair. "That's pretty symbolic stuff, Gainsworthy. Water is a universal symbol for Spirit, isn't it?"

"I believe so, but maybe this was just a dream from my

subconscious about how I want things to be."

"Maybe, but it seems to have had a powerful influence on your life."

"I guess it has."

"So maybe you shouldn't be calling it 'just a dream.'"

"Isn't that what you'd call it?"

"I think you have preconceived notions about me, Gainsworthy. The truth is that I'm open to the validity of mystic occurrences."

Obie was surprised. Adam had been factual to a fault in both military and private life. Maybe he *had* changed; it had been four years.

That speculation caused him to reconsider mentioning a detail he thought might bring up old hurts. "I saw members of your family there."

Adam's eyebrows shot up. "Who?"

"Your Uncle Yarden and Aunt Shira and your cousin Jael."

Obie thought he saw the start of tears in Adam's eyes. "I dream about them too," he said as he cupped his hands around his wine glass, looking ready to say more but remaining silent.

"I was surprised to see them there on the steps of a Christian church."

"Yes, that would be a stretch."

"Yarden told me that there's only one Spirit."

"Meaning one God?"

"That's how I interpreted it."

"And that's from your subconscious?"

"Maybe, but it's affected my theological thinking."

"Obie, maybe you've been smacked in the head with the truth. Don't dismiss it as something else."

Obie waited, but apparently, Adam had no more to say on the subject. "So that's my story," Obie said.

"I'm glad for you, Obie. However, your joining the Army again is another matter. What *are* you thinking? You've paid your dues. Why can't you just let somebody else do it?"

"It's different this time. I'm not an infantryman. I'll be a chaplain. I might not even go to Korea."

"Yes, you will. They'll be delighted to get someone with your experience. And, you'll probably make a career in the Army."

"I'd have to think about that. I expect I'll have to serve

some time somewhere in the States first, but I'm looking forward to Korea. I can provide the supportive help needed in battle zones. I've been in battle. I can make a difference."

"I'm sure you will." Adam paused to refill his glass from the wine bottle. "Are you leaving behind any women this time?"

"No, there's nothing like that in my life, and there won't be."

"I thought you and Cassie would make a go of it. As you know, I tried to help it happen. Your father said you hadn't made up, but he didn't give me any details."

Obie felt the pain again, as always when he heard her name. "That was a terrible time," he admitted.

He'd called Adam twice in the space of a few weeks, once to thank him for traveling to Stafford Rest and talking to Cassie, and then again to tell him about their breakup.

Obie retold the story, briefly in detail, while struggling to avoid venting about Laura's part. He said, "As for Cassie, it seems I've lost even her friendship."

As usual, Adam spoke frankly. "You're still a fool, Obie. You should have camped on her doorstep until she let you in. She would have, I suspect, from what your father says."

"No, it's over. Anyway, how can *you* give me love advice? You hardly dated at Berkeley. Is there someone in Israel?"

"No, but there's someone here in the city. It's another reason I came back. The main one, really."

"Tell me about her."

"She's a doctor, a physician. Rachel is her name. I met her some months before I left for Israel. We corresponded. She's returning with me this time. We'll be married there."

"Adam, you rascal!" Obie reached out to grab Adam's hand. "You had that news and weren't telling me? How could you?"

Adam laughed. "I was getting around to it, just waiting for the right moment."

"Congratulations! I wish I could meet her. You should have brought her tonight."

"I was going to, but she was called in to work. She's a resident at Presbyterian. She's anxious to go to Israel. Physicians are much in need there."

"What does your family think of her?"

"Rachel and Naomi are good friends. Father doesn't know

about our engagement yet, although he's met and likes her. I'm hopeful that she and Naomi can help smooth things between Father and me. This is the happiest time of my life. There's Rachel . . . and it's the first time I'm doing something I truly enjoy."

After dinner, they parted with promises to meet again.

"Until next time," Adam said.

"Until next time," Obie echoed.

* * *

Obie had been in Korea for three months. His request for Korean duty was granted after two months as an assistant chaplain at Fort Benning. Although he'd been encouraged to hone his "pastoral skills" longer in a benign environment, he pressed the matter. Whether through persistence, or luck, he received new orders and, not long after that, boarded a troop ship in San Diego with two other chaplains. He was glad for the ship chaplain's invitation to assist with services on a rotating basis, for it kept his mind off seasickness.

His Korean experience was proving more difficult than anticipated. There was never enough time to finish any job. He held regular services when he could, but units were constantly moving, making it hard to keep up.

The past three days had been relatively quiet, and Obie was dispatching endless paperwork. He looked up from his wooden crate desk as someone approached.

"Lieutenant Gainsworthy, sir." The emphasis was on the "sir." The lanky soldier stood at attention and executed the correct military protocol. "Sir, Private First Class Anthony Gladstone reporting for duty, sir!" The man's thick glasses magnified his eyes to owl-like proportions. Obie's first reaction was a silent question: *How could anyone with those eyes possibly be in the Army?*

"At ease, private."

The slouch-shouldered soldier assumed a stance resembling the parade-rest position. He looked about twenty-one, maybe a little older. From his speech patterns, Obie guessed that he was a mid-westerner.

"Are you my new assistant, Private Gladstone?"

"Yes sir, I am indeed, sir."

Obie smiled. "Relax, Gladstone. Sit." Obie indicated an upended wooden box like the one on which he was sitting,

31

furniture a sympathetic cook had supplied. "I've been expecting you. Tell me about yourself."

Obie had been without help for more than a week. His former assistant had finished his tour of duty and returned to the States. Obie missed Stevens for his endless repertoire of sanitized jokes and his bravery. He'd been willing to go anywhere Obie went, which sometimes had an element of danger. He hoped Gladstone was the same caliber, despite first impressions.

Gladstone appeared tired, which was understandable once he explained that he'd been in a group ferried from Japan to Pusan, farther south. After that, they'd taken a train north to the front. That ride had been an exercise in patience; add to it the anxiety of entering a war zone, and it was no mystery why some men often arrived in a bewildered state of mind.

Obie was right about the accent; Gladstone was from Wichita. He was twenty-two, had graduated from Kansas State the previous May, and was immediately drafted. He'd planned to enter seminary.

"I want to be a Methodist minister," Gladstone said. "When I was drafted, I told them I'd rather not kill people. So, I guess this is my seminary for the present. I asked the Lord to put me where I could be the most service . . . and here I am."

Obie was curious. "What about your eyesight? You'll have clerical work, and we go often into the field. It's important that you function well enough to help me there." Nothing was gained by avoiding a subject where lives are at stake. "Is it going to be an issue?"

"No, sir." Gladstone removed his glasses. "I can see well enough without them." His squinting did nothing to convince Obie.

Gladstone continued, "You don't have to worry about it, sir. I'm strong, and I'm swift." Obie was unsure if he was speaking of his speed of foot or his mental capacity.

Obie had been writing letters to families of men killed in action, a heartbreaking business. Causalities had increased each month since his December arrival. By April, the numbers had become overwhelming. So he put Gladstone to work typing letters on company typewriters when available and writing by hand when not. He found his new assistant more than capable of those chores.

Until the end of February, Obie had been well back of the

battle lines. He'd since been ministering to men retaking contested hills from the Chinese. Old wounds to his mind were reopened on the first day when he bent down to a man on a stretcher with an arm and a leg blown away.

"God, will we never learn?" he had said aloud.

While assigned to Chaplin Jim Forrester in Italy, he'd learned important lessons useful in these new situations; as the chaplain had modeled, Obie tried to be a conduit between God and man. He made himself accessible to everyone who needed him.

Services were usually held in the open, regardless of the weather. He avoided giving flowery messages, speaking plainly and simply, soldier to soldier, about surviving the war in body and spirit.

North Korea had forced its communist ideology on the citizens, but pockets of dedicated Christians still existed, and Obie tried to contact them. Some came forward as word got around. Together with a Catholic chaplain, Mass, and his own services, were held in secret locations. Although a few other chaplains did the same, one of his superior officers questioned the practice. "You'll get them killed if we pull out and word gets back to the communists."

Something else learned from Forrester was that the relationship between a chaplain and those with whom he worked must be one of friendship and trust. While Obie and Gladstone observed military protocol, Obie encouraged his assistant to openness. He probed him about his religious background not long after his arrival, more to get him talking than to pry.

"I come from a long line of ministers," Gladstone said. "My grandfather moved from Virginia to Kansas in the eighteeneighties. He was a Methodist turned Presbyterian. All the rest of my family were solid Methodists."

"What happened to change your grandfather?"

"He had a falling out with my great-grandfather. It was so bitter he changed churches, as well as location."

"How far back can you trace your Methodist line?"

"There's an unbroken string of preachers back to Francis Asbury. Asbury's not in my ancestry, of course, because he had no children. What I meant was that one of my ancestors was one of his circuit riders . . . an iterate preacher."

Gladstone had become comfortable with Obie, who let him

ramble on. The young man had great faith, something he would never discourage. Obie asked him, "And you don't want to break the string of preachers in your family? Is that it?"

"Yes, sir, that's it for sure. But my ambition goes further."

They were unpacking boxes of books Obie had ordered to make available to service personnel. He said, "I'd like to hear about your ambition, Tony."

"It's pretty simple. I've studied early Methodism and known the modern-day church firsthand. There's a big difference between then and now. So much has changed over the years."

"Don't some things have to change? We live in modern times."

"True, but in my opinion, it's gone too far."

"And you want to reverse that?"

"As much as I can, sir. Christianity is a serious undertaking. It changes lives in a demonstrative way. First, all sin must be stripped from the sinner, and then Christian friends should hold him accountable."

"Hold a spiritual gun to his head, so to speak?"

"Yes, sir. No sir! I didn't mean it to sound so strict. I meant it in a framework of love."

Obie may not have agreed with the urgency of such an undertaking, but he admired Gladstone's zeal.

"After all this is over," Obie said, "I want us to stay in touch. I want to see how your 'ambition' plays out."

"Yes, sir. I will. I promise."

Obie injected a dose of reality. "You spoke of being where the Lord put you. Let's not forget where we are, Tony. It's okay for us to talk doctrine and church ideology, but I must warn you that once we're on a battlefield, theology and ideology will seem quite far away. You'll see and do things that will test your faith."

"I trust my faith is strong enough, Lieutenant Gainsworthy. How soon will our regiment be going up?"

"Any time now. Tomorrow, most likely."

"I'll pray that we can be of the utmost service to Him."

"Tony, we'd better have that prayer now. Once we start moving, time, even for prayer, will be at a premium."

CHAPTER FOUR

April 1953

Their regiment was moving to the front. Obie had been briefed about their destination. He'd hoped there would be no more "going up," that the constant starts and stops of recent weeks would become a permanent "stop." Optimism blossomed with Eisenhower's promise of ending the war and his resultant presidential election last November. However, even as negotiations intensified, the fighting became harder.

It was very early morning when they moved out. Obie prepared himself, as he always tried to do, for whatever lay ahead. The road was a quagmire of mud. In the dark, he maneuvered their jeep around several mired trucks. They'd been warned against turning on their lights. In the right-hand seat, Gladstone held on as Obie gunned the vehicle across roadside ditches.

Usually, an assistant would do the driving, but as much as he trusted Gladstone with other duties, driving wasn't one. Obie doubted he could see beyond the hood; he must have had an enemy on his draft board.

The sound of guns came closer. At a checkpoint, a captain told Obie, "It's damned fierce up there. The Chinese have overrun us several times. You'd better stay back here until things settle down. We'll secure the hill eventually. Right now, conditions are bad."

"We'll go on," Obie replied.

"Be careful, chaplain."

The first light of the morning sun filtered onto the landscape. They folded down the jeep's windshield and went on for another five minutes until an MP sergeant motioned them to a stop. "You can't drive any farther," he said, pointing up the slope. "A thousand yards in that direction, there's more Chinese than you can count."

"Many causalities?"

"Yes . . . many. Over there," the sergeant said, motioning toward a group of trucks.

35

Obie drove to them. A couple dozen men on stretchers were inside an enclosure formed by five vehicles. Three medics were there. A corpsman pointed, indicating a stretcher on the ground. "In a bad way," he whispered to Obie. "Gut wound. Won't last long."

Obie opened his small leather-bound Bible, a gift from his Aunt Izzie. He spoke to the soldier, a black man not over twenty years old. His eyes were glazed, and he kept closing them.

"What's your name?" Obie asked.

The voice was barely discernible. "Dennis Chapman, sir. Am I going to die?"

"No, you're going to be fine, Dennis. I want to pray with you, anyway. Can I do that?"

"Yes, sir, please do. My momma prays for me all the time. She prays for my brothers, too."

"How many brothers do you have, Dennis?"

"Three. All but one is in the military."

"That must keep your momma pretty busy?"

"Yes, sir, it sure does." Dennis groaned.

"God is with you, Dennis. Let yourself lean on him."

"Blessed Jesus," Dennis prayed, "Help me with this . . . and watch over my brothers, too."

Gladstone leaned across Obie's shoulder as he read the Twenty-Third Psalm. Dennis was in a great deal of pain. Obie held the young man's hand and prayed aloud. Dennis died before he finished. In Italy, he'd learned to recognize when the spirit left the body. That memory had been refreshed in the past months.

"Is he gone?" Gladstone asked.

"Yes, he's gone."

"What do we do now?"

"We go on to the next man."

The full light of day came. Even as they talked, ambulances pulled up and loaded stretchers and men. Other medics arrived from the hill with walking wounded and those on stretchers. From there, they would be taken to a battalion aid station where a surgeon would determine who went on to a M.A.S.H. unit. Obie moved from one to the other, making swift decisions about who needed him most. The drama of new causalities arriving while others were being moved out seemed never-ending.

A corporal with a mangled arm walked in, staring into

space and unaware of where he was. Another, on a stretcher, had half his face blown away. He made strange and unintelligible sounds, trying to communicate with a mutilated tongue and voice box. Obie bent and placed a hand on his forehead. He kept it there as he prayed for the man, who grew silent. Obie saw second lieutenant bars on his collar underneath his fatigue jacket. A memory serge carried him back to a day in Italy when Adam had given him statistics about the grim chances of a lieutenant on the battle line. Some things never changed, it seemed. This man was not likely to survive a trip to the aid station.

Obie helped wherever he could with words of comfort. Gladstone followed him like a frightened puppy. Gunfire from the hill finally slowed, as did the stream of causalities.

In the lull, Gladstone said, "I never dreamed it would be like this, this bad."

"Sometimes it's worse."

"I don't know if I can do this."

"Do you remember what I told you right after you arrived, that your faith might be challenged? Out here, there isn't much standing between a man and God. You can't tell whether they are Methodist, Presbyterian, Baptist, or Jew."

"You're right; I can't."

"But, Tony, you *can* do it. You have to. Look at it this way. You want to be a minister. If you're like all the other would-be preachers, you've worried about whether you'd be the kind of shepherd who can handle difficult problems. If you can do this, what else could be a challenge? That's how I try to look at it."

"It's still hard . . . but I'll try to think of it like that."

Obie picked up his field pack. "It's time to go back if someone hasn't stolen our jeep."

Gladstone looked relieved. "Good. I'm drained."

Obie said, "Don't get ahead of yourself. There will be time for rest later, maybe. Right now, we're going to the aid station. We'll follow up on these men and see a lot more."

* * *

It was late evening when they returned from the hill area. Obie hoped for a few hours of sleep. Gladstone threw up their tent in the dark, a shelter barely large enough for two men and their packs. He couldn't find the chaplain's flag, so he shaped a cross from a coat hanger, covered it with remnants of a red sweater, and tied it to the ridgepole. Gladstone was soon snoring, and Obie was removing his boots when someone came to their tent.

"Sir! Chaplain Gainsworthy!" Obie recognized the voice of their mail clerk. "Captain told me to deliver this letter to you." The man slipped an envelope through the tent flap. Obie found a flashlight and went under his blanket. Since arriving in Korea, he'd received mail from several people, including his father, Angie, Adam, and Matt Burroughs' mother and sister. He was astonished to see Cassie's return address. He quickly tore open the envelope.

Dear Obie,   *April 9, 1953*

    This letter, several years late, will be a complete surprise, I am sure. I'm sorry, Obie, for how I have treated you. I threw our friendship away along with the other thing that didn't work out between us. I only hope that it's not too late to retrieve the friendship. I hope with all my heart that you will forgive me.

    I've talked to your father about where you are and what you are doing. I'm so proud of you for serving the spiritual needs of our troops. But you're in danger again, and I worry as I did during the last war. I don't know how I would manage if something happened to you. So please, Obie, be careful.

    I am still teaching here in Stafford Rest, normally first grade, but sometimes second grade. I have an apartment over the hardware store. For one who grew up with a rebellious spirit, I lead an austere life. Most of our classmates have moved away because of marriage or to find work elsewhere. Our town, like so many in the Adirondacks, doesn't have enough work to keep people here. Dad employs about thirty workers, and Mom has four employees in Evergreen at the real estate firm she opened there a few years ago. She got tired of working out of her car. So, my family is doing its part in supplying jobs, but that is an exception.

    I see your Uncle Abner and Aunt Claire occasionally. They seem well, although Abner has spoken of selling the farm and moving into town. I don't think Claire wants that, at least not yet. Ken and Angie are buying the Johnson place on White Pine Road where they moved to after their marriage last June.

But you probably already know that. The old place on Black-berry Hill looks so forlorn with no one living there. Ken finally got rid of his truck, and they have a car now. They are going to the Catholic church in Evergreen. Dad says Ken is the best foreman he's had. It's incredible how he's changed his life around. It must seem strange, your aunt being your stepmother. I can tell that they're in love. Love strikes in odd places, doesn't it, Obie? Angie's daughter, Cleo, is a junior at Evergreen High. Martin, her son, is a senior at Albany State and comes here only occasionally.

Ernie Boswell's dad died, and Ernie is running the store and marina and talking about opening a restaurant there. He and Cora have two children. Chester is eleven, and Linda is eight. I had her in my class. She's a bright child. "Chet" is smart, too, although a bit wild. I occasionally see Ed Baum-gartner when he comes to visit. He's a professor at Columbia and not married. Mom says he's a homosexual man. I don't know if it's true, nor do I care. He's just Ed to me.

Laura comes home about twice a year. They are doing well. Ben is a brilliant doctor (according to Laura.) Danny is a beautiful little boy (he is nine) and really intelligent. During the summer, he stayed a couple of days with "Aunt Cassie." We had a great time. Laura and Ben are talking about going to Europe next summer, and she may send Danny to Stafford Rest, which would be for several weeks.

I guess I'm approaching the age where I'll be considered an old maid. I haven't been much interested in dating or men in general (in case you are wondering). The most exciting thing along those lines happened last summer. A man named Ed Jackson came to see me. I met him in San Francisco when I came to see you. My friend, Judy Ramos, introduced us. He's a salesman for a California earthmoving equipment company. He had been in New York and remembered me. He came to Stafford Rest and stayed for three days. We had a great time together. He's coming again in June. We'll see how it goes.

Your last letters went unread, and I regret that. It would serve me right if you don't answer this one. I hope and pray (yes, I do that now) that you will. I'll be forever sorry for our failed attempt at matrimony, but we must remain friends.

Love always, Cassie

Obie read the letter through twice more before switching off his flashlight. He lay in darkness, eyes wide open, hearing big guns booming in the distance. The letter caused both joy and pain. Years had passed since hearing from Cassie. Her letters had sustained him in Italy; this one had come as he needed support again.

He'd dreamed of Cassie numerous times, most often as a teenager. Sometimes the dreams were erotic, leaving him with subjugated longing. *He had made a massive mistake by not trying harder.* He tried to picture her face against the blackness of the tent top. It eluded him until he remembered her as a girl, her golden hair bobbing crazily while she shouted angry insults at Laura and sometimes at him. Balancing those incidents were make-up times with her looking down at the ground and saying, "I'm sorry," then quickly glancing up with an expression that revealed she wasn't.

Laura was to blame for their breakup—and possibly Abigail. Not hating was hard, maybe impossible. He feared what might happen if he ever came face-to-face with either.

What should he read into Cassie's letter? Was there a chance she still desired more than friendship? No. Mentioning Ed Jackson was likely her way of letting him know she had moved beyond that. Although painful to accept, he must keep reminding himself that his decision not to marry was good; he would defuse the erotic thoughts. Nevertheless, he must answer her letter to restore their friendship.

He didn't remember sleeping and was sure only minutes had passed when a voice awakened him. He sat up and opened the tent flap a few inches.

"Lieutenant Gainsworthy," the runner said, "You asked to be called if there were major changes. The Chinese have broken through. There are many causalities."

"Thanks. We'll be right along." He nudged Gladstone. "Get up, Tony! We've had another call from God."

* * *

As Obie drove along a crowded road, there was the usual confusion of men and machines operating in a war zone. Sounds of battle intensified, as did the danger. Obie stopped the

40

jeep to get directions to the battalion aid station, which had been moved.

"It's over there," an MP told him, pointing, "but they may be getting ready to pull out again. If the Chinese advance, we'll all be pulling back."

The situation at the aid station had approached chaos. Medics brought in streams of wounded, which seemed to have no end. A doctor and nurse were doing their best to keep up with causalities, which Obie deemed impossible. Several stretchers were lined up outside the tent. Many men had severe wounds. Obie went from man to man, bolstering spirits. Gladstone helped the nurse and Obie, giving them a hand when he could.

Two soldiers carrying a stretcher approached. A wounded sergeant was ranting. "My men! I've got to get back up there!" He repeated the words several times, interspersed with profanity.

One of the men carrying the stretcher, a corporal, said, "Sarge, you're out of it now. You've lost a leg. You ain't going anywhere except home. So be glad of it and quiet down."

The men set the stretcher beside the tent. A medic checked the tourniquet over the stub of the sergeant's lower leg. "Leave me the hell alone!" the sergeant yelled. "I'm missing four men! I've got to get them out!"

Obie approached him. "Are you a squad leader, sergeant?"

His eyes showed pain. "Yes, I am."

"What's your name, and who's missing?"

"Brown's my name, Chaplain. I left four men out there. We were withdrawing, and I thought we had everybody. But, in all the confusion, I guess we didn't. It's my fault. We took a direct artillery hit, and I got this." He motioned toward his leg. "And two men were blowed up right there in front of me. I couldn't help that, but those other men didn't deserve to be left behind."

"I understand your concern, Sergeant Brown. However, you must see that you can't go anywhere. I want you to settle down. They'll get to you soon."

Brown had no intention of settling. "I need to do something! I can't leave them out there!"

"Maybe they'll find their own way out."

There was more than a little derision in Brown's tone. "Chaplain, you've never had men in trouble!"

Obie nearly responded in kind but thought better of it. *A chaplain must act like a chaplain.* He said, "Sergeant Brown, I'll see if I can find someone to look for your men. It may require some patience on your part."

He sent Gladstone to company headquarters. He was back in ten minutes. "Nobody wants to listen," Gladstone said. "Everybody has their own urgent problems."

Brown heard him. "See," he said. "It's up to me!" He tried to rise from the stretcher.

"Corpsman!" Obie called. He put a hand on Brown's shoulder. "Hold this man down if you have to." Then, to the corpsman, he whispered, "Sedate him."

"I already did."

"Well, do it again!"

Brown fell back on the stretcher, a forearm across his face in a gesture of resignation. "Nobody cares," he said.

"Listen, soldier," Obie said, "We do care. We care deeply. God cares."

"*God?* God cares?" Lines of sarcasm formed on Brown's forehead. "Where's God in all this? I'll tell you where. He's nowhere! He's about as present as my right foot."

"God forgive you," Gladstone said. Obie gave his assistant a "stand down" look.

Brown wasn't finished. "They're good men. Corporal Davis is married and has a little girl who is only a few months old. He shows everybody her picture. Benton is smart. He's going to be an engineer when he gets out. The other two are young. They shouldn't be here. Should be back in the States playing high school basketball or trying to make it with some pretty girl. They'll all die out there."

Faces flashed before Obie—Rivera, Grugs, Perkins, faces of men in his squad in Italy—men in peril. He said, "Brown, can you tell me exactly where they are?"

Brown stared at Obie. "Why? You and your blind assistant going out to get them?" His laugh was bitter.

"We'll find someone who will," Obie said.

"Not likely," Brown muttered but gave the information. Brown's squad of eight men was separated from their platoon and pinched between two enemy bunkers by crossfire. Two died there. With dawn breaking, Brown rushed to lead them out under increased smoke cover and darkness. He and one man almost reached the American lines when a shell exploded. Brown had his foot blown off. The other man was unhurt and helped Brown to safety. Only then had he realized men were missing. "I don't know what happened," he said. "The shelling was bad; maybe they took a direct hit, too. But they could still be there, pinned down."

"Can you give me more specific directions?"

"Find the first checkpoint north of here. It's daylight now, and if you look northwest a couple hundred yards, you'll see a grove of trees and, above that some cliffs. Trees and cliffs are about a hundred yards apart. My boys are in the draw about mid-way. There's some cover, boulders and shrubs, but it's mostly open. The Chinese are in both the shelter of the cliffs and the grove of trees. I know the rest of our platoon is in the vicinity. If they haven't withdrawn, see if you can get them to send someone in there and get my men out."

Obie commandeered a corpsman and two stretchers. They would drive as close as they could, then go on foot, Obie told them.

"What are we going to do?" Gladstone asked.

"We're going to go find them."

Gladstone was quiet. Obie imagined what might be going through his mind. He remembered the first time he was in danger of close enemy fire. Bradford, the corpsman, said little as they pulled out.

Obie drove as fast as he could without bouncing his passengers out. An explosion in the road ahead caused him to slam on the brakes. There was no way to get around the hole.

"All right, grab some stretchers and follow me," Obie said. They ran the last few hundred yards to an American bunker. The men there had their packs on. A captain told Obie the battalion was abandoning the position.

"Captain, there are four men in the draw over there. Can you spare someone to go get them out?" Obie asked.

"Chaplain, we have orders to move out. I'd like to help, but I can't. There's no one alive in there. Haven't seen any signs of life for the past hour."

"I hear machinegun fire."

"The Chinese shoot at anything. I'd advise you to get out, too."

Obie turned from the captain. "Come on, let's see what we

can find," he said to Gladstone. Bradford followed. They stopped behind a cluster of brush about a hundred feet from the American bunker.

"Here's my plan," Obie said. "I'll take a stretcher and go up the draw. You two stay right here. I'll hold the stretcher over my head. These Chinese aren't known for observing the Geneva Convention, but we can hope they might this time. If so, I'll call you up as well. Be sure to hold your stretchers up. They need to see we're unarmed. Don't do anything sudden. Walk, don't run."

"What if they shoot at you?" Gladstone said.

"In that case, retreat to the bunker. I'll make it back on my own."

"You'd never make it," Bradford said. "Too much open space."

Obie didn't let himself contemplate the truth of Bradford's statement. He said, "Let's be about our business."

As Obie stepped from behind the bushes and held the stretcher over his head, his legs trembled. The bravado he'd tried to muster helped little. He breathed a little easier with each step as he walked the fifty yards toward the next cover. There was no enemy activity. As he reached the cluster of bushes, he was desperate to duck, to remove himself from the sight of riflemen who would have weapons trained on him. Such a defensive action would raise doubts about his intentions. He remained on his feet and signaled Gladstone and Bradford forward. He watched as they approached, his heart beating so hard he felt it in his throat.

They reached him, breathing in little gasps. Obie heard voices from the grove of trees, which was closer than the cliffs. It sounded more like arguing than discussion.

Obie spoke softly. "I figure we're halfway there. There's a large boulder up ahead. I'm not going to stop when I reach it. I'm going all the way down into that dip. I'm betting our men are in there. If they are, and there are wounded, I'll signal for you if you're needed. If I don't signal, you wait right here. Whether there are wounded or not, we'll make it look like there are. I'll figure it out when I get there."

"Sir," Gladstone said, "They have their guns pointed at us. I can see them." His voice shook.

"I know the tendency is to duck, but don't do it unless they start shooting. Can you do that, Gladstone?"

"I think so. I'll try."

"You okay, Bradford?"

"Yes, sir. I'll be fine."

"All right, I'm going."

Obie walked with deliberate strides. There was a slight rise near a little gulch where he believed the men would be. As he topped the rise, he saw them, not four but three, lying close together, heads down. They saw him at once and swung their weapons toward him."

"Whoa!" he called out. "I'm your friend."

They lowered their weapons. "It's a chaplain," a corporal said. That would be Davis. "Get down, sir!" Davis said. "Get down!"

"No, Corporal Davis, they're holding their fire. I'm here to pick up wounded. If I don't stay visible, they'll start shooting."

"Wounded? We're not wounded. DeBren is dead. It's just Benton, Marshall, and me. We thought we'd been forgotten." All three men were muddy with sweat streaks on their faces. Their eyes were stressed.

"Sergeant Brown didn't forget," Obie said. "He sent us to get you."

"Is he okay? We worried he might have been hit."

"He was, but he'll be all right."

"Good old Sarge," Davis said. "He must be fuming. His chicks got scattered."

"I can't believe they're holding their fire," one private said.

"It's the cross on his helmet, Marshall," Davis said.

Benton spoke. "It won't last. We'll be sitting ducks as soon as we try moving out."

That was Obie's fear as well, but he couldn't let these men know it. If they were to survive, they must stay calm.

"Here's what we have to do," Obie said. "We'll make them believe you're all wounded. Marshall, put these around your head." Obie handed him white bandages from his pack. "Benton, you look the lightest, so get on the stretcher. Look dead, or wounded at the least. I'll take the front. Davis, you take the back. Be sure to limp. And leave your weapons."

"With all due respect, sir, we should keep our weapons with us," Davis said.

"They have the firepower to take us out whenever they

wish. Our only chance is showing them a group of wounded being helped from the battlefield."

Nothing would be gained by calling up Gladstone and Bradford. The little group was ready to go within a minute. "Stay close and walk fast," Obie said. "Don't run, whatever you do,"

"It's a trick," one man said. "Soon as we get out there they're going to mow us down."

"We have to chance it," Obie said over his shoulder.

They walked out of the depression. Obie imagined he heard cocking of rifles. He glanced neither right nor left, only straight at Gladstone and Bradford, who, to their credit, had not moved.

Obie's desperate hope that they might pull it off was destroyed with the crack of a rifle, followed by a volley of shots. Earth and rock splinters kicked up all around them. Obie dove for the ground. He wasn't alone.

"I'm hit!" The utterance came from Marshall. Obie glanced back at him. Blood flowed from his neck, under his ear. "Marshall," Obie bellowed, "Press down on it with your hand. That's it. Keep it there."

The firing continued. The "plop" of a bazooka sounded, and an explosion occurred twenty feet away. Up ahead, he saw Bradford in a prone position. Gladstone ran toward the American bunker, turned quickly, and dropped to the ground.

Obie said, "We need to get out of here. We're too exposed. Forget the stretcher. On my signal, run like hell. Go right past me. I'll catch up. Marshall, are you okay?"

"I'm good, sir."

"Take cover where you see that corpsman. From there, we can make it."

Obie saw enemy soldiers move out from the trees, their padded uniforms making them appear larger than life. The patrol was made up of about a dozen men. They would be well-armed and would soon reach them.

"Go!" Obie yelled.

When the last man was fifty feet beyond him, he leaped to his feet. He ran harder than he had for years, and it felt like his lungs were on fire. He was vaguely aware of two things: His men had reached the clump of brush, and figures were moving toward them from the American bunker. The captain must have changed his mind, after all.

There was a sledgehammer-like blow in the middle of his back. His first thought was that an enemy soldier had caught up and struck him with a gun butt. He looked down to see a hole in the front of his jacket with an expanding ring of red encircling it. He found himself face down in the dirt. He rolled over and saw a gun barrel pointed at his face. In a desperate move to save himself, he reached up and shoved the barrel away. It came back. He grabbed it again, twisted it, and jerked until it came free. He looked into the eyes of a Chinese soldier. Obie turned the weapon with brute strength and found the trigger. A look of surprise froze on the man's face as the bullet struck him in the forehead. Obie was losing consciousness as the enemy eyes glazed over. The soldier toppled forward on top of him.

Obie was unable to move. *Was this what it was like to die?* "Oh, God," he prayed. "I tried to keep my promise. I'm sorry."

As his vision dimmed, he whispered, "Cassie. Cassie . . . I love you."

CHAPTER FIVE

1953–1954

Cassie was dismissing her pupils when Ken Gainsworthy came to her classroom door. She saw his red eyes and the telegram in his hand, and her knees weakened. She held onto the door jamb for support.

"I knew you'd want to see this," Ken said.

Under a Western Union Logo, words were pasted to form a message, "Regret to inform you that your son, First Lt. Obadiah Kenneth Gainsworthy has been wounded in Korea in the service of his country. His injuries are severe." She could read no further because her tears blinded her. *He was not dead. Obie was still alive!*

Her voice sounded feeble to her ears. "How bad is it?"

"I only know what it says here, Cassie." He read the rest of the telegram aloud. The wound was in the upper torso, and Obie was in critical condition. He would go to Tokyo when it was deemed safe to move him. More information would follow. "Now, I guess we have to wait," Ken said, his voice exhibiting an uncharacteristic quaver.

The next two weeks were agonizing. Several telegrams followed. Obie was stable, whatever that meant. "Stable" sounded like "no progress." Later, he was "serious," which had its own ominous sound. That was an improvement, according to Ken.

News arrived regularly as the weeks passed. Obie was in a hospital in Tokyo and would soon go to one in San Diego. Cassie was invited often to Ken and Angie's for dinner. Sometimes they were joined by Abner and Claire. The state of Obie's progress was always the main subject.

In June, Ed Jackson made his second visit to Stafford Rest. The situation was awkward, given Cassie's distraction. He appeared understanding. Cassie told him about Obie and didn't understate her feelings.

"Let me get this straight," Ed said. "This is a man you've known all your life, a man you were once engaged to marry, if

only briefly. A man you say shows little interest in anything beyond friendship, yet you're willing to wait as long as it takes for
him to change his mind?"

"That's pretty much it, except I'm still working on retriev-
ing our friendship. I've written a letter to that end, but I don't
know if he received it before he was wounded. I don't want to
hurt you, Ed. I believe you're a good man, but I won't lead you
to believe you and I have a future together, either short or long-
term."

They were necessary words. Better to end it quickly. He
surprised her. "My dear, I'm a persistent guy. If I want to keep
coming here, even if I know it can't go anywhere, I will if you
let me."

"Well, it's up to you, just so you know how I feel."

The war ended with a truce. Then, on a day early in August, Ken called Cassie and asked her to come to their house.
She was there in five minutes. Two letters had arrived, one with
"For Cassie" on the envelope. Angie explained. "He says the
letter you sent him was in his jacket pocket and blood-soaked,
obscuring your return address. He thought you might get this
faster if he sent it to us."

Cassie wanted to be alone when she read it. "I have to go
to a private place," she said. "I hope you understand."

They did. Ken said, "We're going out there to San Diego.
We need to see for ourselves that he's getting better."

White Pine Road from the Gainsworthy house went by the
Methodist church. On impulse, she went in and sat in a pew in
the darkened sanctuary. She opened the envelope. A stained-
glass window let in enough light to read the handwritten letter.

Dear Cassie,   *August 8, 1953*

> *If you expected a fast response to your April letter, then
> you've been disappointed. I'm sure you know why. I received a
> severe wound that has taken a long time to heal. I'll tell you a
> little more about it down the page, but first I want to assure
> you that I am well on the way to full recovery. I've been in a
> hospital here in San Diego for nearly a week.*
>
> *I can't tell you how pleased I was to get your letter. As
> for our long silence, it's as much my fault as yours. I should
> have made a greater effort. To say I have missed our friendship*

would be putting it mildly. Let's not ever let it happen again, Cassie.

 The war is over, thank God. It was so frustrating this spring with negotiations going on, believing that eventually it would end, and us going on killing one another anyway. How stupid we are! I had toyed with the idea of staying in the Army, but I've changed my mind. The only capacity my conscience would allow would be to serve as a chaplain, and I feel I can no longer do even that. The reason is that I took a life. In Italy, it was different. I was serving as an infantry soldier, not as a chaplain. I promised God I would not kill again, yet I did. It is little comfort that I killed because I was about to be killed. You may think I was justified; others have assured me I was, but I broke a vow. Chaplains can request discharge. I have exercised that option and believe the paperwork will come through soon. Whether I can ever serve the Church again is something I have to sort out. Right now, I think I will seek an unrelated profession.

 As I said, I am recovering nicely. A Chinese slug hit me in the back and went through. It missed my heart, broke several ribs, and damaged some other organs that have taken time to heal. I have to admit that it was touch and go for a time. I remember practically nothing until they readied me for the flight to Tokyo, yet they say I was conscious most of the time.

 I owe much to some brave men who removed me from the battlefield. I was told later what happened after I went down. There was a platoon nearby getting ready to pull out. They delayed when they saw us in trouble. They drove the Chinese back before they could kill us. A corpsman who was with me was wounded, although not severely. Marshall, another soldier, had a more serious neck wound but recovered. The one to whom I owe the most was my assistant, Pvt. Tony Gladstone. Without a weapon, he ran to me even before the enemy soldiers had withdrawn and shielded my body with his own. He carried me to an American bunker. He could hardly see, having lost his glasses. I admit I never expected it of him. I could go into a description of Gladstone to help you better understand, but the point is that people surprise. He was superb in his bravery, and I understand he is receiving the Bronze Star. He intends to become a Methodist minister, and I believe he'll be a good one.

I received a medal, too, in a little ceremony here last week. I didn't want it. I set out to rescue four men (there were only three; one had been killed.) I placed them in a situation where we would all have died if the American patrol hadn't saved our necks. I already had a Silver Star from my time in Italy. Now I have two. I was told it was rushed through Congress because some senators thought chaplains should be honored.

The three men we led out were from the patrol of a Sgt. Brown, who insisted somebody go get them. He lost a leg and was with me here before they moved him to Texas. I received a letter from him yesterday. He's already discharged and at home in Dallas, Texas.

There is some irony in the fact that I was constantly in a battle zone in Italy for two years and never received a scratch. I was in Korea for over four months, in a "safer" job, and came home wounded. The good news is that I'm getting stronger every day. Yesterday, I walked (slowly) out to where I could see the bay and watch the big boats come and go. California is beautiful. Do you remember how we spent the day in the park near Berkeley? I may never leave this state.

Your letter was ruined, but I had already read it, and I remember you mentioning a man coming to see you. How is that progressing? You deserve happiness, Cassie. I wish, I really do, that it could have worked out with us. Our brief time when we were "engaged" was the happiest period of my life. Perhaps, though, you're lucky. I'm afraid I would have been a less than ideal husband. Please understand. There is no one anywhere that I love more than you. But the truth is, I'm a broken man concerning such relationships. Sometime, God willing, I might get things together, but that time is not yet. I don't expect you to wait for it to happen.

Please, dear Cassie, take care of yourself. I love you. I do.

Your friend, Obie

Cassie sighed as she put the letter back in its envelope. It was bittersweet. He would recover. He was her best friend again. *He would never be anything more.* Her tears smeared the ink on the envelope.

* * *

"What's your name?" the boy on the dock asked.

"Danny."

"Don't you have a last name?"

"Everybody has a last name."

"Well, what is it?"

"It's Williamson."

"Are you Doctor Williamson's son?"

"My father's a doctor in Boston. My grandfather's the doctor here in Stafford Rest."

"You must be pretty smart, then?" There was derision in the tone. Danny was annoyed; the boy was making fun of him.

"I bet you have a name, too," Danny said, hoping to inflict his own touch of sarcasm.

"Don't be a smart aleck."

"You're the one who said I was smart."

"How old are you?"

"Ten."

"Well, I'm eleven."

"Big deal! You're a year older. So what? I'm as tall as you, anyway."

The boy appeared to consider. "My family owns this marina," he said.

Danny had walked down to the docks several times and had seen this boy, but they'd never talked. Today, he'd detoured and arrived here while on his way to his Aunt Cassie's. He was starting to regret it.

Danny pointed to a big sign over the entrance. "Is it called Ernie's Marina?"

"Gee, you can read. Ernie's my father."

"I know who you are. You're Chet Boswell. My mother told me about you. She went to school with your father."

"Where are you staying?"

"Up there at my grandmother's." He pointed toward Garnet Point. He wasn't sure he liked Chet Boswell.

"Oh, that old witch. Everybody hates her."

Chet's words made Danny angry. His parents had told him it was better to walk away from insults, but he'd never been inclined to do that. "You're a liar," he said, putting his face close to Chet's.

Chet stepped back with a surprised expression. Danny's response was clearly not one he expected. Chet lunged forward and shoved Danny, who fell backward. "You deserved that, you jughead!" Chet said.

Danny sprang to his feet. A roundhouse right connected with Chet's jaw, followed by something resembling a left jab to the nose that sent the older boy reeling.

Chet's nose was bleeding. "I'm going to tell my dad on you," he yelled. "He'll fix you good."

Another voice, an adult one, boomed from a boathouse doorway. "I'm going to fix somebody, all right . . . and it's going to be you!" The man grabbed Chet's shirt collar and yanked him toward the boathouse steps. "I heard what you said and saw what you did. You got what you deserve. Go inside and put a cold, wet towel on your nose." He gave Chet a shove.

The man turned to Danny. "And you, young fellow, you're pretty quick to throw a punch."

"Yes, sir! I lost my temper, I guess. I'm sorry."

"Chet's got a big mouth, but you boys should try and get along. When he comes back out here, I'll make him apologize. Then, maybe you can be friends."

"Maybe. Are you Chet's father?"

Ernie laughed. "Yep! I sure am." He looked as though he were sizing Danny up. "You've got a lot of spirit, like your Aunt Cassie."

"My mom, too."

"Laura's more the genteel kind. Not that it's not good, but they're different, your mother and your aunt."

"Mom says she went to school with you, Mr. Boswell."

"She sure did. Why, we grew up here not much more than a stone's throw from each other."

"How come Chet said that about my grandmother?"

Ernie looked at the sky. Danny thought for a moment that he wasn't going to answer the question. An angry look had crossed his face, something like he saw on his father's face when he and his mother quarreled. Ernie said, "It's a grownup thing, Danny. You kids shouldn't have to think about such things."

"Mom said she liked you."

"Your mother's a good woman. She was pretty as a summer day. Still is." He smiled, apparently remembering something funny. "I wanted a date with her. Never got one. Obie

Gainsworthy, he's the one she liked. I would've taken offense if Obie and I hadn't been friends."

Danny wanted to ask a question, but Chet returned holding a wet towel over his nose. Ernie lectured and made him tell Danny he was sorry.

"I'm sorry, too," Danny said.

"You can come back sometime," Chet said. "I have my own rowboat. We can go fishing."

"I don't have a pole."

"I've got several. Bait, too. How about tomorrow?"

They agreed on a time.

Later in the day, Danny told his mother, "I made friends with Chet Boswell." There was no point in explaining their route to friendship. Something else was on his mind. "Mom, Mr. Boswell told me about your growing up here."

She smiled. "And what did Ernie tell you, dear?"

"Mom, who is Obie Gains . . . Gains something?"

Her smile faded. "What did he say to you, Danny?"

"He said he wanted to ask you for a date, but his friend asked you first, or something like that. So, Mom, did you date him?"

She sighed. "Danny, I guess you're old enough to understand that grownups have things happen in their lives causing them pain. It's something your mother would like to forget. Just a bad memory. Do you understand?"

"Sure. There are things I'd rather forget, too," he said. His parents arguing was one.

"I knew you'd understand, Danny." She seemed to hold her breath but said, "His name was Obadiah Gainsworthy! They called him 'Obie.'" The words came quickly like she wanted to rid herself of them. "We won't need to mention him again. Okay?"

"Okay, Mom."

If it *was* okay, why did her eyes tear up? There was a mystery there, Danny decided.

* * *

Ken and Angie's visit to San Diego was a respite from unpleasant memories, but after they left, and during weeks of recovery from his wound, Obie experienced warring emotions.

Should he give up on Church work in all its forms and find another profession? From the day of his mystic dream experience in the Russian River Valley vineyard, it had been one continuous march forward with that goal in mind. He had felt God's call and answered; he had turned his "belly up to God." Seminary training had strengthened his resolve and his faith. That mindset had changed.

Early on, during his physical healing, he had become friends with Father Bruce, a hospital chaplain who was a good listener. There was some gut-spilling, brutal self-analysis, and much reflection. On learning details of Obie's personal life, Father Bruce suggested he might consider reviving his journalism career until he came to terms with whether to return to "the ministry." Obie saw that it was a reasonable suggestion.

Father Bruce knew a newspaper editor in Oakland who might help. Obie stood by as the priest talked on the phone about him in flattering, even flowery terms, listing his "many" accomplishments. Finally, he handed the phone to Obie. "Doug Carlson, the editor, wants to talk to you. Relax. He's interested."

The editor's tone during their telephone conversation was encouraging, and a face-to-face interview was scheduled. He took a bus to Oakland after his discharge from the Army and the hospital. The job was his within hours of the interview, and by the next day he had rented a small apartment.

Obie's life became hectic. As the newest junior editor, he drew the meanest assignments—and a great many. He waited for a chance to prove he could write something meaningful. He'd quietly set for himself the task of establishing a broader writing career, so he dedicated several hours each evening to writing about subjects of his choosing. He submitted written ideas to Carlson, and the editor smiled as he handed them back.

His tiny apartment in Oakland was inexpensive, although not a quiet place. He adjusted. A fellow reporter bought a new automobile and sold Obie his old one, a 1948 Ford, at a ridiculously low price. The car ran reasonably well throughout city streets; he would hesitate to use it for longer trips. He wasn't up for trips, anyway; his wound had been pronounced healed, although there were days when he still experienced considerable pain.

The job paid little, and the first weeks in Oakland were austere. He had saved nearly all his Army pay while in Korea, so he had enough money to squeeze by even after buying the car. He'd applied for service disability and was told to expect a lengthy wait.

His financial situation improved when Wilford Clark, the pastor at a local Methodist church he was attending, discovered that he was an ordained minister. After interviews with the district superintendent and other church officials, he was hired as a part-time assistant minister. The job included organizing and carrying out youth ministry and filling in for Clark at various times.

It was a hectic schedule, juggling time between his two jobs. A modest church salary and equally meager newspaper paycheck nudged him just slightly above the poverty line. He bought a used typewriter from the newspaper.

He had mixed feelings about returning to church work, although the position was only part-time. Korea, and what had happened there weighed heavily on his mind. He might never return to the kind of ministry he'd dreamed about, but maybe he could work his way back into God's favor by doing the little jobs. Church members seemed to like him. He wasn't sure how they received his occasional sermons; to him, they felt uninspired.

Obie gained confidence about having found a niche in journalism. Carlson finally noticed his efforts and gave him small writing assignments to fill in newspaper space. One, his story about the work of chaplains in Korea, written during evening hours at home, caught the editor's attention. Carlson suggested he lengthen it and submit it to magazines.

"We're just a little rag that reports the daily news, Obadiah," the editor said. "Your literary style is better suited to magazines. Some publication will want it because you have something to say, and you say it with authority."

That assessment was correct; *Cosmos Primer* bought the story, and the magazine editor asked if he had anything more. Obie was delighted. He'd been paid good money for work it had taken less than a week to produce. Over the following days, he wrote another article and submitted it to *Cosmos Prime*. Again, there came a quick acceptance. The piece, a reflective narrative about winters in the Adirondacks, was published, and he was mentioned on the editor's page.

I draw your attention to the article "Adirondack Resting" by Obadiah Gainsworthy on page 34. The description of Mr. Gainsworthy's forest in winter is so vivid that you will believe you are, yourself, drawing in "frosty mountain air that sets your lungs to burning." Gainsworthy writes with a subtle enticement that pulls the reader into his sphere of more profound thought and clarity of purpose. You will not only have visited a forest, you will also remember it in ways you would never have imagined.

The editor's words surprised Obie. He couldn't think of himself as "enticing" readers in any fashion, especially into "profound thought." He'd simply been telling about a world he knew intimately.

Soon after the article was published, Obie received a letter from Charles Lansing. Their intervals between letters had lengthened in recent years. Charles had read the *Cosmos Primer* articles and commented on Obie's writing.

We often discussed gifts and how they can be used for God's purpose. I encouraged you to become a minister or some such church worker. I was disappointed that you seem to have given up that pursuit. But, as I read your articles in Cosmos Primer, my heart soared, for I see you have a gift we gave little attention to back then. Even if you never again administer to soldiers on the battlefield or stand in the pulpit, your words can reach far more people. Use your gift well, Obadiah. My prayers are with you.

Obie had continued writing to Cassie, and they had started calling each other in recent months. They talked every couple of weeks, more often if one had something special to tell the other. He shared his good fortune about his published articles, and she brought him up to date on happenings in Stafford Rest and vicinity. Cassie mentioned her friend Ed Jackson several times. Ed had made four trips back East to see her, she revealed.

One evening in late summer, she called. "I have something special to tell you. I've wanted to call for days but hesitated because I'm not sure what you'll think."

"Sounds serious. Are you getting married or something?"

She paused before responding. "Yes, Obie, I am. Ed has

asked me to marry him, and I've accepted."

A knot in his stomach worked its way up into his throat. He found himself speechless.

"Obie, are you there?"

"I'm still here, Cassie. It's wonderful news. Really!" He was biting his lower lip so hard it hurt. *Why did he feel this way?* He had no right to keep her from happiness, nor even want to. "When is the wedding?" he managed.

"September, and it's going to be in California. Near you."

"Where?" He hoped she wouldn't invite him.

"Ed's relatives are mostly in the Bay Area. He's leaving the location to me. His parents are not churchgoing people at all, so he's open to either a civil or a church wedding."

"Why are you coming out here? Your family and most of your friends are in Stafford Rest."

He detected hesitation. "Ed insisted. It's something to do with his work. Time off, that sort of thing." She didn't sound convincing.

"I hope you choose a church marriage."

"Yes, it's what I want. I want you to marry us, Obie."

His knees were weak. "Cassie, you want *me* to perform the ceremony?"

"Yes . . . *you.*"

"Why?"

"Because you're a minister and my dearest friend."

It wouldn't do at all. He avoided the real reason. "I've barely been here a year, and I've never married anyone. Cassie. I'm just an assistant here in this church."

"You're ordained. I'm sure the minister will allow it."

"He probably would," Obie admitted. "I doubt your mother would."

She laughed. "Obie, it's my life, my choice. You've been gone a long time. I'm my own woman."

He wanted to say that she must not marry Ed Jackson—or anyone else. She must wait until he, Obie, had his life straightened out. He prayed silently, "Give me a little longer, please, God." Finally, he said aloud, "I don't know, Cassie."

"Please, Obie. You owe me, you know."

"And why do I owe you?"

She laughed. "When we became engaged in Berkeley, you promised me a ring. I never did get it."

How could she say such a thing? Was she merely attempting to keep the conversation light? "That hurts, Cassie!"

She hesitated a moment. "I'm sorry, Obie. I didn't realize you were touchy on the subject. It's been nearly six years."

"Oh, it's all right. I've moved on. I know that we're only friends now. I've come to terms with it."

"Well, friends do things for each other, don't they?"

He could never do it. He had to make her accept that. "Cassie, I'd do anything for you. You know that, don't you?"

"Not this, though? Is that what you're telling me?"

"Not the ceremony. If you're looking for a church, you can come here. Reverend Clark can marry you. I'll have a word with him."

"I had my heart set on . . ."

"Cassie, it's impossible. I simply *can't* do it." He was more forceful with his words. "*I won't.* I won't marry you to another man."

He could hear her inhaling and exhaling unevenly as though she wanted to say more. He waited. She said, "All right, Obie. Please give me the minister's phone number. I'll make the arrangements."

"I think it's better this way."

"Yes, I suppose you're right. I want you there, however. You will attend, won't you?"

Had she asked the question first, he would have refused to consider it, but having denied her the other impossible request, he couldn't add further hurt. "All right," he said.

You're not going to back out, are you?"

"No, I won't."

"Do I have your word?"

"You have my word on it."

"Good! You should also know that my parents will be there. We've already discussed it."

"Your mother knows you're inviting me to your wedding?" Old anger surfaced at the prospect of seeing Abigail Hunt.

"Yes, but she didn't say anything. She's learned to stop meddling in my business."

"Cassie, I feel a little like I've been tricked."

"I thought you might. I'm sorry, Obie. I feared you wouldn't attend if you knew she was coming."

"You're probably right." He laughed so she would know he

wasn't angry.

"There's something else, Obie."

"What now?"

"Laura will be coming, too."

CHAPTER SIX

1954–1959

The day preceding the wedding was a typical September day in the Bay Area. Fog gradually rose above the hills until, by ten o'clock, a blue sky dominated.

Obie's sky was not as blue; his nerves were frayed. Cassie had called late the evening before to tell him they had arrived in Oakland and would meet Reverend Clark in the morning for rehearsals. She asked Obie to "please be at the church to make introductions." His first impulse was to decline, but the pleading in Cassie's voice made it impossible to refuse. He paced the narthex for several minutes and watched for their taxi to enter the front driveway.

How long had it been since he'd seen Laura? *Eleven years?* How could it be? What could they possibly say to each other? She, and indirectly her mother, were to blame for ruining his and Cassie's future together. But, with Cassie on the verge of a happy marriage, he tried telling himself that the past should be put away.

Nevertheless, the old feelings were still surfacing. Cassie had said Laura was reluctant to come. Maybe she had guilt feelings—as well as she should.

He was more concerned about seeing Cassie. Exchanging photographs had been enlightening, but it had been six years since they had met in person. They'd avoided talking about what had separated them. He had wanted to ask her if she still believed he'd done something terrible to Laura. Perhaps his hesitation had been to avoid hearing her answer. She'd shown trust in him by asking him to perform her marriage ceremony. *Why had she done that?* She must have known he would refuse. *How could she not know how painful this was for him?*

Two nights earlier, he had dreamed he was performing the marriage ceremony. On reaching the point in the service where he asked if anyone knew of a reason why they should not be joined together, a voice startled him by saying, "I have a reason.

61

I love her, and she loves me. She must not marry this man." He was horrified to realize that he had said the words himself.

He watched now, in a daze, as a taxi entered the church parking lot and approached the front door. Reverend Clark, who would be ten minutes late, had asked Obie to greet the group. He watched five people disembark, two men and three women. He should go out and meet them; he seemed unable to move.

"This is crazy," he said aloud. He had waded into battle without as much dread. He had to get control of the situation, unpleasant as it was. He breathed deeply and went outside.

Cassie was glowing. Her hair, still golden, was her shining feature. Wide blue eyes studied his face momentarily before she stepped into his arms. "Oh, Obie," she whispered, her mouth close to his ear, "It's so wonderful to see you again."

"And you," he said, afraid to utter anything more.

When he looked up again, Laura was standing in front of him. *He must try to do the right thing.* He released Cassie and stepped toward her. She was little changed, except her dark hair was short where it had once been long. If she had gained any weight, it wasn't apparent. A wisp of hair blew across her forehead, and he saw the slightest tinge of gray.

"Hello, Laura." He held out his hand.

She ignored it. "Good morning," she said. Only two words, but delivered without a smile and with a coolness that chilled his heart. Eager eyes he'd once known were nearly devoid of expression; no hate there, only disinterest.

Abigail didn't offer her hand. Grayer, and with a few more wrinkles, she stared straight at him, her expression announcing that she was there under duress and nothing had changed between them. In contrast, Pinky hugged Obie and pounded him on the back.

"How's the factory, Pinky?" Using the nickname felt strange, even disrespectful. "I hear that you've gone national."

"Yes, we have. We're expanding. Business is good, thanks to men like your father. Ken's a good man now that he's . . ."

"Married and sober," Obie finished for him.

"I was going to say 'settled down.'"

Ed Jackson was tall, taller even than Obie, and slender. He shook hands with Obie. "I've heard much about you from Cassie," he said. His expression seemed guarded.

"All good!" Cassie said, cutting off Obie's obvious response.

They went into the church. The rest of the wedding party, comprised of Ed's family and friends, soon arrived. After Wilford Clark came in and was introduced, Obie sat on a back pew to watch them practice the procession, the vows, and the responses. Abigail and Laura sat in a pew in the middle aisle. Obie couldn't help noticing how much alike were their expressions of detachment.

Dinner together that evening was at a downtown restaurant. Obie attended out of respect for Cassie. Abigail came, but Laura begged off. "She doesn't feel well," Abigail told Cassie. "The time lag thing, I think it is."

"Or something else," Cassie muttered, barely loud enough for Obie to hear. He saw Ed clamp his hand over hers, warning her against saying something unwise.

At Obie's probing, Ed filled him in on his background and plans. "I'm a glorified salesman," he stated. "I don't intend it to stay that way, however. I'm going into business for myself. Instead of going out to make sales, I'll have people out there doing it for me. It may take a few years, but I'll get there. You'll see. I'll give Cassie the life she deserves."

Obie observed that Abigail was listening. Nevertheless, her poker face remained rigid.

* * *

Even with the presence of Ed's many relatives, the wedding was small by most standards. Obie sat alone in a pew in the back, transfixed. His dream was still vivid; *"If anyone knows a reason why this man and this woman should not . . ."* He knew, of course, that no modern-day minister included that archaic question. But what if they did? Would he speak up? And what would *she* do? Would she turn and look at him with a question in her eyes? Would there be longing there? As Reverend Clark reached a point near the end of the altar service, the shadows of his dream still lingered. Why not yell, *"Stop this?"* But the moment passed, and as Clark pronounced them "man and wife," Obie realized they were words that would forever separate him from Cassie.

The reception was held in the same restaurant where they had dined the previous evening. Abigail, working long distance, had arranged it all, and, as with most things she organized, it worked out. There was a cake, there was food and wine, there was dancing, and there was well-wishing. Cassie's college friend, Judy Ramos, had come from across the Bay.

Obie drank more wine than he should have, as did many others. Once, he stared into his glass, remembering Jacob's oratory about "making wine." He could hear his grandfather's voice. *When you make wine, you're planning the future. It's a choice. You have to decide whether or not to make wine.* " He'd said something else, too, something that hadn't registered on Obie's teenage mind but later caused him to marvel at Jacob's insight. *That one with the yellow hair . . . Pinky's daughter. She reminds me of Prissy . . . your grandmother. Maybe she'll be your wine.* Obie took a sip from his glass; that wine tasted bitter.

Laura sat at a table, staring straight ahead. Why had she even come? He glanced at her from time to time. She was as beautiful as ever. Her dress was low-cut, revealing cleavage. She hardly looked his way. Why was she so angry at him? What right had she? She was pretending, for whatever reason. She was the one who had broken her word and married someone else; she was the one who had cruelly come between him and Cassie. The fury he'd held in check flared, and the old question arose, as repugnant now as the day he'd learned of her betrayal. *Why did she do it?*

Why not ask her? Cassie had said he should; Adam had suggested it. She was sitting ten feet away. He doubted he would ever see her again. Why did he not simply go sit down beside her and ask her? He formed the question: *"Laura, what did I do to make you stop loving me?"*

"Obie!"

Cassie stood in front of him. Ed held her hand. "Cassie, I'm sorry! I didn't hear you."

She laughed. "You looked like you were a million miles away. What on earth were you thinking about?"

He lied. "I don't know. Just things."

"For one with a skill for words, you seem at a loss." Her grin told him she was teasing. At least, that hadn't changed. "We're getting ready to go," she said.

"When is your family leaving?"

"They'll stay the night and fly home tomorrow. Ed and I are going to the coast for a week. Obie, as I told you last night, we'll live in San Francisco for at least a while. Please come and see us real often. You and I have been friends for so long that it would be a shame if you neglected me. We'll always be friends, won't we? Will you come and see us?"

"Of course. Of course, I will."

"Good! Now, I need to spend some time with Laura and Mom. You coming, Ed?"

"In a minute, Love. I want to chat with Obie briefly if you don't mind."

When Cassie had gone, Ed leaned back and crossed his arms. "I have something to say to you," he said.

Ed's tone was, at the least, serious. "Sure? What's on your mind?"

"You can disregard the invitation Cassie just extended."

"What . . ."

"What, indeed? Cassie has told me about you. The last thing I need is to have an old flame hanging around. I let her invite you to our wedding simply because she begged me to. I hoped you'd have the decency to stay away. You didn't. I don't want her seeing you again."

Obie was sure the hair on the back of his neck was rising. "Now, see here . . ."

"No! *You* see here. Stay away from my wife!" Before Obie could object further, Ed turned and walked away.

Obie's inclination was to follow the man and put him straight, convince him that he and Cassie were now no more than friends. He stopped short because the truth was far more complicated. He and Cassie were much more than friends, and Ed knew it. Despair caused him to slump into his chair. *What had he done?* He'd given up his best hope for happiness. Not only had he watched his future die, he'd also participated in the execution.

Cassie and Ed left, and the wedding party gradually dispersed. Pinky and Abigail were talking with restaurant personnel. He'd already said goodbye to Pinky. Obie sat for several minutes, calming himself until he felt ready to leave.

Just outside the restaurant door to the parking lot, Laura Williamson sat on a bench he couldn't avoid passing. He said, "Laura . . ." He didn't have breath for more.

She glanced up. Her eyes were red; she'd been crying. "Good evening," she said without looking at him.

"What's wrong, Laura?"

She still didn't look at him. "Nothing. Well, yes, I feel sorry for Cassie."

"It's her wedding day. She's happy, it seems."

"Sometimes happiness is an illusion . . . and temporary."

"May I sit down?"

"Suit yourself. It's not my bench."

He sat as far away as the short bench would allow. "Laura, Cassie will be fine." He wasn't sure he believed it. Ed Jackson's possessive words still rang in his ears. "They'll get settled in here. It's a good place to live. She intends to apply for a teaching position."

"She doesn't love him."

"How do you know that?"

For the first time, she looked straight at him. "She told me so. She expects she'll learn to love him. When I told her it wouldn't work, she wouldn't listen."

"Laura, you're her sister, and I understand your concern, but Cassie is strong. She'll make a good thing of her marriage."

She turned toward him again, this time in anger. "You, counseling about love and marriage? Don't you dare! Not to me."

Putting an end to this hostility was the right thing, and it seemed up to him to make the initial move. "Laura," he said as he reached for her hand, "isn't it time we end the long silence between us? I . . ."

She pulled her hand away. "Don't touch me. Don't ever touch me. You should go."

"Laura . . ."

"We have nothing to say to each other. Please leave."

He stood, knowing he should walk away, but the suppressed anger returned. This time the situation was different; she was right there in front of him, in the flesh. What right did she have to treat him this way?

His words tumbled out. "Tell me something, Laura. Have you been happy with your big house and possessions? Has your marriage been better than it might have been with me?"

"You bastard! Why would you say such a thing? You have no right."

"No, Laura! *You* have no right. You chose your life, and it's your fault if you're unhappy. But, at least you have your son. You told me once that you wanted a son."

She emitted what sounded like a sob. "I did what I believed was right. And yes, I do have a good life. I have a wonderful life. I have the son I said I wanted. Danny is the one I love the most in all the world."

Maybe he was being too harsh. Maybe talking about her son would calm her. "Tell me about Danny," he said.

She rose. For a moment, she looked as if she wanted to hit him. He got up quickly to stand beside her. Her eyes were wild with fury. "Don't you ever speak my son's name again," she said. "Get away from me! Leave me alone!"

He turned quickly and walked away. Talking to a crazy woman had no purpose. A part of him wished the conversation had gone better. Another part was relieved that he'd learned firsthand how disturbed she was. Any lingering feelings for her were gone.

CHAPTER SEVEN

1954–1959

Cassie called him a month after the wedding. He wanted to feel happy hearing her voice, but Ed's stinging words lingered.

"I waited for your call," she said.

He wished to avoid an explanation. "How are things with you, Cassie?"

"Very well, thank you."

"And are you settled in?"

"We're still living in Ed's old apartment, but we won't be here long. We're moving to San Antonio. Ed has given notice. He's starting a business in the same field, selling earthmoving equipment. I'm not sure how I feel about the move. In any event, I'm calling to invite you for dinner this weekend if you're free. Can you come, Obie?"

"Cassie, I can't. I have important newspaper deadlines. I hope you understand."

"I suppose so." Her disappointment was apparent. "It'll be three weeks, though, before we leave. When is a good time for you?"

Seeing her again was impossible. Ed had made it clear that Obie wasn't welcome in their home—and he was right to feel that way. Their marriage needed no connection to anyone who shared such a history as his and Cassie's. They'd already put considerable distance between them, but making a clean break would be infinitely hard. He searched for the right words.

"Cassie, I have so much to do that . . ." He stopped, knowing he was avoiding the truth. "The fact is, I should leave you two newlyweds alone. You need time for getting to know each other . . . don't you think?"

"That's ridiculous, you stupid man. How long does your addled mind imagine we need?"

He must say it. "Cassie, it's best that we don't see each other."

"What do you mean?"

"Just that it's not a good idea."

"And for how long should we not see each other?" A keen

edge of anger was now present in her stressed words.

His answer was squeezed out with reluctance. "For good, sweetheart."

"You can't mean that."

"I do mean it. I'm sorry, Cassie."

Although the long silence was a vacuum begging for additional words, he waited. He could hear her crying softly.

At last, she said, "You're my friend, Obie. You're my dearest friend. And I believed I was yours. How can you destroy our friendship? There's no reason you should. We endured years of not speaking. I don't want that ever to happen again. Why are you saying this terrible thing?"

Even the chance of sewing discord in her marriage went against all the ideals he'd set for himself. "Cassie, we have to go our separate ways." *The words were out, at last.*

"Obie, did I do something?"

"No, this is all my doing. And yes, you are the best friend I ever had."

"Then *why?*"

Any answer would be insufficient, for he was pushing the woman he loved from his life—forever.

He chose avoidance. "We must, Cassie."

"I love you, Obie, and I think you're not being honest with me."

"And I love you too, but it has to be."

"I won't let it happen. *I simply won't!*"

He spoke the cruel words quickly, hoping speed might minimize the pain for her and himself. "Goodbye, Cassie. And this *is* for good."

She had the last word. "I'll not call you. I'll wait for you to call me. And if you never do, have a good life, Obie." She hung up.

* * *

Another year passed before Obie concluded that he'd outgrown the newspaper job. It had been a period of creative growth and spiritual regeneration. In an act of faith, he would launch a new endeavor; he would devote full time to writing.

He loved the Bay Area but felt a need to change locations. He did not doubt that his mindset had something to do with

Cassie's ghost, which he encountered everywhere. He said goodbye to his friends at the newspaper and to the church members. The Silvermans gave him a private farewell dinner in their home. The following day he left, nursing his old automobile south along the coast road, through Los Angeles and toward San Diego, stopping numerous times to add water to a leaking and overheated radiator.

He slept on a park bench for two nights before finding a one-room apartment on the second floor of a building that looked ready to collapse any moment. The room had a bunk on one side and a gas cook stove on the other. A bathroom was down a hall and shared with three similar apartments. There was no refrigerator, so he bought food items in amounts that would last a day or two without spoiling.

He found a small wooden table abandoned on the sidewalk beside overflowing garbage cans. Its broken leg was easy to repair; it served as a place to eat and a desk for his typewriter. He paid for a wooden kitchen chair, a cheap buy. The few dollars saved while in Oakland were soon gone, and the modest government monthly payouts for his war wound had not caught up. The money he earned for a few hours a week of janitorial work at a department store would suffice.

Miserable living conditions aside, San Diego suited him, as did his work. His newfound obsession for putting words on paper had a natural feel. Years of pent-up emotions had driven him, sometimes manifesting in anger, sometimes in frustration, and occasionally in joy. He realized that those emotions had propelled him most of his adult life. He considered it positive, congratulating himself that he was now disciplined and focused; journalism had done that.

He had already planned a book and completed some research; he was not a historian, so he spent far more time in libraries than writing. Anyway, the book was not to be just a historical account of twentieth-century wars but an unbiased analysis of their causes and consequences.

Then, not long after he settled in at San Diego, a new thread, the personal element, began weaving its way into the work. Persistent images of his squad members killed in Italy appeared, seeking to influence his thoughts. What would those lives lost in war have contributed to the world? It was a subjective question to be integrated into the work, even if there were no definitive answers.

Throughout the growing manuscript, there appeared a recurring question, not only about each war but about the lesser conflicts, as well. The question was never stated directly, but prominent, nonetheless: *Was the war necessary, and if not, what paths of avoidance could have been taken?* The question extended even to futile battles. Matt had died in Italy in an end-of-the-war combat that could have been easily avoided. And, in Korea, he had bemoaned the fact that even with negotiations in progress and a strong likelihood of an imminent truce, fighting went on. Men died needlessly because commanders pushed them into unnecessary battle situations—perhaps to enhance their careers. He'd once voiced that emerging belief during his last enlistment, inviting hostile stares. Being a chaplain had probably saved him grief. Now, he rejoiced that there were no such restrictions to the words he would put on his pages.

Ultimate Conflict required two painful years of continued research, writing, and rewriting. Pauldine House, a prominent New York publisher, bought it. The advance would be held until "certain details are worked out," said his agent, Andrew Loris.

Obie had never considered using an agent; he had planned to write and submit until someone bought. The hookup with Andrew came about because they were already friends, having met in Oakland. He had spent time with Andrew, a second-generation Italian, speaking Italian to keep from losing proficiency. Andrew had left Oakland several months before Obie to become a literary agent in New York. Aware that Obie was selling articles, Andrew traced him to San Diego through a mutual friend. It was timely that Obie was finishing the manuscript.

"I've sold dozens of manuscripts in two years," Andrew told him. "If your book is anywhere near as good as your articles, I'll sell it for you. Then, instead of worrying about publication, you can go right on to your next book. It had looked like a no-lose situation.

Through further editing and revision, another year passed before publication. Obie had grown impatient throughout the period, but Andrew assured him that the time from submission to the bookstore was often much longer.

He was amazed by the check he received from Andrew for his share of the book advance. To one who had spent three years in a one-room apartment in the poorest section of San Diego, subsisting on a small military pension and money from odd jobs, the amount seemed a fortune. He called Andrew because he feared there might have been a mistake.

The agent laughed. "It's standard for a promising first work. It'll probably sell modestly, Obie, but most first books do. Pauldine is betting on your potential. They think you'll be a major writer. I think so too."

Obie couldn't think of himself in those terms. "I can cash the check, then?" he said.

"At once!"

He bought a new automobile the following day, a four-door 1958 Ford Fairlane, a two-tone red and white beauty. His old Ford had barely made it to San Diego and then sat constantly on the street outside his apartment. A neighbor started the car with a booster cable so he could coax it to the dealership for a trade-in.

Obie walked around the new car several times while it was serviced, admiring everything from flaring fins in the back to double headlights in front. No one in his family had ever owned a brand-new automobile. Abner had purchased a new tractor before the war that was the talk of Stafford Rest and the pride of the Gainsworthys, but this felt even better. He occupied the better part of two days driving around San Diego, into the brown hills, and along the shore.

New housing was next: He wanted something semi-private away from the city center but with an ocean view. It took nearly a week to find what he believed was the perfect place. The second-floor furnished apartment north of the city was one of four in the two-story building. The neighbors were quiet, assuring the privacy he wanted.

Ultimate Conflict had a slow start. Reviews were mixed. Then, three months after publication, it began selling well. Certain factors influenced sales: Nuclear war with Communist Russia was a public concern, and any work offering solutions for easing tensions, however hypothetical, was welcomed by portions of the reading public.

He had, as Andrew suggested, started another book. In its initial stages, it was both factual and fictional, a Plato-like dialogue among shapers of modern forms of government. It followed his evolving theme of "Could there have been a better way?" That focus changed slightly after talking to Charles Lansing.

Charles had read *Ultimate Conflict* right after publication and was not shy in his criticism. He had called to say, "Your writing is brilliant, but where was God in there, Obadiah? As a God-called servant, and you are, you need to construct roads to God. Surely, within your stressing that there are better ways of solving problems than fighting and killing one another, the morality issue could have been stressed more. Where morality is discussed, God can hardly be ignored."

It stung, coming from someone whose opinion he valued and who had been such a significant influence in his formative years. Obie went back to his work in a more prayerful way, inspired to slant the work toward an analysis of how religion had influenced various governments' formation and activities. It was, however, something with which he continued to struggle, especially the balance of power between Church and state.

Charles hadn't asked, but if he had, Obie could state truthfully that he'd not ignored nor neglected God since coming to Southern California. He had private prayer, worship, and study rituals, and faithfully attended Sunday services at a large Methodist Church in the city. Nevertheless, he'd kept his literary work separate from his spiritual life. But, as Charles said, he would be mindful to "integrate God" into his writing.

He'd promised himself never to do pastoral ministry again. His casual relationship with the San Diego Methodist pastor had not revealed that he was ordained. Although he took on little jobs in the church like any other member, he didn't consider official membership.

There was no immediate need to worry about essential finances. He was paying the bills and could easily do that for a while, but he wasn't deluded; if he didn't write and sell his next book before his advance ran out, he would need employment.

He was happy, with only a few exceptions, he told himself: He had his work and his freedom; he was on good terms with his family; he talked to Ken and Angie on the telephone every couple of weeks and, on occasion, called Abner and Claire. In addition, periodic letters passed between him and Izzie.

He had friends, old and new, and his interaction with them was on his terms. He was surprised to receive letters from Army personnel who had read his book. Paul Aimes, settled once more in Tennessee, said he planned to make *Ultimate Conflict* required reading for his high school history classes. Jim Forrester, the chaplain in Italy to whom he became assistant for a while, was a tenured religious professor at Indiana University and was recommending the book to fellow teachers. Albert Howard, his wounded platoon leader whom Obie had carried to safety, was now a colonel stationed in Germany. Howard sent a long letter. In it, he said:

> *I cannot tell you what depth of feeling I had while reading your book. We all came away from our experiences in that war with different emotions. Some take those memories and bury them. You, my friend, have seen fit to internalize them enough to describe our mistakes and make suggestions for helping us be better humans. Indeed, some wars have to be fought; most do not. As you said, let us be "humans first and warriors second."*
>
> *We would all like to go back and do some things over. In Italy, I wish I could have known the men better. As a chaplain in Korea, you no doubt learned that being in command, even in the lower echelons, has its handicaps. I did not know you well in Italy, Obadiah, for there were so many of you, but your book helps me know you now as an individual. I do want to thank you again for saving my life. For that, I'll always be grateful. God bless and keep you.*

There was steady correspondence with Adam. He and Rachel had two children, David and Sarah, ages four and two. They were carving out successful lives in Israel. Adam was a high-ranking officer in the army and had been in the Sinai Peninsula war in 1956.

Correspondence with the Burroughs' had lagged and then stopped. The last letter from Carla, three years previously, consisted mainly of three news items: Matt's body had finally been brought home from Italy and laid to rest in a little cemetery close to their farm; their daughter, Tina, was engaged to be married for the second time, and they had gone to Italy again to see Rosa and their grandson. They believed there was progress in persuading her to come to the United States. He promised himself to write to them, for he missed their letters.

He couldn't think of Matt without thinking of Rosa. When Obie and Matt met her in Nazi-destroyed Naples, she'd been starving, and they had taken her to a restaurant. Matt had fallen in love with her that night. Later, she had walked, pregnant with Matt's child, from Naples to Rome, slipping through Allied and enemy lines to find him. Chaplain Forrester, a division chaplain, had reluctantly married them. After the war ended, and before going home, Obie visited Rosa and her infant son, Matthew. He'd given her the sad details of Matt's death.

It was Cassie that Obie missed the most. His memory of their conversation four years earlier still hurt. Several times during those years he'd picked up the phone to call her. Ken, unrequested, had sent him her San Antonio telephone number along with periodic news that Pinky gave him. Ed's business was doing well, and Cassie had taught school there for a year before becoming pregnant. Their daughter Julie, a Downs Syndrome child, was born two years after their marriage. Obie yearned to speak to her, to give her support. In the end, however, he didn't call.

CHAPTER EIGHT

1959–1960

Obie's San Diego lifestyle was straightforward; he wrote mornings, did research in local libraries in the afternoons, and went for neighborhood walks before dinner. On Sundays, he attended church services and took frequent drives, usually into the hills. His apartment was small; he wasted little time on household chores, although his military experience had instilled the habit of orderliness. He cooked sparse meals and occasionally went to a restaurant for dinner. He was content, he told himself.

The Methodist church collected goods for a food pantry in the city. Obie volunteered one Sunday to deliver collected food to "feed the homeless and the down-and-out." He arrived at the pantry early afternoon with his car's back seat and trunk filled with cans, bottles, and bags. The young woman who came out to help him unload had flaming red hair tied back with a blue kerchief; her every move was quick and sure, as was her tongue.

"Good God, man! Is this all a church that size can come up with? You rich people are certainly tight with your money!"

"We thought we were being generous," he said, smiling.

She cocked her head, and her green eyes projected what he perceived as feigned disgust. "That's the trouble with society today," she said. "Everyone looks out for themselves without regard for the less fortunate. So, what's your name, anyway?"

"Obie . . . Obie Gainsworthy," he said meekly. "What's yours?"

"I'm Annie O'Shane. I'm Irish and proud of it. Don't you think O'Shane is a good Irish name?"

"Well, yes, it certainly is." He held out his hand. "Annie O'Shane, I'm happy to meet you."

Her hand was soft, but she had a firm grip. He scrutinized her, trying not to be too obvious. Although her face was not movie-star beautiful, she was more than pretty with a high forehead, small nose, and wide mouth. Her medium height carried a few pounds more than most frames her size, but she was certainly not fat. Pleasing curves, evident even beneath ill-fitting jeans, caused him some distraction.

It took several trips to carry the food inside. He was surprised when she followed him back to his car after they finished.

"Will you come again?" she asked, leaning into the driver's side window, close enough for him to detect her mild but not unpleasant glandular scent mixed with a light cologne fragrance.

"Perhaps. Other people volunteer, too. Are you here every Sunday, Annie?"

"I'm here every day. I'm a full-time volunteer."

He was curious. "How do you do that? Do they put you up and feed you? How do you manage without a paying job?"

She laughed. "I can see that you've struggled for a living, Obie. It shows in your attitude. If you were one of the rich, you'd assume I have independent means and do this because I can afford to."

"I'm definitely not one of the rich ones." They laughed. "So, how *do* you do it?"

"I have independent means and can do it because I can afford to."

"Is that true?"

"Yes, I have an apartment in another part of the city."

Obie found himself unable to leave. She appeared to want a conversation. Annie was from Connecticut, the daughter of a textile manufacturer. She was twenty-five. She'd been in San Diego for a year after graduation from Columbia. Her father and mother were dead, and she had no close relatives. She received monthly funds from a trust set up by her father. "Not enough to make me rich, but enough so I don't need a paying job."

"Why this?" he said, "Why this mission?"

"I'm a do-gooder, I suppose. Always felt for the poor, the downtrodden. That may sound strange for someone who grew up as I did, but I do have empathy with people who struggle through life."

"No, it's commendable. Are you going to stay here at the pantry?"

"For now, at least. Later, who knows? I live pretty much in the moment." Her hand rested on his arm. "We could go out for a meal."

Such directness surprised Obie, but he was not unpleased. "You mean like a date?"

"Yes, like a date. What else?"

"We just met, Annie."

"So what? I like you. You like me. I can tell. You can't be too bad if you mix with these church people. Anyway, it's nobody's business but ours."

"All right, where can I pick you up . . . and when?"

"Right here will do, at five o'clock."

"Don't you need to go home and freshen up?"

"You can take me home if you don't mind. I don't have a car. I usually take a cab. You can wait awhile at my place before we go out."

Things were moving at a dizzying pace. "Five, it is, then."

"Don't be late!" she said, punctuating her words with a resounding whack on the car roof.

That first date moved at the same reckless speed as their meeting. Obie had envisioned dining out and attending a movie, but they never left her apartment. When he was getting ready to go sometime in the early morning hours, it was with the knowledge that a dam of suppressed emotions had broken.

As he dressed, she said, "I suspect you don't do this often."

"That's right. I don't." Annie inspired honesty. "It's been more than a dozen years," he admitted.

"Why, for goodness sake? It's a gift, a free, wonderful God-given gift . . . if you believe in God. Even if you don't, it's still a wonderful thing."

Undone by her refreshing honesty, he told her about Laura, not in detail, but about the hurt he'd endured. He also spoke guiltily of Mirabella, a girl at the end of the war in Italy with whom he'd spent a night devoid of feeling.

"You poor thing," she said, caressing his arm and kissing his cheek. "If you'll let me, I'll make up for all those lost years."

Before leaving, he felt compelled to give her a brief personal history. *"You're a minister?"* she squealed.

"Does that make a difference in how you see me?"

Her laughter rang off the exposed wooden beams of her apartment. "Indeed, it does! I've made it big time! Now I'm really turned on."

In the following weeks, Annie talked openly and unashamed about her sexual history, which had begun in high school and continued in college. "Here, though," she said, "I've been too busy with other things. You have me all to yourself."

Aside from being aghast at her liberal views on human sexuality, Obie enjoyed her easygoing company. He went often to her apartment, and she went to his on occasion. But he made her understand his need to devote certain hours each day to his work. Being with her made him more efficient since he was forced to organize his time better.

* * *

Months passed. Obie finished *Discourse of Nations,* his second book. Andrew called to tell him Pauldine House wanted it and that an advance would be forthcoming. A major revision was required first, however. The revision would take six months, he estimated. The time required was a disappointment, but he started work on it right away.

During that time, Annie started saying things that annoyed him. She said once, "You keep too much to yourself. You need to do things that help other people."

He felt defensive. "What I'm doing *is* helping others?"

"Obie, you need to go down there with me for a day or two a week to see people who are in need. Sure, your writing *is* important, but you're only feeding minds. I'm feeding bodies." The compromise was that he began volunteering on Sunday afternoons, which didn't affect his writing time.

After the revised manuscript of *Discourse of Nations* was finished and submitted, Obie felt washed out. He decided to take time off to revisit his long-neglected painting. His artist's eye had discovered places in the area that inspired brush and paint.

He also wished to spend more time with Annie. He'd asked her to attend church with him, but she'd declined, saying she was needed at the mission. He'd been disappointed but accepted her excuse. The realization was that he'd come to care for her—but their relationship had troubling elements; looming largest was a growing knowledge that it wasn't going anywhere.

Their intimacy brought pleasure and joy to both, but neither spoke of love. Having decided never to marry, he struggled with the temptation to change his mind. *Maybe he was finally ready.*

He needed to gauge her feelings; it was best to attack the chore head-on. "Annie, what's going to happen to us?"

"You mean as a couple?"

"Yes. Do you want it to stay the way it is?"

"There's nothing wrong with how it is, is there?"

"Well, no. But don't you sometimes want something more?"

"Are you tired of me?"

He laughed. "No, nothing like that. It's just . . ."

"I don't know what more I could do to please you?"

"Annie, you're nearly perfect. The problem is . . ."

"I didn't realize there was a problem."

"Don't you ever want to settle down and have children?"

"Sure, someday. Not for a long time, however. Is that what's bothering you, Obie? Do you want to settle down? If that's it, you'll have to do it with someone else."

"You know there's no one else."

"That's too bad. If that's what you want, you should find someone who feels like you do. *That's not me.* You know what I do . . . what my passion is. That's not going to change. If it disappoints you, I'm sorry, but that's how it is."

"Our relationship means so little to you?"

"It means a great deal to me. But I never expected it to be a permanent thing, however. Did you?"

"I expected it to get consideration."

"Well, in my case, it won't get any consideration." She looked and sounded angry. "Your problem, Obie, is your upbringing, your education, especially in the religious area. It's given you expectations that any intimate relationship must lead toward love and marriage. In my opinion, that's naive."

He hesitated to question her further but knew he must. "What do we do, then?"

"If you persist in this discussion, maybe we'd better go our separate ways."

"Just like that? We've been together for a year. Are we to throw it all away?"

Annie's eyes narrowed, and her expression hardened. "Maybe it's time. I'm extremely fond of you, Obie. Just not *that* much."

He left before his emotions became unraveled. The following day was difficult to get through. She didn't answer his calls. He tried for several more days with the same result. Apparently, she meant what she'd said. Nevertheless, one evening when his phone rang, he rushed, hopefully, to lift the receiver.

The caller identified himself as the Reverend George Dulany. "I'm calling from San Francisco," he said. "Are you the Reverend Obadiah Gainsworthy?"

He'd not heard that prefix lately, nor had he expected to hear it again. "I'm Obadiah Gainsworthy," he managed.

Dulany was a Methodist district official in the San Francisco area; a minister in one of his churches had died, and he was looking for an interim pastor to serve for one year. Would Obie be interested?

He was ready to reply negatively until the uncertainty of the past few days came to mind. His relationship with Annie was over. He'd finished his book and had only vague ideas about the next. Nothing was keeping him in San Diego. Maybe he needed a change. *But ministry?*

"I don't know . . ."

"It's a limited opportunity," Dulany said. "You're not the only candidate. I need a quick yes or a no."

"Yes," Obie said, "I'm interested."

"Good! Can you come to San Francisco in two days for an interview? You should know that we're interviewing two other qualified candidates. One is the assistant minister. He's well-liked but quite young. The other is known to have a drinking problem. But that detail is probably something I shouldn't be telling you."

"Yes, I can be there. I'm curious, though. How did you get my name?"

"I believe you know Anthony Gladstone?"

"Yes. Tony and I served together in Korea."

"Well, he's a distant cousin of mine. We stay in touch. I've been hearing about you for years, Obadiah. Tony is making a career in the Army. He's a chaplain. When I told him of our dilemma, he suggested I look you up. It took some doing to get your number."

"Good old Tony." *That half-blind young man who had carried him from the battlefield.* "He's the best. I'm sorry to have lost touch."

"Yes, he *is* the best . . . and apparently, he's kept track of you."

"You know, don't you, that I've never served a church except in my seminary days and as an assistant in Oakland."

"Yes, I know. I've talked to Wilford Clark. He came out for you in brilliant colors."

"Reverend Dulany, I know how the Church works. You should be meeting with your district elders to find an interim pastor. They're best suited to finding qualified candidates. I think that's what you're required to do."

"This was sudden, and the district is currently short on pastors. I have the approval to proceed with hiring."

"I'm not very good with sermons."

Reverend Clark says differently. Look, Obadiah, there's no sure thing, but with your education and literary accomplishments, I believe you have a good shot at this interim ministry. But, even if you are chosen, I can't promise it will lead to a permanent appointment."

"I'm not looking for a permanent appointment."

Well, in any event, I certainly look forward to meeting you."

CHAPTER NINE

1960–1962

Obie stood on the sidewalk outside Greenleaf Methodist Church gawking at the huge red brick structure. The San Francisco church boasted over five hundred active members, a fact learned after calling Wilford Clark. Obie couldn't remember ever being inside a church building that large, not counting cathedrals in Italy. Stafford Rest Methodist probably never had more than a hundred active members. What was he getting himself into?

Reverend Clark also wondered. "I know pastors who would kill to have a chance at that church, including me," he said. "How in the world did you even get an interview?"

"I have no idea unless knowing a higher-up's cousin helped. Anyway, it's only an interim appointment for one year . . . and I'm not hired yet."

The church's size and elegance did nothing to bolster his confidence. He entered with a tight knot in his stomach. The "Fellowship Forum" interview with several church leaders was intense but friendly. They seemed impressed with his having authored two books, although only one person had read them. "I've read them both," Gus Miller, a college history professor and chairman of the Pastor Parish Committee, said. "The second one, especially, gives some insight into your theological convictions."

He was asked to deliver a "mini-sermon," something he had anticipated and prepared for; he kept it safe, avoiding anything controversial. When he left after the two-hour session that included a guided tour of the building, he was confident he'd done his best, despite a nagging concern that God intended him for something other than pastor of this congregation. He expected at least a twenty-four-hour wait, but Gus Miller delivered the parsonage key to his motel room before nightfall. He could move in right away, Miller told him.

He returned to San Diego the next day to close out his life there. Repeated efforts to meet with Annie were derailed. When she didn't answer her phone, he went to the mission. She had gone home, the manager said, although on driving to her apartment, he found it dark. He returned to the mission. The manager told him again that she wasn't there, but he could see her through a window, working furiously, unpacking boxes without glancing up. It was evident she didn't want to talk. Resigned to the possibility of never seeing Annie again, he loaded all his belongings into a small rented trailer hooked to his car and drove back north.

The previous minister had his own home, so the parsonage had sat empty for over two years. The furnished and musty-smelling house was on a corner of the church property, not far from the main buildings. It seemed immense, with four bedrooms upstairs and a downstairs study adjacent to a spacious living and dining area. The kitchen was equipped to supply an army, it appeared. He noted, with mixed feelings, that the house was more suited for a family, which most ministers his age seemed to have.

The settling-in weeks that followed were not without consternation. Conditions in Vietnam were causing general worry about the United States' involvement there, and it was not unusual for church members to engage Obie in conversation about it.

The period was also a time of adjustment from a solitary life to one placing him in close contact with people. "Busy" had a new meaning; there was hardly enough time to perform his duties of visiting the sick and homebound, counseling, chairing committees, and attending to other administrative tasks. In addition, he delivered two sermons on Sundays and led a Bible study group on Thursday evenings.

His hope of continuing to write, even on a limited basis, proved futile. And notwithstanding repeated efforts to make Andrew understand his time restraints, the agent called often, urging him to start a new book. *Discourse of Nations* had received good reviews and was having a fair run, selling more copies than *Ultimate Conflict* had during its first year.

A delighted Charles Lansing had little sympathy for Obie's complaints regarding his workload. "It's catch-up time," Charles said.

Adam Silverman gave him even less compassion. In a letter, Adam said, "I've seen you working toward this since I've known you, although sometimes your progress has been more of a crawl. Lock and load, soldier!"

At his first monthly meeting with the Pastor Parish Committee, he asked for an assistant minister; the previous assistant had been reassigned after being passed over in favor of Obie. Gus Miller laughed at the request. "We may be big, but we're not rich," Miller said, then added, "We were looking to dissolve the position anyway."

Obie's organizational skills and acquired ability to adjust to conditions eventually rescued him. As the months passed, he fell into a routine that, if not comfortable, was efficient. It became a time of personal growth. As a military chaplain in a war zone, he'd gotten away with impromptu services and makeshift schedules. At Greenleaf, he had to nail down time slots and pay strict attention to the Christian calendar. The church members here were used to the elaborate celebration of Advent, Christmas, Epiphany, Lent, Easter, and Pentecost.

Symbolism as a channel for worship reemerged for him, which was not surprising considering his youthful years in the Catholic Church and his seminary training. One carryover from his Catholic experience was making the sign-of-the-cross. He was questioned about it.

"It's not something Methodists do," Scott Caldone, a committee member, said.

Glendora Sweetwater came to his aid. "John Wesley, our founder, was a member of the Church of England. Those people signed. Don't you think John Wesley did, too?"

When Scott looked unsure, Obie explained. "For me, it's a sign of respect. If it offends, I'm sorry."

"No, it's all right," Scott said. "I understand now." The others nodded, and nothing more was said about it. Nevertheless, the incident validated his suspicion that he was being watched for his "little beliefs," as well as larger doctrinal ones. He would be careful—but not hypocritical.

Funerals were brutal for Obie. Offsetting that unavoidable duty were the marriages and baptisms; he was thankful there were more of those.

Even amid responsibilities, Obie made time for personal reflection; he examined and framed his religious convictions to a degree he'd never attempted before. Then, he integrated those into his sermons and his counseling. Writing sermons was as demanding a chore as writing books, he often told himself during the process. It never became easy, but he gained proficiency in that chore, as in his other duties.

The church building had been constructed in the late eighteen hundreds. Obie developed the habit of walking around the two-acre grounds in the early morning, an act that inspired him for the day ahead.

Glendora Sweetwater, a retired public librarian, sat down with him one day and delivered a lecture on the church's history. She explained that there had been extensive damage to the sanctuary during the 1906 earthquake. Glendora was a child, and her father had been the minister. The Reverend Joel Sweetwater had coaxed and cajoled the membership into erecting a smaller chapel adjacent to the main one to serve their needs before attacking the main sanctuary's more protracted and expensive repair. Sweetwater Chapel was now a draw for marriages and small gatherings.

Obie was happy to renew his friendship with Hershel and Virginia Silverman. He went often to their home, as he and Adam had while students at Berkeley.

Obie still missed Annie. He wrote several times during his first months at Greenleaf—without an answer. He finally became resigned to never seeing her again.

George Dulany came to see him near the end of the anticipated year at Greenleaf. "I've met with your Pastor Parish Committee," he said. "They've indicated they wish to keep you on as a regular appointee. They even want to give you an assistant pastor. So it will become fact if you're agreeable and the district approves." Despite his initial reluctance to pursue pastoral ministry, Obie soon found himself the regular pastor of the large church.

Things went smoothly, and, a month into his second year, he felt that being called "Pastor" was deserved. God had opened a door for him and had forgiven his missteps. Nevertheless, he couldn't abandon his belief that writing was his true calling and that his present position was temporary. Andrew must have believed it, too, for he hadn't ceased nagging him.

One evening, a telephone call came. "Obie," Annie said.

"Yes, Annie?" He waited.

"Obie . . . are we speaking?

"That's up to you."

"I've been a fool, Obie. I miss you so much. Can I come and see you?"

"Of course, but you'll have to take separate accommodations. My lifestyle has changed considerably."

"Yes, I know. I've kept tabs. I called your father. I'm leaving San Diego. It's time for me to move on."

"To where, Annie? Another mission?"

"No, I want something more stable."

"Annie, you need to be honest with me. What are you thinking?"

Obie heard her sob. "I'm thinking that I love you, Obie. It surprises me, but I think about you all the time. Life's so empty here without you. There hasn't been anyone else since you left. Do I still have a place in your life?"

He hesitated. He'd spent a year and a half getting over her; she'd caused him pain. The way she wanted to live wasn't what he wanted. Did he wish to take a chance on more pain?

"I don't know, Annie. I care for you, too. However, I have many questions."

"I'll marry you!"

He sucked in his breath and held it. Her words surprised him, but he didn't want to overreact. He exhaled slowly. "I'm a minister, Annie. It takes a special person to be a minister's wife."

"I can be whatever it takes."

He was hopeful, but he must be cautious. "Why don't you come on up here? Then, we'll see how things go."

She arrived two days later. They spent public time together for three weeks. She attended services at Greenleaf Methodist, listened to Obie's sermons, and was introduced to the congregation. Exactly one month after her arrival, George Dulany, in a special ceremony open to the congregation, joined Obie Gainsworthy and Annie O'Shane in marriage.

* * *

Annie brought a domestic touch to the parsonage. The house was aired out and thoroughly cleaned inside. Old drapes came down, and new colorful ones went up. Victorian furnishings were moved to the attic, and rooms quickly filled with modern furniture, some new, most purchased from sidewalk sales and used furniture stores. Bookcases in the study, which housed

Obie's sparse volumes, also became stocked with vases and knick-knacks. Paintings bought at local art shows, and some of Obie's own, hung on the walls. Flowers adorned tables. The house came alive with physical change, activated by the vibrant personality of Annie Gainsworthy.

The congregation had followed their whirlwind courtship with great interest. Scores attended the wedding, and well-wishers dropped presents off at the house. Obie was thrilled by the way his wife was received. She was quickly sought after for committee work and women's groups, not only in the church but also in the community. Any fears that she might not fit in were soon dispelled.

She attended both Sunday morning services, her scarlet head adorning the front row. Annie seemed a perfect helpmate for a minister of the gospel. "I love it here," she said aloud one day while watering her plants, but within his hearing. *Perhaps he was destined to be there.*

Another surprise came one evening when she said, "Let's go up the Napa Valley for an overnight. I know a little place."

"I didn't know you'd ever been there."

She laughed. "I get around." He ignored what might have been taken as a double meaning. "Okay, it'll be good to get away awhile."

The "little place" was a six-room house with stucco siding and a red-tiled roof. A dusty dirt road, about two hundred feet long, led to the house; it was curved so that the structure wasn't easily seen from the highway. What *was* visible, delighting Obie as he stepped from the car, was an adjacent vineyard spilling back across several rounded hills. A large house, a Spanish-style mansion, sat on the peak of one hill like some ancient manor house ruling its subservient lands. It reminded him of the vineyard in the Russian River Valley where he worked before his senior year at Berkeley, and where he had the dream that propelled him into seminary.

"What a view! How did you know about this?" Obie asked as they carried their overnight bags from the car into the house.

She smiled as she took out a key and opened the front door. "It's mine," she said. "It was a gift from Dad several years ago. He grew up here and brought me here when I was little. But I haven't been here for nearly three years."

"Annie, you're amazing."

"I knew you'd like it. I've saved it as a surprise. You can come here and write."

"If I ever find time for that."

"We'll make time."

In truth, the setting was one in which inspiration might dwell. It felt good being alone with Annie in such a place. She left for a couple of hours on the second day to visit the house on the hill. She explained that she'd long known Matilda, the vineyard manager's wife. The couple also watched over her house, and she needed to talk to them about that. Obie wanted to go along, but she didn't invite him, so he spent the time sitting on the back porch reading and enjoying the scenery.

They stayed an extra night, with Obie letting the essence of the surroundings sink in and Annie working to resuscitate a long-neglected flower garden. He slept better than he had for years; there were not the war memories that came so often to torment him during the night. He was rejuvenated when they returned to San Francisco.

The fantasy didn't last, however. Annie soon became restless. She stopped attending the second Sunday service and dropped out of some committees. Obie watched helplessly as the changes slowly took place; they coincided with national events. Annie had hailed the election of John F. Kennedy to the presidency, only to loudly condemn his Bay of Pigs invasion.

"Some people here won't agree," he told her. "And to keep the peace, perhaps you shouldn't be so vocal."

Her eyes flashed a challenge. "What does it matter what they think? If you know you're right, shouldn't you speak out?"

"Sweetheart, I can't set members of this church against one another. My job is to foster love, not create dissension."

"Never take a stand against anything? Is that what you mean?"

He was defensive. "No! It's *not* what I mean! I *do* take stands. Haven't you been listening to my sermons? Didn't I publicly endorse the Committee on Racial Equality last Sunday? Haven't I encouraged some young members of our congregation who plan to join the Freedom Riders in the South?"

"Speaking of such . . . I'd like to join them."

That surprised him. She'd been outspoken in supporting Dr. Martin Luther King Jr. but had never indicated she wanted personal involvement.

"I forbid it," he said.

"You *forbid* it!" Her anger was apparent. "Obie, I reject anyone's right to forbid me from exercising my convictions." Her tone softened slightly, and she added, "Respectfully."

"It's not safe. That's my objection. People will get hurt. I don't want it to be you."

"I'm not afraid."

Nothing more was said on the subject for several weeks, although he knew it was on her mind. She purchased a television set and they watched the news from the South as it unfolded.

One day she said, "I'm going back to San Diego for a few days."

"Why?"

"I received a letter from Ruth, the mission coordinator. They may have to close for lack of volunteers and funds. I can change it around if I spend a couple of weeks there. I know people who can help."

"Two weeks?"

"Obie, it's something I need to do. I left suddenly and without much explanation."

"How did she get our address?"

I wrote to her a couple of weeks ago because my conscience hurt. You do understand, don't you?"

"I guess so. Is this the reason you've been distracted lately?"

"It is. It's all right if I go, then?"

Her asking permission made him suspicious that she might be using San Diego as a cover for a longer trip. He said cautiously, "I suppose so. Where will you stay?"

"Ruth has offered to put me up while I'm there."

"Are you sure San Diego is where you're going?"

"It is. Listen, Obie, I'm not the perfectly moral person you'd like, but I'm truthful. I'll always tell you the truth even if you'd rather not hear it."

He believed she was sincere. "I'm sorry if it sounded like I doubted your word, Annie. I *do* trust you to tell me the truth." He added, "And it occurs to me that we could use a program like that in our community here. You'd be perfect for heading it. Has that occurred to you?"

"Let me get this other problem out of the way first," she said, "then I'll give it some thought."

Obie explained her absence to the membership.

Nevertheless, it became awkward when two weeks passed and she hadn't returned. Finally, she called to say she needed another week.

When she returned after three weeks, she was revitalized. She went to Sunday services and was a perfect clergyman's wife in every way. She also encouraged intimacy. He was a lucky man, he told himself.

When she hadn't acted on his suggestion about starting a food pantry program in their area, he brought it up. She dismissed the idea as being impractical. She was "too busy with other things."

"But not too busy for going to Southern California?" He feared his words were confrontational.

"Don't worry," she said, "I'm not going to leave you again."

"Is that a promise, Annie? You've become an indispensable part of my life. I miss you even when you go out for a committee meeting in the evening, so you can imagine how I felt when you went to San Diego."

"How sweet," she said as she kissed him on the cheek.

Another month passed before Annie started missing the second Sunday service again. She also cut back on church work. A pattern of behavior was evident.

He decided to face matters head-on. "Annie, what's bothering you?"

She answered with a question. "You know that I love you, don't you?"

"You've not given me reason to believe otherwise."

"Do you take confessions?"

"That's a Catholic thing, but I'll listen to you." He braced himself for what she might be about to say.

"I'm a restless person, Obie. I've always been like that. I need to change location often. When we met, I'd been the longest in one place and was ready to move on. I guess you provided enough variety to satisfy me. I told you that I graduated from Columbia. What you don't know is that I attended three other schools before that. It's the way I am. And I should have told you, but I hoped I could change. I guess I can't. I don't love you any less, but I need occasional space. Can you put up with that?"

"I'll try, Annie. Are you getting ready to leave again?"

"I'm really awful, aren't I?"

"Where to?"

"New York."

"New York? What's there?"

"My cousin. My mother's sister's daughter. I haven't seen her for four years, and she's having a serious operation. She doesn't have anyone else. I'd be gone two weeks."

He couldn't stifle a sigh. "Or longer?"

"Maybe. Obie, I'll come back. I promise. If you can't put up with this, please tell me now." She hesitated. "I'll give you your freedom if you want it."

His inclination was to reply in anger, but she looked contrite. Finally, he said, "I believe in the sanctity of marriage, Annie. If you need to take your jaunts, go ahead. But please don't stay away too long."

"Thank you, Obie! Sometimes, all it takes is a few days. I'll always come back. And I'll be true to you, too. I love you, Obie." She hesitated. "Something puzzles me, however. You've never told me that you love *me*?"

Was it true? He must have sometime said those words to her. *How could he not have?* He searched his memory and came up blank. He *did* love her. He could learn to live with her imperfections.

"I do love you, Annie," he said. He reached for her, held her close, and kissed her forehead, cheeks, and mouth.

She took his hand and led him toward the stairs. "Come on! If I'm going to New York, we need to get ahead."

He needed no convincing.

CHAPTER TEN

1962–1963

Not long after President Kennedy initiated the Peace Corps, Annie announced her intention to join. Obie wasn't pleased, but neither was he surprised. The Corps was meant for someone like her, someone with an intense desire to serve. With Obie's support, she announced her decision to the church; any negative reaction was mitigated by news of five other young people leaving for the same reason.

"Why don't you go with me?" Annie said.

"You know it's not practical. I have responsibilities here."

She'd seldom been overcritical of his work. Now she said, "You serve these people well, Obie, but have you never wanted to serve in other ways?"

"You mean like marching in Alabama?" He knew she felt guilty about not joining that cause, although she'd never said so.

"No, that's not what I meant. There's much ignorance and misery in this world, hungry people to feed or teach how to feed themselves. I'm not saying intellectual and spiritual guidance isn't important. It's just not the most urgent need of the downtrodden. Sometimes helping others means getting down in the ditch with them and getting dirty yourself."

There was truth in her declaration, as far as it went. The seminary had taught him about John Wesley's quadrilateral model, which named scripture, tradition, reason, and experience as the basics for balancing Christian life.

"Experience" was the activist part—Annie's domain. As a pastor, it was necessary to guide with a balanced hand. He supposed that having all sides of the mystical quadrilateral equal was ideal but knew that it was unrealistic. People were different from one another, as were churches and denominations, all serving in unique ways.

Grandpa Jacob was strong on three sides of that quadrilateral; tradition hadn't been his strength. And Annie appeared incredibly lopsided against Wesley's model. Her works, driven by her passion for helping others, didn't need Christianity for success. It may be that her strength was his weakness. Christian faith, however, was something he wanted for her.

"Annie, I agree with you . . . mostly, but I can't simply up and leave."

"Yes, you can. They'd find someone else. They found you soon enough, didn't they?"

"I guess so."

"You shouldn't let yourself get tied down, Obie. There are better causes than this."

He tried not to scowl at her words, although he knew his expression would reveal his disapproval. "This is my calling, at least for the present."

"Not long ago, writing was your calling."

"And it still is. I'll get back to it. But for now, this is where God has placed me. He put me here for a reason, and I must play it out."

She softened. "I didn't mean to disparage your work. It *is* important. It's just that maybe you need to expand your horizons."

"That's probably true, Annie, although now isn't the time for me to attempt it."

A few weeks later, they learned she was going to Africa, to Ghana, for a year. When it was time to part, Annie, at the train station with her luggage gathered around her, said, "There's a blessing in this. My absence will give you time to do some writing. I know I've kept you from it."

Undoubtedly, her words were meant to ease his mind; the effort was appreciated, although ineffectual. He held her face between his hands and kissed her repeatedly.

"You must be careful," he said. "I don't know much about Ghana, but for sure, it's not home."

"Obie, I'll be all right. I'll write at least once a week and tell you all about what I'm doing. You must go often to our house in Napa Valley." She had given him the key a few days before.

For several months her frequent letters came, filled with details of her small group's work. They were introducing modern agricultural methods and building irrigation channels to gardens and fields, for which she'd had no previous skills. She said it required tremendous time and patience but was the most rewarding work she'd ever undertaken.

He was thankful for her letters. They couldn't replace the

warmth of her presence but did ease the pain of her absence. But there were days, especially his more tying ones, when he wanted to be with her, close to the earth, solving problems with real solutions.

Annie had been gone eight months when Obie received word from his father that Aunt Izzie had died. He was still reeling from that news when a letter came from Annie with a section that disturbed him further:

> *Del Greene ... I told you about him. He's a dedicated man, a chemical engineer between jobs who wanted to put his time to good use. He was assigned to our group along with Carrie, Cindy, and me. We did a lot of work until we all became sick with a bug that took everything out of us, and I do mean everything. Del and I recovered from it pretty quickly. I've been lucky, blessed with a healthy constitution, I guess. Carrie and Cindy were so ill that they had to be evacuated. They are on their way home. That leaves Del and me on this project. They intend to get someone else in to help, but it's him and me for now. We get along well. He's thirty years old. We decided it would be expedient for us to share the same quarters. Now, don't worry ... we both know it's only a working relationship. I love you, and only you.*

He did worry. In earlier letters, she hinted that Del Greene was not someone likely to resist temptation.

Obie had, in Annie's absence, tried to write. He went to the Napa house during a two-week vacation and at other times when he could arrange it. Andrew told him that if he could supply an outline for a book, he was sure he could get a healthy advance from Pauldine House. The books in print had returned their advances and now paid a royalty, but sales had slackened, and the amount was far from enough to make him independent. Moreover, the planning and outlining a new book didn't go well. He was unfocused, and worry about Annie, both physical and moral, was a real distraction.

Several weeks passed before he received her next letter. His fears were confirmed. "We've always been honest with each other," she wrote, "and I don't want that to stop . . . even if we hurt each other."

She went on to say:

> *I'll not go into detail, but Del and I have become more than just roommates. You know me, how I am. He just happened to be here instead of you. I can't make excuses for my actions. I'm undoubtedly a sinner in your eyes, but I want you to know he means little to me. It's you I love, and I'm anxious to return to you in a few short months. <u>Please forgive me</u>.*

Obie crumpled the pages of the letter along with the envelope and threw them across the study. "Like hell, I will!" he said aloud, adding, "You slut!"

He could think of little else other than her betrayal. His anger was like a terrible toothache refusing to go away. He couldn't work at writing or pastoring and avoided all situations where he had to give counsel. Then, one evening a phone call came from George Dulany.

"Obadiah, what's bothering you?" The voice held a proper balance of concern and judgment. "One of your members called me to say you seem troubled. Said you've put off talking to her several times. Is something wrong?"

"I may need to take a few days off," Obie said.

"I'll talk to your Pastor Parish chair. Your assistant can handle it. It'll be a good experience for him. Take a week off."

"Thank you, George."

"Is there something I can help you with, Obadiah? Are you ill?"

"George, it's my wife, Annie. You're aware that she's in Africa with the Peace Corps?"

"Yes, I know."

"She's having an affair."

"Good lord . . . not Annie?"

"I'm afraid so, and I'm having a bad time with it."

"I understand. Let me come and talk to you personally. I can be there in half an hour."

"George, I know you give good counsel, but right now I need solitude more than talk. I'm going away for a while. I need to decide what to do about this."

"Very well, Obadiah. I'll pray for you . . . and for Annie. I want you to know that this is just between you and me. Call me when you return."

Obie went first to the Napa house; he left after two days because he saw too much of Annie there. Then, he drove up the coast road, a route he had taken in Adam's old Caddy while in his first year at Berkeley. That time, shortly after the war and soon after he'd entered Berkeley, had been carefree; this time, there was a feeling his world had been broken beyond mending.

As much as he believed in prayer, he was unable to pray. When he drove back south, he chose roads through the mountains and stopped often to walk into woods or along streams. On the last of those treks on the way back to the Bay Area, he walked a great distance in shoes not suitable for backcountry and sustained blisters that nearly crippled him. He reached home after midnight. Instead of going to bed, he took out stationary and composed a letter.

> *Dear Annie,*
>
> *I have given considerable thought about how best to answer your letter. I have been on a trip and am very tired, but it may be the best time to write because I will be less guarded with my words, and this is a time for honesty. The one thing I admire about your letter is your honesty. Therefore, I am trying to respond in kind. I cannot say your disclosure did not hurt me, for it did. I hope my words will convey my decision without causing you as much pain. If not, then I'm sorry.*
>
> *I forgive you, Annie. Nevertheless, I do not believe things can return to how they were before. When we married, I knew of your divergent beliefs about relationships. I was willing to put that aside. Everyone needs a new start, and I believed it was what you wanted. I suppose I was wrong.*
>
> *I'm not asking for a divorce. It's up to you whether you want one. I'll never marry again, so I have no need for a divorce. But, on the other hand, I have no desire for us to live together again. However, you are welcome to come and get your belongings once you return to the United States. If you like, I can arrange to be absent at that time.*
>
> *Sincerely, Obie*

Hobbling on sore feet, he went to a corner mailbox to ensure he couldn't change his mind. Then, he went to bed and slept until the afternoon.

* * *

Weeks of emotional pain followed. Annie didn't answer his letter. Obie went through the motions of pastoring, not letting the congregation believe anything beyond the expectation of Annie's imminent return. Her women's group was planning a welcoming home party. *He must tell them the truth.* He consulted George about how to proceed.

"We'll meet first with Pastor Parish and your board," George said. "The best policy is to tell them straight out that Annie's not returning. We don't have to say why, although I'm sure the question will be asked. We'll let members of Pastor Parish stand with you as you break the news, but you'll have to handle any questions in your own way."

"When?"

"At once."

On Sunday, after it was over, he withdrew to the parsonage, asking that he not be disturbed for twenty-four hours; no one violated his request. When he emerged and assumed his duties again, he was surprised that no one asked questions. *Maybe they knew.* He didn't concern himself with how they might know. He was just glad they were letting it lie.

He eventually returned to his writing on a manageable schedule. He also led a small church group on a retreat to the Napa house, hoping it would make him feel good about the place again, and to some extent, it did. He would return the keys to Annie, but since she seemed in no hurry, he would go there when he could.

He sought out friends. Hershel was strangely quiet after hearing what had taken place. Virginia had much to say. "You no longer love her?"

"I do love her. If I didn't, this would be easier."

"Obadiah, what are the things about Annie that you don't like?"

"Isn't it obvious? She's been unfaithful. No man should have to put up with that."

Virginia leaned toward Obie, her large eyes intent. "Do you believe one bad thing cancels out all the good things about Annie?"

"In my eyes, it does. I'll not put up with it again."

A surprised look appeared on Virginia's face. *"Again? Has she done this before?"*

"No."

"So, what do you mean 'again?'"

Hershel broke his silence. "You're a proud man, Obadiah, and an angry one right now. I can't help thinking your anger is misplaced."

"And how might that be?" Obie said, not trying to hide his annoyance.

His mentor was not deterred. "And the other friend of yours . . . Cassie? I was sure you two were in love. Was she unfaithful to you, too? Is that it?"

"Cassie and I have had a complicated relationship. She's married. No, if I'm angry, it's at Annie . . . and I'm not transferring it from Cassie or anyone else."

"Ah-ha," Virginia said. *"Someone else.* I thought as much. Am I right?"

"I remember now," Hershel said. "My nephew once told me you were broken up about a girl who married someone else after you enlisted in the Army."

"A long time ago." He was aware of clenching his jaw and being unable to stop. "I'm over it."

"What's her name?" Virginia asked.

Virginia could be relentless with her questions. "Does it matter?" He choked back a lump in his throat. "She's Cassie's sister. I've long ago put it behind me."

"No, you haven't," Virginia said. Her laugh was one of revelation. "What's her name, Obadiah?"

He let his breath escape slowly. "Laura. Her name is Laura. See? I can say it."

"And you have tears in your voice," Virginia said, still smiling.

Hershel looked as though a light in his brain had clicked on. He said, "Don't take it the wrong way, Obadiah, but we can harbor anger for a long time. If you had an intense relationship with Laura, it might explain some things."

"Are you two trying to psychoanalyze me?" Obie asked, not caring that he probably sounded angry. "The simple truth is that Annie was unfaithful. No man likes such a role. That's why we're done."

"It's been weeks, Obadiah," Virginia said. "You should be

getting over it. You should be writing to Annie and trying to save your marriage."

"It won't happen. It's over. I won't take her back!"

"Even if she admits she made a mistake?"

"That's right!"

The silence lasted long enough to make Obie uncomfortable.

Finally, Hershel said, "Tell us about Laura."

"Why?"

"Do you trust me, Obadiah?"

"Totally, sir. You know that."

"You might concede that talking about Laura can be cathartic."

"Tell us," Virginia urged.

He hesitated, then words began to tumble out. He didn't tell them everything, but enough. Hershel and Virginia were silent, letting him vent.

When he finished, Virginia said, "How old were you?"

"Seventeen."

"And now?"

"I'm thirty-six. It's been nearly twenty years."

"You were a baby," Hershel said. "And at an impressionable age. Maybe you've harbored anger about what you considered her betrayal."

"It *was* a betrayal. She never explained why she married someone else when she was so much in love with me . . . or so I believed."

"Have you ever considered that there might have been some miscommunication?"

"I don't see how. We had a system all worked out to keep her mother from knowing."

"Sometimes systems break down," Hershel said.

"You know what I think?" Virginia said. "It's Laura you're most angry at." She ignored the shaking of his head. "Is that fair to Annie?"

"Are you saying Annie's not at fault?" He was conscious of his voice rising. "If you are, then you're wrong. She cheated on me. She was aware that a pastor's wife has moral responsibilities."

Virginia wasn't intimidated by his angry words. "Okay, she shouldn't have done what she did, but everybody makes mistakes. Haven't you?"

"None like that."

"What does Jesus do, Obadiah?"

"What?"

"The one you worship . . . does he not forgive? Do you not try to be like him?"

Obie was subdued. He was thinking how best to answer when Hershel said, "Obadiah, we're your friends. We've only seen Annie a few times, but we were starting to love her as we love you. We're trying to help. You say you still love her. Isn't it right to try saving your marriage instead of writing it off? I wasn't at your marriage ceremony, but I'm willing to bet that somewhere in it there was the phrase, 'for better or for worse.' Am I right?"

"Yes, you're right. It still doesn't excuse . . ."

"Hypocrite!" Virginia said. Obie was taken aback because he had never heard her raise her voice. She continued. "Underneath all your pious talk, you're like the rest of us, aren't you? I'll bet if you were in Africa for nearly a year with a beautiful woman, you'd succumb too?"

He reminded himself that he'd lived like a monk for years. "No, I'd manage to resist it."

"I know my men," Virginia said. "I've seen how you look at me."

It felt like being stabbed in the ribs. Since their first meeting, he had felt a mild attraction for Virginia, who was half Hershel's age. He glanced at Hershel to see if he'd heard, then tried to make a joke of it. "Well, Virginia, you are special. Your beauty exceeds . . ."

"Don't try to change the subject. You're just a man. Any woman worth her salt could have you naked in bed within an hour."

Hershel laughed. "She's right, you know. Underneath our human exterior lurks sexual animals."

"I don't believe that," Obie said. "I'll never believe it."

"You delude yourself," Virginia said. "I'm not saying you cannot raise yourself or let God raise you above the level of the masses, but everyone has a threshold where they compromise their beliefs. Evidently, you've not reached yours. It's there, nonetheless."

As he prepared to leave later that evening, Hershel said,

"Obadiah, we mean you no disrespect. We're only trying to help. We would like to see you and Annie patch this up."

"I'm sorry, but it's not likely," Obie said.

Virginia had the parting word. "You're not too good to stumble, you know . . . and someday you will."

* * *

There was no word from Annie; she would have been back for several months. Obie stopped going to the Napa house. It would be awkward if he found her there. Nor had he touched any of her belongings in the parsonage. He should box them up, for they were constant reminders, stirring up memories he didn't need.

He considered divorce. Staying married to Annie would create estate difficulties should either die. He dismissed the idea with a sigh and tried to imagine where she was and what she was doing. Lying in bed at night, he remembered her there beside him, touching him, arousing him. He tried, unsuccessfully, to expel from his head the image of her with Del Greene.

On a day in May, a Monday, the weekday he kept for himself, he drove to Monterey. He'd been there once with Adam. He wanted to see the ocean, watch big waves roll in, and eat seafood in some little restaurant. He was getting over Annie, he told himself. He was putting her behind him at last.

He arrived before noon. There were few people on the beach. Large boulders were scattered between the parking lot and the water. He sat on one, removed his shoes, and rolled up his pant legs.

"I know you." The voice was female.

Obie turned, thinking she was speaking to someone else, but she was alone. The woman, in her late twenties, was lying on a quilt at the edge of the boulder area. She was behind a huge stone, so he'd been unaware of her presence. She was long-legged and deeply tanned. Her bikini left little to the imagination. "Gorgeous" was the word best describing her.

"I'm sorry. I'm afraid I don't remember . . ."

She smiled. "Oh, no, I only meant that I recognize you. You're Obadiah Gainsworthy." She held up a book. It was a copy of *Ultimate Conflict*. "Your picture's on the back cover."

"That's a boring way to spend a beautiful day."

"Not at all. A friend loaned it to me. She said it's brilliant, but so is she. I'm enjoying it. Sort of. At least the parts I understand."

"So, you know who I am. What's *your* name?"

She sat up and reached a hand toward him. "I'm Amy. Amy Gilchrest." Her hand was soft and warm.

"Glad to know you, Amy. I'm not often recognized like that. It's good for my ego, though . . . so thank you."

"Why don't you sit and talk to me." She patted one side of the patchwork quilt on which she sat.

"I'm only here for a walk on the beach." There was no need to let things get out of hand.

"Can I walk with you? It's not every day I get to meet the author of the book I'm reading."

Refusing wouldn't be polite. "If you like."

The wind was up, and waves crashed onto the beach only seconds apart. They walked as close to the water as possible, an erratic course to avoid the surging tide.

She was a nurse in a nearby hospital; she'd been divorced for several years; she had a ten-year-old daughter. She said there had been a boyfriend, but he had neglected her to the extent that she "wrote him off."

When he told her that he was a pastor, she looked surprised. "The blurb on your book didn't mention it."

"Both my books were published before my appointment, although you might have noticed I was an Army chaplain."

"You're a war hero too, aren't you? What do I call you? 'Obadiah' sounds so formal."

"Obie. That's what my friends call me."

"Well, Obie, why don't you tell me more about yourself."

They eventually retraced their steps to the rock where their belongings lay. He had trouble not staring at her. Her blonde hair was cut short; the ocean breeze had ruffled it, creating an unmanageable appearance. It struck him, then—she looked like Cassie—not so much her face, but her hair and body shape.

He needed to end the feelings that were beginning to overwhelm him. "I have to go, Amy," he told her. "It's a long drive back to San Francisco. I have to eat and start home."

"I can show you a good place to eat."

"I don't want to hold you up. You need to get back to your daughter."

"She doesn't get out of school until three o'clock. That's three hours away. It's not far. Come on, you can follow me."

It was hard to refuse. At the sidewalk cafe, no one appeared to mind or even notice that Amy wore a bikini. The day was becoming chilly, so Obie took a light jacket from his car and wrapped it around her shoulders. They ordered sandwiches and soup and, after eating, talked about various things. Obie told her he painted when he could "find the time." He prepared to leave.

"Does your schedule have such a hold on you that you can't stay a few more minutes?" she said. "I have something I want to show you."

She was unbelievably forward. "What do you want to show me?"

"See the building there?" She pointed. "It's where we live. Upstairs. I paint, too. Some people even buy my paintings. Can you take a look and tell me what you think?"

He was reluctant. "I guess, just for a few minutes."

The paintings were good. Her style was individualistic, and her technique was flawless. He understood why people would buy them. Had she brought him there to sell him a painting? He'd imagined something else.

"Amy, these are excellent."

"Thank you. Every artist needs encouragement. But you know that."

"I must go." He spoke the words but stood still.

Her hand was on his. "Don't go," she said. "Stay with me awhile." Her meaning was clear.

"Amy, I'm married."

"You didn't mention a wife."

"I haven't seen her for more than a year."

"So, you're separated?"

"I guess we are."

"So, you're free to do as you wish."

"I'm a minister, Amy. It's a sin for me."

She planted herself squarely in front of him and put her hands on his shoulders. "It's not often two people meet like we have today and feel like we do about each other so soon. Yes, I can tell you like me. I like you too." She laughed. "I'll admit that I was having trouble getting into your book, but I do like its author."

"I like you too, Amy, but I couldn't."

"Maybe God gives us moments like this . . . little rewards. I'm not very religious, so I don't know if it's true. The thing is, if we don't use these moments, they're gone forever."

She leaned against him. He didn't turn away when she raised her head and kissed him. The room whirled. "Put your arms around me, Obie," she said.

He did as he was told. Her feel, her scent, everything about her was intoxicating.

"This way," she whispered, leading him. He followed.

Much later, on the road back to San Francisco, he remembered Virginia's words: "You're not too good to stumble." Even if he believed it, he couldn't have imagined it happening so soon.

By the time he pulled into the parsonage driveway he'd reached a decision. This fall from grace didn't make him an evil man, but it did accent his recurring opinion that he was unfit for the ministry. The reality of today's deviant encounter had convinced him. Tomorrow, he would speak to George and see what steps he must take to resign.

CHAPTER ELEVEN

1963

Daniel Williamson adjusted the throttle of the Cessna and tax-ied along the tarmac toward the tie-down spot. His instructor, Gabe Black, occupied the right-hand seat. Dan had just completed a routine series of "touch-and-goes."

"Stop here," Gabe said.

"We're in traffic," Dan protested, thinking that Gabe was conducting one of his frequent spot checks to keep him "situation-aware."

"We won't be here long."

"What're we doing?"

"It's time, Danny Boy!"

"Time?"

"I'll walk over to the hanger. By the time I get there, you should be back out to the end of the runway and ready to take off."

"I'm soloing?"

"That's right!"

For a moment, anxiety knotted Dan's throat. "Do you think I'm ready?"

"You are! Today's the day!"

A rush of joy came, something like Christmas when he was a kid; after waiting, and working, and more waiting, it was happening. Finally, he was trusted to take an expensive airplane into the sky alone and bring it back without a mishap.

"What do I do?" Dan tried to sound casual.

"What we've been doing. Take her up, around, and down. Then do it two more times and come back here and tie 'er down just like always."

Gabe stepped out and raised his thumb. In minutes, Dan was on the end of a runway that pointed toward the Atlantic Ocean. He informed the tower of his intentions and half ex-pected Gabe to come on to encourage him, but a monotone voice on the radio gave him clearance to take off.

The situation was wonderfully unreal. He scanned the

instrument panel, making sure everything was normal. Flying with Gabe in the other seat was one thing—being alone, just him and the aircraft, was a new feeling but one he relished. He'd earned the right, he believed.

He eased forward and made quick jabs at the brake pedals to line up with the runway's center before pushing the throttle against the instrument panel. Seconds later, he was in the air.

The day was calm with a five-thousand-foot ceiling. He wouldn't be above a thousand feet. As he climbed, he saw waves hitting the beaches below. He stayed in the pattern, making two left turns until he was again lined up with the runway. Decreasing power, he let the Cessna settle to the surface. Seconds later, he went to full power and climbed until he was once more at pattern altitude.

After completing the third landing, he couldn't control his smile while taxiing to the hanger and maneuvering into their tie-down place. Gabe, grinning, came out to help. "Congratulations!" he said.

"How'd I do?" Dan asked.

"Fine, fine. Now that we've got that out of the way, we can do some real flying."

"I'll be gone for the next two weeks," Dan said. "I'm going home to Boston. Christmas break, you know."

"Yeah, you college boys have a real tough time."

They bantered back and forth while putting the Cessna to bed and filling in their logs. Other students and instructors appeared and went through a flight school ritual of tearing off Dan's shirt and writing messages on it. He'd made many friends there in the past four months. After the others drifted away, he talked with Gabe awhile, then excused himself to drive back to his dorm and pack.

Dan was in his second year at the University of Miami in Florida. He'd scorned his Grandmother Hunt's advice about applying to Ivy League schools because he felt there were better ways to spend his time than studying every spare minute. His father lectured him about the many advantages of being a physician like himself and his grandfather.

Dan was unsure about following that career path. Grandfather Williamson had raised the subject several times when Dan was younger, not trying to convince him but obviously wanting him to consider medicine. On the other hand, his father's approach was more like a demand, and Dan had trouble with demands. He had two more years to consider his options, so he wasn't concerned.

Nevertheless, there was a concern preying on his mind, one he shared with many other students; the escalating Vietnam situation made finishing college on time an uncertainty.

He was taking a commercial flight home and would be in Boston until the day after Christmas. He and his mother would then drive to Stafford Rest, a yearly routine. His father hadn't gone there for three years—since the death of the elder Doctor Williamson.

He packed one suitcase and a smaller bag to carry with him. His winter clothing was in Boston. A few items, including his skis, were in Stafford Rest. While there, they would spend at least one day at one of the ski resorts scattered around the Adirondacks or maybe one in Vermont. His mother didn't ski. Aunt Cassie did; she was good at it.

However, Cassie wasn't going to Stafford Rest this year; she'd called his mother to say that Julie was sick. He bemoaned that fact. Cassie was fun, someone who did exciting things. When he was little and spent time in Stafford Rest during the summer, he went often to her apartment on Main Street. She had all kinds of art supplies and games and sat on the floor with him and in the sand on the beach.

He was eleven when she married Uncle Ed. After that, he'd not seen her during summers. She'd never failed, however, to return for Christmas, even after Ed stopped coming. He would miss Cassie and Julie. Julie was seven and, even with her handicap, often seemed the mature one at their family gatherings.

Dan's fondest memories were of Stafford Rest. His grandmother was a pain at times, but his jovial granddad more than made up for it. His dad disliked the town and said the only reason he ever returned was his sense of duty to his father. Dan had spent limited time with his Grandfather Williamson, for the doctor lived alone and could be called out at all hours. So, by default, Dan became closer to his mother's family.

Dan and his mother made other trips together to Stafford Rest during the year, and he thought it a mystery why she usually descended into periods of depression as soon as they arrived. Something about Stafford Rest upset her; he hadn't figured out what it was.

This holiday season would be bleak, with Cassie and Julie absent and the country still grieving over its murdered president. His father would have a dark mood as well.

His estrangement from his father was an old story. As a child, Dan was unable to avoid angry outbursts. As an adult, it was still unpleasant, but now he could walk away. He was glad his father no longer went to the Adirondacks.

Dan went to bed right after packing. His flight was scheduled to leave at seven o'clock.

* * *

Would she heal in time? Cassie had called Stafford Rest to say they would not be coming for Christmas, telling her mother that Julie was ill. She called later to say they might make it after all. As she examined her face in a mirror, she realized she might have to call again. If it were one black eye or one other singular injury, they might believe a story about falling down the porch steps or being hit by a door. With multiple bruises on her face and arms, such a lie would not do. And the other painful bruises that covered her body would likely give her away. She would wait two more days before deciding about the trip.

Why did she put up with it? The question was one she'd asked herself repeatedly for several years. Ed was a man with two personalities. His angry side flared in unreasonable ways. But after a blowup, he was humble and caring for long periods. For some reason, he never lashed out at Julie, and Cassie was thankful for that. If he had, she would have left long ago.

He provided for them in a way she couldn't do alone. Julie would need special care all her life. Her parents would help if she asked, but Cassie had exchanged so many divisive words with her mother that crawling home was not a pleasant option. Even being there at Christmas often felt unnatural.

In a way, Ed wasn't to blame, for she provoked him. She didn't take kindly to being told what to do. In addition, she didn't love him, never had, and never would. He knew it, not because she'd told him so, but because she'd never said to him that she did. She'd been honest before their marriage, telling him she was in love with Obie. Ed had laughed at her and declared, "You'll forget him. I'll make you forget."

For the most part, their lives were comfortable: The

business had boomed; they lived in a large house on the outskirts of San Antonio; she had a late-model automobile; they lacked nothing material. She preferred teaching, but taking care of Julie was a full-time job. Anyway, Ed wouldn't have allowed it.

His last blowup, two weeks before, was the worse by far. It started because she'd left Julie with a babysitter and gone into San Antonio to pick out material for new living room drapes without telling him.

After the babysitter left, Ed said, "If you went for drape material, where is it?"

"I didn't find what I wanted."

"It's more likely, I think, that you didn't go for drape material at all. Isn't that right?"

"No, I *did* go to get drape material . . . as I told you."

"Don't give me lip, Cassie!"

"I'm giving you the facts!"

"Your version of the facts, but not the truth?"

"Are you going to start one of your tirades again? If you are, I will take Julie and leave until you simmer down."

"You're not going anywhere unless I say you can."

She wouldn't stand such abuse. "Go to hell, Ed! I'll do as I please!"

He had struck her. His fist hit her cheek and knocked her backward, causing her to fall over a couch. "Don't you ever talk to me like that again!" he shouted.

She saw Julie standing in the doorway, a horrified expression on her young face. "Mommy," Julie said.

Ed went to her. "Honey," he said as he kneeled and pulled her close. "Mommy and me are just having a little argument, the way grownups do sometimes. We'll stop. Okay?"

Julie didn't answer. He held her and rocked her back and forth for a full minute. "Okay?" he asked again.

"Okay, Daddy," she said.

"I'm going to take you to bed now, sweetheart. Okay?"

"Be good to Mommy, Daddy."

"I will, sweetheart. I'll take care of Mommy." He glanced at Cassie as he said it.

Cassie went into the downstairs bathroom to nurse her aching cheek. A whelp had risen. She hoped that would be the worst of it.

When he returned several minutes later, she was sitting on

the couch with an ice pack on her cheek. "Tell me about your trip to town," he demanded.

"I did tell you. Unfortunately, you didn't listen."

"Cassie, who is it you're seeing? Who's the son-of-a-bitch you're fooling around with?"

"You're crazy! Absolutely crazy!"

"Is it one of the locals, or is Gainsworthy here?"

The accusation angered her as much as anything he might have said. "I fool around with every man who wants me. There, does that satisfy you? Let's see . . . there's Tom, and there's Dick . . . and, oh yes, there's Harry."

"And don't forget Gainsworthy!"

She stood and placed herself toe to toe with him. "You bastard!" she said. "You're the only man I've ever been with, and I was nearly thirty years old then."

He struck her. She fell across a chair and slid to the floor on her back. "Liar!" he said, straddling her and repeatedly pounding her face and body. Before she passed out, she said, "I wish Obie were here! I wish he were here!" Then, she saw Ed's fist coming down, and everything went dark.

She awoke the following day in bed. Someone was lying beside her. Was it Julie? She had trouble seeing and tried to focus her vision. Then, after a moment, she realized that Ed's face was next to hers on the pillow. There were tears in his eyes.

"Cassie, I'm so sorry, sweetheart. I'm so sorry." His hand was on her shoulder.

She remembered and let her fingers explore her face, which was swollen and painful everywhere. "What have you done to me?" she said, sitting up.

"You'll be okay. It's only a few bruises."

"You beat me. I passed out."

She got up. She was dizzy. She still had on yesterday's clothes. She made her way to their bathroom. What she saw in the mirror frightened her. Her eyes were so swollen that she had to tilt her head back to see. The front of her dress was covered with dried blood. There was nowhere on her body that didn't hurt; her ribs, on both sides, were especially painful. She thought some might be broken.

Ed came up behind her and placed a hand on her shoulder. She turned quickly and went back into the bedroom. He followed. "Cassie . . . please forgive me. I don't know what came over me. It'll never happen again."

"I know it won't," She said, "I'm leaving you. I'm taking Julie and leaving."

"Please, Cassie, we're a family. It's not right to break up families."

"It's not right to beat on your wife, either."

"I know. I do know. You're right. Please, please, Cassie? I promise it will never happen again. I'll never lay a finger on you like that again."

"You've said that before, and look where we are."

"This time, it's different. I'll get professional help to find out why I'm doing this. I'll do anything. *Anything.* Tell me what I can do to fix it up between us."

"What about my whoring around?" She couldn't control the sarcasm. "Can I keep doing that? I wouldn't want to give that up."

He took one of her hands in his, "Oh, Cassie," he said. "I know you wouldn't do that. I don't know why I said it. Maybe a psychiatrist can straighten me out. I'll make an appointment today."

In the end, she had relented. Perhaps therapy would help. She would try one more time. She wasn't one for giving up on anything. Marriage was important. She would give it time, a little, anyway.

She glanced in the mirror again. She and Julie could still go to Stafford Rest with a few more days and a little makeup.

CHAPTER TWELVE

1963–1964

Dan's Grandfather Hunt threw another log into the fireplace. The fire roared and cast out sparks that looked menacing but landed harmlessly on the stone hearth just short of the polished oak floor. Dan felt the heat from several feet away.

A recently-cut burly spruce dominated a corner of the room, its strong coniferous scent mingling with that of burning dry wood. Store-bought icicles gleamed from the tree's branches, and its colored bubble lights created random glimmers in the corner. When Dan turned to look out the broad picture window, he saw the eastern end of Diamond Lake and next to it a portion of the village, white from a dusting of December snow. He loved this place.

There had been a pleasant surprise when he and his mother arrived. Cassie and Julie had made it to Stafford Rest, after all. It was like old times with the family gathered in the living area. Grandfather Hunt finished rearranging the burning logs with a poker, turned his back to the fire, and picked up a glass of red wine he'd set aside.

Dan's grandmother was on a settee pulled up beside the hearth. Julie sat at a small table dressing a doll. Cassie, seated on the huge leather sofa facing the fireplace, was also drinking wine. She had a woolen scarf still around her neck after having carried firewood in from the woodpile. His mother stood by the window, looking pensive.

Not one argument had erupted during the twenty-four hours they'd been there. He grinned; it might be a record, but a little disappointing. One attraction he counted on was the entertaining bouts of verbal assault members of this family could heap on one another. He was sure the peace couldn't last.

The wait wasn't long. "Cassie," his grandmother said, "Julie's hair is all snarled. It looks as though it hasn't been washed for a week."

"I washed her hair this morning," Cassie said, "We used your shampoo. I asked you if I could. Don't you remember?"

"Well, evidently, you didn't use enough. I'll do it over for her." She motioned to Julie. "Come here, dear. I can fix it." Julie came running.

Cassie rose and took a couple of steps toward her mother and daughter. "Julie," she said. "Go back and play with your doll." Then, to her mother, she said, "One hair-washing a day is quite enough. I never had even that when I was growing up."

"Well, your hair was unmanageable, unlike Laura's."

Laura came quickly to Cassie's defense. His grandfather tried negotiating peace, a position he often took and one he seemed never to master. Cassie glanced at Dan and shrugged her shoulders. "What else can you expect of this family?" she said.

After things calmed down, his grandfather said to Dan, "So you're getting a pilot's license?"

"Sure am. I soloed a few days ago. It'll take a few more months to get my license."

"Good boy!" his grandfather said. "No one else in the family has ever done anything like that, although I'm not surprised. You've always done things differently."

"Flying is dangerous," his grandmother said. "You could kill yourself."

"Abigail," his grandfather said, "he's doing something special, something he takes pride in. A young man needs to stretch his wings . . . no pun intended."

Dan's mother spoke. "I can't help worrying about his flying. But we did leave the decision up to him. He has a good head on his shoulders."

"Oh, it's safe enough," Dan said. "I'm getting good training."

"I'm sure," his grandfather said. "How far do you expect to go with it, Dan?"

"I want a private pilot's license. Someday, I'll have my own airplane when I can afford it. And maybe I'll use my flying skills when I enter the service."

He heard his grandmother gasp. "Don't you even think about it," she said. "No grandson of mine is going to Vietnam! I'll take you to Canada first! Getting involved in this war is our country's worst mistake."

It was a touchy subject, Dan knew. The United States had gradually moved from advisor to the South Vietnamese to engagement in combat missions against the Vietcong. Protests were taking place in various cities around the country. He'd heard some men say they would refuse to go when drafted. Nevertheless, despite his doubts about the war, he registered for the draft, as was required of all eighteen-year-olds. He would go if called. Military service was part of being an American male. There was even a sense of adventure attached to the idea. He would not, however, express such thoughts to family members.

"I'll do my duty," he said.

"You wouldn't leave school?" The anxious question came from his mother. Surely, she must have considered that possibility.

"It depends. I guess I would if men were needed that badly."

"You're not a man. You're still a boy," his grandmother said.

"Grandmother, I'm nineteen."

"No young man should have to go to war," Dan's mother said. "Let the politicians go, instead."

Cassie, who'd been quiet, asked her father, "What do you hear of Obie?" The question was simple enough, but Dan noticed that she leaned forward expectantly and cocked her head as though the answer was the most important thing in the world. His mother moved away from the window and looked intently at her father. Dan sensed more than casual interest.

"You haven't asked about Obie for a long time," his grandfather said. "I thought you'd kept in touch."

"Who's Obie?" Dan asked.

"We haven't," Cassie said.

"Who the hell is Obie?" Dan came close to shouting the words.

"Watch your language, Danny," his grandmother said. The others ignored his question.

Cassie caught her breath. "I haven't seen him since my marriage in California . . . nine years ago."

"He left the ministry, you know," his grandmother said. "And I wasn't surprised. I can't think of anyone less suited for it."

"Who is he?" Dan repeated, trying a softer tone.

His grandfather seemed the only one willing to acknowledge his inquiry. "Obadiah Gainsworthy. Obie. That's who we're talking about." He took several minutes to tell Dan about Ken and Vi, her position as housekeeper with the family, and how the three children had been so close.

Dan remembered hearing the name, which brought a memory from long ago. His mother had not been complimentary toward the man. Dan had been curious then and still was. "Nobody seems willing to talk about Mr. Gainsworthy." He studied all their faces in turn.

"Obie has had a varied career," his grandfather said. "He served in Italy during the Second World War. He was a war hero. Earned the Silver Star for Gallantry. Earned another one in Korea as a chaplain."

"So, he was in two wars?"

"Indeed. He's also an author. He's written two books and has a third coming out soon. Ken, his father and also my foreman at the plant, tells me that he's the editor of a magazine in San Diego."

"He tried being a minister and failed at it," his grandmother said.

Dan thought it strange how she seized every opportunity to say something nasty about the man. Could he be so bad? Having observed her propensity for impaling others on her sword of judgment, he doubted it. Her judgment was sometimes irrational.

"Yes, he did give up the ministry," Dan's grandfather said as he gave his wife a dark look. "I'm sure it was to do something he's better suited for."

"It sounds as though you admire him," Dan said.

"I do. I watched him grow up under some trying conditions. He was a good young man, and I'm sure he's still good, regardless of what some people might think." He glanced at Dan's grandmother. "Your mother used to date him," he added. "They didn't think we noticed, but we did."

Dan watched his mother's face. She said nothing but grew pale. "What do you mean by 'dated?'" Dan asked.

"Nothing, really," his grandmother said. "Teenage crush. That's all."

"I meant the question for Mom," Dan said, turning to his mother. "Was it that, Mom? Or was it more serious?" He was probing but, having started, was determined to follow through.

His grandmother said, "That's a very personal question,

Danny."

Dan ignored the remark. "Mom?"

She said, "Dan, we were young. We thought we were in love. But then, he broke my heart. We've hardly spoken since."

"And you can't forgive him, is that it?"

"I'll never forgive him." Her words were without apparent emotion and managed to send a chill up Dan's spine.

He couldn't help asking, "Did you know Dad then?"

"I'd met him. It was soon after that I turned to him for comfort."

Cassie fairly exploded off the couch. "That's a lie, Laura, especially the part about Obie breaking your heart! You know it is! He never understood what he did to turn you against him."

"And what else did he tell you, sister?"

"A lot. Do you have any idea what hell he went through going off to war with that on his mind? We wrote all through the war and later, too. I saw what it did to him."

"He had no one to blame but himself. It was all *his* doing."

"If that's true, prove it. I've believed for years that there's more to it. Right now, with all of us as witnesses, give us the whole story so we can decide for ourselves who's to blame."

Dan had never seen Cassie so angry. It had certainly turned into an exciting day. There had been fussing in the family, but this was becoming a special event. He looked at the others to see how they were taking it. His grandfather had a look of horror. He must think things were out of control. Fortunately, Julie was still bent over her doll, unconcerned about the proceedings.

His mother's mouth was open, indicating a desire to say something. However, when she did speak, her voice was calmer. "Cassie, you were taken in by Obie and his lies. I realize you've always been in love with him. You've made no secret of that. However, love can blind a person. You see only the good."

How interesting—Cassie in love with a man his mother once dated. He didn't doubt that his mother and aunt loved each other, but he'd also noticed some indefinable friction, something he'd been unable to explain away. Could this be it?

"And what's the bad?" Cassie asked. "If you know what it is, don't we all deserve to know?"

His mother looked perplexed. She put a hand to her forehead and glanced toward his grandmother. The look passing between them was puzzling. His mother, with a determined expression, stood straighter. "There are things I don't want to discuss," she said. "Sometimes we need to protect others. It's not that we want to avoid talking about certain things, but sometimes we must."

Cassie wasn't placated. "Protect us from the truth? Is that what you're saying, Laura? In the absence of the truth you refuse to divulge, I have my own thoughts about Obie. He has a conscience. When he tells me he doesn't know why you broke up, I believe him. I didn't believe it once . . . and it has cost me dearly."

She paused a moment, obviously collecting her thoughts. "He couldn't live with himself if it were a lie. Have you read any of his books? They're full of his passion for truth. But I don't need such confirmation. *I know the man.* I know his heart." Cassie's voice trailed off as though she were out of breath. Dan saw tears in her eyes.

Although Dan had been feeling some amusement in the exchange between sisters, he became aware that this was not simply one of the Hunts' little squabbles and was ashamed for encouraging it, if only in his mind. Nevertheless, there was a mystery—some family secret. He agreed with Cassie; it should come into the open.

"No, I haven't read his books, and I won't," his mother declared. "There are things you don't know, Cassie, and things I can't tell you. I wish I could, but I can't. Please forgive me."

His mother's response and her teary eyes did nothing to decrease his desire to understand what ugly thing had happened in his family.

"Go to hell!" Cassie said. "Julie and I are going home."

* * *

Cassie seethed in her old bedroom. Someone was watching Julie, she supposed. Maybe she had overreacted. Nevertheless, Laura had no right to blame Obie for some secret she refused to reveal. Her sister's words, "You've been taken in by Obie and his lies," still resonated in her ears. Such an accusation had caused Obie and Cassie's breakup—and here it was again.

Was it possible? Could he have done something bad enough to make Laura feel as she did? Cassie had defended him as being too upright to hurt anyone. Although prone to little lies as they were growing up, Laura had been truthful in essential matters. Whatever Laura believed about Obie, as crazy as it was, was truth to her. But did any of it make a difference now? It had been so long ago?

She decided to go for a walk, hoping it might soothe her emotions. The weather was mild, and the skim of snow wouldn't require boots. She took a light jacket, slipped out the back door, and started down the road, hoping no one would miss her. The mid-afternoon sun cast up prisms of light from Diamond Lake. The lake began to freeze along the edges during an earlier cold spell, but mostly open water remained.

Cassie had intended to cross over Garnet Creek bridge into town. But when she reached the Lake Road cutoff, she changed her mind and walked past the marina and up the road. She'd not seen Abner and Claire for years. Maybe she would spend a few minutes with them. She heard footsteps behind her.

Laura, hurrying to catch up, grabbed Cassie's arm. "I'm sorry, Cassie," she said. "Our discussion shouldn't have gotten so . . ."

Cassie faced Laura and grabbed her hands. "My fault, entirely. Let's forget it."

"You're going to stay?"

"Of course. I just lost my temper."

"Some things don't change much, do they?"

"Some things not much, and other things not at all. Mom's a good example of the latter."

"She'll always be like that."

Cassie let the statement stand without comment. "I'm on my way to see Abner and Claire. Want to come along?"

"Didn't you know? Claire died nearly a year ago. Abner sold off all his livestock and is living in a little house in town next door to Ken and Angie. Mom is still trying to buy his farm."

"No, I didn't know. I'm sorry. I'll go see Abner. Ken and Angie too. Go with me, Laura."

Laura hesitated. "I'll skip it, Sis. Ken Gainsworthy never liked me much. In addition, I wouldn't discuss anything with him concerning Obie. I hope you understand."

Cassie changed the subject. "Did I hear Dad say Ken is retiring?"

"Next month. Dad's throwing a party for him at Ernie's restaurant."

"Will Obie be there?"

"What do you think? He's abandoned his family and everyone from his younger years. That's what he does best. He abandons." Cassie held her temper, and Laura continued, "I'm going back to the house now that I know everything is okay between us."

"No, Laura. Wait a minute. Let's talk a bit. All our conversations of late have been in the company of other people. Let's talk like we used to when we were teens."

"All right. Stafford Rest has a coffee shop now near the Diamond Inn. Let's go there. There's still time for you to visit the Gainsworthys."

Ward's Coffee Shop was small, and a table they found in the back was private. Cassie waited, not speaking. She wanted to ask questions without stirring the same coals that had ignited the last fire. When she thought the time was right, she said, "Laura, I know how deeply you feel about whatever happened between you and Obie. So, if you don't want to talk about it, we won't."

"Well, I'm glad because I won't discuss it. I want to let it rest."

"I respect that, but I would like some other information about Obie, not from the distant past, but in the last few years since we were all together in California. I get back here once a year, and most of my time is spent with family and dealing with family concerns. I've had no discussions with anyone about Obie. But you're here three or four times a year. You must hear things."

"I thought you kept in touch with him."

"He told me not long after the wedding that he wanted no correspondence with me. It left me angry and confused. But I believe I know why he did it. I think Ed threatened him."

"Obie's not one to be frightened off."

"No, he isn't, but he'd look out for my interests."

"That's debatable, and what difference does it make, anyway? You're married. He's married. You've gone separate ways and . . ."

"He's married?" The question required an answer, and for an instant, she wished she hadn't asked.

"You didn't know? I guess you *have* been away."

"It would seem so. But tell me what you know. Please,

Laura?"

"Why? Why does it matter to you? It's a love lost. There's that in nearly every life." The words carried more than a hint of bitterness.

"Don't you ever miss him, Laura?"

"You said we were going to talk about recent things."

"All right, we will. What do you know about his wife?"

"They met in San Diego after he went back there to write. Then, after he became pastor of a big San Francisco church, they were married there. I heard she left him, which is why he quit the ministry."

"Who told you that?"

"Dad. He likes Ken, and Ken tells him a lot. Ken and Angie went out to California a few months ago. They didn't stay long. Ken said Obie was so busy writing and running the magazine that he had little time for them. They said they wouldn't go again, that they'd wait for him to come to New York. That'll never happen. As I said, he abandons people."

Cassie fought the urge to counter but asked, "Are you happy, Laura? In your marriage, I mean?"

"Of course. Aren't you?"

"No . . . I'm very unhappy."

Laura placed her elbows on the table and leaned forward. "Why? What's happened? Has Ed found someone else? Have you?"

Cassie laughed. "I don't know about him, but I've had no such luck. Our problem is something else."

"What is it, Cassie?"

The light in the café was not the best. Cassie moved closer. "Look at my face. What do you see?"

Since arriving in Stafford Rest, Cassie had tried to hide her bruises. Now she wanted Laura to see. "You mustn't tell anyone about this," she said, leaning forward.

"Your eyes look swollen," Laura said.

"Look closer."

Horror clouded Laura's face, followed by anger. "You have black eyes! Ed did this to you?"

"You should have seen me two weeks ago. That's why I almost didn't come."

"Does he hit Julie, too?"

"No, he's good to her."

"You should leave him. Why does he do it?"

"He accuses me of having affairs. The real reason is that he's frustrated because he knows I don't love him. I've not been a good wife in that respect, but I can't be something I'm not. I'm partially to blame, I guess."

Laura delivered an angry monologue about the dangers of staying with an abusive husband. "You're asking for trouble, Cassie. I'll worry about you if you stay with him. Leave him! Come live with me. We can protect each other." She put her hand to her mouth, apparently regretting her words.

"Do you need protection too? What kind of men do we attract, Laura?"

"Ben has never laid a finger on me. He does have a sharp way with words, to both me and Dan. He sometimes makes me feel small, if you know what I mean. He's a good man, otherwise. He'd watch what he says more closely if you were there with us. That's all I meant." She sighed and added, "Not such a good idea, I guess. It would be no life for you."

Although Laura's mood became casual, Cassie detected a disturbing undercurrent. Was it fear? She'd known Laura too long not to recognize it. Cassie had her own troubles, but her sister's were as pressing, although different. She wouldn't be surprised if they would need each other in the future.

*　*　*

Another year passed, and the Christmas season came again. Pinky Hunt pretended to read a book. He was, instead, observing Laura as she sat at a table by the window. He'd taken the day off, a luxury he enjoyed more often. His seventy years might be catching up with him, but his shift in thinking about what was important made him seek more leisure. Abigail, at sixty-two, was still going strong. She was in Evergreen, putting in a full day in her real estate office. She had few other interests.

It should have been a pleasant time, with Christmas only a few days away. It was not. Cassie wasn't coming—for sure this year. Laura had come alone, and Dan was far away.

Laura had hardly moved for the last ten minutes, nor touched a glass of wine he'd placed on the table beside her. She was looking out the window toward the lake, but Pinky suspected she was gazing at something far beyond. He was sure of one thing; Laura was bearing troubles she was unwilling to discuss.

Both daughters were unhappy, and that made him unhappy as well. The reasons for their unhappiness might be guessed at, but they kept their feelings to themselves. How much better life would be if his family members were more open with one another. Despite being vocal, and sometimes excessively so, they kept secrets. One veil of secrecy had nearly dropped last year when everyone was home. As much as he hated discord, his daughters had revealed certain things about themselves.

Although Cassie was more outspoken, inclined to air her feelings, she was hiding something. She had, long ago, told her parents of her love for Obie, a tragedy Pinky thought she had left behind. Seeing those feelings surface again had been heartrending.

As for Laura, whatever happened between her and Obie affected her significantly. Ken Gainsworthy's son was a common factor where his daughters' emotions were concerned. Whether Obie was the root of Laura's unhappiness was unclear; it was suspect, however.

Dan's absence was problematic for her, too, Pinky concluded. The situation was stressful for them all, especially so for Laura. He asked, "Laura, Honey, how often does Dan write?"

"I've had two letters, but he's only been in Vietnam for two weeks."

"He has a noncombat job, doesn't he?"

"Yes, at present. He's in a supply company on a post in Saigon."

"Let's hope he stays there his whole tour of duty."

"I was so angry at him," Laura said. "He could have stayed out of it . . . at least until he finished college. The war would probably have been over by then."

"You know how young men are, especially those with a strong sense of duty. I'm sure he'll finish college when he leaves the Army. But, unfortunately, he's not alone in having to make such decisions. Many men are going away to war from here, too, like in the past."

Her expression changed. She sighed, got up, and went to stand by the fireplace. Her eyes were teary.

"What is it, Laura?" he asked.

"Nothing, Dad."

He should push the issue and make her talk about her problems. After all, he was her father. He would help if he could. "No, something *is* troubling you." He went to her and put his arms around her. She snuggled up to him.

"Oh, Dad," she said, "Life is so complicated."

"Tell me about your problems, Honey."

"I worry so much about Dan in a war zone, afraid I'll lose him too."

"Too?"

"Wrong word, I guess. I was thinking about some things I gave up when I got married. College was one, although I've been taking business courses at Boston University. And I've missed Stafford Rest."

Pinky knew she was making up things to conceal her slip. "You don't miss Stafford Rest," he said. "You have an active social life in Boston. There's no comparison."

Her laugh was a nervous one. "Yes, it's a good life, though there are empty periods."

"Are you happy, Laura?"

"I guess about as happy as any forty-year-old woman whose only child is in a war zone can be."

He released her and stepped back. "Is that the only thing? You haven't said much about Ben lately."

Laura looked perplexed. He suspected that she didn't want to talk about her husband. She finally said, "We live in the same house. There isn't much communication."

"I'm sorry, Laura. I really am."

"I've considered leaving him, Dad."

"Will you?"

"Probably not."

"Does Dan know how you feel?"

"No, but I doubt it would surprise or even bother him if I left. He's never been very close to Ben."

"I think there's something else, too . . . something you need to get off your chest. I think it's about Obie."

Her eyes flashed anger. "Don't, Dad! Don't bring that up!"

Pinky tried to make eye contact with his daughter; she turned her head away. He placed a hand under her chin and gently turned her face toward his. "I'm your father, Laura. I love you. I want the best for you."

"I know you do. I love you, too. There are some things I

can't talk about. I'd like to, but I promised Mom."

Pinky wasn't surprised. He'd long believed Abigail knew more about the Obie situation than she admitted. Cassie thought so, too. He must, nevertheless, proceed with caution. "You and your mother have a secret, don't you?"

"That's become obvious, hasn't it?"

"Secrets are one thing, Sweetheart, but when it's clearly causing you pain, can you blame a father who wants to help."

"There's no help for it, Dad. It's over and done with. It's been more than twenty years. How can there be any help for it?"

"You still love him, don't you? Obie, I mean?"

"No, of course not!"

"Love can be forever. I love your mother despite our differences, but I get mad at her sometimes. Several years ago, I told her I would leave her if she didn't stop trying to get me to go into politics. I wouldn't have, of course, but she must have believed me because she didn't nag me anymore, at least about that."

"I don't love Obie, Dad. How could I after what he did?"

Pinky said it as casually as he could. "And what was that?"

"I can't tell you, Dad. It would hurt you . . . like it hurts Mom."

"I've heard snippets of conversation indicating he simply stopped writing. Is that true?

"Yes."

"Isn't there something else, too?"

"Yes, Dad, there's something else."

"And your mother knows?"

"Yes, Mom knows."

"It might help to talk about it."

"No, it would just cause you pain. And me, too, to see your pain."

She was upset. He'd wanted to help but had made it worse. "All right, Sweetheart. It's okay. It's not something I have to know."

He turned away, but she said, "Dad, if I tell you this, you must never tell Mom you know. I promised her long ago that the secret would remain between the two of us . . . and a couple of other people. Now I realize it's not fair to you. You have the right to know."

"I won't reveal it."

"Let's sit down. I might have some trouble getting through the story."

The next few minutes were emotional. Finally, when she finished, they clung to each other without either speaking. Then, she got up quickly and left the room.

Pinky sat quietly. He finally understood his wife and daughter's anger toward Obie Gainsworthy, for he now shared it.

CHAPTER THIRTEEN

1965

Months earlier, when Dan Williamson sat in his college dorm room firming up a decision to enlist in the Army, he'd not imagined becoming a supply clerk or that his duties would keep him so far from the real action. Instead, his expectation had been more about victorious skirmishes against the enemy.

The adventures he imagined hadn't happened except for occasional guard duty and token patrol maneuvers. He feared he might spend a whole year in Vietnam and never see a single Vietcong. He nursed his discontent for a month after his arrival before an opportunity arose; it came about because of his friendship with Corporal Norman Lasher.

"I'm being reassigned," Lasher told Dan one evening over beer in the enlisted men's club. "When I was at Regiment, I ran into a first lieutenant I knew from back home. Becker's his name. Josh Becker. He was a couple of years ahead of me in high school. A sharp guy. Has a special assignment here. Recon work. He maps out safe routes for transporting high-ranking officers and diplomats. He needs two GIs to accompany him. He asked me, and I took him up on it. It's better than sitting here in Saigon twiddling my thumbs and hating all the paperwork."

"What responsibilities will you have?"

"That's the beauty of it. Officially, I'll be his assistant. My real job is to protect him while he carries out his duties."

"Bodyguard, eh?"

"That's about it, I guess. He said we'll travel by air and sometimes on the ground."

"You lucky dog. I'd like something like that."

"Well, Dumbo, it's why I'm telling you. He's authorized to have two assistants. I'll put in a good word for you if you want me to."

"Hell, yes!"

A few days later, Lieutenant Becker called Dan to regimental headquarters for an interview. Becker was professional but personable. He said, "Private Williamson, the war's changing fast. Troops are pouring in at an unprecedented rate. We'll take it to the VC, and it wouldn't surprise me if we're bombing the far north real soon."

"Yes, sir. We must, especially after the recent strikes against us." Becker would know he was referring to the deadly VC attacks at Pleiku and Qui Nhon.

"It's going to be hotter all over. What I'm saying is that I'll be going over the place, real hot spots, and I don't want people with me who would rather be someplace else."

"I understand. I want the chance to go with you."

"I'll let you know in a couple of days. No more than three, because that's when I start this duty. Be ready to leave at a moment's notice once I confirm your assignment."

Dan wanted the job and had trouble thinking about anything else. Needing a diversion, he asked Lasher to go into Saigon with him to kill time. The city was dangerous, some spots more so than others. Lasher led him to a beer joint he sometimes frequented. After speculating over a couple of beers about the advantages and perils of their upcoming assignment, they exited the building intending to return to the post.

The girl outside the beer joint was standing by a lamppost. The provocative effect she was trying to project was subjugated by such apparent shyness that he nearly laughed. She was slender; the nipples of her small but shapely breasts thrust out against the fabric of her white blouse.

The Army position was that military personnel were not to fraternize with civilians; friends were not easy to distinguish from foes. Dan was well aware of how things worked in Saigon and everywhere in the world. When boys meet girls, hormones begin a dance that makes it hard not to join in. The girl by the post didn't resemble an enemy in any way.

Lasher whistled softly. "Say, Williamson . . . you or me?"

"She's only a kid," Dan said.

"I'll flip you for her." Not waiting for an answer, Lasher pulled a coin from his pocket, tossed it in the air, and said, "Heads!" He caught the coin. "Tails! You win!"

"I was supposed to call it."

Lasher smiled. "I've been doing okay. It's your turn."

"I don't know," Dan muttered.

He'd been informed about the decadence of Saigon and had managed to stay away from it. Images of college classmate

Myra Waters had helped. He and Myra became intimate several months before his enlistment. Although there had been other girls, she was special. He'd not imagined he would go through a year in Vietnam without female companionship, but picking up girls off the streets felt sordid.

"Live a little," Lasher said. "Look at her. She's certainly quality . . . for what she is."

"She may well be. However, I'm not interested in prostitutes." He wasn't sure; he'd a good look at her in the light of the lamppost.

"Well, you'd better figure out something to keep from hurting her feelings because she's coming over here. And she's looking right at you. Anyway, I'm going." Lasher whirled and walked away but said over his shoulder, "You're on your own. Have a good time."

She stopped in front of Dan. "I am Ly Yen," she said. "What is your name?" Her English was excellent. She was numerous levels above "pretty" with velvety skin. Her raven black hair, shining in the lamppost light, was pulled back and bound with a bright blue kerchief.

"I'm Dan," he said.

"Hello, Dan. I have a place . . . a room. We can go there." She sounded nervous, not like a prostitute at all.

"Ly . . .?"

"Ly Yen."

"Ly Yen, how old are you?"

"I am seventeen."

"You should be home with your family." His own words surprised him. Who was he kidding, pretending he cared about her welfare? She was a prostitute, and trading sex for money was what she did. What he thought or said would make no difference in her life.

"My family is not here," she said. "My mother and father live beyond the edge of the city. We once lived in Tay Ninh until the Vietcong came.

"No brothers or sisters?"

"No . . . no more. I had two brothers." Tears trickled down her cheeks. "They have died."

"In the war?"

"Yes, more than a year ago. One came home with great wounds. He died at home. He told of the death of my other brother. My parents still cry for them."

"I'm sorry, Ly Yen."

"We go to my room, yes?"

"Yes." He astonished himself by agreeing, for he'd just decided to fight his erotic feelings. After all, he could find someone better suited than a prostitute to satisfy such needs.

They went through back alleys, increasing his apprehension. He followed her, stepping around piles of garbage and human feces. The insanity of being alone in Saigon had been drilled into service personnel. "Avoid Saigon altogether if you can, and never go there without a friend," rang in Dan's ears as he followed this girl whom he had known for only a few minutes. What might she be leading him into? He teetered on the edge of fear.

Ly Yen stopped in front of a low wooden door that would require stepping down to enter. "This is my room," she whispered.

She went through, and he followed. She pulled a chain on a bare light fixture hanging from the ceiling and turned to close and bolt the door behind them. The dim light revealed a tiny room, empty except for a bunk in a corner, a wooden straight-back chair, and a battered old chest. Yet, even with such austerity, it was clean. She turned toward him, and her voice quivered. "I will require five American dollars."

He stared at her. She would turn heads anywhere. His attraction toward her hadn't subsided. Nevertheless, he heard himself saying, "Maybe we could just talk."

"*Talk?* You would pay me to talk?" She looked disturbed. "Maybe you do not wish to pay me at all?"

He quickly fished a bill from his wallet. "No, it's all right. I'll pay you."

She smiled. "Thank you, Dan." She quickly turned quizzical. "Do you think I am not attractive? Is that why you want only to talk?"

"No, that's not the reason at all. You're quite attractive. You're one of the most attractive women I've ever met."

She laughed, surprising him. "You are either one who avoids truth or you have not known many women."

He laughed, too. Not only was she pleasing to look at, she was also intelligent. "Ly Yen, I like you," he said. "Maybe we can be friends."

"Yes, if you wish."

"How much time does the money give me?" he asked.

"One night." Then, with a more serious expression, she said, "But we can be friends as long as you like. What is your whole name? Americans have big names, yes?" She stretched her hands apart as far as she could reach.

"Some do. Me, too, I guess. It's Daniel Pinkerton Williamson. The one in the middle, 'Pinkerton,' is the name of one of my grandfathers. My mother gave it to me to honor him. You can call me 'Dan.'"

"It is good to honor grandparents in such a way. I would do such a thing."

They sat and talked at length, he in the uncomfortable chair and she on the bunk. He told her about Boston, Florida, and Stafford Rest. She told him about her brothers who had been older than her, about her parents who were elderly and ailing, and about her religious beliefs. About the latter, she said, "My parents are of the Cao Dai religion."

"Is it your religion, too?"

"No more."

"What *do* you believe?"

"I am a Christian, I have decided. When I left home of my parents and came to Saigon three months ago, I lived with nuns at orphanage. They have taught me about Jesus. They also fed me and helped me with my English. They sent some money to my parents. They stopped because they are poor also."

"I'm not much for religion," Dan said. "It's not that I don't believe in God or an afterlife. I just don't have much interest in such things. It seems like living to get ready to die. I'm going to live my life *now.*"

Her grin widened. "The nuns would love to talk to you. They would teach you a better way."

"I'm amazed you learned English so well in only a few months?"

"I knew some English, but most of what I learned was with American sisters."

"Why did you leave them if they cared for your needs?"

"It was for my parents. They are sick. They need medicine and food. The nuns can take care of only me, not my parents. I will earn money. I go to them once in a week."

"Once a week? Is it far?"

"It takes half a day if I walk. I had a bicycle. It was stolen. Now I walk. It saves money to walk."

"Is it dangerous?"

"The city is very dangerous. The countryside is dangerous also. It is hard to find a safe place anywhere in our country."

"So, you turned to prostitution to get money to care for your parents?"

"Yes, it is best way to make money. Many girls do it. One girl taught me things I have to do and say."

"What about this place? This room? Do you pay for it?"

"I do not pay. It was empty. I came in. I cleaned it. It is sufficient, except for rats."

Her words caused Dan to make an anxious survey of the dark corners. "It must belong to someone," he said. "What if they return?"

"Then I will go someplace else," she said as though it were the most obvious answer.

"How long have you been doing this? You know . . ."

"Only today."

"Today?"

"Yes, this is first time. You are first I have asked."

He didn't believe her and told her so. "You seem to know what you're doing," he said as he shook a disapproving finger at her.

"Dan Williamson," she said, "It does not matter if you be-lieve me, for after tonight I will not see you again. To lie is a sin, sisters told me. Why would I lie with nothing to gain for the lie? No, I do not lie. I believed I would become a prostitute tonight. I am not yet. Tomorrow, I will be, but not tonight . . . unless you choose me."

There came a strange sadness for her, a sentiment falling short of pity, for she had too much dignity to foster that emotion.

"Ly Yen," he said, knowing he was a fool for what he was about to say, but saying it anyway, "Maybe I can help you."

"Help me? How?"

He hesitated, wondering why he was making such a serious commitment. "Impulsive," his father had often called him after losing his temper about some "stupid" thing Dan did.

He plunged ahead. "Ly Yen, I can get some food for you." Lasher had access to mess hall and commissary goods and was not above using some of it for his own purposes. He must work fast, though, for Lasher would leave in a couple of days. Lasher had seen her; he would understand.

Dan told her, "But you'd have to do something for me."

"What would you have me do?"

"Stop trying to sell your body. As you say, you're not yet a prostitute. It can stay that way."

"Does it mean you believe my words?"

"Yes, Ly Yen, I believe you. I believe this is the first time you've done this."

She was studying his face. What might she think about him? She frowned. "I am not untouched. I am not a virgin. I was with a man when we lived in Tay Ninh. He was my age. He loved me."

"Did he tell you he loved you?"

"No, but I knew. I can tell when a man loves." There was sadness in her words.

"Couldn't he have taken care of you . . . kept you from having to come here like this?"

"He went with my brothers to war. He is dead, too."

"I'm sorry, Ly Yen."

"I tell you this because I do not want you to think I am better than I am. It would be like a lie."

"I understand. I don't think any less of you because you've loved someone."

"He was a good man, as were my brothers. It was a sad time. My parents did not want us to live in the outskirts of Saigon, or for me to come here. I thought for a while they would manage with what sisters sent each month. When that stopped, I knew I must earn money myself."

"How much were the sisters sending?"

He was surprised the amount was so little, less than he would spend on a night out. "I'll tell you what," Dan said. "I'll give you that much for them each month if you promise to stop doing this."

Her eyes opened wide. "You would do that for me?"

"Yes, if you promise."

"Why do you believe I will honor such a promise?"

He made sure she saw his smile. "Because you've decided not to lie."

She stood, leaned over, and kissed the top of his head. "You say you have no interest in religion or God. It is a puzzle because you have acted toward me as sisters say Jesus would act. Can you explain it?"

"I guess it's because I like you, Ly Yen."

"We will be friends," she said, touching his shoulders. "And I promise I will not sell my body. I will be only your woman."

"Ly Yen, I'm not asking you to be *my* woman." Despite the statement, she'd elevated herself in his eyes over just a few minutes. Making her *his* woman was something to consider.

"Jesus must have sent you," she said.

He told her he had to go, for it had grown late. As he slipped through the door, dreading the walk back toward lighted streets, she put the bill he had given her into his hand.

"No, you keep it. Please send it to your parents. Consider it the first installment of our agreement. I'll come back with some other things, too," he added.

"I will wait for you."

* * *

Dan went back the following evening to help Ly Yen move. During the day, he'd slipped away to find her more suitable quarters. The apartment consisted of two small rooms on the second floor of a dilapidated wooden building. Devoid of furniture or amenities, it was at least away from back alleys where most crimes occurred. The elderly man who lived downstairs looked at him suspiciously but took his money without comment.

Dan took her a large bag of items that Lasher had "rescued" from the commissary, mostly nonperishable food. He was determined she would not go hungry. After she was settled, he hurried back to the post, not wanting to miss a message about his request for reassignment.

The NCO in Charge of Quarters held papers toward him as he entered company headquarters. The orders reassigned him to special duty under the direct command of Lieutenant Joshua Becker. The assignment period was for three months, with the possibility of renewal. However, his primary assignment would stay the same; he would still be attached to the same company and live in the same quarters while in Saigon. He was to report to the airfield the following morning.

They were gone three days on the first trip. Space was

limited on the four-place OH 23 helicopter. Most legs of the flight were short, with considerable ground time. Neither Dan nor Lasher had taken their bedrolls, a mistake because one of the night stops had no quarters for them. As a result, they spent a miserable night taking catnaps under the helicopter with one eye on the perimeter for a possibility of attack.

They arrived back in Saigon tired and sleepy. Becker reminded them that they were on a two-hour call. They must return to Becker within two hours, whether on-post or off-post. "And don't show up drunk," he warned.

That time window presented difficulties. Dan wanted to spend time with Ly Yen. She had occupied his thoughts constantly while they were away. He and Lasher solved the time problem by devising a schedule where only one would leave the post at a time. Each would know the whereabouts of the other.

The interlude between the first mission and the second stretched to four days. Becker told them such leisure would not be a regular occurrence. On the contrary, the activity would increase, he assured them.

Dan spent a part of two evenings with Ly Yen during that period. They made love the second evening. She seemed happy about it. "We are friends," she said, "and now we are more than friends. Is it not true?"

"Yes, it *is* true."

Missions became routine. They flew in a variety of helicopters and small aircraft. Their pilots were numerous, although many rotated regularly back into the schedule. They traveled vast areas of South Vietnam to observe enemy troop movement and map out safe routes that changed daily. Once, while on foot to investigate a suspicious site, they were approached by a small VC patrol. Becker made them lay low until the soldiers passed.

"We could have taken them," Lasher complained, patting his weapon.

"You'll have an opportunity, I wager," Becker told him. "Now isn't the time."

Dan's hands had shaken, and his breathing had quickened while they hunkered in the grass. Back in the air, he worried; would he be a coward? He'd entertained visions of conducting himself well under fire. Was that a reality? He feared bringing disgrace on himself or his friends.

They traveled with few encumbrances. Becker insisted on

it. Their helicopters were small, and their light fixed-wing air-craft had no more than four seats. Lasher wanted to lug along a Browning Automatic Rifle and mentioned even heavier arma-ment, but Becker nixed that. Lasher ended up with a Thompson submachine gun. Dan carried his M-16. Both wore belts laden with grenades and other items. All three men had side arms.

Dan was always happy to return to Saigon and to Ly Yen. She clung to him when he left and welcomed him with tears of joy on his return.

The apartment underwent a transformation. New furniture items, cooking utensils, and stoneware appeared, from where she didn't say but likely scrounged from dumps or alleyways. Ly Yen was an expert at making do with the barest of necessities.

He struggled to understand the kind of poverty she en-dured. He took money for granted; his parents and grandpar-ents were wealthy by most standards. His mother and grand-mother sent him supplemental funds adding up to much more than his Army pay. "Pocket change," Grandmother Abigail told him in a letter. He accepted their money without question but didn't live extravagantly. He was even accumulating a bank ac-count.

One night he encouraged Ly Yen to tell him more about her family. "When my parents could work," she said, "and my brothers were at home, we did well. We were not the most pros-perous family in our village, but we thought my brothers would go to a university."

"You made a living from the land?"

"Yes. We controlled rice paddies and two groves of coconut trees. My parents no longer have control of those."

"I wish you would take me to Tay Ninh sometime."

"I would like that also. But it is dangerous. That is why we left. I need to go outside Saigon soon to see my parents, and I do not think you could go there with me. You must stay nearby for when you are called."

"Yes, unfortunately."

Months passed. The demographics of the war changed. VC buildup, with their units pushing south, caused fear everywhere. Panic spread even to Saigon. President Johnson authorized more United States troops. Enclaves along the coast were strengthened. During the summer, a large cavalry division landed at Qui Nhon and spread west. Many outfits ended up at

An Khe to assist tactical operations there. That airfield became one of the busiest in Vietnam. Marines landed at Da Nang Air Base in August.

Lieutenant Becker's little group continued hopping from place to place, performing their assigned duties. They avoided trouble. Once, they were away for ten days. Ly Yen clung to Dan on his return. "I worried so much," she said. "You have never been away so long. I worried that you might be dead."

"As you can see, I'm fine."

"Many times, I wonder if you have changed your mind about me."

"You needn't worry about it, Ly Yen. I'll never desert you."

He had uttered the words through the joy of being with her again. Later, he wondered if they could have been better chosen. At the very least, he should have added, "While I am in Vietnam."

He knew how much she hated lies and valued commitment. Later that night, in his bunk, he examined his feelings. What would happen after he left? He could set up a fund for her, an account that would eventually be exhausted. Then what? The next time they were together, he said, "Ly Yen, I worry about how you'll manage after I go home. I have only four months left."

She extracted herself from his embrace and held him at arms-length. "Dan, you have been kind to me and my parents, but you are not responsible for me. I will survive. I must survive to care for my parents."

"Are they no better?"

"No. When I went there last week my father could hardly walk. It is because of an accident he had years ago. He is sick too. My mother sits and cries all day. Sometimes, she seems not to know me or my father."

"I'm afraid that once I leave, you might go back . . . you know, back to the streets."

"No, I will not do it again. I made a promise to you. Do you not remember? I would die first."

"Yes, I believe you would."

She put her arms around his waist and her head on his chest. "Dear, dear, one," she said, her voice like a pigeon's coo. "You have changed my life. You have brought me much joy, and I shall never forget our time together. But it is . . . I am not sure of the word. It is . . . a limited time."

"An interlude?" The word hurt.

"Yes, that is it. It is an interlude. We will enjoy our time together. But then, it will be over. We must understand and accept it."

"How old did you say you were?"

"Seventeen. Soon eighteen."

"If I didn't know better, I'd say you were sixty or so."

She laughed. "You must not worry. I will find a way."

They made love, a gentle union accompanied by light caresses and soft words, unlike any intimate encounter he had ever experienced.

* * *

They stood in a little room he called a "kitchenette." Ly Yen said without emotion, "My father has fallen and is injured. I must go and stay with them."

He didn't try to hide his disappointment. "I have only two more months here," he said. "Will you come back?"

"I do not know. Fate will decide. But I will try. What is date of your leaving?"

When he told her, she said, "If I cannot come sooner, I will come back three days before, so we can have our last days together."

She stood on tiptoe as they kissed. He noticed that she was pale. "Aren't you feeling well, Ly Yen?"

"I will be all right. I have just a small dizziness. It is because of parting from you, dear one."

"I'll keep paying the rent for the rooms so you'll have a place to return to. Do you promise to return?"

"Yes, I promise."

Leaving her was difficult. She cried. His own eyes filled. "I'll look forward to seeing you in two months," he said.

"Your army will not send you into battle, will they?"

"I've been told that my duties won't change until my rotation date. However, with the Army, there's no such thing as a promise kept . . . until it's kept."

"I will pray to Jesus that you will go home unhurt, not die, as did my brothers."

"I won't die. I promise you."

"Another once told me that."

"I'm sorry you've been so hurt," he said.

They stood at the apartment door. Ly Yen faced him and held his hands. "Thank you, Dan Williamson, for being so good to me."

They kissed once more before he tore himself away. He was afraid to look back. *What if he never saw her again?*

CHAPTER FOURTEEN

1965

Corporal Dan Williamson had less than a month left in Vietnam. The frequency and direction of his little group's information-gathering flights had become more unpredictable as pockets of VC converged in a growing number of locations. Finding safe corridors became harder.

Becker was promoted to captain. Dan and Lasher expected to be sent back to their supply jobs to finish their tour of duty, but Becker begged for extensions, and word soon came that they would remain with him until their rotation date.

During the first months of their assignment, there had sometimes been time for relaxation between trips. But now, having more than a single night off duty had become a rarity. That wasn't a concern for Dan because Ly Yen wasn't there. Nevertheless, he went twice to her rooms, where he sat in the dark, missing her.

Early on, Becker learned of Dan's private pilot license; when they flew in winged airplanes, he insisted Dan occupy the right-hand front seat. "In case our pilot decides to take a nap," he said.

They all knew what he meant. Most flights, however, were in helicopters of various kinds. Piloting a helicopter looked much harder than flying a fixed-wing airplane, and Dan saw it as a challenge for some future time.

In early November, on a route by helicopter toward An Khe, they crossed the flight paths of several Hueys on a course toward the Ia Drang Valley. Below, against the jungle foliage, Dan could see three helicopters strung out several hundred yards apart.

"What's going on?" Lasher asked.

Lieutenant Benedict, a pilot with whom they had flown several times, said, "Hell of a situation over there! VC regiments are pouring in off the Ho Chi Minh Trail. We've been ferrying troops from Plei Me to the Pleiku Province all day, particularly to LZ X-Ray. Hueys are taking more fire on each trip."

Pointing, he said, "I'll bet those birds are taking fire right now." He paused and leaned forward. "Do you see that? One is in trouble for sure!"

Dan spotted a trail of black smoke extending across a green canopy of jungle. Benedict announced, "I'm going down there to see if we can help!"

They dropped swiftly to treetop level. Dan tried to keep the Huey in sight. "There it is," Becker said, "Seven o'clock . . . on the ground."

He'd no sooner uttered the words than an explosion from the downed Huey sent up a cloud of black smoke. Benedict swore. "They've ignited!"

A pinging sound reverberated across the bottom of their own helicopter. They swerved sideways. "We're taking fire too!" Lasher yelled.

"I'll get some altitude," Benedict said.

Becker moaned and slumped forward. Lasher, next to him, froze. Dan grabbed and held the captain's shoulders to keep him from bumping his head. A gush of blood came from Becker's mouth, and his eyes became fixed. Dan had never seen anyone die, but instinct told him that Becker was dead. "Hell!" he muttered.

Dan's eyes stung as smoke filled the cabin. *It was unreal.*

Again, there was the sound of bullets hitting the undercarriage. "We're losing power!" Benedict said. The helicopter dropped, then leveled off. They were skimming treetops. Benedict remained calm. "Going to set her down. Help me find a spot."

During Dan's flight instruction, Gabe Black had drilled him repeatedly about the constant need for picking emergency landing sites. Gabe said, "If you're up there and that prop stops turning, you're going to land, and it's best to know where." Occasionally, Gabe would reach across Dan's legs and turn off the engine. Scouring the landscape had become second nature.

Out the right side, Dan spotted a large bare-topped hill with a stream weaving in loops down its near side. They wouldn't have enough altitude to reach the hill. Several hundred yards farther right was a thicket where he saw men scurrying.

"To the left, about twenty degrees," Dan shouted over the noise of the sputtering engine. "There's a clearing beside that rock formation."

Smoke rolled from the front, and Benedict struggled with the controls. "I see it!" he said. "Hang on!"

Beyond the miniature clearing Dan had identified, and in another section of jungle, he saw smoke rising from the downed Huey. Their own helicopter engine was sputtering, and when they were twenty feet above the ground, it quit; they nosed down and hit hard. Dan was thrown forward, his shoulder striking a window.

For a moment, everything was silent. Then, Benedict said, "Help me!"

Dan struggled to release the dazed pilot from his harness. Blood flowed from a cut on his forehead. Lasher helped, removing Benedict's helmet. They soon had him out and lying in the grass.

Benedict tried to sit up. "The big rocks we saw going in. Let's get to those." His words were slurred.

"Negative, sir," Dan said, "Vietcong are in there."

The lieutenant couldn't stand, and after several unsuccessful attempts, collapsed onto the jungle floor. In addition to a six-inch gash on his forehead, blood was forming on his left pant leg. He raised himself on one elbow. "Where's Captain Becker?"

"He's dead," Dan told him.

After a moment, Benedict said, "You saw VC in the rocks?"

"As we were coming in."

"Then we need to go somewhere else. They'll be swarming in on us soon."

"Get on the other side," Dan told Lasher. "We have to carry him."

"Get Captain Becker out first," Benedict said. "We can't leave him in there. There's fuel all over the place. It could catch any second."

"He's dead!" Lasher said. "What's it matter? We have to hurry."

Benedict was not too injured for anger. "It matters a hell of a lot! I want him out!"

Dan agonized over the time it took to unfasten Becker and drag him out. When they finally stretched the body on the ground, Dan said, "Sir, we can't take him. It'll take both of us to help you."

"All right. Drag him away from the chopper. They can pick him up later. There's a thicket over there that might provide cover for us." Benedict pointed.

"We can't go there, either. There's at least a patrol in there."

"You saw them?"

"I did."

"All right, corporal. Do you have a suggestion about where we *can* go?"

"There's a stream coming off the hill. It may offer a place to hide."

They moved toward the clearing's edge. Dan and Lasher held the officer up between them. Dan slung his M-16 over his shoulder, and Lasher carried his Thompson. Although Benedict tried moving his feet, it was necessary to drag him to make progress. His leg wound was still bleeding but had slowed. Dan saw that the head wound was more severe than he'd first believed. Nevertheless, the pilot was fighting to stay conscious. They stopped at the edge of a jungle thicket.

There was a muffled explosion. Gas tanks on their chopper had ignited. Whether their location had been discovered was unknown.

"We have to move out and get deeper into the jungle," Dan said. "We need better cover."

They walked as fast as conditions allowed. Dan wished for darkness; it would put another layer of safety between them and the Vietcong.

They reached a thicket where several logs of various sizes had fallen across one another. It would provide fortification of a sort.

"You think we should stay here?" Lasher asked.

"Until it gets dark. After that, we'll see."

"Let's ask the lieutenant what he thinks."

"He doesn't even know where he is," Dan said. "It's up to us to decide."

"What about that other Huey? That explosion looked bad, but maybe somebody survived it."

Lasher was right. They should find the wreck and provide help if needed. It might be a fool's errand. Nevertheless, they must try.

"Let's get Lieutenant Benedict as comfortable as we can.

Then, one of us will have to go look for the Huey."

"Can't we both go?" Lasher said.

"Someone has to stay here to keep him quiet."

"Where did they crash? Do you know?"

"That way!" Dan pointed. "I saw it just before we went down."

"You'd better go, then."

"Keep him still. Stuff something in his mouth if you have to."

"You want the Thompson?"

"No, I'll be fine. Do you have your compass?"

"Yeah."

"If I don't return by dark, you'll have to carry or drag him."

"To where?"

"See where I'm pointing. Take a heading in that direction. You should run into a stream. Follow it up the hill. There's a good-sized clearing on top. It's the most likely place for a pick-up."

"They should have been here for us by now. Someone must have seen us go down."

"They're not here, though, and it's not long until dark. For a night rescue, we'd have to give them a lighted signal, and that's risky. They'll get here tomorrow, for sure, and they'll expect us to find the best pickup place."

"Where?"

"On top of the hill. Head for it. I'll return here before dark if I can, but don't delay. Start as soon as it's dark. I'll catch up."

Dan's confidence about knowing the direction of the crashed Huey waned as he set off through the jungle. The foliage's thickness disoriented him. He followed his own advice and used his compass to set headings. Nevertheless, he doubted his ability to keep on the original heading. Even if he found the Huey, survivors might have fled the wreckage.

He skirted several ponds and waterlogged areas, making headway difficult. The wreck should be spouting smoke, but he saw nothing. He stopped often to listen. The jungle was not a quiet place. Birds and wild animals, species about which he could only guess, made their presence known in a cascade of sound.

The scent of a burned-out fire soon reached his nostrils. He followed it upwind for a hundred yards to the smoldering Huey remains. He stood still, watching and listening for several minutes before venturing closer. Twisted and partially melted metal was scattered across the jungle floor. In one section, the outlines of seats were barely recognizable. They held charred remains of human figures.

A couple of intact bodies lay farther away, possibly thrown there by the impact of landing; the heat had scorched their clothing. One had corporal stripes; the other was a private. Dan saw no signs of other bodies, although they could have incinerated inside the aircraft. He guessed a Huey could carry seven or eight men with full gear, plus the pilot.

The chance of anyone escaping this crash was unlikely. Two hours had passed. The VC had probably been there and left. There was nothing to do except retrace his steps and get ready to ascend the hill.

Someone coughed. Dan flipped his M-16 off his shoulder. He had the man in his sight when he realized that an American was standing in front of him.

"Hey!" the man said.

"Hey, yourself," Dan replied as he stepped out. "You walk away from this?"

The man nodded. He seemed dazed. His face was blackened, and dried blood on one cheek indicated an injury. "Who are you? You weren't on the chopper," he said in a tinny voice.

"Williamson," Dan said. "That's right . . . I wasn't with you. We saw you go down. We were grounded too. Are you alone?"

"There's four of us. The other three are injured. We all managed to crawl away from the chopper. We're over there in the woods." He pointed. "These others didn't make it. One was my friend."

The man's name was Bevins. He'd returned to the Huey in search of armament. Bevins told Dan that no one had escaped with weapons except a sergeant who had a sidearm.

Private Bevins led Dan to the other survivors huddled together under a rocky overhang about two hundred yards away. The situation looked gloomy. The sergeant had a head wound, and his speech was incoherent. There were two other privates. Dennis had his broken left arm tied against his body with a belt. Coats was lying on the ground, groaning; secured to his right leg with strips of cloth was a crude splint made from two tree branches. "Busted good," Bevins said. "Bones sticking out."

Dennis explained that they had arrived in Vietnam only a short time ago and had never seen combat. "Except Sergeant Jones," he said, "He served in Korea."

Jones was sitting up with his helmet off. A four-inch flap of his scalp hung over his forehead. He appeared to understand the situation. "These men are in my squad," he whispered, "and I'm in no condition to get them out of here. Corporal, you'll have to do it."

"Sergeant Jones, we'd better move farther away. The VC may have already been at your Huey. They'll probably be beating the bush all around us."

"I agree. We stopped here only because we couldn't go any farther."

Dan explained their own circumstances and why his plan for getting on the hilltop was the best chance for rescue. "We must get back to the lieutenant and Lasher before dark," he said. "We'll figure out how to go from there."

"How far are they?"

"Three-quarters of a mile . . . maybe a little more."

The trip took time and great effort. Dennis and Bevins helped Jones, supporting him between them. The sergeant kept passing out, becoming dead weight. Bevins did most of the lifting because of Dennis' broken arm. Dan had difficulty assisting Coats, who hopped on one leg and dragged his broken one. Darkness was descending as they struggled into the enclosure with the fallen trees.

"God help us!" Lasher said as he surveyed the group.

Benedict was lucid again. Dan told him about his trek and finding the other group. "You're in charge, sir," he said, hoping the lieutenant would comprehend. "You need to tell us what we should do."

"I'm in no shape to lead this group, corporal. Neither is Sergeant Jones. I'm giving you the responsibility. You seem level-headed. I'm counting on . . ." His voice trailed away, and Dan feared he had passed out again.

Dan turned to Lasher, who nodded his approval. The seven men were close together, and Dan kept his voice soft, barely above a whisper. "Listen up. It's grown dark, and we're moving out. There's a stream maybe a half-mile away. I know approximately where it is, so I'll lead. Once we get there, we'll follow the stream up to the hilltop. When daylight gets here we'll be in a good position for rescue."

No one questioned his plan. They started moving with men helping men. Lasher supported Benedict. The night was black. Dan went forward with deliberate slowness, hoping not to fall into one of the many holes he believed were present. He tried going in a straight line, depending primarily on guesswork. He heard the labored breathing of the men following him.

Although he knew the general direction of the stream, he remembered it as curving in several directions. He was startled when he tripped and slid down an embankment. Benedict went with him and groaned in pain.

Dan stood to find his feet in water only a few inches deep. He helped the others down the bank. They huddled close together.

Dan said, "We'll rest here for a few minutes."

Benedict roused. "Set up the guards!" he said, louder than Dan liked. "I've lost a bird! It won't look good on my record!" He was hallucinating.

"To hell with your record," Lasher muttered under his breath. "We've got other worries."

"We have to be quiet, lieutenant," Dan whispered, putting a hand on the officer's shoulder. "Do you understand me, sir?"

Benedict calmed. Maybe he was asleep. That would help. After several minutes, Dan said, "We're moving out. Is everyone ready?"

"It's too dark," Lasher said. "We can't see anything."

"I have a flashlight," Bevins announced.

"No lights," Dan said. "No lights and as little sound as possible. Vietcong are somewhere here. You can be sure of it."

"I can't go any farther," Coats said.

"Me neither." That would be Dennis.

"Williamson," Lasher said. "How much farther to the top?"

"I'd say maybe a thousand yards if we follow the stream. Why?"

"We're pretty busted up. Why can't we rest until oh-three-hundred? We can still get to the top by daybreak."

"Might make sense. Jones, what about it?"

Jones groaned and muttered. "Sure, whatever you think." Little help was coming from him.

"All right. Does everyone understand? We'll rest here awhile. This streambed's deep, so it'll give us some protection.

147

We're light on weapons. Lasher, Bevins, Dennis, and me, we'll take turns on watch. We'll pull out at oh-three-hundred hours. Understood?"

It grew cold and uncomfortable as the night wore on. Dan lay against the creek bank, M-16 in hand, shivering. His eyes had adjusted to the night. He watched dark outlines of trees and bushes before him, searching for movement.

Even extreme vigilance didn't keep him from reflecting. He had trouble believing he'd been in Saigon just a few hours ago. Now, Becker was dead, and they were in a vulnerable and miserable situation somewhere in the jungle. He had tried preparing himself for a situation like this; he and Lasher had discussed it. They had known the risks. However, the stark reality was something else.

Fear, and his reaction to it, had been an unknown. Would he be brave? He had often asked himself that question. He was glad to see that, though fearful, he wasn't overpowered by it. The night passed slowly. It became apparent that there was no immediate search by the VC. They would be waiting for daylight.

His thoughts turned to Ly Yen. She would return to Saigon before he left for home, even for only a few days. He was confident he could find time to be with her.

What was there about Ly Yen? Was it bearing, physical beauty, or her long black hair spilling over strong velvety shoulders? There had been other beautiful girls in Boston and Miami. He'd never wanted for female attention.

Until the past few months, Myra Waters had stood atop his register of admirable women. She'd continued writing, apparently not discouraged that he had answered only a few of her letters. Nevertheless, all previous interludes with women, pleasant as they were, paled compared to his time with Ly Yen. Being with her was pure happiness.

Was it possible that he was in love? Other men had been stricken by Vietnamese women. A few had even married their girlfriends.

What would his mother think? She said the day he boarded an airplane from Boston to San Francisco, "Don't fall in love with an Asian girl." Although she made it sound like a joke, he recognized a measure of fear behind her statement.

What about his grandmother? His present situation, even

in the chill of night, did not keep him from smiling. For her, it was all about how it would look. He loved Abigail Hunt despite her many flaws. But she would never approve a wife for her grandson who was not white, Anglo-Saxon, Protestant, and rich.

Anyway, he doubted that Ly Yen would marry him. She had given herself to him without reservation, but since their first meeting, he'd believed it was a matter of survival for her. She was too devoted to her parents to leave them. Once he left Vietnam, he might never see her again. She had said it herself. It was a sad situation. Considering his present position, however, it might be a concern without merit.

* * *

Dan slept despite the cold. When he awoke, he knew immediately that he'd botched it; the first evidence of daylight was creeping onto the landscape. He'd planned to climb the hill under darkness. Now, it must be accomplished in the light of day. "Damn!" he muttered.

The morning air was cool and still, but the sky was clear. The men huddled close together. A portion of the streambed they occupied was lined with stones placed by human hands, probably to prevent erosion of the steep banks. The stream looked smaller in daylight. He was surprised to see a culvert twenty yards downstream. About five feet in diameter, it went under a dirt road. They were in a bad position, one easily seen from the road.

Coats was in great pain, although conscious. "Not even any morphine," Lasher said. "He's got guts."

Benedict was another story. He slipped in and out of consciousness several times. "Concussion!" Dan heard Bevins say. Dan told Bevins to sit next to the pilot and hold his hand over his mouth if he started to cry out. Jones was awake, as well. He was suffering.

"We're going in a minute," Dan told them.

"I don't think I can make it," Coats said. Fear clouded his eyes.

"Leave me," Jones said. "You can travel faster. You need to get up there. I've already heard choppers. They're out looking for us. Get up there quickly. You can come back for me later."

"Sarge, we're not leaving anybody behind," Dan said.

A distant sound made Dan realize that something was approaching on the road above them. He heard Lasher whisper, "We're in for it, now!"

A half-dozen soldiers were walking along the road in their direction. "When they cross the culvert they're going to see us," Jones whispered.

"Let's get upstream," Lasher said. "There's a bend about fifty yards away where we can hide."

"No time for that," Dan said.

"Maybe we can get in the culvert."

"They'd see us go in. We'd be trapped in there."

"Well, what *are* we going to do?"

"Fight, if we must. If we're lucky, they might not see us. But chances are, they will. Ready your weapons. Be perfectly still, and pick out a target as soon as they get above us. Get as many as you can before they take cover. Any left can lay on the road and pick us off. We'll retreat up the stream and take whatever cover we can find."

Dan took the thirty-eight from Benedict's holster and gave it to Dennis. He saw Jones draw his sidearm and hand it to Bevins. Lasher leaned against the stream bank, cradling the Thompson in his arms. Dan knelt in the water, finger on the trigger of his M-16.

The enemy soldiers were only a few steps from the bridge over the culvert. Dan picked out a stocky figure destined to come into his most direct line of fire. His heart pounded so hard he could hear it.

The soldiers were above them. One turned in their direction. Dan saw a look of surprise on his face.

"Fire!" Dan shouted.

The man Dan had targeted collapsed onto the road. Other figures above the culvert fell as Lasher's Thompson sent out its torrent of bullets. Some enemy soldiers were taking kneeling positions to fire back.

In seconds, Dan formed a plan. He had three grenades on his belt. At least three enemy soldiers were left on the road. With his carbine over one shoulder, he ran toward the culvert pulling the pin of a grenade at the same time. He was conscious of bullets striking stones in the streambed. When a few feet from the culvert, he tossed the grenade as high as he could, hoping it would reach the road and not fall back on him.

The explosion was loud. He felt the percussion as he flattened himself against the bank that slopped up to the road. The firing from above stopped. Weapon in hand, he scaled the bank in four or five steps and leaped onto the roadbed. It was strewn with bodies. One was still moving. A soldier, face bloodied, was pulling a rifle from under the body of one of his comrades. Dan shot him. He lay still.

Dan looked up the road. Although no one was there yet, he was sure there soon would be. He went back down the bank and scurried up the stream.

"Damn good job, Williamson," Jones said.

"How are we here?" Dan asked.

Lasher said, "Don't know how, but nobody was hit."

"All right, let's get moving." He hoped they understood the urgency. "We're heading to higher ground . . . around that bend in the stream."

Even as the wounded groaned, they made it around the bend quickly. Benedict was heavy, and although he tried moving under his own power, he needed help. They were now out of sight of anyone on the road; Dan spurred them on, anyway. Every yard they moved away from the known enemy was another yard closer to rescue.

They heard a helicopter but couldn't locate it through the thick foliage. "They're searching for us," Lasher said, sounding hopeful.

The stream petered out. They moved cautiously and stopped often to listen. Dan hoped the soldiers at the culvert were part of a transient group, one not likely to make an extensive search. The sun was well up when they topped a rise leading from jungle undergrowth onto a bare field.

"We'll rest here until we're sure there are no VC in the area," Dan said.

The wounded were in bad shape except for Benedict, who was reviving again. His eyes were open, and he gazed around, trying to orient himself. Dan couldn't imagine how much pain Coats was experiencing. Makeshift splints only partially immobilized his compound fracture. Jones sat, hugging himself. A bandage cut from his shirt kept the red flap of his scalp from hanging over his sagging face. Dennis was in pain, too, but didn't complain.

Dan wanted to scout out the top. Jones tried to get him to reconsider and send Lasher. Dan went, anyway. He was gone half an hour.

"Nothing there except an old observation tower of some kind," he told them after returning. "There's a road coming up from the other side but no sign of activity. Plenty of places to land a helicopter, too."

"Sounds almost too good," Lasher said.

Benedict was awake and had been limping around. He was still not entirely coherent. Dan spoke to the group of exhausted men. "We're going on up. I've found a spot where we can wait out of sight and get out quickly for pick-up. I'll go into the open and wait for a chance to signal an aircraft. They'll be looking for us."

Several times throughout the morning there was the sound of distant helicopters. The Hueys' loud engines made determining distance difficult. From his position on a knoll, Dan could hear them again. None came close. He returned to the group several times. He worried because the wounded were getting weaker. Dan's greatest concern was for Jones and Coats. Coats was running a fever.

Bevins relieved him on the knoll. Dan went to sit beside the others, wanting to rest for a few minutes. Bevins soon came running back.

"There are two choppers!" he shouted. "One flew over the other valley. I waved, but they didn't see me. There's another one that looks like it's coming this way."

Dan jumped to his feet. "Let's get up there!"

They moved toward the highest open space visible, about a hundred yards from the observation tower. The helicopter Bevins had spotted disappointed them by veering off in another direction. They waited as time passed. Eventually, there came the sound of another helicopter. Dan had never seen such a beautiful sight as the machine coming over the crest of the hill. It hovered above them briefly before resting on the spot he had marked with broken branches.

The pilot motioned for them to come forward. Dan helped carry and assist the wounded until he was alone on the ground. Then, he bent to retrieve the M-16 he had leaned against a bush.

When he glanced back at the helicopter he saw the pilot gesturing, urgency contorting his face. Lasher was jabbing an excited finger toward the tower. A truck was there, and figures were piling out. The Huey had left the ground and was doing a little up-and-down dance. Dan lunged toward the machine, trying to find something to hold onto.

There was immense pain in his right side. He tried again to grab something solid on the helicopter but missed and fell forward. His face struck the ground. His eyes were full of dirt. He lost consciousness.

CHAPTER FIFTEEN

1965

If anyone had suggested to Obie, even a year earlier, that he would find himself back in uniform for the third time, he would have believed them deluded. When he left the Army after Korea, he'd been content to consider service to his country complete.

Two factors influenced his decision to join again. The first was dissatisfaction with his editorial position in San Diego. An over-analytical colleague called it a "midlife crisis," but he recognized it as the latest visitation of a recurring discontent, the origin of which had long been a mystery.

The other factor was an incident that brought his allegiance into focus: His annoyance had grown for several months because of anti-war demonstrations around the country. He disagreed with the war, believed the United States had no right to a presence in Vietnam, and wanted the country to find a way to withdraw. In addition, he couldn't condone the reality that the hate generated by the demonstrations was often directed toward military service members. He was already considering contact with the Chaplain Corps when a chance encounter with a young naval officer at a bus stop caused him to make up his mind.

Obie had initiated a conversation. The ensign was from Ohio; he'd arrived a day early for his new duty and was trying to see some of San Diego before boarding his ship. Three other people, two males and a female, also stood at the bus stop. They were college students, judging by their ages and the books they carried.

"You sound as though you might be a veteran yourself," the sailor said to Obie.

"Two wars. One as an infantry soldier, another as a chaplain."

The girl shifted her book bag from one shoulder to the other and said to Obie, "A chaplain should be against war. It sounds like you're a war lover. Isn't that true?"

For a moment, he was silent as he considered how to

answer. He said, "No, Miss, I don't love war. The fact is, I hate war. I . . ."

She had turned to the ensign. "You're going off to murder people, aren't you?"

"Look, Miss," the sailor answered, "It's really none of your business. I was having a conversation with this gentleman."

"Not *my* business? Yes, it's my business. This evil war must be stopped. But people like you, blindly following orders, keep it going. Why don't you refuse to go? If enough people did that, the war would stop."

One male student spoke up. "That's right! Tell them you won't go!" He chanted loudly, "Hell no, I won't go!" The other young man joined in, chanting the same words several times.

Their level of anger surprised Obie. He sought to bring calm. "It's not quite so simple," he said. "What you suggest would bring anarchy. I agree with your purpose. The war should be ended as soon as possible, but I'm afraid I disagree with your way of going about it. You shouldn't criticize this man for doing his duty."

"There's no excuse for him or any other soldier going to Vietnam," the girl said. "You either refuse to go, or you become a killer . . . a murderer."

"That's absolutely right," the male student who had spoken first said. "There's no compromise."

Although Obie wanted to respond, the firmness of their jaws and the intensiveness in their expressions convinced him his words would have no impact. Finally, the bus came, and when they got on, Obie and the sailor took seats apart from the students, ending a conversation that had nearly become a confrontation.

The encounter bothered Obie. Was this desertion of reason typical of how the young felt? The country had become polarized over the war, but there must be a retreat to a middle ground with level heads prevailing, both civilian and military.

He decided that evening to brush off his spiritual ideals and place himself at the intersection of war and compromise, go where the men were to help them face their demons—and maybe his own. He recognized ambivalence in his willingness to serve in chaplaincy and not in civilian ministry but refused to let himself dwell on it.

Events didn't play out as he imagined they might. He was

welcomed back and given the rank of captain, but from landing at Qui Nhon on the eastern coast of Vietnam and settling in at his appointed base of operations, he'd had no major contact with anyone except officers who managed support elements. He believed he was being purposely kept away from other chaplains and chaplain duties. He wanted to be near the fighting men. He went to see his superior, Colonel David Atwood.

"I need some answers," Obie told Atwood. There was no point in wasting words.

The colonel's annoyed expression changed little as he listened to Obie's complaints. After Obie had vented, Atwood said, "Don't be impatient, Gainsworthy. Command feels you're best suited for the duties you've been assigned to here."

"With all due respect, Colonel Atwood, I've been here a month, and all my duties have been within Regimental headquarters. True, I've been loaned to other regiments for a couple of assigned duties, but well back from any combat zones."

"Are you asking to go into a combat zone, Captain?"

"I'm asking to go where I can perform the real duties of a chaplain in wartime. I've been doing little except paperwork."

Atwood studied his face. "How old are you, Captain?"

"I'm thirty-nine."

"We have younger chaplains in the field. They undergo the same hardships as fighting troops. It's a tough life."

"I've been in the field, Colonel."

"Yes, I know you have." He opened a folder on his desk. "You have two Silver Stars, one earned in Italy and another in Korea while serving as a chaplain there. That's exceptional"

Obie was still determining where the conversation was headed. "They're only medals," he said.

"The Pentagon doesn't give out Silver Stars indiscriminately. I'm sure you earned both of yours. But that's not the issue here. If I hear you correctly, you want to leave the relative calm of this command to go where you'll be with combat troops. Is that correct?"

"That's correct, sir. I can do more good there than here."

Atwood sat up straight, obviously irritated. "Well, I think you're wrong. You're in a perfect place." He got up, poured himself a cup of coffee, and offered to pour one for Obie, who declined. Obie was too keyed-up for more caffeine.

"Colonel Atwood," He said, trying not to sound

confrontational, "I'm good at giving men council under fire. I'm good because I've been under fire. I've lost friends in battle, and I know how it affects thinking in battle zones and even later in life. That's exactly why I enlisted a third time . . . to use those skills."

Atwood opened the folder again. "Why not take advantage of a chance to sit it out?" It sounded like pleading. "You can perform a great service right here supporting the troops. The front lines are for the young. A thirty-nine-year-old doesn't belong there unless he's a combat officer."

"With all due respect, sir, several older clergy are in the thick of it." He was unsure about the truth of his declaration and paused to gauge Atwood's reaction. Then, with as much certitude as he could muster and without it sounding like a command, he said, "I want a change of assignment."

Atwood sighed. "There's something I need to tell you, Gainsworthy. I didn't want to, but your persistence requires it. This isn't military approved, so I need you to tell me it will go no further."

Obie had no choice if he was going to make any progress. "All right," he said.

"You and I have a mutual acquaintance. Albert Howard. Do you remember him? He was a first lieutenant when you knew him?"

"He was my platoon leader in Italy until he was wounded and sent home."

"Yes, and he was also the man whose life you saved. He's still in the Army and stationed in Washington. He's followed your career, or should I say 'careers'? He called me when he found out you were assigned here. The thing is, I've been instructed to look out for your safety. General Howard said he'd have my head if anything happened to you, and he holds the rank to do it. Scared the hell out of me, if you must know."

Obie was speechless for a moment. He'd not heard from Howard for years. Nevertheless, he felt the need to press the matter. "Colonel, I appreciate your concern, but I don't need protection. In fact, I don't want it."

"I thought you'd feel that way. It's why I hesitated telling you. I was hoping to persuade you, appeal to your good sense."

"I've been told I'm sometimes lacking in that."

"You're not going to change your mind, are you?"

"No, I wish reassignment."

"There's paperwork. It'll take time."

"Not too much time, I hope, sir."

"Something occurs to me. You've learned, no doubt, that chaplains in this war operate differently than in previous wars: In those, chaplains were operational predominately within a regiment or some other well-defined unit. Here, chaplains usually spread out, serving several units. They cover more territory and move around a lot more. That's both good and bad. Ranging farther afield brings chaplains into contact with many people. But, in my opinion, it also keeps them from forming solid relationships with one another. We need more ways to bring them together. It would increase morale among the chaplains. Would you be interested in heading up such a program?"

"You mean like retreats?"

"Yes, that's part of it. Retreats are good. It's being done in many places. But this is separate. There must be other ways to get your people together. I'd leave it up to you. Would it interest you?"

It took Obie only seconds to respond. It was short of what he had in mind, but it might be the best he could hope for. "Yes," he said, "I'm interested."

"Good! Let's make it so."

* * *

Obie was soon released from regimental command and, much to his surprise, allowed to go and do pretty much as he wished. A major project was the organization of a three-day retreat for protestant chaplains who served on or near battle lines. If he couldn't be with men at the front, at least he could be with men who served those men. He chose An Khe because of its central location, and although he wanted to hold the retreat sooner, it took two whole months to make it a reality.

An Khe was a busy base the day he and his assistant arrived. The airfield was a hub for much of northern South Vietnam's United States military activity. Obie had planned to drive the fifty miles to Qui Nhon, taking Route 19 as he had the month before. However, he'd been recently advised against doing so again because of increased Vietcong activity along the east-west route.

Their flight on a Caribou was a short one. Several incoming troops, also on the aircraft, were soon sorting out their bags and other gear the crew had tossed onto the tarmac. Obie and Corporal Fields had traveled light. They walked away from the still-idling Caribou that was readying for a return flight to Qui Nhon.

A jeep pulled up, and the driver identified himself as Private Elkins. "I'm assigned as your driver for the three days you'll be here," Elkins said.

"Your duty will be light, private. We'll be confined to one area most of the time."

"Yes, sir. In any event, I'm at your service if you need me."

Obie and Fields climbed into the jeep. "We'll need you to show us a few locations," Obie said. "I've been here once before, but it looks to have changed."

"Changes daily. It's hard to keep up. Where would you like to go now, sir? I believe you're attending a retreat at Regiment. Would you like to go there, or to your quarters?"

"Our quarters. The retreat doesn't start until tomorrow morning. No! Wait. Take us to the hospital."

The hospital visit was not a random decision; he had planned to go there, but not so soon after arrival. When they reached the conglomeration of old and new buildings, primarily low wooden structures, he dismissed Elkins with the proviso that he'd call him when needed. Obie had spent most of his time at this hospital on his last visit. He reminded himself daily that a chaplain must not forget his primary duties. *That was why he came to Vietnam.*

"Is there someone here you wish to check on?" Fields asked.

"No one in particular." Fields was new to Vietnam and to the duties of a chaplain's assistant. His only real qualification was a love for singing hymns. That alone was good enough for Obie, whose musical talents were just short of dismal. Fields could learn the rest, as Obie had learned from Captain Forrester in Italy. Obie added, "I'm sure all the men I saw last time are long gone. But, sadly, there are always others taking their place."

"It looks like they're getting lots of business today."

Even as they spoke, two ambulances pulled up to a side door and another approached from the airfield. Inside, liters lined the walls. There hadn't been such congestion the last time.

During the past two months, he had educated himself about the hospital system. Having been given an assignment with few parameters and disconnected from normal chaplainry, he structured his job as he wished. His highest priority was visiting as many units as possible to form a network connecting far-flung chaplains. He wanted something more personal than anything available. No one questioned him; orders were cut at his request and transportation was made available on demand. He tried doing what he'd want to be done if he were a chaplain in a hot zone.

He'd also visited surgical units and field hospitals wherever he went, not only American units but also those of other nationalities. Some of those were in terrible want of supplies and medicine. He helped, on one occasion, to "redirect" some supplies from American stores to an Australian unit near Saigon. For that, he was called on the carpet. Nevertheless, he considered it his duty to do the moral thing, regardless of the consequences.

In the hospital at Nha Trang, busy nurses saw the cross on his collar, but no one asked him if he wanted to see anyone in particular; he went about as he wished, speaking to wounded from various parts of the country. Most came from Pleiku Province. All beds were filled, and hallways held stretchers with wounded soldiers awaiting attention.

"Is this normal?" he asked a nurse.

"No. Hospitals everywhere are having the same problems. Fighting has been fierce along the Cambodian border. We're getting some severely wounded."

Obie introduced himself to another Protestant chaplain. Together, they gave comfort, collected family contact information, and helped nurses and orderlies transport men to operating areas. Fields stayed at his heels.

It was after midnight before Obie prepared to leave. The other chaplain thanked him for his service. They were on their way out when a soldier in a bed near the front entrance motioned to him.

"Chaplain, sir," the man said when Obie approached his bedside, "I need to get a message through to someone in Saigon."

The young man's face was covered with grime, typical of others on beds and stretchers in the ward. His lips were swollen and his eyes were red. A large blood-soaked square of gauze was taped to his right side. A bloodied jacket with corporal stripes was tucked behind him on the bed.

"Girlfriend, I bet," Obie said, smiling. "How about your family?"

"My family will know I'm all right soon enough. However, my girlfriend might not know if no one tells her."

"I'll be here two more days," Obie said, "but I'm going to Saigon after that. So, if you don't mind the delay, I'll carry your message."

"I'd appreciate it, sir." The man eased himself back until he was lying flat. It was apparent he was in pain.

"What happened to you?"

"Copter crash. I was hit just as they were pulling us out."

"How many with you?"

"There were four from a crashed Huey and three of us from another wreck, including the pilot. That's him over there."

A hand went up from a bed a few feet away. "I'm Lieutenant Benedict, Captain. Seven of us survived our little adventure." He cleared his throat, "Before Corporal Williamson continues his story, I want you to know that he played a big part in our survival. I believe he deserves some recognition."

Obie turned to Fields. "Write down what the lieutenant says." He asked Benedict, "Who else is here from your group?"

"Sergeant Jones is recovering from surgery, and Privates Coats and Dennis are being attended to down the hall somewhere. Private Bevins and Corporal Lasher weren't injured, so they're returning to their units."

"Write down everything you hear from these men," Obie told Fields. "I'll sign their statements and give them to one of the chaplains who'll know what to do with them. Then, if Corporal Williamson deserves commendation, he'll get it."

"I was only doing my duty."

"It's out of your hands, Corporal. Relax and let others decide about it."

"I thank you, anyway, Sir."

"My pleasure. What's your injury?" Obie pointed to the bloody bandage.

"Spent bullet bounced off a rib. It's not as serious as they thought when they brought me here. But they believe there are still fragments in there, so they're going in to see as soon as they take care of the more seriously wounded. I have a concussion too, they think."

"Give me the name and address of your girlfriend in Saigon. I'll need that information to find her." Obie tried not to appear judgmental. Many men had liaisons with Vietnamese women, most ending badly. This would probably be no exception.

"I'll write it down for you. Just so you know, Ly Yen might not have arrived there yet. I might even get there ahead of her. Anyway, I'd appreciate your looking in to see if she's there. If she is, I'm sure she's worrying about me. I don't want that."

Such concern deserved credit. "I'll check, Corporal."

"Another place you might find information about her is at the orphanage near the airfield."

"Yes, I know where it is. I've meant to visit them."

"By the way, sir, what's your name? Your jacket covers it up."

"I'm Chaplain Obadiah Gainsworthy," Obie said, holding back a portion of his jacket so the young man could see his name label.

The blond head jerked up quickly from the clipboard. "Sir, are you from upstate New York?"

"Yes, I grew up in the Adirondack Mountains."

"Stafford Rest?"

"Yes. How did you know?"

The truth dawned even before the corporal could answer. Williamson was not an uncommon name, so he'd had no reason to suspect.

It was confirmed. "I'm Daniel Williamson. I believe you know my mother and her family . . . the Hunts."

From the dirty and bruised face, Laura's blue eyes stared up at him. "Yes, I do." Obie felt like he was squeezing the words out, like toothpaste from a spent tube. "I know them all. I can see the family resemblance."

"I'd heard you were back in the service," Dan said. "My Aunt Cassie told me. I'm glad to meet you, sir."

"It's a small world," Obie managed. "I hope you'll be feeling better soon. They'll take good care of you here."

"I'll tell my folks I met you."

Every instinct wanted to shout, "Please, don't do that." Instead, he said, "Yes, of course."

Later, after Obie sent Fields on to their quarters, he sat in a chair by a nurse's station, waiting to hear the results of the exploratory operation on Dan Williamson. The surgeon told him there was no permanent damage and that he should heal quickly. His hospital stay would be only a couple of weeks, provided there were no complications. He was near rotation, so he'd soon be out of the war. Obie was glad.

He reached his quarters at three in the morning, exhausted after the long day. He would have to get up at six o'clock to have breakfast with the chaplains who'd traveled there for the retreat. But he lay awake for another hour.

CHAPTER SIXTEEN

1965

There was little time for reflection during the retreat. Later, on the flight to Saigon, Obie mulled the ramifications of meeting Laura's son. The young man was a mystery, someone whose existence he recognized but whose physical presence had no relevance in his own life.

The troubling Laura situation was many years behind him, and those years had dimmed the memories and blunted his reaction to them. Nevertheless, on meeting Dan face to face, it all came back as fresh as yesterday: His and Laura's promises to each other, their tortured parting, and then her betrayal that brought renewed pain. He saw Laura in young Williamson's face, in his eyes, even in his manner of speaking. That evening, after landing in Saigon, and while resting in an officers' transit barracks, the old anger threatened to emerge.

He tried to control his ire with a silent prayer. "Lord, my heart is troubled. My mind knows it's foolish to dwell on this, to bring up old and hurtful issues. Let me forgive the guilty and not blame the innocent. Create in me a new heart, full of love and forgiveness."

By the following morning, he was sure he had Daniel Williamson in proper perspective; he was a young man caught up in war, as Obie had been. He was also in a romantic involvement. That, too, was something to which he could relate. Obie had promised to find his girlfriend. As a chaplain and as a man of his word, he was obliged. He would help.

Ly Yen wasn't at the apartment, nor was there any sign of her recent presence. He located the orphanage. Sister Lydia was Mother Superior of the convent of American nuns that had a presence of twenty years in the city. She welcomed him warmly, and seemed starved for conversation. After Obie answered numerous questions about his background and work, they finally discussed Ly Yen.

"Yes, she stayed with us for several weeks, a beautiful and intelligent young woman," the nun said. "Her family was having difficulty. They were destitute. We helped where we could, but there are so many needing help."

"Do you know where I can find her?"

"We haven't seen her for several months. She was receptive to God's word, and we were surprised when she left without notice. We worried she might turn to prostitution, something we've seen happen to many girls. Maybe you can find her and enlighten us about what happened to her."

"All I know is she became friends with a young soldier named Daniel Williamson. He was putting her up in an apartment here in the city. He said she was his girlfriend."

"Then he must know where she is?"

"All he said was that she'd gone away but would return. He was wounded in battle and was afraid if she came back and found him gone, that she'd worry. I was hoping you could tell me where she might have gone."

Sister Lydia snapped her fingers. "Actually, I can. During the time we were sending funds to her family, she told me they had precarious health issues. Her greatest purpose, it seemed, was providing for them. If she went away, that's probably where she is. I have no clue about how to get there. I had a trusted courier deliver the money. He's no longer available, but I do still have an address. If she's there, you'll come back and tell us, won't you?"

"I'll search for her tomorrow and tell you what I find."

Obie gave Fields a day off and took a young Vietnamese translator with him. Binh, whom he'd commandeered, and who knew the area well, drove their car.

After they found the small house, better labeled "shack," Binh's language skills were unnecessary; Ly Yen was there. Obie sent Binh back to guard the car and introduced himself as "Chaplain Obie."

She was helping her father into a chair inside the front door. Her mother sat on a bench across the room, head drooped, appearing uninterested in her surroundings. Ly Yen led him into the adjoining room.

Her expression was one of alarm as he told her his reason for being there. "Are Dan's wounds serious?" she asked. "How is he?"

Obie was quick to explain. "He's recovering. He was shot at long range with a wound in his rib area. There were small fragments of the bullet to be removed. They'll keep him at the hospital in An Khe until he's fully recovered. He wanted me to tell you that he'll return to Saigon in time to meet with you."

Her face showed relief. "Oh, I am so glad. Will you see him again? Please tell him I will meet him in Saigon as we have planned."

"Ly Yen, I doubt I'll see Corporal Williamson again, but I'm sure he'll return to Saigon in time to see you."

Her eyes were sad. "I would like to see him one more time before he goes. I have something to tell him . . . something he does not know."

She seemed an earnest young woman, and Obie could not help being intrigued. A memory of Matt and Rosa's romance in Italy came; he'd doubted its permanence, and he'd been wrong. Maybe this relationship was a serious one after all. "You'll surely see him again in the future, won't you?" He hoped the question was not too direct.

"I do not know."

"Are you planning to stay in Vietnam?"

"Yes, I will stay here. My parents need me. It is what I must do. As you can see, they are very ill."

"Is it what you want . . . to stay here?" He hoped he was not pushing the limits of decorum.

"I do what I must."

"Nevertheless, is it what you *want?* Have you talked about it with Corporal Williamson?"

She looked at him intently. "The cross on your collar? Is that the cross of Jesus?"

"It is."

"Did you see the sisters?"

"They gave me directions for finding you."

"I follow way of Jesus, too."

"I'm happy for that, truly, but you've not answered my question."

She hesitated. "Jesus says you must not lie."

"Yes, he said something like that."

"I love Dan very much," she said as she drew in a breath. "No, I have not told him that I will stay with my parents. He does not know."

"Why haven't you told him? You must realize that he'll have to know sometime."

He could see her struggling for words. "If he does not love me, he will go away and never come back. That will be end of it. There will not have been a need for mentioning it to him."

"And if he *does* love you?"

"He has not told me that he does."

"But *if* he does?"

"It will cause him pain. I will have to tell him I will not see him again."

"You must tell him, regardless . . . not only of your plans but also that you love him. Maybe he loves you too."

"Do you think so, Chaplain Obie?"

"Ly Yen, I don't know Corporal Williamson very well. I know his family in America, but I had never met him until a few days ago. We talked for a few minutes in an Army hospital. I can't say what he feels. I'm sorry."

"I have a friend who also knew an American GI. She was disappointed and hurt when he left and went back to United States. He did not write as he promised. I sometimes fear I will never hear from Dan again after he leaves."

"I can't make predictions about it, Ly Yen. Love is strange. I will say that my first impression of Corporal Williamson was that he is honorable. I believe he would speak the truth. You must talk together."

"*I will tell him.* I will tell him I love him."

"Yes, you should."

"At least he will know that . . . and the other thing I have to tell him?"

"You could find another way to care for your parents." Even as he said it, he feared he might be pushing her.

Her expression was one of dismay. "No, my mother and father need me."

"Tell me more about your family, Ly Yen."

She told him about her brothers, and then said, "I am my parents' only hope."

A sad situation, he realized, not unlike that of Rosa, who had also sacrificed so much for her family. The night he and Matt met Rosa, they had taken her to a restaurant where she wolfed down her food. When Obie told her, in Italian, to slow down, she had asked him a question. "GI Obie, have you ever been hungry?"

He had admitted that he hadn't, and Rosa's words had

shamed him. She told him that her mother and two brothers and two sisters were always hungry, that she ate swiftly because she was afraid that, at any second, Matt or Obie would say, "That is enough." Rosa's mother, sisters, and brothers had survived the war, but he didn't know if her father had ever been found.

Obie wished he could tell Ly Yen what he thought, that in their condition, her parents wouldn't last much longer and that she was giving up her only chance for happiness. Instead, he said, "Promise me something, Ly Yen."

"If I can."

"Promise me you will find a way to correspond after he leaves. Things change, and so do situations."

"Dan has told me some things about his family. I wanted to send a letter to his mother. He did not think it a good idea."

"No, it wouldn't be," Obie said, as much to himself as to Ly Yen.

"You said you know his family . . . his mother?"

It took effort to say, "Yes, I know his mother, but that really isn't . . ."

"What is she like? Is she pretty?"

"Yes, she's pretty, but I haven't seen her for several years."

"Is she good, like Dan?"

His own prayer words, recently uttered, sprang to mind: *Create in me a new heart, full of love, full of forgiveness.* "Yes, Ly Yen, she's good."

"You must also know his father?"

"Not really. He's a physician. I saw him around sometimes when I was a boy. But, no, I don't really know him."

"Is Boston a big village?"

He smiled. "Yes, it is."

"Is it as big as Stafford Rest?"

Obie laughed. "Yes, it is to Stafford Rest as Saigon is to this village."

She smiled, seeming to understand. "If I wrote a letter to Dan, would it reach him in such a village?"

"I'm sure it would, Ly Yen. Yes, it would."

"If he tells me where to send it."

"I don't know his parent's address in Boston, but I can give you his grandparent's address in Stafford Rest. You can write to them for information if you miss seeing Dan before he leaves."

He took satisfaction in the suggestion. Abigail Hunt would blow a gasket knowing her grandson was romantically involved with someone beyond her approval.

Ly Yen said, "I would smile on you for that. However, I would need help with letter. I speak good English, I am told, but I cannot do the writing. I will find someone to help me."

Obie had another thought; Abigail might try sabotaging her grandson's romantic endeavors as she did with her daughters. "Listen, Ly Yen. I'm going to give you a different address, one that might get faster results." He nearly said, "one more trustworthy," but restrained himself. He wrote on a slip of paper and handed it to her.

She looked puzzled and said, "I cannot read English. Who is this person to whom I can write?"

"His name is Charles Lansing. He no longer lives in Stafford Rest. I'm sure, though, that he'll help you in case you ever need to find Corporal Williamson. He's a good man, Ly Yen." He added, "He loves Jesus too."

* * *

Obie was called back to Qui Nhon without explanation. Although he knew Colonel Atwood was probably behind it, he decided to go ahead with plans for revisiting all the contact points established in past months. He would slither under Atwood's radar.

In the meantime, he was preparing for a Sunday service scheduled for a post near Qui Nhon. His concentration wasn't good, however. Meeting Daniel Williamson had resurrected old emotions that refused to go away.

Why did some memories, lying dormant for years, surge back to disturb the mind? Why could they not be ordered, labeled, and shelved as the Army shelved outdated equipment, thereby solving the issue? Life wasn't that way, it seemed. Yet, he was aware that joining the Army again had, in part, brought order to his own chaotic life, at least until recently.

His sermon at the outpost was delivered rote-like, and afterward, loneliness settled on him like a persistent disease. Had he not been in the Army, he would have stayed in bed and stared at the ceiling. For several days he secluded himself when possible and even avoided sitting with friends in the officers' mess for fear they would notice his malaise and ask questions.

He managed during the day but dreaded nights. In the dark, family members and old friends marched by, their images nostalgic and often accusing, causing regrets for his neglect. Where were Ernie, Chuck, Ed, Tommy, and the others from his youth? What had happened to Rosa? Had she gone to the United States? He'd heard from no one in the Burroughs family for several years.

Nor had there been contact with anyone from Stafford Rest except his father and Angie. Abner was ill; he'd never written, anyway. With Izzie gone, the only communication he had with his mother's family was Angie, whose Christmas cards always had short messages. She sometimes added a comment to his father's infrequent letters, as well. She had, for a time, kept him up to date about relatives in Italy. But, unfortunately, that was no longer the case, probably because he'd not expressed interest.

There were a couple of bright spots: Charles was still faithful in his correspondence; Obie and Adam Silverman continued to write, exchanging long letters about twice a year. Adam's letters always held exacting details about his work in the military and on the farms. In addition, he was involved in politics, and Obie suspected he aspired to some high office.

And, what of Annie, his restless wife, a wife in name only? She'd been in the habit of showing up in San Diego two or three times a year—a woman who considered her service to humanity too essential to consider a family of her own. The civil rights movement wasn't only her passion; it had become her obsession.

He would have taken her back after the initial shock of her infidelity wore off—or given her a divorce. She had shown no interest in pursuing either option. On her visits to San Diego, she had merely asked for a place to stay for a few days. They were cordial to each other, but neither initiated intimacy. She'd lectured him about the war and sent him a letter after his reenlistment, condemning his "poor judgment."

Their situation had gone on too long. When he returned home, he intended to start divorce proceedings.

As always, it was Cassie he missed the most. His father had informed him of her troubled marriage. She deserved better. Obie had come to accept the reality of his love for Cassie, rationalizing that it was not a sin of some sort but simply a fact.

He'd been foolish to let her go. God had placed her right in front of him many times, and he'd blundered worse than a blind man stumbling down a rocky trail.

Daniel Williamson, her nephew, had said she knew of his reentry into the Army. *But did she ever think of him?* Did she monitor his whereabouts, or had she simply overheard some random conversation on one of her trips to the Adirondacks?

Her last words after he severed their correspondence were, "I'll wait for you to call me." He hadn't. His reason was noble then, not wanting to cause difficulty in her marriage. If he could turn time backward, he would do it differently.

Eventually, over the span of a week, Obie was able to cast off such debilitating images. It was time to get out from under Atwood's thumb.

* * *

Orders were cut, and processing was complete. In a few minutes, Dan would board a bus to transport him and Lasher to the airfield for a long trip back to the United States. Nearly every GI in Vietnam longed for that moment. Lasher was jubilant. For him, however, it had become a time of desperation.

He'd been in the hospital in An Khe longer than predicted and had returned to Saigon with only three days to spare. He wasn't supposed to leave the post, but with fewer than six hours until departure, he'd managed to get into the city with help from Lasher and one of Lasher's friends.

"I'll cover for you as best as I can, but it's up to you to get back here in time," Lasher said, and added, "She must be something to make you crazy like this."

He went to the apartment first to find it broken into and empty, not only of life but also of furniture and personal items. Dan had paid the landlord two months in advance, thinking it would keep everything safe. It had not. He searched for indications that Ly Yen had been there, for some clue she'd left, some sign of her presence. He found nothing.

She must be in the city. If she'd returned to the apartment and found it emptied, the orphanage was the logical place for her to go.

Sister Lydia listened with compassion. "The Army chaplain came a couple of weeks ago, also asking about Ly Yen," she said.

"He returned later to tell us that she was home with her sick parents. If she has returned to Saigon, we don't know of it. I'm sorry."

He walked through the streets for three hours, going to all the places they'd frequented. In the end, he concluded that she was not in Saigon. He returned to the post with only an hour and a half to spare.

They boarded the bus. Dan's chest hurt, filled with grief he couldn't articulate. He didn't trust his voice above a whisper. Lasher, who sat beside him, tried to make conversation. "Williamson, we're going home! Is it true they gave you a medal in An Khe?"

"No, not true. It's still being decided, I think."

"You deserve it. Taking out the VC on the road that day saved our necks. They sent an officer to ask me about it, and I told him all about what you did."

"Lasher, I don't feel like talking."

"It's the girl, ain't it?"

"Yeah, it's the girl. Ly Yen promised to meet me, but she wasn't there."

"There'll be other girls, Williamson."

"Something must have happened to her."

"You really liked her, didn't you?" Lasher's tone often bordered on sarcasm but now sounded serious. "There's a lot to be said for these Asian women, even those from the streets."

"She's no whore, Lasher."

"Yeah, I know that now. You did a good deed, Williamson. You saved her from that way of life, even if you never see her again."

They traveled through parts of the city toward the Air Force base. A high chain-link fence separated a section of the road from the street. Dan caught sight of a figure on the outside. The girl clutched the metal links, a look of despair on her face. It took an instant for him to recognize Ly Yen.

"Stop the bus!" Dan shouted.

He saw the driver recoil. The bus screeched to a halt. "What's wrong?" the man said. "We under attack?"

Dan ran up front. "I need to get off!"

"No way," the corporal said. "I'm not supposed to stop, and we're late as it is."

"Please, I only need a few minutes." Dan put his hand on

the door opener.

"You take your seat right now, or I'll have the MPs pull you off. He reached toward his radio.

"Please," Dan repeated. "This is important."

"No! Sit down!"

Dan became aware of someone behind him. Lasher gave Dan a nudge to one side and stepped in next to the driver. "Say, Cummings, you know me, right?"

Cummings looked up at Lasher. "Sure, I know you. Is this okay?"

"It's okay, Cummings. He wants three minutes. It's the most important three minutes in his life. You understand, don't you?"

Cummings opened the door. "Three minutes. No more!"

Dan ran back to where Ly Yen was standing, disbelief showing on her face. He placed his fingers through the fence on top of hers, and for a moment they gazed at each other. His voice trembled when he finally spoke. "I looked for you. I looked and looked. Where were you?"

"My father fell again. I had to get medical aid." Her tears flowed freely. "I came as soon as I could, an hour ago. Oh, dear one, I am so happy to see you and know you are well."

"How did you know to come here?"

"One of our soldiers. He brought me." She motioned toward the road behind her. Dan saw a car with a uniformed Vietnamese driver standing beside it. "He said you would pass this way."

"Ly Yen, I have only a couple of minutes." He clutched her hands tighter.

"I have worried so much about you, dear one. The chaplain you sent to me . . ."

"The nun said he found you."

"Yes, he came to my parent's house. He said you were wounded and that you were getting better. I worried anyway."

"Ly Yen, I love you."

"And I love you also, dear one. I have wanted to tell you."

"I want you to marry me . . . be my wife. As soon as I get to the States I'll start making arrangements for you to come to me."

She stared at the ground. "It cannot be."

"Why not? We love each other."

173

"I must care for my parents, or they will die."

"Ly Yen, surely someone else can look after them. Can't you can find a way."

The bus horn sounded. The driver put his hand out the window and motioned.

"There is no way," she said.

"You should have your own life. You have a right to happiness."

The horn sounded again.

"I desire to come to you, but it is impossible."

"In my country, a man has more responsibility toward his wife than his parents."

"Then it is good we are not married."

"You know what I mean."

Cummings stuck his head out the window and yelled, "I'm going, soldier. You'd better get here right now!"

"You will forget me, dear one."

"Never!"

"Yes, I know you will not forget. I would not want you to forget our love. But you will not yearn for me after a while. Go back to other one you told me about. Myra Waters, you said was her name. She will comfort you."

"Ly Yen, there will be no comfort for me without you. You must change your mind. I'll go ahead and make what arrangements I can, but, you *must* come to me."

She put her small fingers over his. "Dear one, I cannot. You must understand. It is not likely we will see each other again." Her tear-filled eyes gleamed. "But I will have much to remember you by."

"I want to be with you?"

"I carry your child," she said. "It will be with me."

He groaned. "A baby! You're going to have a baby?"

"Yes, our baby."

The horn blared again. "Ly Yen, I love you . . . and I love our unborn child. It's even more reason for you to come to me. I'll send for you."

"No, it cannot be." She was sobbing as she turned and ran toward the car.

"The bus driver yelled, "I'm leaving!"

Dan scurried to the bus. Faces stared down at him, some with amusement. He didn't care. As he boarded, he turned again to call after her, "I'll find a way! I'll bring you to the States! I'll never stop trying. See if you can find the chaplain. He'll help you keep in touch with me." He could see her getting into the car. "Do you hear me, Ly Yen?"

No answer came. He was living the worst moments of his life.

CHAPTER SEVENTEEN

1966

Charles Lansing took the envelope received in the morning mail from his desk drawer for the third time. He had, for over an hour, put off acting on the information it contained. Even prayer and reflection while gazing out his study window at the expanse of Lake Champlain and the hills of Vermont beyond had failed to prompt him to action.

The lake waters were irritated on this mid-March day, stirred like the emotions that made him reluctant to do what he must. Events he'd tried to purge from memory crept back; this would mean dealing with them again—and with Abigail Hunt. Was not the slow downturn of his health punishment enough?

He opened the letter again. The script was large and not unlike the writing of a child.

> *Deer Rev. Lansing*   *March 7, 1966*
>   *My name is Ly Yen. Please ecuse my writeing. I can speak in English well but not so well with the writeing. I have taught it to myself and I have mush to lern.*
>   *Amerikan GI Dan Williamson is one I must find. A man give me you address. He was army man of Jesus with cross on his colar. He say you are good man. Say you tell me where to find Dan. Say you know how to talk to mother of Dan or to grandmothor and grandfathor. You please talk to them and they will tell you where I find Dan my deer one. We love each an-other and wish to be marry. The man of Jesus tell me to write letter to you. Yes?*
>   *Dan no I will have babee. That will be in 2 moonth. He is fathor of my babee. He will send for me to come to him. He tell me that. He will be surpise becuse I tell him I not marry becuse my parents are very ill. They are better and say I marry with Dan. Say that I do for them so that I and my babee will have safe life.*
>   *Army man of Jesus say you love Jesus. I love Jesus to. Please to thank you.*

Her address was written at the bottom of the second page. The handwriting there was more legible, obviously written by someone else.

The letter was sad, and he wished he hadn't received it. He had a pastoral duty, however. Would Daniel Williamson welcome such news? Many GIs had liaisons in foreign countries that they would rather their families not learn about. That might be the case here.

Should Daniel receive this news? *Absolutely.* It was the delivery problem that bothered him.

Although they'd never met, Charles had tried to follow events in the life of Laura's son. He would speak directly to Daniel if he knew how to find him. Charles hadn't talked to anyone in Stafford Rest for weeks, not since calling Miles Carmody's drugstore to order a product he was unable to find anywhere else. Miles told him that Daniel had been wounded in Vietnam but had stayed in the Army and was attending a military school in the States.

Getting Daniels's address meant asking a family member. Laura and her husband lived in Boston; he didn't have their address. Cassie lived in Texas; he wasn't sure where in Texas. That left Abigail and Pinky. Talking to Abigail was the prospect that made him anxious.

Years before, he'd left Stafford Rest Methodist with mixed feelings. He'd acted in the church's best interests by giving it a new education wing, but there was often a feeling that he'd made a deal with the Devil. It was prayers, lots of them, that had brought forgiveness.

Nevertheless, this letter and thoughts of dealing with Abigail again opened old mental wounds and brought real physical distress. The usual discomfort in his lower abdomen had become a persistent stabbing pain. He decided to get the call over with as quickly as he could.

He found the Hunt number and dialed it. He hoped Pinky would pick up the phone, but Abigail answered. Her voice was cold. "Charles, why are you calling?"

"I have a letter to read to you, Abigail. It was written about two weeks ago and came today."

"Well, read it. I'm listening."

He read it all through, editing to distract from the errors.

When finished, he asked, "Will you get this message to Daniel, along with her address so that he can contact her?"

"I'll take care of it."

"You should know that I also intend to answer Ly Yen's letter telling her that I've talked to you. You could give me Daniels's address to pass along to her. I could also forward her letter to him."

"This is a Hunt family matter, Charles."

"Even so, she did contact me. I'm obligated."

"Send the letter to me."

He must draw a line somewhere. "No, Abigail, this letter was sent to me. Daniel is the only one I'll give it to."

There was a brief silence before she said, "This is to go no further. Do *not* tell anyone else of this. Do you understand?"

"I don't intend to tell anyone. I'm a pastor, remember? It's confidential information. Haven't I kept things confidential, Abigail?" He made the question as pointed as he could.

"I suppose you have. But, you'd better."

He fought down the old familiar fear; she couldn't hurt him as he'd once imagined. Anyway, she wouldn't dare risk someone discovering her secrets. "So, you'll give Daniel the address I gave you?" he said.

"I said I'd take care of it." She hung up.

He sat a long time sorting his feelings. Christians, particularly preachers, weren't supposed to hate. Abigail Hunt made that difficult. Would she give her grandson Ly Yen's address? She might bury it so no one else would ever know. As she said, it was a Hunt affair. Nevertheless, was he not obligated to tell the girl he'd tried? Yes, he would write to her. Not wanting to delay, he took stationary from his desk drawer.

He hesitated. Were there times when compassion overruled confidentiality? He'd never met this woman who lived in Vietnam, but her cry for help had reached him across cultures and over many miles. Although she might never hear from Daniel Williamson, she should not be ignorant about the family of her baby's father.

"Lord, forgive me," he said aloud as he picked up his pen and started writing.

*   *   *

The forest air was nostril-searing cold, and snow was hip-deep where Pinky Hunt and Ken Gainsworthy stood. Pinky still took pleasure in such outings, despite there being pain involved. He supposed some primal instinct compelled men to go out and "bring in the kill."

They were well-removed from any signs of civilization, at least a quarter-mile north of the ridge that encircled Stafford Rest. A small stream, with a name Pinky couldn't remember, flowed from the ridge in the opposite direction from Cedar Creek. Ken had assured him that the narrow valley between the ridge and the next hill over was a place deer liked.

They'd hunted many places, usually farther away, but never here. He and Ken, accompanied by Ernie Boswell and his son Chet, had driven north two miles to where the stream intersected the highway. The four men trudged a half-mile up the little valley to the spot they now occupied.

Pinky had arrived out of breath. They remained there, under the lower branches of a huge white pine nearly an hour while Ernie and Chet walked to the head of the valley. They planned to circle around and come down the streambed, driving deer that had taken refuge from the cold. But there was still no sign of the Boswells, nor of deer. Pinky was shivering. If Ken was feeling the chill, he wasn't showing it.

"We're not far from town, are we?" Pinky said as he stomped his feet to keep circulation going.

"It's just over the ridge, there."

"We could have walked up Blackberry Hill and then down here."

"Could have. Hard walking, however. I used to."

"We'd have managed it," Pinky said.

"You're not as young as you used to be."

Pinky laughed. "Neither are you. You're my elder by several years."

"I've been climbing hills and mountains all my life, Pinky. Coming up here, I could hear you breathing from ten feet away."

"I finally stopped smoking my pipe, but I fear the damage is done."

"Where the hell are they?" Ken was getting impatient.

"They'll be coming soon. Ernie's a lot younger than us. He's about Obie's age, isn't he?"

"He is, about that."

Pinky had been looking for an opportunity to converse with Ken; this seemed like an opening. "What do you hear from Obie?"

"He recently returned from Vietnam and is living in San Diego. He was discharged from the Army again. I wrote to him after Abner died."

Pinky waited. During their friendship that covered many years, Ken had never been exactly forthcoming with information on any subject. Pinky wanted to use this opportunity to gauge his knowledge of Obie's relationship with Pinky's daughters, particularly with Laura. Did Ken know? Had he even guessed what Obie had done? Should he not be told? Pinky knew it might destroy their friendship if Ken refused to believe him. Nevertheless, he should know the truth, even if telling him it brought Abigail's fury down on Pinky's head.

Ken hadn't reacted to Pinky's probes beyond giving Obie's present location. Pinky tried again. "Why does he keep going back into the Army?"

"Don't really know. One war was enough for me. He's been in three."

"Do you know that he saw our grandson, Dan, over there?"

Ken showed surprise. "No, how'd that happen?"

"Dan was wounded in November of last year. Obie visited the hospital he was, as Dan tells it. They got to talking and discovered their Stafford Rest connections." Pinky searched Ken's face. It showed nothing behind his inscrutable expression.

"Dan is fully recovered, isn't he?" Ken asked.

"Oh, he's fine. He's been back a year. Stayed in the Army and is training to be a helicopter pilot. He's going to Boston on leave, and he and Laura are coming here for Christmas, just like old times."

"They'll send him back to Vietnam, won't they?"

"Probably. I keep hoping and praying that this war will be over soon. Lots of our young men are dying over there. Ernie told me that Chet's going into the service."

"It's not likely to end anytime soon," Ken said. "When you're sucked into quicksand, you don't leap right out."

Pinky decided to dig deeper. "Ken, why has Obie never

come back home?"

Ken's expression fell somewhere between annoyance and anger. He was slow to answer. "Well, you must know, don't you?"

Their eyes met. "No, I don't know," Pinky said, feeling only mild regret at the lie. "Do you?"

"Sure, I know. You do, too, if you'd think about it a minute. Everybody in town knew how much Obie thought of Laura. You knew too, didn't you?"

"I thought it was a teenage crush. Most kids get over those."

"Well, he didn't. He doesn't come back because he can't stand the memories."

"What memories?"

"Memories about the way Laura treated him."

Anger surged for a moment. Pinky fought it. The conversation could go sour. "How Laura treated *him*?"

"Yes, her marrying Ben Williamson just as Obie shipped out on his way to war."

Pinky struggled to put things in perspective. He couldn't blame Ken for what he didn't know. Pinky wanted it out in the open, no matter who was hurt—even if it meant the end of a friendship.

"Ken, there's something I have to tell you . . ."

Two things happened simultaneously: Four deer, three females and a buck lopped into the clearing below them, causing Ken to turn and raise his rifle; Pinky felt a sharp pain in his chest. A heavy overpowering burden hammered him to his knees. He pitched forward, his face enveloped in cold snow.

CHAPTER EIGHTEEN

1967

After his return from Vietnam, Obie rented a San Diego apartment across the city from his most recent residence. It was not far from where he'd lived after his first book sale seven years earlier. The neighborhood showed signs of both progress and decline, with new and decaying structures sometimes sitting side by side. It seemed a wash, much like the course of his life during the same period; those seven years had delivered him to a place where he sat with his hands in his pockets, waiting for something to happen. What that 'something' was, he was unsure.

He had left the Army for the third time with a feeling of frustration. Unlike the previous two tours, where he could measure his contribution, he returned from Vietnam disappointed because of his limited inability to interact with the fighting men. Colonel Atwood, who finished his tour a few weeks ahead of Obie, confided that Obie was considered a "loose cannon" and had been "reigned in." Until that news, he had planned to extend his stay in the military, even indicating that to the Methodist Conference. Instead, he exercised his right to a discharge. It seemed like one more failure.

He'd been back in San Diego for several months—idle months. He'd planned to look for work, knowing that work might bring a feeling of purpose. He procrastinated, however, and now with an uncertain future and a past filled with professional and personal failures, he stared at a wall of despondency.

Time dragged by in a succession of secluded days and sleep-disturbed nights—and the problem intensified. Finally, searching for peace of mind, he recognized his need for human companionship.

Hopefully, he went to a service at the Methodist church he'd previously attended. Another minister was there who preached "hellfire and brimstone" sermons more apt to frighten than to persuade; he didn't go back. He went to the spot where the food pantry had stood, where he had met Annie. The building had been torn down and a parking lot was in its place.

He'd sold his car before his last enlistment and now considered purchasing a new one. Driving into the hills through a different landscape might give him a sense of who he was. However, he failed to act on that idea; the effort seemed too great.

Annie came in his dreams, saying lighthearted things that seemed extensions of her personality. Although love, the kind a husband has for a wife, had flown, he loved her the way a parent might love a wayward child. She would always be a part of his life. He experienced regret about what might have been; he could have handled the situation with more compassion.

Despite their difficulties, he didn't want to lose contact. Through a mutual acquaintance, he'd discovered that she was in Los Angles and heavily involved in human rights projects. He sent a letter, using an address he thought might reach her, to let her know she could visit whenever she liked. "So that you may take rest with an old friend," he'd written, phrased that way to make sure she knew she was welcome but that their relationship could be nothing more.

His apartment had far more space than he needed. The kitchen was merely a place for making coffee, which he drank on his patio where he could stare at the ocean. A restaurant down the street provided sufficient fare. He skipped meals for lack of interest or simply because he forgot. Pain from his old wound came during rainy weather. His general health was good. Nevertheless, he lost weight. No one was there to tell him; his bathroom mirror and baggy clothing revealed it.

Prayer was difficult. He'd delivered sermons to service members warning them of spiritual crisis; he worried that he was on the edge of that condition.

Andrew Loris called one day. Pauldine House was open to a fourth book deal, which surprised him because his last book, his third, had been something of a failure. Critics had called it "uninspired." Obie promised to write an outline but soon gave up on that. If Andrew called again, he'd tell him there would be no book deal.

Along with other meager possessions, he recovered his art supplies from a storage facility rented while he was in Asia. He finished a painting in a park overlooking the bay and quickly destroyed it, dissatisfied with something so inferior. The art supplies went into a closet.

One evening in February, a call came from George Dulany.

They hadn't talked since his resignation from Greenleaf Methodist four years earlier.

"How did you find me? Tony Gladstone again?"

George laughed. "It was. He thinks the world of you, you know."

"I'm not sure how he gets my number. The funny thing is, he never calls me."

"He credits you with instilling him with courage. He's left the military but still has contacts in the Army. Maybe that's how he keeps up with you. He served as a minister in a Methodist church in Kansas before becoming a district superintendent, one of his conference's youngest."

"Good for Tony," Obie said. The reason for George's call had not become evident. "How have you been, George?"

"Good. I've been Good. Obadiah, I have a proposition for you."

Obie appreciated George, if for no other reason than his straightforwardness, but he had to be blunt himself. "I'll not take a church."

"I have a good one, not as large as Greenleaf, but a good place for regaining your pastoral legs."

"No, George. Have you forgotten why I resigned?"

"No, I haven't forgotten. You sinned. You confessed your sin to me and to God. That was years ago. I understand you just spent twelve months in Vietnam. Isn't that contrition enough? Obadiah, you're a good minister. I'm convinced that you've been 'called.' You have a gift. I should say *gifts*. You're still a young man with many years ahead to do God's work. I'd be overjoyed if you returned to us again as the Reverend Obadiah Gainsworthy."

"George, I can't."

"Obadiah, what's *really* troubling you?"

"George, I'm exhausted in spirit. I'm unable to work, and my faith isn't strong."

"Talk to me, Obadiah."

For the next few minutes, Obie poured out his bottled-up feelings about his hopeless life in San Diego, his relationship with his wife, and his inability to write or paint. George listened quietly until Obie finished.

"It's the war," George said. "Or wars. I won't ask what kinds of things you've seen in three wars. I can imagine, though.

Three wars, Obadiah! That's unusual and not healthy for a sensitive mind."

"Nor to the body, I suppose."

"Yes, one affects the other. In my opinion, it's all catching up with you. Have you seen a doctor?"

"You mean a shrink?"

"Yes."

"No. Do you think I should?"

"You do seem to have symptoms of depression. It's nothing to be ashamed of, Obadiah. You should see a physician. See how that goes, and I'll get back in touch in a few weeks. This job won't be open long, but we could find something for you. We want you back."

"Thanks, George. I appreciate your thinking of me."

"You must also go back to church. You need Christian fellowship."

"Yes, I know. I'll try."

"What about Annie? What will you do about her?"

"I'll see a lawyer about getting a divorce. It's gone on too long."

"Is there any chance of reconciliation? I liked Annie. Everyone did."

"No chance. It's better to sever it."

"If it's the only way."

"It is."

They ended their conversation with George repeating his promise to call again. As Obie sat, wanting to digest the contents of their conversation, the phone rang again. He picked up the receiver, thinking George had forgotten to tell him something.

"Are you Obadiah Gainsworthy?" a male voice asked.

"Yes, who is this?"

"Mr. Gainsworthy, I'm Godfrey Lawrence from Castone, Tomes, and Lawrence, a law firm in Hartford, Connecticut. It's taken us a while to track you down. I'm calling concerning your wife, Anna O'Shane Gainsworthy."

How timely. He had just told George he was going to file for divorce. Annie, it seemed, had beaten him to it. "Mr. Lawrence, I'm sure we can work out some reasonable terms."

"Mr. Gainsworthy, I don't think you understand. I'm the bearer of bad news. Mrs. Gainsworthy was killed two days ago in Los Angeles. It happened in an anti-war riot of some kind.

I'm sorry."

Tears stung Obie's cheeks. The phone slipped from his hand.

* * *

Annie's body had been taken to Connecticut. Obie flew there for the funeral. Everything had been prearranged; Annie had taken care of details long ago, even before she met Obie, the funeral director told him. The casket was closed, and the service was short. Not many attended; there were some cousins on her mother's side of the family and a few high school classmates. It was a cold winter day, and only a half-dozen people went to the cemetery where she was buried beside her parents. Such clocklike precision surprised Obie, being so unlike Annie. Planning was not a trait he remembered; she had "lived for the day."

Not so, Godfrey Lawrence told him the following morning at his firm's office where Obie's presence was requested. She had made several provisions, some within the past year.

"Are you familiar with your wife's financial situation?" Lawrence asked.

"Nothing except that she had income from a trust her father established before his death."

"Yes, Mr. O'Shane set it up several years ago. He wanted to protect his daughter, as I recall. He thought . . . forgive me, Mr. O'Shane believed she would not be diligent in handling finances. He was afraid she would give away her inheritance."

Obie was about to say that her father's assessment was justified until an image of her jovial face, framed by amber hair as full and unfettered as her spirit, came to mind. "Mr. Lawrence," Obie said, "You should know, if you don't, that Annie and I have been separated for some time."

Lawrence was surprised. "No, I didn't know. She never told me."

"We've not lived together since sixty-two. She came back occasionally but didn't stay long."

"She never indicated there were marital problems. She spoke highly of you. Said you're a minister. I guess I should address you as 'Reverend.'"

"I'm no longer a minister. Call me 'Obadiah.'"

"I have a letter for you, Obadiah."
"From Annie?"
"Yes." He removed an envelope from an accordion folder. The date indicated it was more than a year old. "She instructed me to give it to you only in the event of her death. I'm sure she never expected it to be delivered. Unfortunately, here it is."

Obie opened the envelope and unfolded the pages. Annie's neat handwriting was familiar.

> *Dear Obie,*   *January 18, 1966*
>
> *Did you ever write a letter you hope is never delivered? Well, it seems this one has been, which means you are now thinking of me in the past tense. Oh, lighten up, Obie. Death is something that happens in life. Does it surprise you that I would say such a thing? We never really discussed death, did we? That, and a lot of other things.*
>
> *There are times when I miss you so much. We loved each other, didn't we? I often long for that feeling, to have your arms around me again. I messed things up and wish I could have undone my mistake. However, it's too late for that and I hope you can at least be happy for me that I went forward and did the things I was intended to do on this earth. Once again, and for the last time, it seems, I ask you to forgive me and put it behind you. Find someone who can be what I couldn't. Be happy, Obie, for me. Please.*
>
> *Let's get on to more serious matters. You never thought I could be serious, did you? I have to tell you about my finances. That's something else we never discussed because you never seemed interested. I did tell you that my father owed a factory in Connecticut. O'Shane Textiles was quite large and prosperous. It benefitted greatly during the Second World War, something that always bothered me. Dad sold the factory while I was in college (colleges, if you will) and set up a fund for me, his only child. I won't go into why he put the money in trust except to say he believed I would run through it in short order. He was right, no doubt. My idea of wealth is to put it where it's most needed. My ideas about that and my father's ideas were at great odds.*
>
> *The funds I received each month were certainly substantial. I kept only what I needed to live on and gave the rest to*

charity (*Godfrey will supply you with a list of those charities since he takes care of that end of it*).

I am leaving it all to you, Obie. Why, you may ask, do I not simply go ahead and give everything to the charities I believe do the most good for humankind? It is because, regardless of what you may think, I love you, and I want to prove my love in this way. I trust you to do what is right. You have many accomplishments, but you are somewhat confused about your life's purpose. If my gift will help you in any way to discover that purpose, I am pleased. I give you a big responsibility, Obie, about how to use the money.

I do have one request I hope you will honor. <u>Please</u> keep the property in Napa Valley. I kept that secret from you for a while. I will not apologize, for it was a good secret, don't you think?. You love the place. I know you do. Remember me when you go there. The property is already in your name, and I have established a fund for its upkeep. I am sure Godfrey will give you details if he hasn't already. A more direct contact is Mr. Lyle Augustine, whom I have placed in charge of the property. He is paid from the fund I mentioned. I have tried to make it so everything can run without involving you, unless you want to concern yourself, for I know you hate to be distracted from your work.

I place no strings on any of this. You can keep all the money and live a life of luxury, debauchery, or both if you wish. I suspect you won't do that, but you can if you want to. Having said that, I hope you will not forget my charities list.

Once again, Obie, have a good life. I really, really, truly, do love you. I wish we could have found a way.

Your Loving wife, Annie

Obie had wiped his eyes several times in order to see the words. Lawrence took out documents and laid them on the table between them.

"This is her will," he said. "No one else is involved, so I'll read it to you."

Annie's father had set up the trust to dissolve upon her death. *The entire O'Shane fortune was open for him to use as he wished.* Obie was numb, shocked, and grieved by Annie's death, but he was also awed at the significance of what the lawyer was telling him.

"The will must be executed, and the estate settled, and it'll take some time," Lawrence said, "but I see no real problems. There are no other heirs, and as far as I can determine, there are no substantial debts against the estate. So we'll get right on it, Mr. Gainsworthy."

"There's no hurry."

"Mr. Gainsworthy . . . Obadiah . . . forgive me, but you seem somewhat casual about this. Do you have any idea how much money is involved here?"

The will gave no monetary figures, although Obie couldn't help being curious. "Annie never discussed it with me," he said.

"The amount she received each month was one thousand dollars after monthly charities were deducted."

"She never seemed to want for money."

"That was only a small part of her monthly trust dispersal, which was, in fact, ten percent."

"So, she was receiving ten thousand dollars a month?"

"Yes."

"And she gave most of it away?"

"She did. Anna was a truly generous woman, one of a kind."

Obie regretted not knowing sooner. "Annie mentioned a list of charities in her letter," he said. "Those are where the money from this estate should go."

Lawrence studied his face. "You're not serious about that, are you?"

"I am."

Lawrence looked incredulous. After an awkward pause, he said, "You have no idea, do you?"

"I know only what you tell me."

When he heard the dollar amount of the O'Shane estate, Obie sat in disbelief.

Lawrence said, "Mr. Gainsworthy. You're a wealthy man. A wealthy man, indeed."

When Obie was a teenager in Stafford Rest scraping together enough money to feed himself, he dreamed of having plenty, even riches. His rational side had consistently recognized it as an impossible dream. Now, in the law office in Hartford, he forced himself to accept the reality.

If he kept the money, he would be rich beyond anything he

could have imagined. He would never have to work again, never need to hope for a book contract nor negotiate a salary. He could travel, paint, and live wherever he wished. He was surprised at the power of the temptation.

Perhaps he could keep ten percent as Annie had done. Even that would be an amount that would set him up for life. He could have the finest things of everything and never worry about money again.

"Yes, very wealthy," he said. He was numb.

"There's also a deed for a property in California. Anna put it in your name some time ago, so it's not mentioned in the will. However, it's a valuable property with a trust attached for its management. We can sell it for you if you wish."

"No, she wanted me to keep it. In her letter, she mentioned a man . . . Lyle Augustine."

"Yes, I'm in contact with Mr. Augustine. Our firm has handled the trust for the property for some time. Through Mr. Augustine and his administration of the property, funds are shuffled to and from the trust. Do you wish to assume day-to-day control? You can even dissolve the trust if you want to."

"No, your firm may continue administering it, at least for now." Such detail seemed gross overkill for a six-room house on two or three acres. Later, he'd handle it all himself, but he was presently in no mood for thinking about it.

"We'll send you detailed accounts of all transactions involving the property," Lawrence said.

"You just take care of it, whatever needs to be done. Send me details at the end of each year, if you wish. That's all I need. I only want to find it clean and livable when I go there."

"The cottage, you mean?"

"Yes, that and the grounds. Yes, everything."

"All right, we'll administer it in conjunction with Mr. Augustine. And how shall I proceed with the rest of Anna's estate?"

Two faces flashed before Obie. Annie was mouthing the words she had written in her letter: *"I trust you to do what is right."*

The other face was his mother's. Her words were from long ago, when she had offered her advice: *"Money can do many things, but it must not keep you from doing God's will."*

A third face appeared, that of Grandfather Jacob. The old man's words were from one of their many conversations: *"If somebody was to give you a whole big pile of money . . . money you hadn't earned by your own sweat, what would you do with it?"* He had, at first, told Jacob that he might keep the money but, with his grandfather's encouragement, came to a more charitable conclusion. *Had anything changed?*

Lawrence repeated his question and said, "Well?"

The temptation was great, but Obie said, "The money will fund Annie's charities, and I'll add my own. A substantial portion will go to a trust in Stafford Rest, New York. There'll be others I'll want to benefit from this money, as well. I need time to think about it. I'll also need to study the legal ramifications of distributing the money. I'll discuss that with you later."

"You'll want to provide for your needs, too, won't you? I can suggest several investment strategies."

Obie wanted to make the lawyer fully understand, and he needed to do it before he changed his mind. "My goal, Mr. Lawrence, is to give it all away." With the words out, he felt relief.

"Mr. Gainsworthy, I admire your generosity, but in my opinion, it is foolish to give away so much. As your attorney, I advise you to secure your own future first. Consider for a moment what you could do with this money. It's the beginning of a business empire. And you can still make Anna's charities quite happy, as well as your own."

"The money *will* go to charitable causes, Mr. Lawrence. But I'll keep the property in the Napa Valley, as Annie wished."

"At least let us give you an advance of some sort. I'm sure we could arrange that."

"I'll manage, thank you."

* * *

Obie grieved, mourning Annie's death and the lost opportunities to have made amends. She had loved him, and he'd scorned that love. So, prayer took on new meaning; forgiveness and rejuvenation went hand-in-hand until he eventually cast off his cloak of misery.

Two months passed. One day, when a warm spring breeze blew in off the ocean, he was surprised that he felt better than he had for some time—better about himself and life in general. The feeling persisted the rest of that day, and the next, and into the following week. *He was ready to go back to work.* He called Andrew Loris.

"I have an idea for a book I want to run by you," Obie said.

"That's wonderful news, Obie. Tell me about it."

"I've decided to write about justice issues, our responsibilities to one another, governmentally and individually."

"That's pretty vague, and if it's what I think you're saying, it's a departure from your other writings."

"I know it is, but it's what I feel I must do." He could feel Annie looking over his shoulder. "My next book will deal with our treatment of minority groups in this country. I have it pretty much outlined in my mind. And, there are enough injustices beyond that to keep me busy with other book projects for years."

"Why don't you write a proposal for me. I'll send it to Pauldine House and get their reaction."

Obie spent several days on the proposal. Andrew called back two weeks after receiving it. "I have good news," he said. There was some uncertainty in the agent's tone. "They're tentatively ready to sign a contract. And it's a substantial advance, much more than previous ones."

"That's great news, Andrew. I've already started outlining it."

"You may want to hold off on that." Andrew cleared his throat, and Obie waited. "The contract is not for the book proposal you sent me. It's for a book they want you to write, one for which they've given me an outline. You should take a look at it."

Obie hesitated. "I don't know," he said. "I'm geared up for this. Had it in my head awhile."

"Why don't I send it to you? It can't hurt. You're not abandoning your idea, only shelving it."

Obie agreed, making it clear he was reserving judgment. The prospect wasn't appealing. A book must come from his own need to write it. It must come from "his own gut."

On reading the outline, his fears were justified. He called Andrew at once. "I can't do this," he said. "I would if it were a subject I could adopt as my own, or at least believe in. But no, not this."

"What's your objection?"

"I hardly know where to start, but I can tell you with certainty that I'm not writing a blatantly anti-war book."

"Why not. It seems to be the majority thinking in this country right now. Obie, this book would sell. You're already something of an authority on the subject. Pauldine House would like to cash in on it. I agree with them. Because of the times, such a book could be a bestseller."

Obie tried to keep emotion from his tone. "This outline, if followed, would produce a work denigrating the military and military people. I'll have no part in it. This particular war should not have been fought. I'll concede that, but I'll not enable misguided elements that want to rip apart our government and military structure. It's an extremist viewpoint. I stand for a middle course . . . a reasonable one."

"In case you haven't figured it out yet, Obie, it's all about money, about the bottom line. We all compromise our beliefs occasionally. This is too good a deal to pass up. Swallow your pride and do the book they want. You owe it to them. And, it will further your career, not to mention your bank account."

"There's more to life than a bank account, Andrew. That's something I just learned. I must live with myself."

"So 'no' is your answer?"

"I'm saying 'no.'"

"You do realize this can hurt your writing career? Pauldine House is powerful, and I happen to know there are some vindictive people there."

"I have to be true to what I believe."

Obie waited for a response. When Andrew did speak, he sounded decisive. "This affects a lot of people, including me. You're letting us all down. If it's what you intend, I'll have to drop you as a client."

The words stunned Obie. "Andrew, there's no need to . . ."

"I'm sorry, Obie. It's best for us to dissolve our agent-client relationship. I've valued your friendship, but I have to make a living."

Their parting saddened Obie. Nevertheless, he wouldn't let himself sink again into a quagmire of melancholy. After some long soul-searching walks on the waterfront, he put aside his "new book" project to let it percolate. In time, he'd find another agent and publisher.

Although he still had sufficient funds for basic needs, he started looking for a job. After two fruitless weeks into that pursuit, he considered the vast fortune he could tap; it would take away his money worries. He quickly purged the notion. As in the past, he would stand on his own feet. Self-reliance was a part of himself he was unwilling to lose.

One day, after returning from a "we'll let you know" interview with an independent newspaper, he received a phone call. "Hello, old friend," a familiar voice said.

"Adam? Is it really you?"

"It's me, Gainsworthy! In the flesh."

"Where are you? Israel? New York?"

"Neither. I'm in San Diego in a phone booth, and as near as I can determine a block or two from your pad."

An emotional reunion took place five minutes later. The two friends hugged, slapped each other on the back, hugged some more, and went to sit on the patio. Obie had trouble deciding what questions to ask first. "What are you doing here?" seemed a logical start.

"I wanted to see you."

"Who told you where I'm living?"

"Your father, same as last time. He also told me about what you've been up to. I'm sorry about your wife."

"Annie and I hadn't been together for a long time. I do miss her, anyway."

"I'm sure you do. Are you well? You've lost a lot of weight?"

"I'm fine now. But you didn't come all this way just to see me? I'll bet you have other business here as well."

Adam Silverman stretched out his long legs and sipped from his wine glass. "There's a family here from whom I hope to extract a sizable amount of money."

"I thought so. You're still collecting money for your adopted country, are you?"

"The answer is 'yes' to your question, although I want to correct your thinking on calling Israel my 'adopted country.' In modern understanding, we've been a country only since 1948, but you need to understand, my friend, that Israel has been a nation in the hearts of people for thousands of years. I've always been a citizen in that sense. The actuality is something I've been a part of from nearly the beginning. I've fought for both my countries, this one, and the one springing from the hearts of my people."

"Things are heating up there again, aren't they?"

"The fighting will continue, I fear. Syria and Egypt are threatening."

"Will you be in combat, Adam?"

"No. They consider me more valuable now as an advisor."

"That's good. You've had enough front-line business. So have I."

"God has walked with Israel, and we have prevailed. And we will again. Still, I've not yet been able to visit and pray at the Western Wall in Jerusalem. When I can do that, I'll feel complete."

"Will you ever have peace there?"

"I believe we will, and it will be a just and lasting peace for us as well as for the Arabs."

Obie studied Adam's face. He was little changed in appearance, heavier by a few pounds, but he looked more youthful than his years. "How is your family," Obie asked.

"Rachel is still my lovely bride. Still a physician in one of our local clinics. David and Sara are growing up." He went on to tell about their lives in Israel, about the perils and the joys. "David speaks of becoming a rabbi," Adam said.

Obie laughed. "So, you're to have a man of God in your house. Serves you right."

"I never criticized you for your beliefs, Obie. The fact is, I envied you. By the way, how's that going?"

"I've had a dry spell where faith and some other aspects of my life are concerned. It's something I'm still struggling with."

"Why don't you explain it to me?"

"Well, for a while now I've been a painter who doesn't paint, a preacher who doesn't preach, and a writer who doesn't write. That's pretty much the sum of it."

"I'm sure there are specifics."

Obie gave Adam more detail about his depression, Annie's death, and about his rejection of a book contract. He even spoke of the fortune he was scorning, something he had divulged to no one else. Adam listened intently until Obie finished, then slowly shook his head.

"You're either the most moral person I know or the most foolish," Adam said, smiling.

"The latter, no doubt."

"You're giving away all that money, and now you're looking for work?"

"Ironic, isn't it?"

"Well, fortunately, I have a solution for you." When Obie didn't comment, he continued. "My sister, Naomi, has left

Silverman Publishing. She's getting married, finally. Moving to Portland, Oregon. Father is searching for a replacement. You'd fit in perfectly."

"I've forgotten; what was her position? She was editor-in-chief, wasn't she?"

"That was her title. But, in reality, she ran the company. She was good at it."

"And you think I'm qualified?"

"Why not? You have a degree in journalism, and you have writing and editing experience. You've no doubt developed administrative skills. I don't pretend to know anything about publishing, but it seems perfect." Adam leaned back in his chair and waited.

The idea took root in Obie's mind as he mulled possibilities. "How do I apply?" he asked.

"Simply tell me you're interested, and I'll set up an interview with Father. And yes, we're on good terms."

"I'd have to leave California." The words were more for himself than for Adam.

"You can't have everything, Obie. Anyway, New York's not so bad."

"Do you think I'd have a chance at this? I've been a magazine editor. This is something else, though. If I also need business skills, the job may be beyond me. Your father will surely find someone better qualified than me."

"I think you can have the job if you want it. There are two good reasons. Three, if you count my putting in a good word for you. Here's why it'll work. First, when Father hears how you're trying to give away a fortune for a principle, he'll count it as moral fiber. He puts a lot of stock in that. The other thing is, he won't have to pay you as much as he paid his daughter. He'll like that, too."

"Well, then, what else can I tell you but that I'd appreciate your putting my name in the hopper."

"I'll talk to him the day after tomorrow when I return to New York. I believe you can start packing your belongings, my friend." Then, Adam's face took on a more serious expression. "There's something else I'd like to know. Have you talked to Cassie lately?"

Obie stared out at the ocean. "No, Adam. We've had no contact for nearly thirteen years."

"That long? How tragic! So, you haven't tried to call her?"
"No. I doubt she'd even talk to me."
"Did you know she divorced her abusive husband?"
"No, I didn't know."
"Your father told me. He said she had recently returned to Stafford Rest and will begin teaching school there next week."
"Maybe I'll write to her."
"You're a fool if you don't contact her." Adam poured himself another glass of wine. "Gainsworthy, you've been looking at me peculiarly, and I believe I know why. You're looking for the 'me' you knew years ago, the one who scoffed at religious belief and thinks there's nothing to life except what we make of it. You won't find that person. I'm not like that anymore. My wife, children, new friends, and experience have taught me that life has great meaning. Our paths are strewn with opportunities. We have only to bend down and pick them up. They're divinely placed in our way if you will."

"That's strange, Adam. There have been times when I've doubted those things. It seems we might have changed places. How can that be?"

"Maybe because I've picked up opportunities laid in my path and kept them, and the ones you've picked up, you've examined and put down again?"

Obie's conscience was pricked. "And consequently, I find myself with little in my hands."

"Yes, that's a way to think of it. You still have your hands, though, and you can still stoop and pick up."
"Are we talking about Cassie?"
"We are, and of other things as well."
"What should I do?"
"What you know you should. I have something for you." Adam pulled a small piece of paper from his shirt pocket.

The paper had a telephone number written on it. Obie recognized the area code as part of New York State that included the Adirondacks.

"Whose is it?" he asked, although he knew.
"She'll welcome your call," Adam said. "Don't be a fool again."
"I've become rather accomplished at it."
"If you're afraid you won't have anything to say, you can always talk about what your father did."

"What was that?"

"You mean you haven't heard about that, either? It was nearly a year ago. It was in all the papers up there. Your father and Mr. Hunt were out deer hunting. Mr. Hunt had a heart attack. Your father carried him across a big hill to reach medical aid. I looked up the news stories. One article had a headline that said, 'They don't make men like they used to.'"

"He never breathed a word to me about it, and I've talked to him several times. But, then, getting anything out of Dad is tough."

"Yes, you're right. I had to pry the story out of him."

"How's Pinky? Did he say?"

"He's okay, I guess. He's back working, according to Mr. Gainsworthy. I'm sure Cassie will feel some gratitude toward your family."

After Adam had gone, Obie sat a long time watching the sun set over the bay. Then, as darkness gradually enveloped the neighborhood, he went inside. He stood by the phone and fingered the slip of paper. Once, he picked up the receiver, only to put it down. Nothing would satisfy him more than talking to Cassie, but an overpowering feeling convinced him it wasn't the right time. He folded the paper and put it in his wallet. *Had he become too comfortable in the fool's role?*

CHAPTER NINETEEN

1967

First Lieutenant Daniel Williamson had been piloting Medevac and Huey helicopters in Vietnam for nearly a year. Initially, he congratulated himself for his "nerves of steel," an illusion that moderated as the months passed. Most missions in later months were harrowing, and he often returned to base with aircraft damage from enemy fire and mental images of torn bodies lifted from battlefields. Afterward, he collapsed onto his bunk with nerves jangling. Hours often passed before sleep came.

But on this day, as he trotted beside a young Vietnamese soldier along a twisting jungle path, his expectations soared, and his heart pounded harder than any other time during this second tour of duty. They were headed toward a row of small buildings at the edge of an expansive rice paddy. Quan had driven him as close as was safe to this small village near Saigon.

The trail was soft with wet fallen leaves, rendering their footsteps silent. Dan continually searched the perimeter for signs of anything unusual. Vietcong was known for unexpected appearances.

Would he find Ly Yen and his child at last? Were they here? Since returning to the war-torn country, he'd been frustrated by the lack of opportunity to search. He'd been in the Saigon vicinity only twice. The first time, three months earlier, was of such short duration that there was only time to visit the latrine. On this stop, however, he had twenty-four hours of free time. The building in Saigon, where she had lived, and they had fallen in love, was no longer there. Sister Lydia, at the Orphanage, had not seen Ly Yen but gave him her parent's address.

With the soldier's help, the village was reached easily. As they broke from the jungle edge, Quan pointed to their destination, a squat two-room building.

While in flight school in the States, Dan pursued several options to locate Ly Yen. He hounded Red Cross officials and various aid agencies, civilian and military. Unfortunately, nothing resulted from those efforts.

He'd even asked his family for help. While still in flight training, he and his mother went to Stafford Rest during the Christmas holidays. That holiday season, with his grandfather recovering from a heart attack, was a poignant time. Pinky had recently returned home from a ten-day stay at the Albany Medical Center. Dan had, at first, cringed at the sight of him sitting in front of the fireplace wrapped in a blanket and looking particularly vulnerable.

Cassie and Julie were there. Cassie was stressed, with dark circles under her eyes. Minutes after they arrived, she announced that she had separated from her husband and filed for divorce.

In Boston, Dan had observed that his mother and father were also having difficulties. Although his mother said nothing about the situation, her anxiety was apparent. With several strands of family fabric fast unraveling, he hesitated to reveal his problems but knew he must. They were gathered around the hearth before a roaring fire. It had been a cold evening, and they were sitting close together.

"I have to tell you all something," Dan said.

"We know you'll be going back to Vietnam," his mother said. "It's pretty much a certainty, isn't it, considering your training?"

"No doubt, but this is something else. Something I haven't told anyone in the family about."

"Well, for heaven's sake, tell us," Cassie said. She sounded impatient.

"There's a girl . . . someone I want to marry." He saw that he had their attention. His grandmother gasped, and what then came from his mother's mouth sounded more like a sigh. He steeled himself. "She has a child. My child!"

His grandfather's laugh was one of wonderment rather than amusement. His mother said, "Where? When?"

His grandmother said, "Who is she?" There was not the element of surprise in her question that Dan expected.

Cassie said, "I'll be damned!"

It all tumbled out, his and Ly Yen's time together, their absence from each other, their last meeting near the airfield, and his fruitless quest for help from military and civilian authorities. He didn't stop for reaction until the story was told.

Silence lingered longer than was comfortable. His mother

had tears in her eyes. Pinky was smiling. His grandmother's mouth was open; she avoided looking at him.

Cassie was the first to speak. "Well, now, nephew! I thought I'd livened up our family gathering, but you've outdone me. You must find this girl, this *Ly Yen*. What a beautiful name."

His mother said, "She was about three months pregnant when you left Vietnam, is that right?"

"Yes, I calculate about that."

"She would have given birth during the summer. The child would be five or six months old now."

"I hope you haven't told anyone outside the family about this," his grandmother said. "Think how it would look."

"I haven't told anyone, Grandmother, but it's not something I'm . . ."

"You don't have to marry her. She sounds like a tramp."

"I love her," Dan replied, trying to avoid anger. "She's good. I want to find her. I want to marry her."

"But she's Asian."

"She is, and your great-grandchild is half Vietnamese." For a reason he didn't want to explore, he took pleasure in the words and the expression they brought.

Abigail wasn't sidetracked. "Danny, you don't know if the child was even born. Maybe she miscarried, maybe she didn't want it and . . ."

"She wanted our child, Grandmother!"

"It might not even be yours."

Her words angered him. Trying to maintain control, he looked away at the ceiling, the floor, the fireplace, and anywhere other than her face. Then, keeping a steady voice, he said, "Grandmother, I believed you might help me. I guess it was too much to expect."

"Help you? I don't see how I can help."

"You know people, politicians, people with pull. Or am I wrong in thinking that?"

"Abigail," his grandfather said, "We know our congressman. You've also met Robert Kennedy."

"And Jacob Javits, the other senator," she added.

"Could either help me find Ly Yen," Dan asked.

"I don't really think so," his grandmother said. "With all the unrest in this country, I doubt they'd have time for something like this."

"Abigail, you can try," his grandfather said. "It means the world to Dan and should to us too. Life's too short not to help people, especially those in love."

His mother said, "Mom, I have a grandchild somewhere. If you can help, please do."

His grandmother was visibly annoyed but said, "Oh, all right. I'll see what I can do. Just don't expect too much. I don't know these people all that well, and they may not have time, anyway."

Nothing came of his request. Dan suspected her efforts had fallen short, although he had no way of knowing for sure. Her attitude had been strange, as though she wanted to say more but held back.

Now, Dan and Quan stopped at the cottage door. A woman came out and seemed ready to talk. Another woman behind her held a small child by the hand. As Quan spoke, Dan tried following the conversation, the meaning, if not the words. When Quan turned to Dan, his expression revealed that the news was not good.

"These people have lived here about half a year," Quan said. "As they moved into the empty house, a young woman was leaving with a bundle under her arm. They did not speak to her."

"Ask them if the woman had a child about a year and a half old."

The two women talked together. Quan said, "They are sure there were two children with her. I am sorry. They do not remember more."

"Two children? Then, that couldn't have been Ly Yen."

"Perhaps not."

"Maybe this isn't the house. Let's go door to door and see if anyone knows anything."

The women started to go inside, but one turned and said something to Quan. With animated urgency, Quan told Dan, "We must go!"

When they were a couple of hundred yards away, Quan said, "She warned us. The Vietcong have been here. She said they would return soon."

Dan could not have cared less about Vietcong at that moment. His world, where he'd entertained hopes of finding his lost love, was shattered. There seemed nothing else he could do.

*   *   *

Dan was wounded again shortly before the end of his second tour. He was carrying troops into a landing zone in western Vietnam when a bullet struck him in his lower right leg, causing him to set his chopper down hard, but without injuring anyone on board. After two weeks in a clinic in Nha Trang and a flight to the United States, Dan found himself convalescing in a Washington, DC, hospital.

He was weary of war. His latest injury destroyed muscle, making possible his early release from active duty. His doctors were confident his leg would eventually heal without lasting effects. Except for last-minute paperwork, he was a civilian on his hospital release three weeks after arrival.

That day brought a pleasant surprise. As he exited the hospital, someone tapped him on the shoulder. He turned to find himself looking into Myra Waters' smiling face. He put his arms around her and drew her close; it felt natural. He had received her letters through both Vietnam tours and answered some, but he hadn't sustained interest because of his preoccupation with Ly Yen.

After graduating from college in Florida, Myra returned to Cincinnati, where she lived with her parents and worked as an assistant at a law firm. One of her letters had caught up with him in Washington, and he had answered it there.

They went to sit on a hallway bench. She insisted on holding his hand. She told him that coming to Washington was an impulse, unexpected even to herself. She'd arrived on the day of his release by chance.

"Five minutes more, and I'd have missed you," she said.

"But you didn't, and I'm glad."

"Come home with me," she urged.

"My mother is expecting me in Boston."

"Surely, that can wait a few days. She's seen you, hasn't she?"

"She was here for a week right after I arrived."

"You and I haven't been together for years. I want to get reacquainted."

He agreed to go home with her, but only for three days. His mother, when he called, wasn't pleased but accepted his decision gracefully. Myra skipped work, and they went for long drives along Ohio country lanes and ate in out-of-the-way restaurants. Myra chose the eateries, Dan suspected, for romantic seclusion. Her parents may as well not have been there the first two days, so little did Dan see of them.

His war years were over, but elements of an internal battle were gathering. Nothing seemed natural; he felt misplaced, not belonging anywhere. Finally, after three days, and at Myra's insistence, he called his mother to extend his visit. In his present mood, he might as well be in Ohio as in Boston or Stafford Rest.

"When *are* you coming home?" Laura asked, disappointment evident.

"Mom, I don't know. I need some more time. But don't worry, Myra and her parents are treating me well."

"Can you give me a date for coming home?"

He told her merely that he would come when he could. That didn't satisfy her, but he wouldn't be rushed. First, he must work through the feelings that disturbed him.

Myra listened as he told her everything, keeping no secrets. During their five days together, there had been no more intimacy than holding hands; he knew she was being patient. In her letters, she had made no secret of wanting more than friendship. His reserve was a protective posture, but it mustn't continue. That would be unfair.

Myra went back to work. He became better acquainted with her parents during the daytime hours. Leroy Waters was an artist. He worked at home, designing ads for newspapers and magazines. Melinda Waters kept busy with community projects and activist causes, particularly woman's rights. They were well off, judging by their house and property. Dan's bedroom and bath occupied more space than any in the Boston home.

They pried. He couldn't blame them. Myra was their only child. She'd brought home a stranger of whom they had no actual knowledge. He told them about his parents and grandparents and wondered if those credentials met with the couple's approval.

On the seventh day of his visit, Myra initiated a serious discussion. "Dan, what are you going to do now concerning us?"

"Sounds like what a father would say to someone dating his daughter. 'What are your intentions?'" He wanted to keep things light.

She laughed, a nervous laugh. "I know a lot has happened to you since college. The war, falling in love with Ly Yen, not being able to find her and her child . . . but you need to decide. Will you continue searching for them all your life?"

They stood close together on a stone walkway leading from the house to a flower garden. There were no flowers at that season, and the weather had grown cold. He sucked in his breath and held it. Her question was one for which he had no answer. Nevertheless, in fairness, he must let her know where they stood. "Do you know what Ly Yen once said? She said I should forget all about her and go back to you."

"You told her about me?"

"I did, and she understood."

"I must know, Dan. *Are* you coming back to me?" She touched his arm.

"Forgive me, Myra, but I don't know. I really don't."

"Do you love her too much to decide? Is that it?"

"I don't know." He took her hands and pulled her a little closer. "You must understand, sweetheart. My emotions are raw. Maybe part of it *is* how I feel about her, but part is about the war. Against your wishes and against what you believe about Vietnam, I went, and I fought. I served my country and feel good about it, but I've paid a price. I'm unsettled right now. I have nightmares. I get flashes of combat situations I've been in, in all their gory details. The truth is, I don't feel fit for human company. I'm not sure I ever will be. Can you understand my problem?"

She hugged him and said, "I do understand. I want to help you, Dan. Will you let me?"

"I guess I'll take help in whatever form it comes."

"Let's just be together, as we were in Florida. That was a time of passion more than love, but it might be a doorway for your return to normal. If it doesn't work, what's the harm? If it does, we can see where it goes from there."

What could he say? A beautiful and desirable young woman had suggested intimacy. "All right," he said. "Just don't expect too much. And I must be truthful. I do love Ly Yen, but I'll probably never see her again. I'll need some time, Myra."

"Yes, Dan, I know, and I understand."

He stayed another week. Myra took time off, and they drove south into Kentucky and rented a small cabin for three days. The chill winds of war gradually slackened. There was, at least, the promise of peace of mind, a condition for which he longed.

"I must go home," he told her as they drove back to Ohio.

"I'd like to go to Boston with you, but I can't right now," she said.

"I'll send for you when you can get away. We'll visit Stafford Rest, too, and I'll show you around there."

"How long will that take?"

"About five minutes."

"Aren't you planning to live in Boston? It's your home."

"Boston is my base for the present, but I think of the Adirondacks as my home. I'm enrolling at Boston University for next year, so you'll get to see it, but I've never felt as though I fitted in there. My parents were active in many organizations, had social contacts, that sort of thing."

"That environment, their contacts, could create stepping stones in whatever career you pursue."

"Make me globs of money, you mean?"

"Well, there are worse things." She looked defensive but quickly regained her composure. "I want to see you happy."

It's the Adirondack life I want. It's where I'll live."

She sighed. "You will call me, won't you, or is this the end? I must know."

"I *will* call you. But, remember, I told you to have patience with me."

"I'm trying, but you must see I'm serious about us."

"Myra, I need to get my life in order, and I know my well-being affects you as well. But I *will* get it sorted out. I've made progress, and I have you to thank for it."

On the evening of the day before he was to leave, he called his mother. "I'd planned on being there tomorrow, but I have a slight change in plans. I found out Mr. Waters has some connection with Cessna Aircraft in Wichita, Kansas. You know I've been saving my money to buy an airplane. He can arrange a deal in Wichita or someplace else around the country. This may be a chance to get a good used aircraft."

"Where would you keep it?"

"There are several little airports around Boston. We could fly to Stafford Rest in a fraction of the time it takes to drive."

"And where would you land there? On Diamond Lake?"

She sounded dubious.

"That's not a bad idea, Mom. I may look at floatplanes. It seems more practical for the Adirondacks."

Four days later, she met him at a Home Base Operation site on the Charles River. The Cessna floatplane, bought from a veteran aviator who lived near Chesapeake Bay, was an ancient one; he'd never been prouder of anything. As soon as he tied up at the HBO, he jumped from a pontoon to the dock and hugged his mother.

"Welcome home, darling," she said. She wasted little time. "Tell me all about Myra."

He did as they went through the city. Dan drove her Lincoln while she pointed out changes that had taken place while he was away. "I'm sure I told you about her back when I was in Florida, but I may not have told you that she wrote all the time I was in Vietnam . . . both times."

"Have you given up trying to find Ly Yen?"

"I don't know what else to do. Myra understands about Ly Yen."

"I'd hoped you'd find her. Does that sound odd?"

"Not at all. You want to know your grandchild. That's natural. I also think you want to see Ly Yen and me together because you're a romantic at heart." He glanced sideways at her to gauge her reaction.

She stared straight ahead, pursing her lips. "You're wrong, Dan. For me, romance has been dead a long time."

"Mom, you're too young to think that way." He waited a few seconds. "Are you and Dad still having difficulties?"

"Yes, big time."

"Why don't you tell me about it."

"What good would it do? You have enough to think about without worrying about your parent's problems."

"I'm your son. Your problems are my problems, too."

"If you must know, he's found someone else, someone younger. I offered him a divorce. He doesn't want that. He wants us to go on living together while he plays around with her."

Her revelation should have shocked him, but it didn't. His father was a strange man who often seemed not present, even when he was. "Who is she?" Dan asked.

"Simone L'Amour. She was one of his secretaries."

"I remember her. She's only a little older than me." Her expression told him that he'd said the wrong thing. "Sorry, Mom. I didn't mean . . ."

She dismissed it with a wave of her hand. "I don't know how much longer I can put up with his foolishness. I'm thinking of leaving him, Dan. Would it upset you?"

"Sounds like he deserves it, but would you like me to talk to him?"

"When has he ever listened to you, or to anyone for that matter?"

"He *is* my father. I should try."

She was silent for a full minute. "No, let it go. He'd yell and scream. I'll work it out. Now, about Myra?"

"There's not much more than what I've already told you. I'm going to invite her up here next month if it's all right with you. We'll probably go to Stafford Rest, as well."

"When a man takes a girl home to see his parents, it's pretty serious." She smiled, a welcome sign.

"It's becoming serious, Mom. I still have a lot to deal with, but I'm coming to understand that Ly Yen will become merely a memory of something good that happened in a horrible time and place."

"Your memories, at least, will be good ones."

CHAPTER TWENTY

1967–1969

Obie first met Ira Silverman in the Silverman Publishing building in New York City. Ira was an older version of Adam, although more intense.

"Well, Obadiah, at last we meet," Ira said, extending his hand.

"Thanks to Adam."

"My son has told me much about you. I feel I already know you."

Obie grinned. "That could be bad news for me."

"No, it's good. But, are you really giving away over a million dollars to charity?"

Obie was shocked at the directness. He shouldn't be; Adam had warned him.

"Not yet. I'm working on it." There was no point in telling him the actual amount. "It's taking the lawyers time to sort things out."

"Your generosity says a great deal about you, although it may also show an impulsive nature. I've talked to Hershel about you, too. He and Virginia raved. She did mention that your love life needs some repair." Obie was hopeful that the slight curves in the corners of Ira's mouth framed a smile.

"There's room for improvement in many areas of my life, I fear."

"I'm not interested in modesty, Obadiah, so you needn't resort to that." Obie hoped his face wasn't reddening as Ira continued. "What matters is that my son believes in you, my brother believes in you, and from every indication, I see no reason I shouldn't believe in you as well. You have a degree in journalism from a prestigious university, you're an accomplished author, and you've also been a magazine editor."

"A small magazine," Obie volunteered.

Ira ignored the remark. "You were the minister of a large Christian church, so I'm betting you picked up administrative skills from that. What it all adds up to is that I'm giving you the opportunity. Naomi's apartment is empty now. That's a part of your remuneration package."

"Sir, I'm delighted. I'm happy to accept . . ."

"This will be your yearly salary," Ira said as he slid a typed sheet of paper across his desk toward Obie. The amount was far more than he'd imagined it might be. Ira continued. "If that's unacceptable, it's negotiable, within reason."

"No, it's fine. But honestly, I wasn't sure how much an editor-in-chief is paid."

"Your salary is a bit above the norm, Obadiah. There's a good reason for that. My interests and time are mostly with Silverman Financial. Naomi ran this company by herself without me having to expend much effort. I'm expecting you to take her place. However, I'm still your commanding officer with the final say. If you're not okay with that, you'd better tell me now."

"No, it's all right." He wouldn't admit it, but he still doubted his qualification for such work.

"And there'll be bonuses if we have a good year. Those come in the form of shares of Silverman Financial."

There was still the feeling that he was in over his head. "Mr. Silverman, I hope I can live up to your . . ."

Ira's stare silenced him. "Obadiah, you're going to be worth every cent because you're going to change this company for me. I've wanted an opportunity like this for some time. Naomi was good at running things but set in her ways. Now that she's gone, we can clean house and make some constructive changes. That's my dream for this company."

"Can you tell me what changes you have in mind?"

"Here's what I want." Ira leveled his intense gaze at Obie. "I want a publishing company in touch with the world as it ought to be, not one trying to capitalize on the latest trend. I want us to sign not only the best authors in the land but also the most popular. I want someone who'll beat the bush to find good works to publish. You can do that, can't you?"

"Yes, sir, I believe I can." That, at least, was not an idle boast, for he was on familiar ground. His magazine experience had taught him how to find good writers.

"For perspective, it bothers me when I see an author's name on a book cover larger than the title. What should matter is the work, not its author. Will you keep that in mind?"

"I will."

"I'll expect you to begin tomorrow. Better yet, today."

Obie had a moment of panic. "I have an apartment in San Diego. I need time to close it up, pack, and move."

"Nonsense!" Ira said. "I'll send someone there to get all your things. They'll be in your apartment here before the end of the week."

"Sir, you're very kind."

"Kindness is relative, Obadiah, so don't lose perspective. I'm giving you a lot of power. In return, I expect results."

The year that followed was not all roses. Ira was demanding, as Adam had warned. Obie gave him a personal report every week defending expenditures and outlining strategies for improving income. Obie expected more involvement in the hunt for authors and the care and nourishment of established ones. He soon learned that, in practice, it didn't work that way. His real job was to find and instruct people who would do those things. Ira didn't hesitate to have Obie fire someone if they didn't perform at a certain level or simply if Ira didn't like them. "The dream," Obie suspected, was not Ira's priority. Profit was.

Obie's short visits to New York City in the past didn't compare with living there. Everything seemed to move at double speed. The train ride to and from his apartment on the Upper East Side was primarily underground. There was no sense of going, of enjoying the ride and scenery, only the starting and arrival. In between, he threw his mind into a lower gear and reflected in silence about green pastures and lonely mountain passes.

Nevertheless, Obie's confidence grew; he was sure he wasn't disappointing Ira. At the end of a year on the job, there had been a complete revamping of the editorial staff and a crystallizing of the goals Ira had said he wanted.

But why were the days becoming more frustrating, subway rides longer, and meetings with Ira more contentious? Obie often awoke during the night, longing for San Diego. There also came recurring thoughts of Stafford Rest . . . and Cassie.

* * *

A second year in New York City passed. As Obie sat at his desk one day looking out the window at crowded streets, he realized his discontent had escalated, as had a dull toothache he'd managed to ignore. When he could no longer stand it, he had his secretary make an appointment with a dentist to take care of the tooth; he wasn't sure what to do about the discontent.

His father noticed it. He and Angie came about every three months, stayed a few nights, then left. "You look like you hate it here," Ken had said on their last visit. "Can't say I blame you. Hell of a place to have to live."

"I do miss San Diego," Obie said.

"There are other things you miss too, son, but you still haven't figured that out."

Obie's next meeting with Ira, the day after having the tooth fixed, was vexing. Ira came to him, which was unusual. They sat on facing couches across the room from Obie's giant desk.

"This office is bigger than mine," Ira said.

"If you remember, I told you on my first day that it was too big. I don't need this much space. You insisted."

Ira ignored the remark. He never admitted anything that challenged the superiority of his judgment.

He got right to his main reason for being there. "How are the three latest books doing?" he asked.

"One is doing well, one poorly, and one so-so."

"And what are you doing about the poor and the so-so?"

"Paul Sherman is handling them. I met with him yesterday. He's increasing the exposure of both authors to the media. He's also generating more reviews. Favorable ones."

"Obadiah, the problem with these books, as well as previous ones, is there's not been enough prepublication build-up. Hype, if you will."

"All three are good books, Ira. They have substance, and they won't disappear overnight. They'll be in print for some time."

"Perhaps. However, I want material that comes out the gate ahead of the competition. He dug into his briefcase, pulled out a volume, and held it up. "Tell me Obadiah . . . what's wrong with this?"

It was a book by a well-known author whose books had been published by Silverman Publishing for many years.

"Nothing," Obie said confidently. "It's a great book, one of our best sellers."

"Look again." Ira pointed at the cover.

"Ira, it looks fine to me."

"This is a major author. Well-known. Why is his name not larger than the title?"

"I thought we agreed that . . ."

"I thought you would know there are exceptions. We must leverage anything that will increase sales. It's good business."

"I'm sorry. I guess I misunderstood."

I'm not complaining about your work, Obadiah. You've done a great job in the two years you've been here. You've increased sales and found sound authors. This is a minor thing, and I know you'll learn from it."

"Yes, Ira, I'm still learning." He wondered where the discussion was leading.

"I believe we have some serious deficiencies in our staff."

Obie's defenses rose. "About whom are you thinking?"

"Paul Sherman. He's dragging his feet."

"Nonsense. Paul's one of the best in the business. We practically stole him from Pauldine House last year. It's been him, by the way, who found the latest new authors, not me."

"You've approved his choices."

"That's right, because I believe in him."

Ira rubbed his chin. "He should be replaced with someone more aggressive."

"Then you'll have to do it yourself."

Ira sat back on the couch, looking thoughtful. Obie stared him straight in the eye. Finally, the older man said, "Obadiah, are we having a disagreement?"

"It seems we are." *The air needed clearing.* "Ira, when I took this job, it was my understanding I'd been given free rein. You outlined goals you wanted to accomplish, good goals of which I approved. It's your right to set goals. I believe, however, that it's up to me to figure out how we get there. Frankly, I'd like *more* leeway and freedom to do my job. It would be best if you stopped looking over my shoulder every minute. And I'll decide whom to hire and whom to fire."

Ira's face had turned red. "Now, look here," he said, his voice higher than usual. "This is *my* company. If I want to dictate day-to-day activities and override decisions at *any* level, I'll do it, by God."

Obie sat back, keeping his body straight. He crossed his arms. "You can do that, and at any time you like. As you say, it's your company, but if you take away *my* authority, I'll not be here long."

"You're threatening to quit?"

"I'll be out of here quicker than my Uncle Abner could shuck an ear of corn."

"That's damned ungrateful, don't you think? I pay you a big salary."

"I earn it."

Ira appeared to relax. His color returned to normal. Obie waited.

Ira said, "Obadiah, it's not like us to fight. We accomplish nothing in doing that. Let's say we have some issues to work out between us. We can do it later. In the meantime, work with Paul. We'll see how it goes."

Obie wasn't going to be forced into a corner. "I don't like arguments either, Ira, but I'm not firing Paul."

Ira got up to leave but turned back at the doorway as calmly as though there had been no angry words between them. "Adam's coming home for a week. He'll be here tomorrow."

Obie already knew, for Adam had written. "I look forward to seeing him again."

"As do I," Ira said.

Obie had held his temper during their exchange. For Ira, it was business as usual. For Obie, struggling with deciding whether to leave, it was troubling.

The issue was more a matter of living in New York; the city was sucking the life from him. A smaller city would be a pleasant change, somewhere with mountains he could see and climb.

He might leave Silverman Publishing but didn't want it to be on bad terms. He would smooth things over with Ira. He had a candid conversation with Adam the day after his arrival.

"I know precisely what you're going through with Dad," Adam said. "That's one reason I left."

"I want to leave, too, but I don't want to hurt him after he's been so good to me."

Adam's laugh came with gusto. "You think you'd break his heart by leaving? Nobody breaks Dad's stony heart unless maybe it was Mom when she died and left him." His expression changed. "Nothing Naomi or I have ever done has fazed him much, so you don't have to worry about it."

Adam went to Portland to visit his sister but promised to see Obie again before leaving for Israel. Those few days while

Adam was gone were soul-searching ones for Obie.

Was he a fool for planning to leave? He was sure that if he straightened out a few issues with Ira and made some concessions, he could have a place of security as long as he wanted. He was making more money than he had ever dreamed possible and even had a sense of accomplishment in his work.

He had received a letter from Charles. Later, he took it from his desk to read again. His old pastor and mentor had never given up trying to persuade him to return to the ministry. A few lines of the letter stayed with him:

> . . . *My dear friend, Obadiah, do you know what I think your problem is? You have wandered far from your roots. God puts us in a place for a reason. Sometimes, not always, he expects us to stay there. You once told me of your desire to serve God here in Stafford Rest. Do you remember that? Yes, I realize those were youthful yearnings, and perhaps you were a little naive, but there's some truth to be realized there too. And I'm not saying the things you have done aren't good. They are, and you are a fine man with many accomplishments, but I think everyone should retain something of the seed from which they sprouted. There are answers in there among the early impressions that the Father gave to us. Don't you think?*

Elsewhere in the letter was a message giving Obie pause:

> *I've not been well lately. If anything should happen to me, death or disability, I mean, I have put aside a small box for you in my study desk, top, right-hand drawer. It has your name on it. You will find the contents interesting.*

Was Charles seriously ill? The question disturbed him for several days. Some things were expected to go on forever; Charles Lansing was one of those. Although Obie had answered his letters throughout all those years, he'd never considered going to see Charles or even inviting him to come for a visit. Most certainly, he should have invited him to New York.

The letter brought memories of those early years when his mother was sick, and Charles had taken them under his pastoral wing. What would his mother think if she were here? He tried to picture her. How long had it been since her death? Thirty years? Impossible. Of late, he'd struggled to see her face and hear her voice. She might think he had not turned out as she hoped. She desired him to become a "special servant of God," an undefined term that could have led in several directions. He had tried pastoral ministry, more than once, and it hadn't worked. It never would. That part of his life was over.

He pushed back from his desk and faced a window that framed the towering buildings of New York. "I'm sorry, Mom," he whispered. "I'll try to be a good man . . . a Christian man, but I don't think I can be what you wanted."

Adam returned from Portland, and they had dinner together on the eve of his departure for Israel. The restaurant, Adam's choice, was homey, with bright green tablecloths and comfortable chairs that swiveled. As usual, they ordered a bottle of wine.

After the meal, Adam said, "Have you decided? About the job, I mean?"

"I have. I'm resigning."

"What are you going to do?"

"I don't know?"

Where are you going?"

"For the long haul, I'm not sure. But for the short term, I'm going home."

"To San Diego?"

"No . . . to Stafford Rest. God help me . . . I want to climb Blackberry Hill again. But above all, I want to see Cassie."

Part Two

1969–1970

Return to Blackberry Hill

CHAPTER TWENTY-ONE

Early Summer 1969

By noon on a day late in June Obie was traveling north on the New York Thruway. He'd emptied his bank account and crammed remnants of personal belongings into an old Chevrolet station wagon hastily purchased from a neighbor. The car wasn't worth the price, but it suited his purpose of escaping New York City as quickly as possible. Earlier that morning he had placed his meager accumulation of furniture on the sidewalk with a "take" sign. All the items were gone within thirty minutes.

Once on the road, a great burden had lifted from his shoulders. The concrete ribbon on the west side of the Hudson River led away from a distressed life toward one ripe with expectation. He was in no hurry and stayed within speed limits. After two years of enduring overcrowded city streets, it was refreshing to see redwing blackbirds foraging terraced creek banks and to spy an occasional woodchuck rearing on hind legs at the edge of the roadway. High long-ridged mountains, the Catskills, lay first ahead, then on his left; nearly an hour passed before they disappeared from his rearview mirror.

Resignation from Silverman Publishing had not been the onerous chore he dreaded. Ira feigned understanding; Adam had probably given him a heads-up. Nevertheless, saying goodbye was bittersweet.

"Must you leave?" Ira asked on Obie's last day. "I can give you more money if it's what you want."

"I must go," Obie said. "I've enjoyed my work here and cherish the friendships, especially yours, but it's time to move on. It's a personal thing, Ira. I need old relationships reestablished . . . and I want to find peace with myself."

"I honor your decision," Ira said while shaking Obie's hand, "and I wish you the best." He added, "You've found us good writers during your stay. You're a good writer, too. We'll look at your manuscripts should you want a publisher."

"I appreciate it, Ira. I'm not sure yet how that's going to play out."

When he reached Albany, he could have taken the Northway, the new "super highway" that provided fast and easy access to the Adirondacks and Canada. Instead, he drove west past the Schenectady exits and left the Thruway at Amsterdam. He preferred a familiar route north.

Barely into the Adirondack Park, he stopped in the village of Northville, where the Sacandaga River flowed into the Sacandaga Reservoir. After dinner in a small unpretentious restaurant on the main street, he continued up the river, through Wells and Speculator, through the villages of Indian Lake, Blue Mountain Lake, and Long Lake. Some modernization was evident in new building styles and the types of establishments, but most of what he saw retained their unique Adirondack character.

A reflective and pleasantly expectant mood descended, one he carried to the crest of Garnet Point, a hundred yards above the Hunt residence. A grove of trees obscured that house. Dusk was draining daylight from the scene, hiding details of the white cedar-covered hills north of town.

He parked beside the highway and went to stand on a high point, a prominent gray boulder that was part of a crumpled rock wall. This was the Griffin family home site, its members long gone before Obie was born, one of the many facts Ken had casually tossed out to his young son about the area's early residents.

Town lights were starting to wink on. Despite daylight's retreat, he could see the expanse of lake, village, and the closer surrounding hills. Diamond Lake, to the west of town, cast up red reflections from a sky still absorbing rays of the sinking sun. In the other direction, beyond the town, lay "the Morass," the place many called "swamp." But that wasn't descriptive of its true character, for varied and abundant life flourished within its boundaries.

At the end of the Morass, a jagged stone-faced cliff was visible but indistinct in the dying light. He remembered the spot on the top where he'd kissed Cassie; they were sixteen. Twenty-eight years had not erased details of that encounter, nor had it dimmed memories of the varied landscape at all points of the compass. From this vantage point, it all looked familiar.

Obie returned to his car and drove down the hill toward Main Street. The Hunt residence still occupied the dominant position south of town. The house was dark as he passed; it appeared smaller than he remembered.

He began to see differences: A profusion of homes sat along the road from the Hunt house down to Lake Road; several new dwellings existed where he remembered only three. On the right, a paved road followed the south side of Garnet Creek, replacing what had once been a path.

He slowed. A Volkswagen bus came up behind him, honked, then passed, displaying its colorful flowered surfaces. He drove across Garnet Creek Bridge and onto Main Street. Buildings were closer together than he remembered. Most open spaces were filled. A sign introduced "White Cedar Street." He smiled at that indication of progress; it had once been "White Cedar Road."

The Methodist church was down that street about fifty yards, and another two hundred yards would bring him to Ken and Angie's house—with Cassie's next door. According to Ken, she had recently purchased the home, the same one his Uncle Abner owned after leaving his farm. For a moment, Obie was tempted to turn down White Cedar Street. He fought the urge; it wasn't yet time.

He crept along, studied storefronts, and looked for things familiar. A pickup truck came up behind him. The driver in his rear-view mirror might have been a younger Ernie Boswell. Obie stuck his arm out and motioned him around.

The drugstore was still there, as was Hoover's Hardware, the Diamond Inn, and Mercer's grocery, now named "Carmichael's Old Country Store." There were also new and refurbished small business buildings. He traversed Main Street's four "blocks," crossed the venerable metal bridge over Cedar Creek, and turned up Cedar Creek Road.

That, too, held a surprise. Houses lined the north side of the road before it curved up the hill. Blackberry Hill proper had more homes than the three or four he remembered. He passed the place his father had often left his truck. The road, still steep, now had a smooth paved surface that gave good traction. The evening had grown darker; he turned on his headlights.

On reaching the house, he saw no discernable driveway. They had never needed one while he lived there since few vehicles could make the grade. Weeds slapped the underside of the station wagon as Obie pulled in, facing the house.

The little house sat forlorn. It had been empty for fifteen years. The front door was boarded up. Loose wooden shingles extended over an edge of the roof. A window cast back his head-lights like two shining eyes. *Had he really grown up in this tiny place?* Whatever its present state, it was his, or so it said on the deed his father had sent him years before. He'd paid taxes on it when-ever a bill came without consideration. After all, he hadn't ex-pected to return.

A flashlight from his travel bag illuminated the way as he walked around the outside. The other sides of the building ap-peared in no better condition than the front. The Arctic entry-way was the best way in. The door was locked. Tomorrow would be soon enough to go inside.

On the way to the barn, weeds brushed his legs, indicating heavy growth in the area. The beam of his flashlight revealed that the barn was in far better shape than the house. Exploration of its interior could also wait until morning. Mental images of small animals residing there made the decision easy.

Since the chance for rain was negligible, he removed items from the station wagon and piled them up outside, freeing enough space for stretching out in the back. For one night, it would suffice.

The sun was up when he awoke. He was surprised to have slept so well. He located a stone large enough to break the lock at the side entrance. Inside, dust a quarter inch deep covered everything. But, except for dust and the clutter left by feathered and furry residents, little was changed. He half-expected to see his mother's treadle sewing machine still by the doorway, but the space was empty.

There were no tables or chairs. Ken must have removed those or sold them. He tried the pump over the sink. There was no resistance when he moved the handle up and down. The spring may have gone dry, if it even still existed. Anyway, pump gaskets would have dried up long ago. If he decided to live here, a water supply would head a long to-do list.

Kitchen wall cabinets contained little. A few rusty cans without labels sat on a shelf. One was bulging. An old bed in a far corner was bare, its exposed springs rusted. A bed in the sec-ond room was in no better condition. The scene was depressing.

The barnroom was also locked; he was ready to smash the padlock when he remembered a key hidden on a rafter in the other part of the barn. Incredibly, it was still there. It turned hard in the lock, but the bolt slid open. As in the house, dust covered the interior. His old cot, after he removed the yellowed sheet that covered it, looked in good shape. There was no evidence of animal invasion. His mother's instructions during the renovation ensured that the room was tight. He lifted a tarp under the big window to see his easel and painting supplies, probably just as he had left them in his hurried retreat from Stafford Rest.

Outside, heavy brush and small trees grew on the hillside where the vegetable garden had been. The outhouse leaned and was missing its door; he found it in weeds several yards away.

What was he going to do? The amount of work required to make the house livable was daunting. Would it not be better to find a motel room somewhere until he could buy a house in the village? He might even consider building a new house on Blackberry Hill. The property was his; he could do with it whatever he wished.

Later, he drove the length of Main Street and back, looking for a breakfast place. Either of the two small cafes looked cozy. He remembered Beth's Café. He settled on the diner in the forks of the road north of Cedar Creek Bridge. Rudnick's blacksmith shop had once stood on the spot. The right fork was the state highway that went up and over the north hill; the other fork went into the Indian Knob section that appeared to have grown far beyond the collection of small summer homes he remembered. A motel, consisting of half-a-dozen small cabins, was just beyond the diner. Several cars were in Caleb's Diner parking lot.

Caleb, identified by Dorothy the waitress, was a large, barrel-chested man who worked the grill. He wasn't someone Obie recognized.

"You at the motel?" Caleb asked.

"No, I'm up on the hill."

Obie was glad Caleb didn't pursue it; he needed time before talking with anyone. The scrambled eggs and bacon were good, and he took his time eating. On leaving, he brought coffee to go and a sandwich for later. Shopping would soon be in order; there was a large grocery store on the other side of town bearing the name "Cam's Supermarket." Closer, on the corner of Cedar and Main, a Stewarts Shop looked to carry essential items.

Back on the hill, Obie mulled his situation again. Behind the house, the metal pipe connected to the kitchen hand pump was severely rusted. As he suspected, the pump gaskets had dried up. Anyway, the spring above the house had all but disappeared.

A simpler life was one he'd contemplated. Life would certainly be simple on his property in its present condition. With no electricity, no indoor toilet, and no plumbing, he'd have to adjust his ways. If he grew his own food, it would mean clearing land, a project that looked formidable. On the positive side, all the tools he'd need for carpentry and gardening were in the barn. He would need basic furniture, too. A few miles back down the highway, he'd passed a barn converted to a store; it appeared to sell new and used furniture.

He lowered the station wagon tailgate and sat on it, drinking coffee while looking out over the town. It had grown, even within its restricted boundaries. Pinky's furniture factory near the Morass had tripled in size, and a chain-link fence enclosed it. Clearwater Road encircled a much larger portion of land, its loop including Stafford Rest Furniture. The Morass was little changed. Bare ghostly trees still pointed at the sky, although many had fallen.

There were still the three small farms between the factory and the main part of town: The Van Alstine farm, the farthest south, now held a circle of homes surrounded by corn fields; the other two irregularly shaped farms, formally belonging to the Buress and the Hamilton families, were little changed and in cultivation. The closer and larger Matthews farm at the foot of Blackberry Hill was also in full production. Tommy Matthews had inherited it from his father, according to Ken. Obie looked forward to seeing Tommy again.

He picked out other places he remembered from his youth. Abner's old farm along Lake Road was visible but too far away to see detail. The Eps farm, on the town side of Abner's land, had homes on it. The Hunts would undoubtedly still own the narrow strip between the Eps development and the Boswell Marina, their access to the lake.

Obie's house still had the highest elevation of any residence on Blackberry Hill. It would stay that way since he owned everything up to state land. Isolation was a thing of the past; he'd heard a car go by during the night. In the light of day, he was surprised to see that the road that had once ended at his house went farther. It curved east beyond his barn and crossed Cedar Creek on a small concrete bridge.

The village or the township probably maintained the asphalt road. From the bridge, the road extended another two hundred yards beneath the north cliffs. He walked far enough along the road to see two lived-in homes, with three more under construction.

The view below, as always, was magnificent; his house site was the best in the area. That observation helped him make up his mind. He would restore his old home, but he'd not live in the primitive conditions he once had.

The basic house structure was sound. He would repair it, add rooms, install electricity and telephone, add a bathroom, and have running water. He'd move into the barnroom while he worked on the house. With summer ahead, there would be time enough before the winter snows came. *This would, once again, be home.* This time, it would be on his terms.

* * *

From her back porch, Cassie scanned Blackberry Hill with practiced eyes. It was a routine followed nearly every day since buying and moving into Abner Gainsworthy's empty house in the village. It wasn't a planned action, only something she did, sometimes daily. She had watched Blackberry Hill all her life. Obie's absence hadn't broken the habit.

This was something new, however. The object was still there, whatever she'd observed the day before—and the day before that. The distance prevented making out details. There had been a light that first night, probably from the barnroom. Yesterday, she told Ken about it across the picket fence separating their properties.

"What's it look like?" he had asked.

"Well, look for yourself. Don't you see the brown something in front? Sometimes, there's a flash from there like sunlight off glass."

Ken shaded his eyes. "I have good eyesight, Cassie, and don't see anything out of the ordinary."

"Well, I'm going up there. Squatters might have moved in.

It's happened in other places, you know."

"The place is a wreck. Don't know if even a squatter would stay there."

"I'm sure someone's there."

Ken's laugh had a hint of amusement. "Maybe it's Obie come back."

She saw no humor in the situation. She had let Ken talk her out of going. Today, however, she decided to find out what was going on. She told Julie they were going for a ride. Julie squealed her delight.

Her jeep took the Blackberry Hill incline without hesitation. As she went over the last hump in the road, she saw the brown station wagon and pulled in behind it.

"You wait in the car," she told Julie.

As Cassie approached the station wagon, she became apprehensive. It was a squatter—or someone who shouldn't be there. Thieves were known for stripping old barns of their beams and other ancient wood. She wished she had brought her pistol.

No one was in sight. A few male clothing items were in the back of the station wagon; they gave little clue about the owner. The passenger-side front seat was filled with books, so she concluded that only one person was involved. She walked toward the house. Several sheets of plywood were stacked against the side by the entranceway. She was startled by the sound of hammering within the house.

She hesitated. She could go back and get Ken, or call Tony Atlee, the sheriff. Someone was in there renovating a property they didn't own. He must be a fool to think no one would notice. Her anger overrode caution, and she stormed through the door to confront the intruder.

He glanced up, obviously startled. "Can I help you?" he said as he laid his hammer on a sawhorse.

He wasn't what she expected. He was tall, slender, and unshaven, with sawdust in his hair and clothing. Light in the interior was subdued, but judging from what she could see, he didn't appear dangerous.

"Can I help you?" he repeated.

"Well, yes, you can tell me what you're doing here. This house belongs to Obadiah . . ."

His startled expression changed to amusement.

"Cassie?"

"Yes, I'm Cassie Jackson. Who are *you?*"

"Cassie . . . it's me. Obie!"

She stared at him, barely believing what she'd heard. "Obie! Obie! Is it really you?"

"It's really me!" He held out his arms, and she went into them. Her heart raced. The feel of his body and his breath on her cheek made her dizzy momentarily. His voice brought her back to reality. "It's good to see you, Cassie."

"I can't believe it!" She pushed him back to arm's length. "This is unreal. What are you doing here? When did you come? What are you doing to the house?"

"Whoa! One question at a time."

"The last I heard, you were an executive in New York. Head of a publishing company, or something like that."

"That's over, Cassie. I've returned to the simple life."

She stared at him. Not much had changed except for a few more lines on his face and the stubble of a beard that hadn't seen a razor for several days. She went to him again and put her head on his shoulder. She smelled the scent of newly cut pine lumber on his shirt. He held her, rocking gently from side to side. Her hope, her dreams, all but dead, sprang to life.

She placed her hands on his chest. "You're fixing up the house. So . . . have you come to stay?"

"Yes."

"You said you'd never return. What changed your mind?" The answer she wanted to hear was that he was back because of her. "What changed?" she asked again.

"Much of my life has been spent searching for something I haven't found yet."

"And you think maybe you'll find it here?" At once, she feared her words had an unintended edge of sarcasm.

"I don't know, Cassie. I do know I haven't found it anyplace else."

"I'm glad you're here." *If only he knew how glad.*

I'm not even sure what I'm looking for, but I need an anchor."

"And Stafford Rest is your anchor?"

"I'm hoping so. I'm hoping I can regain what I've lost."

"And what is that, Obie?" *Please, God,* she prayed.

"Hope. A future."

"Faith?"

"That's part of it."

"Obie, you've not lost your faith, have you?"

"No, I haven't. My desire to serve God hasn't diminished, but I've had trouble figuring out what he expects of me." He stopped and smiled the broad smile she remembered. "I'm a little surprised by your interest in the subject," he said. "As I recall, you were something of an agnostic."

"I talked that way, but I've reformed. I've been going to church and taking Julie. Carl Enslow, the pastor, is old, but he's good with children."

"How long has he been here?"

"He and his wife, Hallie, moved here from Kansas about the time I came back. She grew up in Tupper Lake and wanted to return to the Adirondacks. When he retired from a conference out there, they packed up and came east. He took the job with the understanding that they'd soon find a full-time pastor. So far, they haven't found anyone who suits our Pastor Parish Committee."

"I suppose your mother still runs that committee?"

"Mom has a hand in everything in the church."

A voice came from the doorway. "Mommy!" Julie looked confused.

"Sweetheart, I told you to stay in the car."

"I worried, Mommy when you didn't come back."

Cassie hugged her. "I'm all right, Julie." She turned her daughter to face Obie. "This is Julie," she said. "Sweetheart, this is an old friend of Mommy's. This is Mister Gainsworthy. Or should I say Reverend Gainsworthy?"

"Definitely not Reverend. Julie, why don't you call me Obie."

"Okay," Julie said, smiling.

"Obie, how long have you been here?" Cassie asked. "From the looks of things, it's been a few days."

"Nearly a week."

"That's scandalous. It really is! You've been here all this time and haven't let Ken and Angie know?"

"I'll get to it, Cassie, in my own time."

"How long would you have waited? Didn't you realize I'd want to know you were here?"

He took her hand and studied it as though looking for some

flaw. He was thinking about what to say in typical Obie fashion. She was reassured in knowing some things hadn't changed.

"It wasn't that I didn't want to see you, Cassie. I needed to wait until things felt normal . . . my being here, I mean. Coming back has been emotional, and I don't want to be overwhelmed. By working on this house, I can gradually get things back to normal."

"Well, I suppose it does make *some* sense. Hasn't anyone recognized you?"

"I've seen several people I remember, but they don't seem to know me. Caleb and Dorothy at the diner have displayed more interest than anyone. I finally admitted that I was fixing up a house on Blackberry Hill. He'll ask a lot more questions."

"It's all going to come out now because I'll spread the word."

"You wouldn't do that, would you? I want to do things on my own schedule."

"Well, all right, but only if you go see Ken and Angie."

"That'd be like making a public announcement. Because of Angie, I mean, not Dad."

"Anyway, I want you to go see them."

"I'll go tomorrow."

"No, you won't. You'll go today. Right now."

Julie grabbed his hand, "We'll go see Uncle Ken and Aunt Angie."

"She started calling them that on her own," Cassie said. She didn't want Obie reading something more into it.

He said, "I can see I'm outnumbered. I'll follow you down. Dad's house is next to yours, isn't it, on White Cedar Road? *Street*, I mean?"

"It is. I bought Abner's house from Ken. It's the right size for Julie and me."

On the drive down the hill, Cassie attempted to settle her nerves. *What did Obie's return mean?* It was an event about which she'd often fantasized but never expected to happen. What would their relationship be? He looked like Obie. Was he who she remembered? For that matter, was she still the same person? She had a failed marriage. Ken had told her that his had been an unhappy one, as well.

In addition, there was the question she'd avoided—the secret about Obie that had turned her sister into a bitter woman

231

and kept Cassie from marrying him. That must be confronted. For now, though, she simply rejoiced to see the brown station wagon in her rear-view mirror.

* * *

"What the hell do you mean by staying up there at the old place for a week without letting anybody know?"

They sat in Ken and Angie's dining room around a large table. Obie and his father sat on one side; Cassie and Julie sat on the other. Angie served lemonade. The fan in the kitchen drew fresh air through the open window at the front end of the room.

"I'm sorry, Dad. I should have come here first." He realized, now, that his thoughtlessness showed disrespect.

Angie, who had hugged him about ten times, said, "Ken forgives you, Obie. We're so happy to have you here once again. It's like old times."

His aunt, also his stepmother, still retained the spark of life he'd always admired. He'd been close to Angie and Izzie while growing up, but adjusting to Angie as his father's wife hadn't always been easy. She had her own family from her previous marriage. Her son, Martin, was the manager of a department store in Hartford, Connecticut. Angie's daughter, Cleo, was a teacher in Buffalo. Ken and Angie's brief visits, first in San Diego and later in New York, were not long enough for him to fully adjust to the relationship. Nevertheless, they'd been married fifteen years, longer than his dad had been married to his mother. So, he rejoiced in their happiness and marveled at how she had turned his father's life around.

"I'm glad to be back," Obie said, patting Angie's hand.

"And you must take your evening meals with us," she said. "You'll need a place to shower, too."

Obie laughed. "Cedar Creek's my bathtub, at least for the present. Dad, you must remember that secluded pool near the house. As for meals, I won't burden you with that. Okay, maybe once a week? And I'll take us all out to eat once a week. I've been sampling the eating establishments." The remark was aimed at Cassie as well as at Angie. He wanted to pave the way for seeing Cassie as much as possible.

Cassie told Ken, "Obie has done a lot of work already."

"I can help out," Ken said. "Four hands are better than two. Are you going to stay, or are you fixing it up to sell?""

"I'm staying."

Obie smiled at Cassie, and she smiled back. She was still beautiful. There was no grey in her hair. She was a picture of health. Would he have come back had it not been for Cassie? Maybe, but she was the most important reason for his return. Sometime, maybe soon, he would tell her that.

He watched Julie across the table. Her handicap was apparent. Nonetheless, there was surprising and unfathomable wisdom in her eyes.

"I'll come to visit you, Obie," Julie said.

"Please do. You can bring your mother too."

Everyone laughed. His father brought out paper and a pencil. "Show me what you're doing."

"I have it all figured out, Dad."

"Show me anyway." Ken was determined to have a hand in it.

Cassie and Julie left to meet Cassie's father at the coffee shop. Obie stayed through lunch. When he was ready to go, Ken said, "Son, I'm happy you're back. It's been too long. And about the other thing I've mentioned . . ."

"Is this about Cassie, Dad?"

"Yes, about Cassie. I hope you've finally come to your senses."

In the past, that statement would have annoyed him. Instead, this time it bolstered hope. Impossible things appeared possible.

CHAPTER TWENTY–TWO

Summer 1969

By the middle of his third week on Blackberry Hill, Obie had decided he needed help from someone with carpentry skills who could plan the order of jobs, get proper town permits, and hire plumbers, electricians, and other skilled laborers. From Caleb at the diner, he learned that Chet Boswell was the man for the job—if he was "available and sober." Following that lead, Obie went to Ernie's Marina, which had grown into a complex of docks, store, motel, and restaurant.

The first person he saw was Ernie, stooped over an outboard engine that lay in several pieces on a rickety table under the big oak. Ernie was at least fifty pounds heavier than Obie remembered. His old friend extended a grimy hand and said nonchalantly as though they had talked last week, "I hear you're doing over the old place?"

"I've started it." He pointed to the table. "Thought you'd have someone else doing your grunt work by this time."

"I like to keep my hand in what's basic around here . . . and it gets me out of the restaurant. Bet you're looking for Chet."

"That's right, I am."

"He's on a job over at Evergreen. Should be finished in a couple of days. I'll tell him to go see you."

"I'd appreciate it, Ernie. How've you been?"

"Pretty good. Cora's been poorly, though. How've you been? Thought you were living in California."

"I've been in New York City for the past two years."

"Have you come back to marry Cassie Hunt?" Before Obie could think how to answer the forthright question, Ernie surged ahead. "Say, ain't you a preacher, now? I heard that. Ken says you've been in three wars. Man, that must've about used you up. In a way, though, I envy you. I ain't never been out of the state except to Vermont and Massachusetts. Went up to Canada once, though. I tried to join the Army not long after you did. They wouldn't take me because of my trembly heart. You were married, too, weren't you?"

Obie believed the best way to avoid answering the first question was to answer the last. "Yes, I was married. Tragedically, Annie was killed three years ago."

"What happened?"

"Riot in Los Angles. You know . . . this war thing." he hoped he wouldn't have to give details.

"Sorry you had to bear that, Obie." Ernie sighed. "Are you back to stay?"

"I believe so."

"You gonna marry Cassie?" Ernie was as persistent as ever.

Obie laughed. "I'm too busy with this building project to think about anything else."

"You have Huntitis, don't you?"

"What?"

"Huntitis! You know. The Hunt girls. First Laura, then Cassie. But I think you're gonna marry Cassie."

Ernie could still ruffle him. "What makes you think that?"

Ernie touched a forefinger to his head, winked, and assumed a knowing look. "Deduction, Obie, pure deduction. Cassie dumped her poor excuse for a husband and came back. And now you're back too. Everybody knew how she felt about you, everybody but you. You were too busy chasing after Laura. My guess is that you finally figured it out."

"Cassie and I are good friends."

"Yeah, I hear you." He paused. "Do you know that Laura's also getting a divorce?"

Already shaken by Ernie's candid observations, Obie muttered, "No, I didn't know. I'm sorry to hear that."

"Don't feel bad about not knowing. She told me some time ago. I think she had a weak moment. Said not to mention it to anyone, especially her family, since she hadn't told them yet."

Ernie smiled the same crooked smile that Obie remembered from their youth. "Aw, come on, Obie. I know you must take some pleasure in that, with her running off with Doc Williamson's son that way. I like Laura but don't some part of you think she deserves it?"

Did the whole world know his business? He looked Ernie in the eye. "Listen, it's water under the bridge. I don't want to talk about it or hear what people know or think they know."

If Ernie noticed Obie's objection, he failed to show it. "Their witch of a mother is still up to her old tricks, too. See the stake over there with the flag on it?" She sued me about the property line. Went back to old deeds over a hundred years old to try and prove she owns twenty-five feet of my land. If she wins the suit, it'll take three feet of our restaurant. I'd have to rebuild this whole wing and take down some docks."

"Sorry to hear that, Ernie. Is there a chance she might win?"

"There's no chance she's right. I have deeds to prove it. But that doesn't mean she won't win. Money is powerful. The Hunts have money."

"Looks like you're doing okay too, Ernie."

"We get along, but the Hunt family is still atop the heap around here. Has been as long as I can remember."

"Why don't you talk to Pinky? He's a good man."

"I guess he is, but he's wrapped around her little finger." Ernie sighed and added, "I'll be sure to have Chet go up to your place to see you. Now, let's you and me catch up on some things. I'm glad you're back."

* * *

While not perfect, Obie's building project's cadence was productive. He beat the sun up most mornings. Ken came often to help. In deference to his father's age, Obie attempted to give him easier jobs; that seldom worked. At eighty-four, Ken was still strong and agile. Obie observed him with wonder. When asked about carrying Pinky Hunt over the ridge after his heart attack, Ken shrugged and said, "Couldn't find either of the Boswells. Somebody had to bring him out of there."

Obie realized one day that his strength and endurance had increased substantially. He felt better than he had for years. Besides work on the house, he had cleaned the barn area, cut weeds, grubbed out a section above the house for a small garden in time to plant some late vegetables, cleaned the spring, and rebuilt the pump to get a trickle of water into the house. Shortly after his arrival, he dug a new hole for the outhouse in preparation for repairing and moving the small structure. It was a temporary solution.

Chet Boswell became a consultant more than a worker, although he often stepped in on a project when Obie reached the limit of his skills. Chet was indispensable, as Caleb Doddridge had predicted, for he knew the order of jobs and what preparations were needed for each contractor.

"Telephone can wait," Chet told him. "We need to get electricity into the original section as soon as possible so you can toss the antique saw and get some electric tools." It took three weeks to get electricity. However, that worked out well because the electrician wiring the house was working on several jobs at once and seemed in no hurry.

As Obie drove down the hill one day, he saw two high school-aged boys kicking a football on the elementary school playground. They looked strong, and Obie needed help with the bull work. Both were on the Evergreen High football team and needed "to toughen up some."

Chet had laughed at the "dribble" of water from the spring-fed pump. A well-driller was essential, Chet told him. Within a week, a drilling rig was in place a few feet above the house. Two days later, they struck water. The flow was enough "to handle the needs of three families," Chet assured.

Obie hired help to put in a septic system. The addition of two new rooms and a bathroom was taking the most time. He laid a foundation, mixing concrete himself, put up framing with the football players' help, connected and finished off the new roof, added siding, and prepared for wiring, plumbing, and an oil-fired central heating system. Chet showed up each morning to advise him on the next steps. Each phase required more time than expected and was harder to accomplish than he'd imagined.

"That's just the way of it," Chet told him after Obie vented frustration. Chet never seemed hurried. Obie said to him one day, "Your dad and I have been friends for a long time. You two look alike, but Ernie was more . . . more excitable."

Chet laughed. "Yeah, that's Dad, all right. See, the thing is, I was in Nam. Seen some awful stuff there."

"Yes, that's a mess."

"Makes my head want to explode, sometimes. Swore I'd never sweat the little things again. I keep to that pretty much. I don't rush. I've been told, though, that I drink too much. And I guess that's fairly accurate. Dad says you were in Nam too, a chaplain."

"I was there for a year."

"He says you write books."

"I've written three."

"About Nam, I bet."

Obie started to answer negatively until he realized Chet had hit on a truth. In a sense, his writing had been inspired by his war experiences. If he ever picked up the pen again, he should find a new course. He'd put all the "awful stuff" behind him.

Summer marched along. Obie, Cassie, and Julie watched the first moon landing on television at Ken and Angie's house. As Neil Armstrong and then Buzz Aldrin stepped on the lunar surface, Obie said silent prayers of thanks; perhaps it was a sign that humanity was advancing, putting such effort into ventures like this instead of war.

The hour was late for Julie; she went to sleep with her head on Obie's shoulder. With her sleeping on one side, her breath coming in little contented snorts and sighs, and Cassie sitting close on the other side, he felt more at peace than he could remember.

Despite delays and occasional misdirection, the house renovation made progress. Obie was on target for finishing by winter. As exciting as was the building project, Cassie's company was more so.

He saw her nearly every day. He was relieved by her acceptance of his presence in Stafford Rest. But, considering what had happened between them years earlier, he feared she might still harbor distrust. He hesitated to speak about that terrible time for fear of upsetting a delicate balance.

She came often to Blackberry Hill bringing lunch or lending a hand with the work for an hour or two. At other times, they met for dinner at a restaurant. Julie sometimes came along but usually stayed with Angie.

Obie made excuses when Cassie asked him to attend church with her. As much as he wanted that, he delayed; Abigail would be there. He'd seen her around town but kept his distance. He would work his way up to church attendance and hoped Cassie would not lose patience with him.

He sensed people were starting to view them as romantically linked, and he wished that were true. However, an aura of hesitation lay between them, and he was unsure how to remove it. Their reserve didn't extend to casual conversation, which was as uninhibited as ever. Nevertheless, he longed for more.

But maybe she wanted only friendship. Considering her bad marriage experience, she couldn't be blamed for any mistrust she might feel. The delicate barrier separating them was troubling, but he was content simply being with her, at least for the present. He knew, however, that they must soon talk—a real talk.

* * *

In late July, Charles Lansing received a phone call. He would have been no more surprised if it had been from Princess Grace of Monaco.

"Reverend Mr. Lansing," the pleasant female voice said, "I am Ly Yen. I am calling from San Francisco."

"Oh, my goodness!" He had formed a mental image of her from her letter two years before, and now her few spoken words projected a new image far different from the one he had imagined. "This *is* a surprise."

"I thought it would be. I was not going to call you since I have sent a letter to you already telling you about my new city of residence."

"Ly Yen, I didn't get a letter."

"I only mailed it the day before yesterday, so you should receive it soon."

"It's probably in today's mail. Should I go look for it?"

"Oh, no, you may read it later. It has in it only what I will tell you now. After I posted the letter, I thought how good it would be to talk to such a nice man. I called an operator to give your name and the name of the church where you are the minister. She found your number at once, and now I have called you."

"I'm so happy you did. I've thought of you often, Ly yen, ever since we exchanged letters. I should have written again to see how you were doing."

"My parents both died after we wrote. I was sad, but I am thankful they could see my children before I come to the United States."

"Children? You have more than one child?"

"I have two children. A boy and a girl."

In her other letter, she'd not mentioned another child. Maybe one had been born later. "What are their ages?" he asked.

"My twins are more than three years old."

Twins! Daniel Williamson had fathered twins. Questions he might ask tumbled over one another in his mind. *Did Daniel know? Was Ly Yen aware of the latest circumstances surrounding Daniel?* What effect might it have on the young woman and her children? As great as was his curiosity, he should proceed with particular care.

"That's wonderful, Ly Yen. Have you been in San Francisco long?"

"It is one year that we have been here. After my parents died, I took my children to Qui Nhon on the east coast of Vietnam. There, nuns helped us get to the United States. It took much time. Much talking and paperwork."

"I'm happy you made it. Are you managing all right in San Francisco?"

"I work in restaurant. I am saving money."

A question had long puzzled him: "Ly Yen, in your first letter, you mentioned the chaplain who gave you my address. However, you didn't tell me his name. Do you remember it?" Charles believed it had been Obadiah, but he wanted confirmation.

"He said his name was Chaplain Obie. He was a nice man, although there was something sad about him also."

"Yes, he *is* a nice man." Obviously, she knew Obadiah only as a man who had stepped out of his way to help her. Charles couldn't help smiling. *How great was God as he worked in his mysterious ways.*

"Reverend Lansing, do you . . ."

"Ly Yen, call me Charles."

"You are a man of Jesus. You should be called a name with respect."

"Call me Pastor Charles, then. It's what everyone around here calls me."

"All right," she said. He waited, unsure where the conversation was going. Finally, she asked, "Pastor Charles, do you know where Dan is?"

The question revealed much. "No, Ly Yen, I don't have his address or phone number, and I've had no recent contact with anyone in his family. I can find out . . . but don't you already have that information?"

After another momentary pause, she said, "After I received

your letter, I waited and waited; I waited for much time. I believed Dan would write to me after he got my news. But there was never a letter. I told myself many things, that the mail is slow, that Dan did not get my message. Finally, I went back to my parents. All the time, I thought there was some mistake. The grandparents of Dan would not forget to tell him."

He heard her sigh. "After I came to San Francisco, I wrote to Army place in Washington. They said Dan is no longer in Army. They would not give me his address. There are telephone numbers for many Dan Williamsons. I called many, but I could not find my Dan Williamson. Now, I call you. Can you help me?"

"Yes, I believe I can. I know this has caused you great pain, and I'm sorry, but Daniel may have never known about your letter." Charles hoped that was true, for if not, it meant Daniel had chosen to abandon his children.

"How could he not know?"

"I should have made more of an effort to find him. For that, I'm sorry. I'll do what I can to help you, Ly Yen, but there's something you should know."

"Is it bad news you will tell me?"

"From your perspective, I'm afraid so. I found out about it myself not long ago from someone who knows the family. Daniel has become engaged to a woman from Ohio. Her name is Myra . . ."

"Waters," Ly Yen said.

"Why, yes. So, you know about her?"

"Dan told me she was his love before he met me." Charles heard the pain in her voice. "It is fitting that he returns to her, is it not?"

"Maybe, maybe not. I believe an injustice has been done to you and your children, Ly Yen. If Daniel didn't receive your message, he should be told. If he's marrying this Waters woman thinking you've never tried to contact him, he needs to know the truth."

"No!" The word was delivered with an impetus that startled him.

He continued as though he hadn't heard. "Even if he does learn of it, you should be prepared for the fact that he may want to go ahead with his marriage plans. He lives in Boston, and she lives in Ohio, but I understand they have visited each other regularly for over a year. The wedding is set for early in September, I think. That's over a month away. I'll get his number and call him . . . or you can call him."

"No, Pastor Charles. I will not call him, and I do not want you to call him either."

"Why, for heaven's sake? He should know."

"It is his life as he has planned it out. I do not want to interfere."

"It's not interference, Ly Yen. He's the father of your children. I believe that he never received news of your correspondence. He deserves to know you tried to find him. He can help you financially if nothing else."

"Pastor Charles, I will continue my life in California, and Dan will continue his life as he has planned it. Please promise me you will not tell him about me."

"I can't make a promise like that, Ly Yen."

"You must. Dan must not know I have come to the United States."

"It's a hard thing you ask of me . . . and of yourself."

"It is what I wish."

"You'll change your mind later, maybe after it's too late."

"No, I will *not* change my mind."

He sighed. "If it's what you want, against my better judgment, I'll not tell Daniel about you, but I urge you to change your mind. You have my phone number. I do hope you reconsider."

"Thank you, Pastor Charles. It is the correct thing for me to do."

"May I call you to see how you're doing?"

"Yes, I would like that."

A few minutes later, he walked out to the church mailbox. The letter from Ly Yen was there. He opened it and saw that her handwriting was far more legible than in her first letter. Other nuances of her English had improved, as well. She had made good use of her time.

He read the letter, not anticipating new information, but found something unexpected at the end. Charles laughed out loud. In his letter three years earlier, he'd revealed information to her that he believed she had a right to know. If Daniel Williamson took the initiative to find out about Ly Yen and her children, secrets long held could become public knowledge.

CHAPTER TWENTY-THREE

August 1969

The ringing telephone took Cassie from the porch to the kitchen, annoying because she was deep into lesson planning for next week's school opening.

"Cassie, I'm coming down to see you," Abigail said.

"Why, Mom?"

"We need to talk."

Cassie wanted to derail her mother's intentions, for she suspected the topic. "I'm pretty busy with lesson plans."

"I'll be right there."

When Abigail arrived, she brushed by Julie on the porch steps and plopped down by Cassie in the swing. Abigail's face showed concern. "Is it really true, what I heard, that you're engaged to Obie Gainsworthy?"

Cassie sucked in her breath. "Where did you hear *that*? No, it's not true, and you know it. No one told you that."

"I heard it. Never mind the source. You're lying, Cassie. Don't lie to me!"

It only took only a few words from her mother to elevate Cassie's blood pressure. As much as she wanted to exercise self-control, she found it difficult.

"Mom, I don't want to have this conversation. I'll tell you again what I've told you before, and I hope you'll listen this time. Obie and I have renewed our friendship since his return, and we spend time together. However, he's shown a lack of interest in anything more. And I respect that. I believe he's still grieving over his wife."

"She died three years ago. Anyway, they were separated. But that's beside the point."

"The point being?"

"You must not get involved with him. He's not worth your time, my dear."

Cassie looked away from Abigail but was powerless to keep from muttering, "Where have I heard this before?"

"Yes, and you'll hear it again and again from me. Your infatuation with this man, even a friendship, is a slap in the face to me . . . and to your sister."

"It's an old story I've heard too many times, that there's something Obie did to make Laura angry, but it's something we can't talk about. Well, I'm tired of hearing it, Mom. If there's something I need to know, then you can damn well spit it out."

"You don't need to swear at your mother. It should be enough that you believe it when I tell you to stay away from him."

"It sounds like you're giving me an order."

"I *am* giving you an order. *Stay away from him!*" Abigail stood and stomped her foot on the wooden porch floor.

Cassie had decided not long ago that she would never endure abuse again, either physical or verbal. "I'll do as I like," she said, keeping her voice even. "The truth . . . and you already know this and won't accept it, is that I love Obie. I love him deeply, madly, hopelessly, and have as long as I can remember. I'd marry him today if he asked me. And I pray every day that he will. If God should ever answer my prayers, I'll be the happiest woman in the world."

Abigail's face was flushed. She leaped to the steps and knocked over Julie, who fell onto the grass, crying. She stopped at the gate and turned. "You're not welcome in my house ever again," she screamed. "You're no longer my daughter! I'm taking you out of my will! You'll not get a thing! I'm giving everything to Laura! Do you hear me?"

Cassie rushed to Julie, who appeared unhurt. "I hear you!" Cassie shouted after Abigail. "I hear you. It's fine with me. You can take your will, and your money, and everything else in your miserable existence that you value so highly, and you can . . ." She ran out of breath.

Cassie watched her mother get in her car, spin the wheels, and take off in a cloud of smoke. She heard the automobile roar down the street and waited to hear a crash at the stop sign, half hoping she would.

There had been angry words before. But, this time, Cassie believed a point of no return might have been reached.

* * *

Dan's mood was as dark as the early morning sky he planned to fly through. His conversation with his mother on the way to the floatplane base on the Charles River was becoming contentious.

"Are you sure you love her?" she asked again. She looked away from the road, watching his face.

"I love Myra," he said. "Mom, keep your eyes on the road! I want to make it to Cincinnati."

"I'm driving safely. We're talking about marriage, a lifetime commitment, or that's what it should be."

"Why don't you like Myra?"

"Oh, I do. In the year I've known her, I've learned to like her. I like her a great deal. But that has nothing to do with seeing my son committed to a lifetime with her, with someone he may not truly love."

"Mom, how many times must I say it? I love Myra, and she loves me. We're getting married a month from now. I don't want to hear any more about it . . . please?"

She became quiet, but Dan knew she wanted to say more. He was determined to keep his feelings under control. Taking out his frustrations on her would be indefensible. She had enough to contend with. His mother's discontent always lay just beneath the surface.

A few silent minutes passed before he said, "All right, Mom, what is it? Something else is bothering you."

"Before you went back to Vietnam, when we were visiting Stafford Rest, you told us about the girl there, Ly Yen. You said she was having your child. You said you loved her and that you were going to find her. Well, you didn't find her, and you haven't said much about it, or about her. Why?"

"I did tell you. I told you about searching and all the dead ends I'd run into."

"You haven't talked about your feelings, however. When you first told us about her, you were so descriptive that I could visualize her appearance. Your love seemed to ooze out with your words. That image stayed with me. I think about her often, and about a grandchild that I may never see. I like Myra, I really do, but I don't have that kind of feeling for her, and, honestly, I haven't been able to see that you do, either."

"That's because Myra was here with us in the flesh. I don't have to tell you *about* her. She was there for you to see, for God's sake."

"I don't want you to make a mistake."

"I'm not making a mistake. I've thought this through. Do I love Ly Yen? I do. I probably always will, but she's vanished from my life. I've accepted the fact that I'll never see her again."

"Nor your child?"

"That too. It's a fact. There's nothing I can do about it. To quote a cliché, I need to 'get on with my life.'"

"Dan, there's no rush. Myra and her family aren't making a big deal of the wedding . . . and I find that strange in itself, so maybe you could postpone it for a bit so you can both think about it. There's nothing worse than spending your life with someone you weren't meant to be with."

She sounded bitter, and for a moment Dan wanted to let the comment pass. However, she needed to face her own issues, so he struck out boldly. "Are you thinking about life with Dad?"

She stared at the road ahead for seconds before saying, "Yes, that's right."

"Mom, you're unhappy, aren't you?"

This time, she didn't hesitate. "Yes, Dan, happiness seems to have passed me by."

"I'm sorry, Mom. You can do something about it, however."

"How did we get from talking about your future to mine?"

"Our futures are intertwined, aren't they?"

"I suppose so. We're all tied together in some fashion. It seems once we know someone, they're always there, either helping us or haunting us." She gripped the steering wheel so tightly that her knuckles turned white.

When they arrived at the parking lot by the HBO she pulled in, facing the water, and turned off the engine. Neither seemed anxious to exit the automobile.

"I believe I know what you're thinking," Dan said. He made a sword thrust into the dark. "You're speaking of Obadiah Gainsworthy, aren't you?"

"Yes." The word was barely audible.

"Are you ever going to tell me about that part of your life?"

"No more than you already know."

"Which isn't much."

"It's all you need to know, Dan. It's water under the bridge."

"You know that I met him in Vietnam. Yet, you've never asked me anything about that. Why?"

"I know enough about him."

"He seems like a good man. He did me a favor. He carried my message to Ly Yen."

She turned to face him. "Did you talk about anything else?"

"We talked a bit about Stafford Rest. He said he knew our family. But he didn't seem anxious to continue that part of our conversation. Might that be because he didn't want to talk about you?"

"I suspect so. Did he ask personal questions about you, about your life?"

"Not much. Why would he? Remember, he was a chaplain doing his duty. I was only one of many he was trying to help."

She became silent, looking thoughtful. Their conversation had taken odd twists and turns. Did her introspection indicate she planned a major change in her life, that she really was going to leave his father?

She confirmed it. "I'm filing for divorce, Dan. In fact, I already have. Your father won't give up his little whore."

"It's about time. He's being a real ass."

They grinned at each other about their naked candor. Then, she said, "I'm seriously considering going to Stafford Rest to live."

He was surprised. "When?"

"Soon. What do you think of that idea?"

"For me, it's a good one. You know how I feel about the town and the Adirondacks. But would you be happy there? You have your circle of friends here, not to mention the organizations you belong to. Let's face it, there's not the high society in Stafford Rest that one finds in Boston." He said "high society" with proper emphasis to show his disdain for that way of life.

"It'll be different, although I'll have responsibilities. Dad wants me to take over the factory. He's recovered from his heart attack but feels his vulnerability and wants to retire."

"So, you've told them about divorcing Dad?"

"I did, finally, just last week. Mom took it hard."

"Do you think you can run the factory? It's become quite an enterprise."

"I'm sure I can handle it. Don't forget that I've earned a business degree in my spare time. And I learned about wood long ago from Dad. He'll teach me anything else I need to know."

"What does Grandmother think about your returning?"

"She's miffed. She's happy about my return but hoped I'd go into her real estate business with her."

"Myra's been bugging me to take up real estate. She has friends in the business who say they'll hire me when I get a license. I guess it's as good a way as any to make a living. But, of course, that depends on us staying in that area."

"I'd hoped you would stay in school and get your degree. You're nearly there. Then maybe med school? Even being the bastard that he is, I'm sure your father would help you."

"We'll see. These are things for Myra and me to decide."

"Danny, I don't want you to marry someone you don't love. It's a big step, so please consider it. I should not have married Ben . . ."

He held up a forefinger and grinned. "Except you got me. Don't forget that."

"Yes! Yes, I have you, don't I?" She reached across to touch his arm,

"I'll see you in Cincinnati next month, then?"

"Unless I hear something different from you." She sounded hopeful.

* * *

There was time to ruminate during the legs of his flight to Ohio. His mother's talk about Stafford Rest had stirred a longing. The Adirondack town was where he was most likely to find happiness. Myra had said she liked it there; he suspected she might have said it to please him.

Why had his mother brought up Ly Yen? Just when he'd managed to ease her from his mind, she was back. Her face and voice became intertwined with the constant roar of the airplane's engine as he neared Cincinnati. Issues his mother had raised were ones with which he was still struggling. A question that had plagued him numerous times was back with emphasis. *Should he marry Myra?* Such a serious step as marriage should not be taken with those questions still hanging. Was he making a mistake? Was his mother right in saying they should think about it a little longer?

As he let his thoughts dwell on the life they might have together, another question persisted. *What was he willing to give up for her?* During the descent toward the Ohio River near Cincinnati, with light rain blowing back over the windscreen, he made up his mind that he was going to live in Stafford Rest. Myra could decide if she wanted that, as well.

CHAPTER TWENTY–FOUR

September 1969–February 1970

Exactly one month after the flight to Cincinnati, Dan was making another water landing. He could hardly contain his excitement as he cut power for a decent toward Diamond Lake. There had been moderate turbulence above Lake George, and his mother had complained of airsickness, so he wanted to get her down as soon as possible. They approached from the east, dropping in over the cliffs at the end of the Morass and losing altitude over the town. His eyes scanned the area for boats.

The lake was smooth. He set the Cessna down gently, slowed, turned left past Ernie's Marina, and applied just enough power to ease into the narrow slip leading to the Hunt dock. He'd hoped someone at the marina would help him tie up, but no one came.

He switched the engine off, shed his harness, and hopped out onto a pontoon. The airplane drifted in close enough for him to grab the side of the dock. He unhooked a rope and soon had the floatplane secure. He assisted his mother with a long step from a pontoon to the dock before unloading their baggage.

It was late afternoon and chilly, as the waning days of September in the Adirondacks often were. Bushes around the dock and across the road by the stone steps going up the hill to his grandparent's house showed more red than green. During the flight over New England, the changing colors created a colorful carpet stretching endlessly in all directions. The seasonal wonder was even more apparent after they crossed Lake George. Even so, peak fall colors were yet to come.

Up high on the steps, he saw his grandparents descending; they were excited about the homecoming. They knew the approximate arrival time and must have watched them land.

For both Dan and his mother, this return to the Adirondacks was life-changing. They'd left Boston for good, she to take over Stafford Rest Furniture and he to sell real estate and give flying lessons. A life in Stanford Rest was what he wanted.

Myra would not be with him. She'd broken their

engagement two days after his arrival in Ohio. "I can't live there," she said. "You choose. Me . . . or the Adirondacks."

He'd chosen and, despite the hurt, wasn't sorry. Nevertheless, the day two weeks earlier when they would have been married was a sad one.

The Adirondacks was his home now, not merely a place to visit. He was arriving with little more than his airplane and not much of a plan. His mother had sold her car and expected her furniture to come when she had an apartment.

His grandparents helped them carry their baggage across the road and up the long steep column of stone stairs. His grandfather had a lighter handbag and stopped to rest every few steps. Dan slowed to keep pace with him while his mother and grandmother went on ahead.

"What now?" the older man asked.

"I'll find a place to live, but I'd like to stay with you a few days while I look if you don't mind."

"As long as you need to. Your grandmother has some apartments for lease right in town. She's readied one for Laura. You might consider one of those for yourself. Is something like that what you have in mind?"

"For the present, but like Mom, I'll eventually want a house. She's making plans for building somewhere. I think she wants to stay here with you awhile, too, until she gets her furniture from Boston."

"It seems impossible that you're both here to stay, Dan. I hope it works out. This isn't Boston, you know."

"If it were anything like Boston, I wouldn't be here. Grandfather, this is exactly what I want. As for Mom, she may have some adjusting to do."

His grandmother had "thrown together" a salad and ordered pizza from Charlie's, a new restaurant near the Garnet Creek bridge. After eating, they sat around the kitchen table. Dan was relaxed and on his second cup of coffee.

"Why isn't Cassie here?" his mother asked. "She knew we were coming. I sent her a note."

"She stays busy with her schoolwork," his grandmother said.

"Abigail, that's not true, and you know it," his grandfather said. "Well, she does work hard, but it's not why she isn't here."

"Pinky, you keep quiet about . . ."

"They have the right to know. They'll find out anyway. Cassie didn't . . ."

"Pinky!"

"Laura, your mother has told Cassie that she isn't welcome at our house. That was nearly two months ago, and they haven't spoken since. It's gone on long enough. Cassie's my daughter, too, and I want her and Julie to come as often as they like."

"What's the problem?" Dan's mother asked.

His grandmother said, "Well if you must know, she's been seeing Obie Gainsworthy. They're seen together almost every day."

"Obie?" His mother's mouth was open. "How could that be?"

"He's back. He's come back for good, they say."

"He's fixed up the old place on Blackberry Hill," Dan's grandfather said."

His mother recovered her composure. "Mom, Cassie's entitled to her own life. If that's her choice, it's her own business, isn't it?"

"Laura, how can you, of all people, say that? You know what he is. Is that what you want for Cassie? You didn't always think that way."

"Dad, what do you think?" his mother said. The look passing between them was more than a casual one.

Pinky said quickly, "Same as you. It *is* Cassie's business. And maybe it's time for all of us to start looking to the future."

"I'd like to, Dad, but I don't know if I can. You know what I'm talking about." She looked sorry for having spoken.

"Well, I'm not getting over anything," Dan's grandmother said. "Furthermore, Cassie will have to stop what she's doing and beg for my forgiveness before I let her in this house again."

Dan knew Cassie well enough to know that such an apology was not likely. Cassie might never be within these walls again. This was no way to start their new life here.

* * *

Cassie had known for days that Laura was returning to Stafford Rest and hadn't told Obie. She knew she should not have withheld that information. There was only mistrust between Obie and her sister, so what was it she feared?

With Laura back, she must tell him, or he'd find her silence strange when he learned of it. They were having lunch together at the diner.

Halfway through the meal, Cassie said, "Laura came home yesterday." She paused to gauge Obie's reaction. She saw no change in his expression. "She came to see us last night."

"So? How long will she be here?"

"She's back for good, Obie. She's taking over for Dad. She'll run the factory."

Several seconds passed. "What about her husband?"

"She's divorcing him. It's not final yet, but it should be soon."

"That's too bad."

"Neither Hunt girl chose a husband wisely, it seems."

"Marriages aren't what they once were." His words sounded bitter.

"It needn't be that way, Obie. When the right people find each other, it's a beautiful thing . . . I hear."

"What happened? With her marriage, I mean?"

"Ben found someone else. He finally moved out and left Laura. She's getting a whole lot of money to disappear from his life. That's what she said, not my words."

For a moment, a look passed across his face, one that might be interpreted as compassion. "Anyway," he said, "I wish her the best."

* * *

News of Laura Williamson's return irritated Obie. He'd found peace in Stafford Rest and didn't care to share that space with her. He had no use for Abigail either, but she was what she was and had never tried hard to cover it up. Laura had betrayed him once—and there were the lies she'd made Cassie believe about him. He had no desire to see Laura Williamson. Nevertheless, Stafford Rest was a small town, and he recognized the inevitability of their meeting.

It happened in Cam's Supermarket. He pushed his cart around a corner and bumped into her cart coming from the other direction.

"Sorry!" he said before recognizing her.

She stared at him. "Hello, Obie?"

"Hello, Laura," he muttered, not without some initial confusion.

She wore slacks and a bright green sweater that looked homemade. She was a little heavier, although not enough to distract from her still excellent figure. Her face was little changed except for deeper lines about her eyes and forehead. A few streaks of gray in her hair were enhancing. In the few times he'd thought about her, he had imagined an older version. That image was nothing like the woman taking a provocative stance before him.

"And how are you?" she said. But the words were cool.

"Good! I'm good. You?"

"Good. So, you're back?"

"Yes, and you too. I fixed up the old house. Rebuilt it, actually?"

He wanted to add that he'd worked on the barnroom too. He wanted to say, *"Remember the barnroom where we said how much we loved each other?"* He stopped short.

"Cassie told me. What will you do? I mean . . . you'll need work, won't you?"

"I expect I will, eventually." He could have told her he planned to write, but she would have no interest or understanding. "Right now, I'm getting reacquainted with this slow pace of life." He might tell her he was also painting for the first time in a long time; it would mean nothing to her. "I hear you'll be running the factory. Cassie told me."

"Seems as though Cassie is a go-between."

Why would they ever need a go-between? "I thought it unlikely that we'd be talking directly." He wished for the words back; why stir up things?

She stared at him for an uncomfortable span of seconds before saying, "We can't avoid running into each other, but I'll be civil to you if you'll be civil to me."

"That's fair, I guess."

He saw her take a deep breath. "Obie, I appeal to you not to hurt my sister. She's had enough hurt in her life."

"Laura, I would *never* hurt Cassie. She means more to me than anyone."

She laughed, a nasty laugh. "We both know what you're capable of, don't we?"

"That's not being civil . . . nor truthful."

"You're right about the civil part. I shouldn't have said that, but it's difficult for me not to have concern for my sister."

He wasn't going to comment on such drivel. "I met Dan in Vietnam." He remembered that the last time they talked, she'd ordered him not to mention her son's name again. Doing so felt satisfying.

"I know. He told us about it. I guess you do deserve thanks for your part in helping him communicate with his girlfriend."

"How did that work out?" Cassie had told him something of the cascade of sad events; he just wanted to have a reasonable conversation with this woman.

"It didn't. He's been unable to find Ly Yen, and he's miserable about it. He was going to marry a girl from Ohio until he recently broke off the engagement. I think it was because he can't forget Ly Yen."

"She's memorable. I was quite impressed with her."

"She was pregnant, you know."

"Cassie told me. It certainly puts a different face on it. Is he continuing to look for them?"

"Don't pretend you care, Obie."

"Of course I care." He wouldn't let himself get drawn into another verbal battle. "I might even help him in his search."

"Obie, Cassie's one thing, but I want you to stay away from Dan. He'll never be anything to you."

"Isn't it for him to decide?"

She pushed the front of her cart against his with a loud whack. He couldn't tell if she was angry or faking it.

"I mean it," she said. "You stay away from Dan. You have no right to interfere in my family!" She went around him and headed toward the front. She looked back once and said, "I mean it!"

He could make no sense of her rant. She reminded him of Abigail. It made his stomach churn.

* * *

Obie's occasional glass of wine was normally taken with a guest at home or within a social setting. He surprised himself the day after Thanksgiving by strolling into the Diamond Inn and sitting at the bar. He had walked past the building hundreds of times while growing up but had never been inside.

After he inquired, Bill, the young bartender, told him that the previous owner, Harold Freeman, had been dead for many years but had sold the Inn to Bob Hinky in the nineteen-fifties. Bob was dead, too, and his son, Chuck, now owned the business.

"Chuck and I were classmates and friends," Obie said.

"He'll be on duty tonight if you want to see him," Bill replied as he poured the Charbonneau Obie had ordered.

"I'll catch him some other time. No hurry."

"I'll tell him you were in. What's your name?"

"Tell him Obie Gainsworthy stopped by."

A figure moved from the shadows adjacent to the bar and stood beside him. "I couldn't help overhearing," the man said. "We meet again."

It took Obie a moment to recognize Dan Williamson. He looked less vulnerable than he had in the hospital in Vietnam. Dan held out his hand, and Obie shook it.

"Sir, I never had a chance to thank you for your help over there."

"Think nothing of it. Meeting your young lady was my pleasure. But I was recently told that you've been unable to find her. That's too bad. You'll keep looking, won't you?"

"I will, but it's discouraging. I'm not sure what else I can do." Dan sat on the stool beside Obie and motioned to the bartender. "Bill, bring us a couple more here."

Obie had hardly touched the first glass, but he didn't protest. He wished to talk to this young man again. Laura had ordered him to stay away from her son, and the demand only increased his interest. He and Dan had experiences in common that she could never understand.

"Don't give up on finding her," Obie said. "It's never too late."

"I don't have much luck in the romance department, it seems."

Obie grinned. "You and me both. I hear you'll be a real estate agent with your grandmother?"

"Yeah. I can't get too excited about it."

"What would you really like to do?"

"I'm going to give flying lessons if I can find the students." Dan appeared thoughtful. "Medicine interests me. My dad, and his dad, were physicians, and most of my schooling has been in that direction. Maybe it's in my blood. Mom prods me toward the field every chance she gets."

"You joined the service before you finished college, didn't you?"

"I did, but I attended Boston College all last year. Combined with work credited in Army flight school, that leaves me only a few credit hours short of a degree. I plan to take a course or two at Albany State as soon as I get settled here."

"I wish you luck with that. Now, tell me about your second hitch."

"I saw a lot more action. I flew helicopters."

"I heard."

"I got off lucky compared to some."

Obie saw in Dan's eyes what he'd seen in scores of veterans before. "It's a bad war! Sometimes I wonder if it'll ever end."

"It will if we keep bombing the hell out of the north."

"Lots of people dying on both sides. Any chance you'll be called back."

"No, I'm out of it. Leg wound." Dan slapped his leg to empathize. "I'm even getting some disability pay."

"You'd been wounded when I saw you in the hospital at An Khe on your first tour. I don't remember the details."

Dan told the story again. Obie listened with interest. "As I recall," he said, "you were up for a medal for that action."

"I received a Bronze Star. Undeserved."

"The men you were with believed you deserved it. They would know."

"Grandfather Hunt told me you have two Silver Stars. Now, *that's* impressive."

Obie gave him brief descriptions of those actions, downplaying his part. Nonetheless, the younger man's eyes showed a glint of respect.

They talked of other things, weather, flying, and local politics, but when Dan tried to order more drinks, Obie said, "No, Dan—no more for me. Two's my limit. In truth, one is."

Dan grinned. "Oh, yeah, I forgot. You weren't only a chaplain. You were a minister, too. But something Grandmother said makes me think you might have given that up."

"I've given up pastoral ministry."

"I'm not religious, but how do you give up the ministry? It would be so much of who you are that there wouldn't be much

257

left."

The words jolted Obie. "I hope that's not true, but your observation is thought-provoking, nonetheless."

"I'm sure there's a lot of mileage left in you, Reverend Gainsworthy." He took a drink from his beer glass and set it down slowly. "There's something I'd like to ask you." There was mischief in Dan's voice. "It's about you and my mother. Why are there bad feelings between you? It's my understanding you were once close, even romantically involved."

Obie sucked in his breath. "We can't discuss that."

"Reverend Gainsworthy, I'm a get-things-out-in-the-open person. Mom, on several occasions, has indicated that you did something that caused animosity between you. My grandmother feels that way, too."

"That's not . . ."

"I'd like us to be friends, but it might present a problem if you're the cause of my mother's unhappiness. Can you see my point?"

His history with Laura was not a topic Obie was going to discuss with anyone, especially her son. "I admire your directness, but we can't talk about your mother. And please stop calling me 'Reverend.'"

Dan was showing determination. "What *did* you do, *Mister* Gainsworthy?"

"I didn't do anything," Obie snapped, "and if she says I did, she . . ." He was ready to say, "is lying," but recovered and said, "She's mistaken." He wouldn't antagonize the innocent son by casting blame on his mother, although that was where it belonged.

"From knowing my mother so well, and from my impressions of you . . . and I'm a good judge of character . . . I believe you two suffered a mix-up, maybe a simple misunderstanding that needs correcting. My Aunt Cassie put that bug in my ear. I'd like to see you straighten it out."

"It's too late, Dan."

"Nothing's ever too late. Didn't you tell me that a few minutes ago?"

"That's a different matter."

"Sounds like my situation and yours, as unalike as they may be, are matters of the heart."

"Dan, believe me, what happened between your mother

and me is no longer a matter of the heart, as you say. Such feelings, if there ever were such feelings, are no longer there for either of us."

After a moment, Dan said, "You're seeing a lot of Cassie, aren't you?"

"Cassie and I are good friends. We just had Thanksgiving dinner together, along with Julie and my dad and aunt."

"I heard. She couldn't come to Garnet Hill. That's your fault, too, isn't it?"

Whether Dan's observation was an accusation or merely a statement of fact was unclear, but Obie felt the conversation had taken on a feeling of impropriety. He needed to end it. "Dan, I have to go."

"You could stay awhile. I still want to discuss this matter."

"I'm not going to discuss anything about your mother, nor Cassie, either." When Dan didn't respond, Obie added, "But I'll help you search for your Vietnamese sweetheart if you wish. I may have some contacts you don't."

Obie had extended the invitation to salvage a budding but potentially frayed friendship. He was unsure what the response would be and was pleased when Dan said, "I may take you up on that."

* * *

Obie felt good about his health that winter. His hands were calloused due to the previous summer's work on the house and his daily appointments with the woodpile.

Although he had grown up chopping wood for his mother's insatiable kitchen woodstove and his stove in the barnroom, he had underestimated the amount of wood he'd need for this winter. He'd believed his new forced hot air furnace would negate extensive use of the rebuilt fireplace. Cassie changed that; every time she came, she threw in wood and lit it, creating an atmosphere where they sat, drank coffee, tea, or wine, and talked.

It was still midwinter, but he vowed to build up the woodpile, maybe even get ahead on next year's supply. He could easily purchase firewood, but downed and seasoned hardwood was plentiful on his land.

He found his old snowshoes in the barn and walked in the woods on the ridge several times a week. He usually went around the Morass to the main road on Garnet Point and then walked back over the same route, the identical two-mile trek taken many times in his youth. He found it little changed. It remained wild because, being state land, it was protected.

"I'd like to go too," Cassie told him one day after arriving unexpectedly as he was putting on his snowshoes.

"I have another old pair in the barn loft," he said, delighted at the request.

She had no trouble keeping up. When they reached the overlook on the high cliffs behind the Morass, Obie experienced poignant memories. He could tell by Cassie's expression that she was feeling something similar.

At sixteen, and standing on this same spot, they had kissed. It had been an innocent encounter, the first kiss of that kind for either. Her words that day should have made him aware of her feelings, but he'd been young—and enamored of Laura.

Were they being given a second chance, an opportunity to get it right this time? Obie had a great urge to tell her what he was feeling. He moved closer and said, "Cassie, do you remember being here alone with me?"

"It was a very cold day."

"What do you remember?"

"You tell me."

"You made me kiss you."

She smirked. "I did no such thing! You grabbed me."

"That's not how I remember it." He moved closer. "We were very young, weren't we?" He wanted to take her in his arms. Should he?

"Not too young for you to be in love with Laura." Her words had turned as icy as the cliffs beneath them. "You gave me the impression you didn't like kissing me."

"Cassie, I'm sorry. I was a stupid and insensitive kid. I didn't understand. If I hurt you, I'm sorry."

"You've always hurt me, Obie. Sometimes, simply being around you hurts me." Then, with those stinging words, she turned and walked away.

Her strides were long, and he had trouble catching up in the deep snow. He wanted to protest, say something to make her know things were different. But her straight-ahead stride through the snow made him wary of saying anything more. *Maybe another time.*

*　*　*

Obie made time for his father that winter and their conversations were relaxed; He had trouble seeing Ken as the same person he'd known while growing up. Topics that might once have caused derision were no longer off-limits.

Ken was candid about his drinking habit. He and Obie were sitting in the living room relaxing after one of Angie's "just a little something" dinners. She was in the kitchen and out of sight.

"She's sneaking her wine," Ken said, his grin showing no accusation. "She does that out of respect for me . . . knowing my problem."

"That's not really a problem for you anymore, is it?"

"No, it isn't. Those were my dark days when you were young. I was frustrated." Ken sighed. "My drinking may have been an addiction, but it was also something more. I wanted to return to the woods, doing the things I loved to do but couldn't make a living at. It was during the Depression, and it was all I could do to keep my head above water. Your mother working for the Hunts saved us, and I had difficulty accepting that. It was stupid. *I* was stupid!"

"You and Mom had some other troubles, didn't you, Dad?" He'd wanted to ask that question for a long time but had never found the right time, or the courage.

"Well, yes, we did. Not big troubles like some marriages. We loved each other. When Vi died, it nearly killed me, too. It still hurts like hell."

"Even after all these years?"

"Yeah." His father's eyes were watering up, but he was talkative. "Angie was what got me through it. She never forced our relationship. She was just there when I needed a friend. She understood. She'd lost her husband in the war. We came to love each other, although it's been a mature love."

"Dad, do you ever think about how the churches here cared for us after Mom died? We might have had a bad time without it." Ken had been skeptical about accepting money from those he called "do-gooders."

"I do think about it." He sighed. "I'm afraid I didn't appreciate it then, not like I should have."

"I received money from that fund Grandpa set up while I was at Berkeley and in seminary."

Ken looked surprised. "You know the story, do you?"

"Most of it, I think. Pinky Hunt once told me how Grandpa saved Bernard Templeton from drowning. After I started at Berkeley, he told me the rest."

"That incident happened in Indian Lake while Papa was a wilderness guide. Templeton was a rich man. He owned that big factory in New England and left Papa a whole slop-pot full of money. So far as I know, Papa never spent more than a few dollars of it on himself and Mama. I guess they never considered it theirs. He put nearly all of it in the fund. The 'Love Fund,' he called it. Said it was for helping people in difficulty and for young people's education. Lots of folks besides you have bene-fited. It's part of our family history and something we should be proud of."

"Did you and Abner know about it all along?"

"Abner knew. I didn't know until after Papa died. I guess Papa didn't tell me because of how I was then. He trusted Ab-ner." Ken's words held no bitterness.

"Pinky told me that, except for him and some bank offi-cials, no one outside the family knows the source of the money."

"Papa and Mama kept it a secret. Abner did too. And I do the same. It'll pass to you after I die, and what you do is up to you."

"I like the secrecy. I think Grandpa would approve. Has Pinky always administered the fund?"

"Ever since Papa started it. He greatly admired Pinky. Pinky sees that everything gets where it's supposed to."

"What part do you play in making decisions?"

"Pinky runs everything by me, though I told him he doesn't have to. He's perfectly capable of deciding who needs the help."

"Grandpa and Grandma were certainly generous."

"They did a heap of good. I believe the original amount was nearly a million dollars. Of course, it's been depleted over the years. But it earns interest, and there's still a goodly amount."

Obie had felt great empathy with Jacob. "There'll be more money soon," he said.

Godfrey Lawrence had written recently, outlining decisions Obie needed to make. For months, he'd dragged his feet about the final details for distributing the money. He must act soon.

Ken had failed to notice the offhanded remark, and Obie let the matter stand. Ken and Pinky had a pleasant surprise coming.

CHAPTER TWENTY-FIVE

February–April 1970

Obie Gainsworthy's reluctance to talk about Dan's mother didn't keep Dan from visiting Blackberry Hill. *He liked the man.* They discussed many and varied subjects while lounging in front of the new fireplace.

Their like-mindedness was the glue for affinity. Nevertheless, they disagreed on some things. The subject of war brought heated debate, and Dan liked that. "I don't understand," he told Obie one evening, just to agitate, "You've been in war. Three wars, for God's sake. You must know that the only thing some governments understand is brute force, yet you sit there and tell me that wars are unnecessary."

"I said *most* wars are unnecessary."

"You're siding with the riffraff trying to tear our country apart. I've been called names and spit on because I was wearing a uniform . . . not in some foreign country, but right here in this country. Is that what you're defending, Obie?"

"Not at all. Placing blame on military men for the sins of governments angers me, too."

"Yet, you defend their right to protest? Did you learn that at Berkeley? That's a hotbed of malcontents, I hear."

Obie laughed. "It wasn't much of an issue when I was there, but yes, it has become excessive during this war. The problem is that the country has become polarized. People are being asked to choose either one of two extreme positions. Reasonable ground, where I stand, has been largely abandoned. So tell me, Dan, if it were up to you, how would you bring this war to a conclusion?"

"I'd put every ounce of our military might behind our efforts. I'd bomb the north into submission like we did the Japanese in 1945."

"In other words, you'd kill until there wasn't anyone left to kill?"

"Well, no, that's not what I meant."

"People in the south would die too. It's easy to talk about

killing if you don't put faces to it. And there are faces there that you know, aren't there?"

The words hurt. "That's not fair, Obie."

"Well, *she* is there. So is your child. I'm sorry I used it as an example." Obie's expression indicated that he really was contrite. "The point I'm trying to make is that some can do deeds of war without seeing faces. I can't do that. I was able to, to some extent, in the Second World War, but it caught up with me when I pulled the trigger on a prisoner in Italy.

That surprised Dan. "You killed a prisoner?"

"I thought he had a gun, and I reacted too quickly. It's no excuse, however. It haunts me to this day."

"Is that why you became a chaplain?"

"Actually, it almost kept me from becoming a chaplain."

"I don't think you should carry guilt about it. You were doing your duty. It could happen to any soldier."

Obie was staring into the flames. "You're the only one I've told about that incident," he said. "I hope it stays with you."

"Maybe you *should* tell someone. Someone who can help. Your shrink, maybe?"

"I don't have a shrink."

"A clergyman, then."

"Perhaps." Obie's expression was one Dan could only label as pain.

Their conversations were often heated, although never angry. Dan was stimulated by dialogue with Obie, and his respect grew. Nevertheless, Obie's refusal to discuss anything about Dan's mother and himself only fed his obsession to discover the truth. He wanted them reconciled, certainly not romantically, but on friendly terms.

He mulled it over for weeks, and on a clear day in March, when lengthening sunlight hours brought the promise of winter's end, Dan devised a plan for getting them together. He would place them in a situation where they would have to talk. He wasn't sure how to do it yet but was determined to make it happen.

Dan's life was busy. He'd rented a small apartment on a short lakeside street off Main, near the park. Buying a house was a goal for the future, so his present residence must do. In January, he'd enrolled in a night class at Albany State University and drove there two evenings each week.

When he wasn't working with his grandmother in Evergreen, he traveled to other towns and over distant back roads to show houses and land to prospective buyers. Abigail wasn't a patient teacher, although a thorough one. It was all part of learning the real estate business, he knew. Her company had grown, with an expanded main office in Evergreen and the addition of a smaller office on Main Street in Stafford Rest.

He noticed the high turnover of agents, probably caused by Abigail's overcritical nature. The agent who'd been longest with her was Bernadette Simon. Abigail's relationship with Bernadette seemed a friendship more than anything else, for the woman wasn't very productive. His grandfather had told him she'd been postmistress in Stafford Rest during the Second World War, a position Abigail had helped her obtain. Bernadette would retire soon, his grandmother said, confiding that she was ill.

He'd arrived in Stafford Rest with his new flight instructor's license and the hope that he could give flying lessons as a part-time endeavor. But, unfortunately, there hadn't been enough time for that, even had the students materialized.

Sundays were reserved for his flying trips. The floatplane was in Ernie's Marina, out of the water and up on blocks for the winter. A little airstrip at Evergreen became his base for winter flying. He rented aircraft on a day-basis, ranging wide in his exploration, covering the Adirondack Park and beyond. He became familiar with out-of-the-way HBOs and airstrips east, west, and up to the Canadian border. Cassie and Julie went with him once. Julie became airsick and told everyone she would "never, ever, go flying with Cousin Dan again."

He made new friends and renewed old friendships. He and Chet Boswell found time together to plan spring fishing trips and to trade war stories over a beer in the Diamond Inn. Dan had expected contentment in the Adirondacks and was succeeding to a degree, but tranquility was elusive. His breakup with Myra was firm in his memory and still caused guilt. Yet, as much as it hurt, it had been the right solution. The marriage could never have worked. No marriage would work for him, for he couldn't forget Ly Yen.

Frequenting the Diamond Inn all winter resulted in brief encounters with women, usually for only an evening or a night; none were satisfactory. Finally, he confided in Obie, who told him, "They never will satisfy. You love Ly Yen. If she's lost to you, you'll have to find someone else to love. Anything else is meaningless." He'd added, "I believe you'll find her."

Obie had suggested several search avenues to explore, and for a time, Dan's dream that she might be found was heightened. But those ideas proved futile. He wasn't ready to give up, would never be, but hope for a successful outcome was diminished.

* * *

Obie was about to enter the barnroom when he saw a man approaching. He hadn't heard the car pull into the driveway. He wanted to spend the day painting and experienced some annoyance at the pending interruption. He waited by the door.

The man was elderly, with white hair framing a thin, lined face. He maneuvered around a couple of puddles left by the melting spring snow. "I'm Carl Enslow," he said as he held out a hand. "I'm the pastor at Stafford Rest United Methodist."

"Oh, of course," Obie said. "I've meant to come to services, but I've been prevented." It was a version of an excuse he'd heard many times, and he knew how feeble it must sound. He couldn't explain the real reason for his non-attendance.

Hoping to avoid further confusion, he added, "I've been busy getting my life in order. I was away for many years. I'm Obadiah Gainsworthy."

"Yes, I know," Enslow said, smiling. "I've been talking to folks. Some don't remember you, but many old-timers do. They know *about* you, and they know your family."

"Reverend Enslow, I'll start attending services . . . very soon." He'd already decided to make that a part of his routine again, even if it meant close encounters with Abigail. He'd been faithful with his private devotions but needed more.

"That's well and good," Enslow said, "but it's not the reason I'm here."

"Oh?"

"I should have said that I regard myself as the *interim* pastor. I took this job two years ago, and I've been trying ever since to get someone else appointed here. I'm encouraged to think I may have, at last, found someone who fits the need . . . Reverend Gainsworthy."

So that was it. He'd cut short that idea at once. "I'm no longer a minister," he said.

Enslow looked him up and down, much as a parent would scrutinize an errant child. "I've talked to the district superintendent. He already knows about you. I can't dictate who replaces me, and the conference has its own selection process, but he agrees you're a qualified candidate. He thinks our Pastor Parish would approve you, and as you probably know, they're particular."

"I can't believe they haven't found anyone."

"Several good prospects, but Pastor Parish either nixes them or the prospects decide they won't put up with such scrutiny."

"Reverend Enslow, I appreciate your kind words, but as I said, I'm no longer a minister."

"You're an ordained deacon. Has that been rescinded?"

"No."

"Are you living in sin?"

"No."

"Have you lost your faith?"

"No."

"While it may be true that your ministerial experience is somewhat limited in a civilian setting, you've been in the military, sacrificing comfort and enduring great hardship to serve our armed forces. You're an accomplished author who embraces moral issues. You've run companies, so you can surely run a church. I can't see any obstacles to your appointment in this conference, whether here in Stafford Rest or elsewhere."

"Except that I don't want it."

The man looked ready to cry. "I had my hopes pinned on you, Obadiah," he said.

"Look, Reverend Enslow, I don't want to seem unappreciative about your faith in me, but things have happened in my life that make it impossible for me to consider it. I'll start attending church, and I'll serve in other ways. However, the clergy is beyond me. I hope you understand."

Enslow nodded but continued. "I also talked to Charles Lansing. He says you have issues from having been in military combat. He didn't go into detail, but I understand what he meant. I was a soldier once."

"I did things . . ."

"Obadiah, we're all sinners. God cleanses his vessels, however. A dirty pot gets scrubbed. Look at his choices of who would carry the gospel to the world. Peter was 'a sinful man' and sometimes cowardly. Paul was a murderer."

"There are powerful elements in the church here that would fight my appointment, and they'd win."

"You don't know that. I believe God decides winners in such circumstances."

"I can't do it, Reverend Enslow. I'm sorry."

"I hope you'll reconsider. This is your element, I suspect."

Later that day, when Obie knew Cassie was home from school, he called her and told her about his visitor. "I'm going to Sunday service. Would you like to go, too?"

"I always go. Well, almost always."

"I mean *with* me. Will you sit with me?"

"You mean like a date?"

"Sure, why not."

"Yes, on one condition. We'll not sit anywhere near my mother."

"Done!"

* * *

Dan believed it would work if he handled it properly. Getting Obie and his mother together would happen; that part of his plan was in place. Getting them talking was the tricky part.

His mother wanted property with a view; Dan had promised to find it for her. Obie had some of the most desirable land in the area, the section above his residence. That he'd expressed interest in selling any of it was immaterial, for real estate was only a ploy for bringing them together. Once that was accomplished, he would entice them into a conversation.

He waited in a small private dining room in the restaurant at Ernie's Marina. His mother would arrive soon, primed and ready to discuss the purchase of land from some unnamed seller. She'd hesitated at first, put off by the secrecy. However, she eventually agreed to come. She wanted to start building early to finish before winter.

He'd told Obie nothing except that he would buy dinner and promised a conversation that would be interesting. That both would quickly see through the plan was a sure thing. Once together, however, he might hold them there long enough to start them talking.

His mother arrived first, driving the new automobile she'd recently purchased in Saratoga Springs. She wore a stylish blue dress. Her hair was short and showed evidence of a recent visit to her hairdresser in Tupper Lake. She looked much too young to be his mother.

As she sat down, she said, "I don't understand all this cloak and dagger stuff. If someone has land for sale, why don't they advertise it?"

"Patience, Mom. He'll be along soon."

"Who is it? Where is the land?"

He placed a hand over one of hers. "Wait, Mom."

Dan ordered a bottle of wine. His mother fidgeted with her napkin. Finally, she said, "At least you could tell me something about the asking price."

"I don't know. We'll have to ask him when he gets here." Dan knew that would be soon, for through the window opposite the lake he'd seen Obie's brown station wagon pull up near the restaurant entrance.

Obie wore no coat, although April winds off the lake were brisk. His green sweater was neat and clean, with only a few visible pulls in the fabric. As he approached their table, his initial scowl changed to an expression Dan interpreted as resignation. Dan nearly laughed aloud at his mother's open mouth as Obie settled into a chair.

She said, "Is this a joke of some kind?"

"No, Mom. It's not a joke. You want land. Obie has land. It's my job as a realtor to bring buyers and sellers together."

"Now, wait just a minute, Dan." Obie protested. "Whatever gave you the idea I wanted to sell any of my land? I've never said anything like that." Obie's tone indicated genuine annoyance.

"We did talk about the land. You said much of it was of little use to you."

"I never said I wanted to sell any of it."

"Obie, I'm sorry if I misunderstood. But since we're here, and since Mom needs land to build a house, maybe you *could* consider it?"

"*No . . . I won't!* Anyway, it's not about land at all. It's about forcing your mother and me to talk."

Dan stuttered as he tried to deny it. "No, Obie! How could you think that? I wouldn't do that."

His mother laughed, a familiar sarcastic sound he knew well. "It's exactly what you're doing. You must think we're fools. If you were any more transparent, we could see right through you." She pushed her chair back to get up.

"No, wait, Mom. All right, I admit it. I'm sorry. I apologize to both of you. I meant well. But let's seize this opportunity."

His mother held up a hand in protest. "There's no opportunity here." She glared at Obie. "That went by a long, long time ago."

Obie said, "Yes, Dan, I'm afraid it's too late for words."

Dan placed a hand on his mother's arm so she couldn't turn to leave. "Both of you, please listen. Mom, I love you. Obie, you've become a good friend in only a few months. It pains me no end that something happening such a long time ago causes all this bitterness. Life's too short to keep doing that. The past is past. Obie, damn it, you're a minister of the gospel. You should know about forgiveness."

"I've forgiven your mother a long time ago," Obie said.

"You've forgiven *me*?" Laura's voice was high.

Dan stepped in quickly. "What about you, Mom? Have you forgiven Obie?"

She looked away. "Yes, I've forgiven, but it's hard to forget."

"Yes, it is," Obie said. "However, the last time we spoke, a few months ago, we said that we'd be civil. We have been, I believe. We nodded to each other in church on Sunday, didn't we, Laura?"

"Yes, we did. Dan, let's leave it at that."

The waitress came to take their order before Dan could say more. "I can't stay, Dan," Obie stated.

"Nor can I," his mother said.

"Neither of you has to go. You came thinking you were going to have dinner. Do you want civility? What could be more civil than sitting down to a meal together? Act like adults."

They sat, and Dan breathed a sigh of relief. It became quiet except for snippets of conversation that sounded intentionally safe. The food came, and they ate with little conversation. Dan had refilled their wine glasses once. As he raised the bottle to do so again, they both protested.

Dan excused himself to go to the restroom. It was part of his plan—give them a little time alone. He had purposely chosen a table by the hallway so he could step around the corner and still hear their conversation. *If there was a conversation?* He listened. A full minute of silence followed.

"He's a good young man," Obie finally said.

"Yes, he is. He's going through some hard times."

"He needs to stay out of the Diamond Inn."

"I've talked to him about it."

"Why is he doing this thing tonight? I'm sure he's not trying to link us up romantically. He knows, or at least suspects, how I feel about Cassie."

"And how is that, the way you feel about her?"

"I prefer telling her that."

"She loves you, you know."

"So you said once before."

"You seem to have great power over her, and I'm afraid that . . ."

"Why did you do it, Laura?"

"Do what?"

"Marry Ben Williamson. Why?"

"You bastard! How can you ask such a question?"

Dan knew he should return, for the situation was getting out of hand. He couldn't move.

"I have a right to know," Obie said.

Her voice rose again. "Your pretense is unbelievable. I almost admire your persistence. And I don't want to hear about *your* rights. You have no rights at all. None!"

"Dan has asked about us several times."

Her tone became a notch softer. "I can thank you, I suppose, for not telling him anything."

"I don't intend to."

"You went against my wishes about befriending him, but I suppose you deserve some credit for keeping silent. He must never know."

"He's savvy. He must have guessed that there was more to our relationship than what you've told him."

"No, he doesn't know. Obie, promise me you'll never tell him. I don't want him thinking ill of me . . . of his mother."

"You can be assured that I'll not tell him anything."

Dan's suspicions were confirmed. *There had been intimacy*

between his mother and Obie. He'd suspected it. Now he knew. If he felt any guilt about eve-dropping, it was limited.

Dan listened, but they had become silent. He wanted to go back into the room but hesitated. Finally, his mother spoke. "We were children, weren't we?"

"Yes, we were. Have you really forgiven me for any hurt I may have caused you, Laura?"

"I think I've forgiven you, Obie. I keep telling myself that you were only seventeen."

"Is it possible for us to be friends?"

Dan had waited all evening to hear that question. He leaned forward.

His mother said, "Real friends like when we were growing up? I believe not. However, as I told you, I'll be civil . . . on the condition that you never talk to Dan about me or about us."

"I told you that I haven't . . . and I won't. You have my word on it."

As Dan prepared to re-enter the dining room, he forced himself to believe that real progress had been made. But his mother's answer damaged that hope.

"For what your word is worth," she said.

CHAPTER TWENTY–SIX

June 1970

A letter from Anthony Gladstone came early in June, the first direct contact with his chaplain assistant since Korea. Tony was still a Methodist district superintendent in Kansas. He explained that Carl Enslow had given him Obie's address. Tony and Enslow had been pastors in the same Kansas conference and remained in touch. And George Dulany had been a point of contact with Tony while Obie was in California. Obie marveled at how many common connections the four men had.

Most of the letter chronicled Tony's life after Korea. He'd overcome many difficulties. One, poor eyesight, was a disability that had become more troubling in recent years. At the end of the letter, Tony made an appeal.

> *You have been a real force in my life, Obadiah, from the moment we met in Korea. You gave me courage. You also impressed on me that I could soften my hard doctrine without compromising my theology ... or my faith. I have carried that ideal with me ever since and probably would not have survived without it. Thank you, my friend.*
>
> *It is my understanding that you have given up pastoral ministry. I will not ask why, although I would guess it might be partly because of what happened in Korea. I am speaking of the fight where you shot an enemy soldier who was about to shoot you. You must put it behind you, Obadiah. God forgives you. God needs you. The harvest is ripe, and the workers are few. You are a gifted man in many areas. I realize there may be other reasons for your decision, but God will put those right, as well.*
>
> *Your service need not be pastoral ministry. I only suggested that because it is what I am familiar with. Your writing can be your ministry, and perhaps that is a better choice. I will pray that you can carry whatever cross is placed on your shoulders. But once called to do His work, there is no turning back. Let the Holy Spirit lead you.*
>
> *Fresh in my mind to this day is a conversation we had in*

our tent one night. At my request, you were giving me counsel about how I should proceed with my attempts to get into seminary and the Chaplains Corps. Neither of us knew whether we would survive the war, but you proceeded as though it was a certainty. You said, "There is already a plan laid out for what you will be. It is up to you to secure it." So, Obadiah, I echo your words. Follow your plan.

* * *

Long June days brought warmth to the Adirondacks. Mirroring the seasonal change was Obie's desire to modify a stagnant routine. Since completing his house the previous fall, he had moved through the winter days with deliberate disregard for anything resembling a schedule. He wrote book outlines in pencil and never moved beyond those beginning phases; his typewriter was never out of its case. He painted in the barnroom nearly every day, capturing frozen wilderness landscapes with an intensity he'd never previously managed. Stress was minimal except for his two brief encounters with Laura.

He continued friendly discourse with Dan Williamson. It was, however, the quiet times with Cassie that Obie savored most. There was the feeling that they were making up for years of absence and, in the process, shucking away many painful memories. Nevertheless, a sense of incompleteness lingered, and Tony's letter intensified the feeling.

The summer season was beginning, and in the spirit of renewed life that was springing up everywhere, he yearned for a new beginning for himself. He spoke about it to Cassie one Saturday afternoon while she was helping him set out strawberry plants. "I'm tired of loafing," he complained. "I need more to do."

"You have several days of planting right here. I noticed you haven't turned over the soil in last summer's bean patch." She pointed with her trowel. "There's lots of work here."

"I'll get the planting done soon enough. That wasn't what I meant."

"What, then?"

"Things that make a difference, beyond feeding and pampering myself."

She rose from her kneeling position and jabbed a finger at

his chest. "Obie, there are tons of things you can do to make a difference. Your writing is the most important. It would be best if you got back to that. There are other things as well if you make the time. Frances Gibbons needs volunteers in the library. For that matter, I could use an aide in my classroom. And you told Reverend Enslow you'd take on jobs in the church. Whatever happened to that promise?"

He experienced a stab of guilt, for only last month he'd been asked to chair a church committee and had begged off. "I try to avoid Enslow," he said. "He won't stop asking me to apply to the conference."

"Maybe you should."

Her words surprised him, for she had never expressed an opinion on the subject. A week earlier, he had read Tony Gladstone's letter to her, and all she had said was, "he makes some good points."

"Cassie, I can't do that."

"Why not?"

"I can't, that's all."

He knew his casual comments over the past months must have given her clues about his spiritual troubles, but he'd never laid it out with words meant to apprise her of his struggle. Maybe it was time.

They worked silently, putting in the last of the strawberry plants. Then, Cassie went to sit on a wooden bench Obie had placed at the edge of the garden. He filled a watering can from the spring and soaked soil around each plant before joining her.

While a western red-streaked sky gradually darkened, he told her candidly about all his reasons for leaving the ministry, including the story of Annie's infidelity and of his own. She listened, nodding, eyes moist. Once she touched his hand, whether for her reassurance or his, he was uncertain.

When he finished, she said, "I'm sorry, Obie, for all those troubles." She dabbed at her eyes with the edge of a pulled-up collar and added authoritatively, "But you must decide what you want to do from now on. You won't be whole until you do."

"I have an idea for a book. It's an idea I explored some time ago, one that I shelved. I believe it's time to resurrect it."

"You must do that."

The idea sprang to life, so real he felt the adrenalin rush. Thoughts about the work required were overwhelming, but he'd done it before; he'd do it again. *It was what he was meant to do.*

"I'll do it, Cassie. I'll write that book."

"And I'll help any way I can." Following a thoughtful pause, she asked, "Will you have to go away to write?" He detected some apprehension in the question.

"No, not at all. I may take trips to larger libraries to research, but I'll do the writing on Blackberry Hill."

Her smile was the one he remembered from their growing-up years. "I'm glad, Obie," she said.

He reached for her hand. "Cassie, I'm here to stay. I hope you know that." He emphasized the declaration, attempting to make it more than casual. He wanted her to know he was serious about a new beginning. He wanted to ensure her that she was at the heart of it.

* * *

Cassie remained at the apex of Obie's world, and he gradually accepted the truth; he'd failed to take advantage of opportunities for ratcheting up their relationship. "The talk" he'd expected was yet to be. *He loved her; he wanted more than friendship.* He let himself hope that she might feel the same.

Sometimes, when their hands touched, she looked into his eyes with expectation. He was a fool not to have acted, and too many years had been wasted. It was time to change that. Cassie, without realizing it, had suggested an outing that initiated a plan.

After finishing lunch at the Evergreen Diner, he had driven up the street by the old high school, which had been converted into a warehouse. "Seems like a long time ago we were here, doesn't it?" he said after parking the station wagon in front of the building.

"You know what I remember, the time you went off mountaineering by yourself? Do you remember that?"

"Indeed, I do. I was caught on Algonquin in a fall snowstorm. Thought I'd had it." The memory of windblown snow whipping his face came rushing back. He'd feared for his life and made promises to God that were impossible to keep.

Cassie's giggle interrupted his musing. "I wasn't going to let you go until you made a promise. Do you remember?"

"Not a clue."

"You promised you'd take me up there."

"To Algonquin?"

"That, or one of the other high peaks."

"And you're going to make me keep the promise? Is that it?"

"You bet I am!" Obie was happy to see her enthusiasm. "I'm ready when you are," she said. "School is out in a week. We can go then."

"All right. You set a date. Will you want to take Julie with us?"

"It would be too much for her. She can stay with Laura."

Obie looked forward to the outing. He'd not climbed a mountain for many years, and although they did shorter hikes together, this was the first time for an adventure such as this.

Algonquin had been something of a religious experience for him at the age of sixteen. But, at forty-four, would there still be something of that mystique on the mountain?

Their conversation led to his uncomplicated plan: He would lead her to a quiet place on the peak where they could talk. As he had in Berkeley, he would tell her again that he loved her. She could tell him if the time for such a relationship had passed and she wanted only friendship. If that were the case, he would be brokenhearted, but their friendship would be intact. The idea seemed logical.

Two days before they were to go, he called her. "We never discussed how long we're staying. Were you thinking about a day trip?" The question was not asked without thought beforehand. Her answer might give him a clue about her expectations.

"What would staying overnight involve? What would we need to take?"

"Packs, sleeping bags, change of socks."

"Where would we sleep?"

"There are lean-tos, and there's a campground near the dam if it's still there. We could even camp off the main trail."

"Any of those would work, but it wasn't what I meant."

"I have a two-person tent. It's small and light."

"And where would *you* sleep?"

"Umm . . . I'd have to find a place, I guess. I've slept under the stars before."

She laughed so hard that he held the phone away from his

ear. "I'm kidding you, Obie. I thought you'd know that. If two friends can't share a tent, what's the world coming to?"

The "friends" definition of their relationship was one she'd used often, and it had become tiresome. He was determined to move beyond it. In Berkeley, years before, she had told him that she loved him, and would forever. *Did she still feel the same?* Although her actions sometimes offered hope, there were no clear indications.

He was cautious. "Maybe it's not such a good idea, at that. Why don't we make it a day trip?"

"Whatever you think, Obie."

He sighed. *Another missed opportunity.* He should have said, "Let's do the campsite," or "Off-trail is best." For someone wanting to move a relationship forward, he was having major difficulty. Was he that provincial? They weren't youngsters, and some things that would have been scandalous in the forties were acceptable now. Yet, it must be her choice.

"I'm going to leave it up to you, Cassie."

He could hear the little clucking noise she often made when contemplating an idea. "I guess," she said, "we should make it just for the day."

Dew covered the landscape on the morning they left for the high peaks. The air was crisp, but there was scarcely a cloud in sight—the promise of a beautiful day. They ate breakfast in Lake Placid. An hour later, they were on the trail up from Heart Lake. Thirty years had elapsed since Obie made that other hike. He wanted to expel the span of years from his mind. A new day had come. *It was a new beginning.* He was with the woman he loved, and he would tell her that before the day was over.

She was obviously in good spirits and matched him stride for stride, even as the trail became steeper. She wore a sweater but later removed it and tied the arms around her waist. Her head was bare except for a red ribbon securing her golden hair. Perspiration lay in beads on her forehead. They were breathing hard when they made their first rest stop.

"This is great," Cassie said. "I don't know why I've never done it before."

They un-stoppered their canteens. "It's a strange thing," Obie said, "people not seeing or acknowledging beauty right under their noses."

She didn't comment. If she understood his double meaning,

she failed to show it. They climbed for two more hours, rested, ate the sandwiches she had packed, climbed some more, and finally sat on the rocky summit. Although they had passed two older couples on the trail, they were alone on top.

The breeze was light, but the air was cool. Cassie put on her sweater again, and he pulled his from his pack. For the next half hour, he pointed out lakes and mountains in the distance. She was a quick learner and recited the names as he good-naturedly tested her. He told her about Heart Lake and the tragic love story of Henry Van Hoevenberg and Josephine Scofield. It seemed best not to mention that Laura had occupied his thoughts the last time he was here.

It was two o'clock, nearly time to start down. Obie sucked in his breath, held it, and let it out, slowly. "Cassie, other people will be up here soon. I remember a spot down in the timber, away from the trail. It's secluded. We can talk there."

She didn't appear surprised, only curious. "All right," she said.

He held her hand as they walked, a deliberate action, more intimate than the helping hand he'd given her across fallen logs and stones as they ascended. The landscape was changed from what he remembered, but he finally located the flat sloping surface of a familiar outcropping. Two pines, hardy and misshapen, grew on the hillside above the little clearing. A rock ledge, the right height for sitting, jutted out from below the exposed roots of the two trees. A ground squirrel scampered through the leaves and disappeared within the roots. There was a feeling of solitude.

"It's beautiful here," Cassie said.

He pulled her close, and she didn't resist. "Not as beautiful as you, Cassie."

Their kiss was tender and lasted more than a few seconds. A great lake of dammed-up emotions drained away. He saw tears in her eyes.

"Cassie! Dear Cassie . . . I love you so."

She pulled back. "That wasn't another kiss like the one on the ridge, was it?"

"No, it was not! I didn't have a clue about anything then."

"And *now* you do?"

"Yes, I do! Cassie, I love you. I've loved you all my life. I hope you can forgive me for my blindness. What happened to us after our engagement is all *my* fault. I should have come to Stafford Rest to get you."

"I bear some of the blame. I was stubborn too."

"When you asked me to marry you and Ed, it nearly broke my heart."

"Asking that was outrageous. I believed you'd stop me from marrying him. But you didn't."

"I didn't know my own mind. But I loved you. It was just that I didn't think I could be a good husband. Cassie, I'm praying it's not too late to tell you these things?"

"Obie, so much has happened."

He'd gotten the burden off his chest and told her his true feelings. Their future, his happiness, maybe hers, now lay in her hands.

"I know this is sudden," he said. "You can't just . . ."

"Sudden! You call this sudden?" A familiar fire lit her eyes. She gave him a series of mock slaps. "Are you awake, Obie? Maybe not! Maybe you've been asleep, trying to outdo Rip Van Winkle. How in heaven's name can you say it's sudden? You say you've loved me all along. Why haven't you told me? You did once, in Berkeley. Since then, you've been silent. You let me marry Ed, a man I didn't love, and told me we could no longer speak to each other."

"There was a good reason for that. Ed told me to stay away."

"Oh, and when were you going to tell me about *that?*"

"I'm sorry, Cassie. I've made a lot of mistakes."

"And just when did you get your head straightened out enough to think that you actually do love me?"

"I've always loved you, Cassie."

"Well, let me ask it another way. When did you decide you wanted to tell me about your feelings?"

Their dialogue wasn't going as hoped. "The past few years, I guess. Ten, maybe."

"And you've kept it to yourself for *ten* years?"

"You were married."

"I've not been married for the past four years, Obie. Where were you during that time? Well, I know where you've been the last year, but what about the previous three years?"

"Why are you angry at me, Cassie? I'm here now, and I love you. Please tell me that my stupidity hasn't ruined everything. *Please tell me.* Is it too late?"

She pushed him away and went to sit on the rock ledge. "Why are you telling me this now? I'd finally adjusted to the idea that we may never be anything but best friends . . . and you spring this on me. You still haven't said why you didn't tell me sooner."

"You were divorced a year before I knew about it. Then, Annie was killed, and I went to New York. My frame of mind between Annie and the job I was ill-suited for didn't allow much time for rational thinking."

She nodded. "Yes, I suppose it would be difficult. And what about the year you've been back? Why have you said nothing? All the time we've spent together, all the opportunities to speak of such things . . . and you've been silent."

"I've wanted to tell you, Cassie. I was afraid."

"Afraid? A man with medals for bravery, a man who's risked his life for others. Afraid? Am I so dangerous?" She curled her lips and growled. "Be careful! I'll bite you!"

"Please, Cassie, try to understand. What I've told you to-day, wanted to tell you since I've been back is so important to me that I've hesitated to bring it up. We've renewed our friend-ship. And, frankly, I've wanted more, but I was afraid I'd de-stroy our friendship. You're the reason I came back, Cassie, and I live in fear that you no longer love me as I love you. I have dreamed that you might. However, I've been afraid to test your true feelings."

"And when did you muster your courage?"

"When it became unbearable."

She was silent a moment. "And you brought me up here to tell me?"

"It's a place that has meaning for me. Cassie, are you going to keep me guessing about your feelings?"

She went to him and placed her hands on his shoulders. "You can calm your fears, Obie. Didn't I tell you once that I'd always love you?"

He took her in his arms again. "I love you so much," he whispered.

"I love you too, Obie, but we must talk about something."

"What?"

"Laura."

He stopped breathing for a moment. Was it this again, the

thing that had separated them before? Was he to be blamed again? "What about Laura?"

"Your feelings for her?"

He hadn't expected that question. "I have no feelings for her!"

"Dan told me about your dinner that he engineered to get you talking. He said you *did* talk. Does it mean that you're friends again?"

"Not in the usual sense. We talked about being civil. She's forgiven me, she said."

"Whatever that might mean."

"Cassie, I have no lingering feelings for Laura. None."

"Her divorce is final. She's free now."

"Listen, there's been bad blood between us for so long I'm not sure we could ever be good friends. If my having talked to her worries you, it shouldn't. You have nothing to be concerned about."

"Promise?"

"Promise!"

They sat on the ledge for nearly an hour, talking quietly with their arms around each other. As they walked down, they held hands or went arm-in-arm where they could. They didn't hurry.

Later, they dined by candlelight in a Lake Placid restaurant overlooking Mirror Lake. Obie didn't want the day to end. He expressed that sentiment to Cassie when they returned to his station wagon.

"It doesn't have to end yet, Obie. I told Laura I might be gone overnight." He guessed that she didn't mean her smile to be seductive, but he found it so. "We can find a place to stay," she added.

"All right."

"Aren't you afraid?" Her tone was teasing. "Isn't this another dangerous crossroad for you?"

"Cassie, I love you."

"I know. And I love you."

Her words were like the grandest music he'd ever heard. He squeezed her hands with his. "This *is* a crossroad, isn't it, for both of us?"

"My love, we've been approaching it for thirty years. You've been a desert mirage, always moving and always just

beyond my reach."
    "I think we may have found an oasis."
    He put a hand on her cheek; he felt her tears.

CHAPTER TWENTY–SEVEN

June–July 1970

On the way home from Lake Placid, Obie said, "People will notice. They're going to know that we were away together."

"I don't care if the whole world knows!" Cassie was aware of how brazen the remark sounded, but she wasn't sorry; she was still in a state of wonderment that threatened to overwhelm any sense of propriety.

He said, "Marry me, Cassie?"

She put a light hand over his on the steering wheel. "Pull over!"

He maneuvered onto the narrow roadside without speaking. She slid over and embraced him. "I've waited a long time to hear those words . . . *again*. Say it once more, Obie, please."

"Gladly! Cassie, will you marry me?"

"I'll need some time to think about it."

"Cassie . . ."

"Yes! Yes! Yes! I'll marry you, Obie Gainsworthy. When?"

"Whenever you wish."

"Tomorrow?" A flashback returned her to a time in Berkeley when they had exchanged nearly the same words. Time may have passed, and as giddy as she was, a need for reason still prevailed. "No, we must be practical. There are things to do, plans to make. This is June. August, maybe? No, too hot. September? School will have started. But I love September. Is September all right with you?"

He engulfed her hands within his and kissed her cheek. "Cassie, you set the date. I'll be there."

She kissed him again. "Late September. We'll have to decide on an exact date, but we can do that later. I'll take a few days off work. I can do that."

Later, Cassie smiled when she remembered giving Obie such a hard time on the mountain. She should feel guilty but failed to muster any significant remorse. She was merely expelling decades of frustration.

Contrary to expectation, no one except Ken and Angie

seemed to have noticed their absence. Angie smiled, and Ken gave them a knowing look, clearly conveying approval.

During the following two weeks, she couldn't remember ever being happier. If school had been in session, she would have been unable to work. She thought of little else except Obie—and the future they were planning.

Julie noticed her euphoria. "Mommy, you are smiling all the time."

Cassie hugged her. "Darling, you're right. Mommy *is* smiling a lot. It's because I'm happy. I have much for which to be thankful."

"Are you thankful for me, Mommy?"

"Indeed, I am, Honey. I love you very much."

"Are you thankful for Grandma and Grandpa?"

"Yes, I am."

"Do you love them?"

She managed to relegate her mother to some dispassionate corner in her mind. "Yes, I do."

"Are you thankful for Obie?"

"I'm thankful for Obie."

She guessed what was coming.

"Do you love Obie?"

"Yes, dear, I love Obie." She must find time to explain about the change coming in their lives. Julie and Obie had established rapport on their first meeting, and the previous summer he'd taken her blackberry picking in the brambles above his house. The three of them spent an evening making jam. Julie mentioned the outing every time she spread jam on her toast.

"Is Obie coming today?" Julie asked.

"Yes, later. We'll take you to the ice cream stand on the beach or to Stewart's if it's raining. Would you like that?"

"Not so much." She giggled. "What do you think, Mommy?"

Cassie laughed aloud at Julie's sense of humor. She wasn't surprised by anything Julie said. Her daughter possessed unexpected insight into conditions escaping more "normal" people. Not long after Obie's return to Stafford Rest, he was telling Cassie about his experiences in Vietnam. Although Julie was in the middle of an artistic endeavor at the kitchen table a few feet away, she said. "It still hurts."

Obie had questioned her, "What hurts, Julie?" He later told

Cassie he believed she referred to some hurt to herself; she attended a rambunctious special education class in Evergreen and
sometimes came home with bruises.

"*You* hurt, Obie!" Julie had said. "Hurt comes out of your
eyes, just like Dan."

Obie had stared at Julie a long time before he said to Cassie,
"Wisdom from unexpected places."

"She does that often."

Cassie loved Julie as much as any mother could love a
daughter. At sixteen, she was a bright light in Cassie's life. Nevertheless, raising a child with Downs Syndrome had its difficulties. Obie and Julie had bonded, but his being with them part-
time was not like living in the same household.

When Obie arrived later that day, Cassie faced reality and
expressed her concerns. "When we marry, we take on each
other's responsibilities. Mine aren't light. Julie will always need
looking after. And, if I should die, it would be up to you. Are
you ready for that?"

"Cassie, you've become my life," he responded. "Whatever
awaits us is what we'll share. Your daughter will be my daughter
and I'll love her as though she were mine."

"I knew you'd say that, Obie. It still means a great deal to
hear it."

Other practical matters, things she had put off, needed discussion. After they returned from their ice cream outing on the
beach, and Julie was in bed, Cassie and Obie sat in the wicker
swing on her front porch.

She'd hesitated to initiate a discussion of their financial situations. She must, however. She believed Obie cared little for
money beyond meeting his immediate needs. She had no idea
whether he had substantial savings or had none. Ken had told
her Obie had inherited some money from his wife but had given
it to charity. Obie had made no mention of it, and she didn't
inquire.

Cassie was sure of one thing; she was marrying a complicated man. He could run churches, edit magazines, write books,
and manage multi-million-dollar companies but, by his admission, seldom took time to balance his checkbook. She did hers
faithfully every month; she might have to oversee their financial
affairs.

The swing squeaked rhythmically as it moved back and

forth. She attacked head-on. "Obie, you've been back a year without any income. And you've spent a ton of money on your house. How do you do it?"

He smiled. "Except for that building project, I haven't spent much. It's all done now, so my miserly ways keep me solvent."

"But now you're getting married? You'll have a family." She held her breath.

"Are you afraid I can't support you and Julie?"

"Well, one must wonder. Julie and I live on my teaching salary, but with the mortgage on this house, we barely get by."

"I experienced poverty growing up. I didn't like it then, and I won't put up with it now. I know my responsibilities, Cassie, and I take them seriously. Being frugal about my needs doesn't mean I'll be stingy when it comes to family. I'm glad you brought this up, for we need to talk about practical things. I've put it off, and I guess you have, too. This seems as good a time as any."

Cassie was relieved and took several minutes to inform him of her situation: Ed had made a settlement to provide for Julie in case Cassie should die or be unable to provide for her. The large lump sum was in a trust and would last Julie a lifetime. Anything left at Julie's death would return to Ed Jackson's estate or his other heirs.

"I could have done better with patience," she said. "I just wanted out. The deal I got was insurance to secure Julie's welfare if something happens to me. You should know that our marriage will relieve him of even that responsibility while you're alive. I didn't expect to remarry, so I thought it unimportant. Unfortunately, it could place an added burden on you."

"We'll manage, Cassie. I'm impressed with how well you support Julie and yourself."

"Mom and Dad offered to help. I've refused."

"Why?"

"Pride, I guess. I haven't talked to Mom for nearly a year. Dad would still help us if I asked him. He comes and takes Julie up there. Mom and I have nothing to say to each other. I don't doubt that if Dad dies first, which is likely, I'll have no inheritance. By the way, I want to continue teaching after we're married. It's an important part of my life."

"Of course, you can do that. And I hope you're not worried

about my solvency. I've waited for the chance to explain some things to you."

"I'm not worried. I'm curious, however. Our future doesn't hinge on how much money we have, but we do need to take inventory. Don't you think so?"

"Absolutely. Let me begin by saying that my present financial situation is simple. I get a small veteran's disability pension from the Army because of the wound I received in Korea. I collect royalties on three books that, amazingly, are still in print. The royalties were substantial once but are much less so now. All three books brought large advances, most of which I was able to save. The salary and bonuses I made at Silverman Publishing for two years were absolutely indecent, and I own several thousand shares of Silverman Financial stock. I have enough in the bank over at Evergreen to last us several years if need be, and I'm going back to work. The bottom line is that you need not worry about money."

"How are you doing with work on the new book?"

"I've nearly finished an outline for it. I've also secured a new agent."

"I'm happy about that. And what about the ministry? Have you given up on it?"

"Yes, and I've told you why."

She wasn't anxious to discuss the incident with the nurse in Monterey, but his attitude about it bothered her, so she broached it. "Annie had all but deserted you, and it was only one time. Wasn't it?"

"I never saw her again."

"You made a mistake, Obie, but a forgivable one. It was human."

"Have you ever made that kind of mistake, Cassie?"

"No, I haven't."

"I was a minister with a flock to look after. Most people can survive such mistakes, but a minister destroys faith when acting in that manner."

"Your indiscretion wasn't common knowledge, was it?"

"No. The higher-ups knew, so it was no doubt whispered."

"Even so, Christians are forgiving people. Isn't forgiveness an essence of Christianity?"

Obie shrugged his shoulders. "My job was to build faith, not destroy it. There's also the matter of taking a life in Korea.

I'd sworn never to do such a thing again, and I failed."

"You'd be dead if you hadn't acted as you did. Don't you think God considers that?"

"Oh, I know I'm forgiven, but that doesn't make me fit again for ministry."

"But you went back and served as a chaplain in Vietnam."

"That's different. It was another way to serve, and I think I was attempting to cleanse myself."

"Apparently, you don't think you succeeded."

His sigh might have indicated surrender to her probing. "Would you like to see me in ministry? Pastoral ministry? You've never shown much interest in spiritual matters."

"I've changed. I probably would not have wanted to be a preacher's wife when we were young. But I've grown spiritually and begun to think differently."

"A lot is expected of a minister's wife."

She didn't want to be his reason for accepting or rejecting any worthy cause. "I just want you to know that if you ever change your mind, I'll stand beside you."

"Thanks, but there's little chance of that happening." Then, after a moment's pause, he said, "There are a couple of other things we haven't talked seriously about. One is about where we'll live?"

"Good question. It's convenient here, although it's small."

"And crowded. Houses are too close together. There's much more space on Blackberry Hill."

"I'm agreeable to living on the hill. I'd like to have a big vegetable garden like Vi had." She remembered something. "Obie, we could still have children." Even in the darkness, she saw his shocked face and was amused.

"Cassie, you're forty-four."

She slapped his leg. "Don't count it out."

"I'd like being a father," he said.

She'd considered their discussion of money finished. Now, she realized she needed to satisfy her curiosity about something else. "Obie, did you really give away money from Annie's estate?"

"Yes, and it's something we must discuss. I've been working up to it all evening. Annie did leave me money, a lot of it. And yes, I've given away a lot. I'm still working on it, but giving away that much is hard."

She hesitated a moment. "How much?"

He revealed the amount so casually that she paused to process his words. She knew her mouth was open and was glad for the darkness. She wanted assurance that she'd heard correctly. "How much did you say?"

When he repeated the amount, she only mused, "I'm speechless."

"My lawyer is still working on it. Annie had many charities, but I also want mine to benefit."

"Does Ken know?"

"Yes, and he used some adjectives describing my stupidity that I'm not repeating. Not many people know anything about it, and I want to keep it that way. The Silvermans and the lawyers know. Dad says Angie let it slip to some lady friends that I inherited some money and planned to give it away."

"I have to ask, why *are* you giving it all away?"

"It's unearned, and Annie's whole purpose in life was to put it where it would help the most people. I let Annie down in many ways, Cassie. Things I told her that I valued, and that I *do* value were things for which I didn't fully support her. She was an activist; I wasn't."

"That's not your nature."

"Perhaps I need more of that nature." She heard him sigh. "I should have gone south with her to stand up for human rights. Not only did I not go, but I also kept her from going. I should have gone to the Peace Corps with her. In the end, she died fighting for human rights. Why would I not want her money to go to causes she valued?"

"You're a remarkable man, Obie. However, I can't imagine that Annie would object to your keeping some of it."

"Cassie, will this be a problem for us?"

"No. No, Obie! It's not a problem. I only wondered."

"I was initially tempted to keep ten percent, following Annie's lead, but I finally decided to give it all away. Now, though, I need to make sure you and Julie are cared for if something happens to me. I'll put enough of it in a trust to take care of that. It's not money I'll touch for myself, though."

"That's what you meant when you said not to worry about money?"

"Yes, I'm looking out for you and Julie. I called my lawyer to set it up. And yes, Annie would approve."

"So, if I murder you, I'll come into some serious money?"

"Sure, you could, but there's this old saying, 'He who trusts in his riches will wither, but the righteous will flourish like a green leaf.' Proverbs, eleven twenty-eight."

"That doesn't apply to me. The quote clearly says 'he.'"

Obie laughed. "In that case, there's this: Proverbs, eleven twenty-two . . . 'Like a gold ring in a swine's snout is a beautiful woman without discretion.'"

She had wanted to lighten the seriousness of their discussion; she loved to hear him laugh. "That's unfair," she said. "You can quote scripture. All I can think of is, 'A fool and his money are soon parted.'"

"I'm sure that's what Dad was trying to tell me. Maybe you think I'm crazy, too."

"I don't think you're crazy, Obie."

"When I was younger, I wanted to be rich. But Grandpa Jacob's philosophy gradually seeped into my system until I came to believe I only needed enough to meet my basic needs. If I had too much, I might believe I didn't have to work. And work is really what it's all about, isn't it?"

"Indeed it is."

He snapped his fingers. "I nearly forgot. There's a house in the Napa Valley, north of Berkeley. Annie deeded it to me before going to Africa, something I didn't know until after her death."

"Are you giving that away, too?"

"No, she specifically requested that I keep it. The lawyer is still handling the details. Bills and taxes are handled by a trust Annie set up, so I don't need to deal with it, not even the paperwork. And that's just fine with me."

"I'm glad you're keeping something."

"The lawyer did send me a copy of the deed. I've neglected the property, I suppose. I should take more interest in that part of it."

She smiled in the darkness. It was what she might have expected of Obie, esoteric in matters of his own choosing and sloppy in approaching the practical. She believed she could help with that.

"Is it a large house?"

"Six rooms. Smaller than the house you grew up in, although larger than my present house on Blackberry Hill. It's a substantial building and in a beautiful location . . . a serene spot. There's a large vineyard on hills adjacent to it. I never met the owners, but Annie knew them."

"A house needs living in. Did you go there often with Annie?"

"Only a couple of times. After that, I went alone. We can go there for vacations. Suppose I put you in charge of the property?"

"All right, but after we're married."

"Is it going to bother you that it belonged to Annie?"

Although that was an uncertainty, she said, "Of course not. She was thoughtful in giving it to you. She must have known you'd give away most of the money, so she went to special pains to see you didn't do the same with the house. I like her."

"Yes, Annie was remarkable in a number of ways."

"Except as a faithful wife. Oh, Obie, I'm sorry I said that. She was human, too."

"Too human, I think."

"You're a prude, Obie, do you know that? You forgive hard. I hope I never do anything I'll need forgiveness for."

"What dastardly deeds are you planning, Cassie?"

She was glad for the teasing way the words were spoken, but she couldn't shake the feeling that Obie was stingy with forgiveness, even for himself.

* * *

Their engagement was announced the following Sunday from the pulpit of Stafford Rest United Methodist Church, and the wedding date was set for September twenty-third. Pinky turned and looked at Cassie with a waned smile. Cassie could see her mother's expression of disgust. Laura stared straight ahead.

Laura had expressed displeasure when Cassie gave her the news. "I know it's your life, sister, but there's no proof that he's changed."

Cassie hadn't argued with her. That Laura didn't intend to change her opinion of Obie was apparent. Her sister was wrong, and Cassie wasn't going to let Laura's attitude interfere with her own newfound happiness. Her family could choose to attend the wedding—or not. She was certain her mother wouldn't attend.

Cassie and Obie planned to go away for a few days to the coast of Maine. Dan had even volunteered to fly them there, although they would probably go in her Jeep.

The day after the engagement announcement, Cassie was preparing sandwiches she and Julie planned to take to Blackberry Hill. Obie was writing, so they would stay only an hour with him.

The phone rang. Her father's voice had an edge of hysteria. "Cassie, it's your mother! She's very sick!"

"What's wrong with her?"

"She threw up earlier this morning and went to bed. She's still there but seems to have a high fever and doesn't appear to recognize me."

"Have you called Doctor Osborn?"

"I called and talked to his receptionist. He's in Saratoga Springs and won't be back for about an hour. Anyway, she said your mother would have to go to his office. I'd have to carry her."

"Don't doctors do house calls anymore?"

"Not unless it's a matter of life or death. Cassie, can you come up here and help me?"

"Dad, Mom has made it clear that I'm not welcome there. Where's Laura?"

"She's in Plattsburgh meeting with a Canadian retailer. I need you, Cassie."

"All right, I'll be there in five minutes." At the back fence, she called for Angie to watch Julie.

It felt strange pulling in beside the house on Garnet Point; she'd not expected to be there again. The driveway had recently been paved with asphalt.

Her mother lay on her bed, fully clothed. Her eyes were closed; she seemed to be sleeping. Her breathing was labored. Her forehead was hot. Her father was right; she *was* ill.

"Dad, call the doctor's office again. Tell them he's to come up here as soon as he returns. He'll come if you insist."

Cassie went to the kitchen, took ice cubes from the freezer, put them in a plastic bag, and wrapped them in a towel. She applied the towel to her mother's head and neck.

Her father came back into the room. "The doctor is coming," he said.

Her mother's eyes opened. "Cassie . . . is that you?"

"Yes, Mom, it's me." She wasn't sure what would come next and braced herself.

"Come closer, dear." Her voice was scratchy but soft. She curled a forefinger in obvious invitation. Cassie saw that she was delirious.

When their faces were close together, her mother's hand went to Cassie's cheek. "My dear, dear, girl. I've treated you badly. Will you forgive me?"

Cassie was taken aback. *How unlike her mother.* She must be out of her head with a fever. Cassie turned to her father, who had seated himself on the other side of the bed. "Dad, has she been like this long?"

"Only in the last hour."

As Cassie moved away from the bed, her mother grabbed her arm and pulled her close again. Her grip was surprisingly firm. "I have something to tell you, Cassie . . . before I die."

"You're not dying, Mom, and yes, I forgive you for whatever."

"Thank you. I *am* dying. I can tell."

"Mom, you have a fever. It's affecting your thinking. Relax. Try to sleep. The doctor will be here soon."

Abigail sighed and closed her eyes as her head collapsed onto her pillow. Then, after about a minute, when she appeared to have drifted into sleep, her eyes opened again, and she spoke. "Don't tell Pinky. He doesn't know."

Cassie looked at her father. He shrugged his shoulders. "Don't tell him what, Mom. He's still here, right beside you, you know."

"No, he's gone to the factory. He won't be back until late. He wouldn't like knowing what I'm telling you. Bernadette knows some of it, though."

Cassie whispered across the bed, "Dad, do you know what she's talking about?"

His face showed concern. "She went to see Bernadette Simon early this morning and came home upset. Something she said led me to believe they might have quarreled, or maybe she was upset because Bernadette is so ill. She has advanced cancer, you know."

Abigail groped for Cassie's hand. When she found it, she squeezed hard. "Cassie, you're really going to marry Obie? Is that true?"

The question sounded rational enough. "I am, Mom. We'll be married in September."

"Then, you should know. You should know the secret."

Her father sat up so quickly that he nearly fell backward. "Not that, Abigail. You shouldn't. You promised Laura."

If Abigail heard him, it wasn't apparent. Finally, she said, "It's about Obie. It's also about Danny."

"Abigail!"

Cassie sat forward, all her attention on her mother's words. "Yes, Mom?"

"Danny is Obie's son."

* * *

The doctor left after giving her mother a shot and prescribing bed rest to combat whatever "summer bug" had attacked her. Cassie washed dishes in the kitchen sink with suspended emotions. She avoided her father's eyes.

He followed her to the driveway and leaned in the driver's side window as she prepared to back out. "Cassie, what you heard . . ."

"Was the truth," she finished for him."

"Yes, it is true."

"Is this the big family secret that I've been hearing about for so long?"

"For the most part."

"How could it be? Obie was gone nearly a year when Dan was born."

"Your mother engineered that deception."

"I should have known."

"Cassie, I've wanted to tell you, but I promised Laura I'd not. She told me about it several years ago. Your mother doesn't know that I know. I'm glad and relieved that you know now. I'd bring it all into the open if it were my choice. It isn't. I intend to honor Laura's wishes, and I hope you will, too."

"Which is?"

"No one outside the family must know, and Dan is not to know."

"Well, Dad, I must say that this secret has been well kept."

"And I'm sure that will continue. And I'm sorry for the way it affects you."

"Why would it affect me?"

"Why, because of Obie. Whether or not to go ahead with the wedding."

"Of course, we'll go ahead with the wedding. We're being married in September. We love each other. Dad, do you think I'd care now about what Laura and Obie did as teenagers? The fact is, I'm delighted that Obie is Dan's father. I never much liked Ben Williamson."

"Ben raised Dan as his own. That deserves some credit."

"I suppose, but I hope you won't ask me to keep this from Obie. He, of all people, should know."

Pinky looked pained. "You don't have to keep it from him, Cassie. He already knows. He's always known."

She gripped the steering wheel to keep her hands from trembling. "Dad, that's simply not true. Obie doesn't know. How could he? I know him better than anyone else in the world. I'd know if he were keeping something like that from me."

"My dear, you don't know him as well as you think. He fooled me for years."

"You sound like Laura, saying such things about him."

"Laura would know, Cassie, and I'm not going to tell you what you should do about Obie, but I hope you'll think about it. You can marry him, but he'll never be a real part of our family because of the way he treated Laura. I loved Vi and came to admire and respect Ken. He saved my life, for God's sake. Obie is another matter. The only good thing I can say about him is that he hasn't told Dan the truth. He has, at least, kept that a secret."

"*The way he treated Laura?* What do you mean?"

"He deserted her, got her pregnant, then refused to acknowledge her letters and phone calls. He put her in the position of marrying a man she didn't love. He broke her heart, and she's never gotten over it. That's the kind of man you're planning to marry." Her father stepped back from the car and raised his hands as though to say he had exhausted the subject.

Hurt and anger were so intertwined that Cassie was unsure where, or how, to direct it, or even if she could. She slapped the gear lever into reverse but didn't move the car. Tears scalded her eyes.

She tried to remain calm and keep her voice level, but it came out as a cry of pain. "I don't believe it, Dad. It's not that

I think you're lying. I think you've been lied to."

"By your sister?"

"I don't know. Maybe."

"Talk to her. She may be back by now. Go see her. See what she has to say. Learn the truth before it's too late."

The tires peeled rubber as the jeep leaped back onto the highway. She screamed at her father, who was retreating into the yard, "I will! I'm going to see her right now!"

CHAPTER TWENTY–EIGHT

July 1970

Following a reckless drive down Garnet Point Hill, Cassie pulled into the park at the end of Diamond Lake, her special place of refuge. She sat in the jeep for a half-hour while controlling her emotions. Then, when she could trust her voice, she drove home and asked Angie to watch Julie a little longer. From there, she walked to the factory by the Morass, thinking the exercise might ease her tension.

Laura's car was in her reserved parking space. Cassie found her sister alone in her office. The buzz of saws and planners from the shops was audible, although muffled by the sound barriers Laura had installed soon after her arrival in Stafford Rest. Cassie flopped into the leather chair in front of Laura's desk.

"Cassie, are you angry about something?" Laura asked.

"Let's see . . . where do I begin?"

"What is it?"

Laura's face grew pale as Cassie told her about the afternoon's events. She leaned back in her swivel chair and looked ready to collapse. Cassie finished with, "Now, it's your turn. No lies, Laura! It's time for the truth."

Laura took a tissue from a box on her desk and dabbed at her eyes. "I'm sorry you learned about it this way. I was going to tell you, anyway. I felt I had to after you announced your engagement. It wouldn't be right for you not to know the full story."

"By all means, give me the *full* story."

Laura came from behind her desk and sat in the chair next to Cassie. "You knew that we'd been intimate, didn't you?"

"I suspected it."

"I never told you directly. I thought you'd know."

"I was jealous."

"We were young . . . and innocent. He told me he loved me, and I thought he did."

"Obie *did* love you."

"Are you going to let me tell this?"

299

For now, she would be patient. "Go ahead."

"We'd started making plans. I was going to college, and we would see each other whenever possible. We were going to get married as soon as we could manage it. Then, Mom found out about us. She caught us together in Obie's barnroom. I was only half-dressed. She was as angry as I've ever seen her. She forbade me to see him again. You know how she is?"

"I know quite well."

"Obie wasn't good enough for her. I honestly think it was that, more than anything else. Later that evening, she told me Obie had volunteered to go away to let things cool down so we could 'come to our senses.' She surprised me when she said she'd allow us to see each other one last time before he left. She even drove me to the old footbridge that crossed Cedar Creek."

Laura wiped her eyes again. "When we met there, I thought of it as a joke because I knew we'd find ways to see each other. So I was devastated when, out of the blue, Obie told me he'd joined the Army and was leaving that very night. I couldn't believe it at first. Hindsight has convinced me he'd gotten cold feet and decided to break up with me. His enlistment was his underhanded way of ending it. Instead of telling me face to face, he took the coward's way."

"Laura, that doesn't make sense. Obie would never . . ."

"He couldn't leave it at that, though. He continued making promises. He said we'd be together as soon as he could arrange it. Said we'd get married."

Laura stopped, and Cassie saw that she was crying. "Are you okay, Laura?" she asked.

Laura recovered. "I'm sorry," she said. "We exchanged several letters. His were full of love and promises. Mom kept telling me to forget Obie. Then, I was sure I was pregnant. I finally told Mom. And I wrote to Obie, thinking he'd find a way to send for me. I thought that we'd be married."

She choked up. "Cassie, I never heard from him again. And during all that time I had to deal with Mom. How hard do you think that was?"

"I can imagine. But . . ."

"She was furious at first, then mellowed a little. I could see that she was as desperate as I was. I kept hoping there had been a mix-up with the mail. Mom was going to let us get married. I'm sure of that. She even helped me phone Obie's post in South

Carolina. An officer there told us Obie was refusing to take the call. So, you see, Cassie, he deserted me, and just when I needed him the most."

Cassie was beginning to feel lightheaded. "There has to be some other explanation."

Laura continued as though she hadn't heard. "I needed a doctor. Mom wanted to take me to Albany. I insisted on going to Doctor Williamson, Ben's father. He'd taken care of us all our lives. Mom's main concern was keeping everything quiet. My state of mind was such that I didn't care anymore."

Whatever the truth, Laura's anguish was real. "I'm sorry, sister," Cassie said.

"On one visit to Doctor Williamson, Mom and I were waiting in one of his little rooms. Ben came in. He said he wanted to talk. He and I had met a few times, and I knew he had feelings for me, but what he said that day absolutely floored me. He told me he knew of my problem. He also said that he loved me."

"He loved you?"

"He'd already told me he loved me, something I hadn't taken seriously. That day, in Mom's presence, he asked me to marry him. I should have been grateful, but I was angry and confused and ran out of the office. I kept trying to get in touch with Obie, still hoping there might have been a mistake in communication."

"Yes, that's probably the explanation."

"Dr. Williamson apparently knew of his son's proposal because he became extremely cool toward me after that. Mom was delighted with the offered solution, and as I became more desperate, she pressured me to decide. I was heartbroken and confused, so I finally agreed. And, as you know, Ben and I were married in September of that year."

"I didn't know any of what was going on. How did you ever keep it from me?"

"Mom kept a tight lid on everything. Even Dad never suspected what was behind our marriage. It was only a few years ago that I told him about it. I kept trying to get in touch with Obie right up to a few days before the marriage . . . to no avail."

"I don't understand how you pulled off such a deception, making people think Dan was born later than he was."

"Mom, again. She stayed with us in Boston until Dan was born. She came up with a false birth certificate. I believe she must have bribed someone. She also sent a fake birth announce-ment to local newspapers here. I don't know all the details. She's clever; you know that."

"You should tell Dan the truth."

"No! *Never!* It would upset so many things in his life. Can you imagine how he would feel if he discovered he wasn't who he thought he was? How would *you* feel in those circumstances?"

"I'd still be me. He'd still be Dan."

"For me, it would be troublesome. I think for him as well."

"Doesn't he have the right to know? He thinks the world of Obie."

Laura didn't seem to hear. "Since Dan and I came back here last fall, I've lived in fear that Obie would tell him. At least that hasn't happened . . . yet."

Cassie wanted to scream at her that Obie didn't know and was ignorant of whatever had happened. But she restrained her-self; she would try a more diplomatic path. "Have you ever talked to Obie about this . . . ever had a real conversation where you referred to Dan as his son?"

"There was never the opportunity nor the need. We both knew what had transpired."

"Are you sure that *he* knew?"

Laura's tone turned angry again. "This spring, during that stupid dinner Dan engineered, Obie told me he would not tell Dan anything about our past relationship. Now, you wouldn't agree to keep silent about something you're ignorant of, would you?"

"Maybe he believed he was agreeing to something else. Laura, I repeat my question. Have you ever at any time actually told Obie that Dan was his son or referred to him that way?"

"Maybe not in so many words. I never felt the necessity of putting it into words . . . painful words for me."

Cassie said against her better judgment, "Maybe you want Dan's parentage kept secret to avoid reflection on you and the Hunt family name?"

"That's not true," Laura said quickly. Cassie thought she had hit a nerve.

"I'm sorry. I shouldn't have suggested such a thing."

"Are you still going to marry him?"

"Yes, I'm going to marry him."

"Even knowing what you do?"

"Laura, I'm going with my heart and what I know of Obie. I don't recognize the person you're telling me about. I'm sorry. I don't think you're lying. But I do believe there was a tragic misunderstanding of some sort."

"Like what? What could there possibly be?"

"I've been thinking about it. Suppose, just suppose, that someone intercepted your mail, someone with the purpose of ending the correspondence between you?"

"You think that hasn't occurred to me? Who would or could do such a thing? I had safeguards."

"Safeguards?"

"Beth Nellis."

"That's a name I haven't heard for a long time."

"She lives in Florida now. We were good friends. Obie sent mail to me through her so Mom wouldn't know we were writing. Beth wouldn't have betrayed me."

"Maybe Mom *did* find out, somehow."

"Cassie, do you honestly believe Mom is guilty of something like that? You should be ashamed."

"I think that's what happened. And, yes, she's capable of it. She thought she was protecting you when, in fact, she may have been destroying your chance for happiness."

"Cassie, I can't believe that. It's preposterous."

"No, it isn't. If she intercepted your letters, it would explain everything."

"No, not really. What about all the years that have passed? If Obie were innocent, why would he not have straightened it out with me?"

"You've seldom seen each other, and when you did, you bristled. I don't think you've ever seriously talked."

"Just a simple apology sometime during all those years would have meant so much. He could have called me or written a letter. He never did."

"I have an idea, Laura. Let's ask him straight out. I'll call him right now, and you can say, 'Obie, I want to hear you admit that Dan's your son.'" She smiled at the mental picture of Obie receiving such a request.

"Don't be silly. He won't even talk about it."

"You're wrong. You *must* talk to Obie, Laura."

"I've agreed to be civil. It'll never go beyond that."

"I wish I had proof, Laura, but I don't. However, I do

believe in Obie."

"I think you'll suffer disappointment."

Cassie walked home. *What a troubling day!* Obie was waiting for her and wanted to know why she hadn't come to Blackberry Hill. She told him of her mother's illness and intended to tell him the secret that would change his life, but drew back at the last moment. It might be dangerous for Cassie and Obie's relationship if Laura and Obie's anger at each other ceased. She hated herself for the thought.

* * *

Cassie was troubled. For the past week, she had withheld important news from Obie, news he had the right to hear. She had planned to tell him during dinner at Ernie's, but the meal passed without her disclosing the information.

Later, as they sat in the swing on her porch, she lost her nerve again. When he had gone, she was ashamed. The barrier keeping Obie and Laura apart was their belief that each had abandoned the other. If those beliefs were proven false, as Cassie believed they were, and Obie learned that Dan was his son, what was there to keep them apart? Obie might still love Laura, despite his protests. *She could lose him. She could never bear that.* After going to bed, she prayed for strength to do what was right and that her recently restored happiness would not be snatched away again.

She was nearly asleep when an abrupt thought caused her to sit upright in bed. It was eleven o'clock. She dialed Laura's number. Her sister had retired and sounded grumpy.

Cassie said, "When we talked a few days ago at the factory, what was it you said about . . ."

"Cassie, it's late. The last thing I want is thrashing through this again."

"Like it or not, I have something to tell you. You said Obie never tried getting in touch, either then or in later years."

"He didn't. He would have if he loved me."

"Laura, he tried to reach you. He called."

"What do you mean? He didn't call."

"Oh, Laura, I'm so sorry that I didn't remember this before, but it was so long ago, and I didn't have all the facts. Obie called from South Carolina while he was in basic training. He called because he was worried that you hadn't written."

"You're making this up, Cassie."

"Damn it, Laura, why would I do that? He called, hoping to catch you instead of Mom. I was home alone and took the call. We talked for several minutes. As I remember, I assured him you were not sick or anything like that. I told him I'd tell you he'd called. He asked me not to. He was afraid you'd believe he was checking up on you or doubting your love. I must have failed to tell you because I was honoring his wishes. I don't remember why I didn't tell you later, except that you kept me in the dark about everything. I'm sorry, Laura."

"Don't be. He had other chances to call or to write."

"Maybe he did write. Maybe his mail was intercepted. Maybe yours was, too."

"He refused *my* telephone call. Don't forget that."

"Tell me again about that call."

"What's the use?"

"Please, Laura, humor me. Tell me if you can remember."

"Oh, I remember, all right. The details are burned into my memory. An officer answered the phone and went to get Obie. He was gone for several minutes. When he returned, he said Obie didn't want to talk to me. That one act of cruelty on his part did more to break my heart than anything else."

"How did the officer sound? Was he surprised at Obie's response?"

"I don't know. Mom did the talking. I was pretty upset. I hadn't been feeling well, either. She made the call and talked to the officer."

"So, you didn't talk to the man at all?"

"No."

"Laura, don't you see? Mom is behind all this. She engineered it, the same as she engineered your marriage and deception about Dan's birth. She deceives. It's what she does best. I'd bet there was no officer on the phone or that the phone call even went beyond this town."

Cassie hoped Laura's silence was a sign that she finally understood. But when her sister did speak, she said, "I can't believe she'd do something that bad. I still believe Obie didn't write."

"Let's use some logic, Laura. I know that Obie *did* call. He wanted to talk to you. You believe me about that, don't you?"

"I guess so."

"Does it make any sense that he would refuse your call? He'd been trying to get through to you by telephone. So why would he not take *your* call? It makes no sense whatsoever. Can't you see that?"

"The mail?" Laura was grasping for any answer. "What about the mail? Why didn't he answer my letters?"

"Mom found a way to intercept your letters, Laura. It's the only answer."

"How could she manage that?"

"I believe I know."

"How?"

"Bernadette Simon. Do you remember that she became postmistress because the postmaster was drafted?"

"Yes, I remember. It was during the war. Mom helped her get the job. But, that . . ."

"The other day, when Mom was sick and out of her head, she mentioned Bernadette. Dad said Mom had argued with her. Bernadette has worked for Mom for years. She's been sick and has recently retired. Dan said she wasn't productive in real estate. Why do you suppose Mom has kept her on the payroll for so long?"

Cassie heard Laura emit a long sigh. "I must admit it doesn't sound like Mom rewarding incompetence, but there must be another explanation. There has to be."

"Laura, Bernadette knows something about this. I'm going to see her tomorrow. She lives on Lake Road in one of the new houses. Let's go together."

Again, Laura hesitated. "I do think we should get to the truth about this, if for nothing else than to relieve your suspicious mind. I'll let you do the legwork, however."

* * *

Cassie had slept little. She was keyed up, speculating what Bernadette might know and how to approach her. In addition, her resolve to get at the truth didn't mitigate her fears that the truth could bring Laura and Obie together again. She even pulled to the roadside to ask herself, "Do you really want to do this?" The answer was that she must finish what she'd started.

Lake Road had been paved twenty years previously. Abigail had long ago purchased the Epps farm bordering Abner and Claire Gainsworthy's property. She divided the farm into building lots, now occupied by modest homes along the road and on three smaller lanes running toward the water. Bernadette lived in one of those houses.

Bernadette was ill, perhaps terminally, so Cassie had waited until midmorning to be sure she was up. She parked in the driveway behind Bernadette's Chevrolet sedan. The woman lived alone, had never married, and had never, to Cassie's knowledge, had a relationship with a man. She was nondescript and blended into the older crowd at Sunday church services. Although she had been her mother's employee for many years, Cassie didn't know her well.

It was several minutes before Bernadette came to the door. She was in her robe. Her eyes were red, and she looked tired. Her illness was apparent. Cassie might be about to add to her misery.

"Cassie, what a surprise. It's good to see you. Come on in."

Cassie declined an offer of coffee or tea. Bernadette sat in a chair, and Cassie sat on a couch where she could face the older woman. She came right to the point. "Bernadette, there's something I want to discuss with you. It might require a little time. I hope I'm not interfering with your plans."

"No, it's all right. What is it, Cassie?"

"It's about my sister, Laura, about her and Obie Gainsworthy."

Bernadette's face became even paler. "Yes, I'm ready to talk about it."

"You are?"

"I'm sick, Cassie. I have cancer. I need to get this off my chest before I die."

Cassie was dumbfounded. She'd been right; Bernadette did know something. Nevertheless, she had expected more work in eliciting a confession. "I'm sorry if this is painful. I don't want to cause you any hurt."

"No, it is I who have caused hurt. I can't undo what was done. I can clear it up, however. I've been planning to tell either Laura or Obie. I'd have done it soon. But, in any event, I'm glad you've come. I'm glad it's you, Cassie. I might not have been able to face Laura. I've watched her and Obie in church. They avoid looking at each other. It breaks my heart to see them that way, especially knowing I had a part in causing it. I changed the direction of their lives. It's almost more than I can bear." She pulled a tissue from the pocket of her robe and dabbed at her eyes.

Cassie sat forward, every nerve tense. "Bernadette, can you tell me exactly what you did? I'll explain it to Obie and Laura."

"Oh, thank you. I've been praying I'd be spared that."

"It was the letters, wasn't it? You intercepted their letters to each other?"

"Abigail had befriended me. I didn't have many friends. I was so grateful when she helped me get the post office job. She told me secrets like she and I were the only ones who would know. Everybody knew how much in love Laura and Obie were. She hated it. She said she'd be forever grateful for whatever circumstances might break it up. She was relieved when Obie was drafted."

"He wasn't drafted. He joined. He was only seventeen."

"So young. He still looks young. But it's been a long time and . . ."

"Did you remove their letters from the mail?"

"To my shame, I did. I broke the law."

"I'm not interested in this in any legal sense, Bernadette. I simply want to know what you did."

"I was putting up the mail in the boxes one day when I noticed a letter addressed to Laura, in care of . . . I don't remember her name. It was one of her classmates, I think."

"Beth Nellis?"

"That was it, I believe. Anyway, I thought it peculiar. Other letters came through with Obie's return address on them. Finally, I told Abigail about it. I guess I thought I owed it to her. I remember us having a long discussion. She invited me to your house, and we sat in your big living room. She asked me to take out any letters from either Laura or Obie and give them to her."

"That sounds like Mom."

"I was horrified and scared. I told her I'd be liable for federal prosecution if I were to do it. I told her she would be, too. She then asked me to take them out and destroy them. My mentioning the criminal thing probably scared her. I refused again. We went round and round about it. Finally, she reminded me that the post office job would only last as long as the war, and then I'd be out of a job. She assured me that if I were to do that little thing for her, she would see that I always had work."

"You sold out to her," Cassie said and was immediately sorry for the words.

Bernadette took out a clean tissue and blew her nose. Tears came. "I wish I could do it over. I was weak. I did great harm, and I'm sorry, but I'm trying to make it right."

"You are, Bernadette. You are."

"Do you think God will forgive me?"

"I'm sure he will."

"What about Laura and Obie? Will they forgive?"

Cassie answered honestly. "I don't know, Bernadette. I really don't. They both speak of being forgiving. But I don't believe either of them put it into practice the way they should."

"You're engaged to Obie, aren't you?"

"I am. We're to be married in September."

"So, in a way, it turned out okay . . . for you, I mean?"

"I guess, in that sense." She couldn't say what she was thinking, that the story still hadn't played out.

"And there's that handsome young man, Danny. If Laura hadn't married Ben Williamson, he wouldn't have been born."

Apparently, Bernadette didn't know about Dan's parentage. Her mother had kept the secret well. "Yes, there is Dan," Cassie said.

"Your mother and me have remained friends, but it's been an uneasy friendship, knowing about what we did. I've felt guilty. I'd never do it now. I was impressionable, and she was so strong and powerful, everything I wanted to be. She also offered me security. I did whatever she told me to do, and she took advantage of it. You know, she's still like that, except now everyone is pretty much on to her."

"Yes, Bernadette, I know what my mother is like."

"She came to see me a few days ago. There was something I always wanted to ask her but never had. I finally did, though. I asked why she even took the trouble to do what she did. What was so wrong with Obie that made her go to such lengths? She got really mad. Said he was trash. I said it hadn't done much good since her other daughter was going to marry Obie. She got madder and called me names. That was when I told her I was going to tell the truth. She told me not to tell anyone. She didn't threaten me, but I felt threatened, anyway."

"That's Mom. I'm sorry, Bernadette. She won't do anything."

Cassie was torn between anger at the woman who had done so much damage to her sister and Obie and wanting to thank her for telling the truth. She chose a middle position and said as she got up to leave, "You've done the right thing, Bernadette, even if destroying their letters was wrong, you're making up for it."

"Wait!" Bernadette said. She went into an adjacent room and soon came out with a large manila envelope. "Here, take this."

The envelope was fat and heavy. "What is it?" Cassie asked. She dared to hope.

"The letters. I couldn't destroy them. They're all there. I never opened a single one."

Cassie had come to Bernadette expecting to gain, at best, a partial explanation, or maybe none at all. Now, her emotions were mixed, knowing that, at last, she held in her hands proof that Obie had not deserted Laura.

CHAPTER TWENTY-NINE

July 1970

Cassie gave no explanation with either message, only a simple "Be at my house at eight this evening. Come prepared for enlightenment." She slipped one note under Laura's apartment door and put the other under the windshield wiper of Obie's station wagon after spotting it in Cam's Supermarket parking lot. She wasn't going to explain until they were all together.

Obie arrived first, and Laura a few minutes later; she looked pale. *She must have guessed the reason for her summons.* Obie's expression was one of puzzlement, but he said nothing. Cassie stood at one end of her dining room table, and Laura and Obie sat on opposite sides facing each other.

"Where's Julie?" Laura asked.

"I sent her over to Ken and Angie's."

It was Obie who asked the obvious question. "Cassie, what's this about?"

"We're going to end the animosity between you two, once and for all."

"That would be a significant accomplishment," Laura said. She was still resistant, but Cassie knew that would soon change.

"All will be revealed," Cassie replied as she turned to Obie. "You need to be brought up to date on this. Laura's going to tell you something that will astound you, so prepare yourself."

His smile was tense. "Not much fazes me. You should know that."

"Tell him, Laura."

"What am I supposed to tell him?"

"What we talked about. What you said he knows, but which he doesn't."

"What's the purpose of telling a rotten apple that it's rotten?"

Obie looked annoyed. "Tell me what?"

"He doesn't know, Laura. He *really* doesn't."

"Of course he does. But this is your show, so if it makes you feel better, you tell him."

"All right, I will!" Cassie bent close to Obie's ear and said softly, "Obie, you have a son."

He laughed. "Highly unlikely, unless maybe Annie had a child I didn't know about."

Laura groaned. "Stop it, Obie," she said. "How dare you keep up this everlasting pretense? You're going to face the facts and stop lying to Cassie."

Obie looked caustic. "Laura, I don't know what you're talking about." Toward Cassie, his tone was only a little gentler, "And I don't know what you're talking about, either. What do you mean, *I have a son?*"

"You know damn well what she means," Laura screeched.

"Laura," Cassie said, "be quiet!" Laura shrugged her shoulders. Her face was crimson. Cassie continued. "Obie, you *do* have a son, and he's someone you know well."

His eyes opened wider; he knew now that she was serious. "Impossible! I've not been . . ." His forehead furrowed, and she could see the question coming. *"Who?"* he demanded.

"Dan. Dan's your son."

She watched the color drain from his face as he turned from Cassie to Laura and back again. "This is for real, isn't it?" He asked Laura, "Is it true?"

"You know it is. Why do you keep pretending?"

He slapped the tabletop. "Pretending? Pretending? Damn it, Laura! You've kept this from me all this time! How could you?"

Cassie saw the pain in his eyes and touched his arm. "Obie, it's not Laura's fault. Nor is it yours. It's a huge misunderstanding brought about by a cruel act neither of you had knowledge of." As Cassie spoke, she took a stack of envelopes from a larger manila envelope she'd casually moved from floor to table. A wide rubber band held the bundle together.

"What is this, Cassie?" Laura demanded.

"Letters, Laura? They're letters. You know where I went this morning."

Laura's mouth was open. After a moment, she said, "Is this supposed to be some sort of proof that Obie didn't abandon me?" Even with her eyes still aflame, her words were subdued. Perhaps the truth was finally dawning.

Cassie removed the rubber band. "These were taken from the mail by Bernadette Simon." Laura gasped, and Obie leaned forward, his hands gripping the table's edge. "She admitted it to me. She's wanted to confess to you for some time. Yes, they're letters written by you both. They're letters that never reached you. They haven't even been opened."

"Dear Lord," Obie said.

Laura stared at the bundle; Cassie could see her confusion and feared she might faint. She felt compassion for them both.

She told them about her conversation with Bernadette that morning, sparing neither Bernadette nor their mother for the part each had played in the deception. Laura and Obie sat, appearing gaunt, neither looking at the other.

After Cassie finished her explanation, it was Laura who spoke first. "Are they really the letters we wrote?" She sounded as though she dreaded an answer.

Cassie felt pity; her sister's belief about Obie, so obviously wrong but thoroughly entrenched, would be painful to dislodge. "They *are* your letters."

"And they're unopened," Obie observed.

Laura said, "I can't even remember what I wrote. It was so long ago."

"I remember what I wrote," Obie said. "The content, at least, if not the words."

Cassie said, "I've arranged them by dates on the envelopes. I'll leave you two alone. After all, they're private, between the two of you."

Laura's seemed drained of energy. "No, please stay. You're part of this."

"Yes, stay," Obie said, not looking at either sister. "The first one is written by you, Laura. How do you want to do this, read it aloud or read it to yourself first?"

"Please, Cassie, I'd like you to read it aloud."

"All right," Cassie said. "The postmark is August 11, 1943."

"I didn't know I was pregnant then," Laura said softly, as though to herself.

As Cassie slit the envelope with a letter opener, she saw Laura look at Obie and quickly glance away as he turned toward her. Cassie read: *"Dear Obie, I have not felt well for several days. I probably ate some bad food, although no one else in the family was affected. I usually feel better in the afternoons. I stayed home from church Sunday. But enough of my complaints. What about you? How are you doing? You* mentioned a long march you were going on. Did that turn out all right? Your friend Matt sounds like a good guy. I too, hope you can stay together.

"Our mail system, with Beth's help, seems to be working quite well, although I can't wait to get to Smith so we can correspond more freely. I've already started packing. Mom is taking me to Saratoga Springs next week to shop. When you get out of basic on September 10th, come straight to me. As soon as I arrive, I'll send the details (address, dormitory phone number, etc.)

"Obie, my darling, I love you so. I can't wait for us to be together again. How am I ever going to study at college? Yours forever, Laura."

Cassie placed the letter on the table after she finished. She had stumbled through the last lines. "This is too personal," she said. "You two should do this together."

Obie still appeared dazed. "No, Cassie, read mine aloud. I want it all out in the open. You're a part of this, Sweetheart. I want Laura to know I didn't desert her. But that was then, and this is now. I just want things cleared up."

"I feel that way, too," Laura said. "Cassie, please, *you* read them."

"I may tear up while I'm doing it."

Cassie read an August thirteenth letter from Obie. He had spoken of love and declared near the end, *"I love you and could not ever love another."* She glanced at him; he was expressionless.

"Laura, your next letter was written the following day before you could have received Obie's answer." She scanned the content. "Oh dear . . . this is sad. Very sad."

"Read it," Laura said, sounding impatient.

Cassie read: *"Dear Obie, Oh, my Darling! The news I give you will, I hope, make you very happy. I am going to have a baby. Our baby! I found out today. Doctor Williamson has set a due date at about the middle of March. I did not dare say it to you in my letter a few days ago, but I think I already knew what he would say. I think Mom did too. I had missed two of my periods before I told her. She is heartbroken and has been in her bedroom crying since noon. Going to Smith is out of the question now. She made me promise not to tell Dad or Cassie. Regardless of the mean way Mom has kept us apart and, although I feel sorry to have brought this grief on her, I'm not ashamed to be carrying your child.*

"My Darling, I must know right away what to do. Please answer by return mail. We must make plans. I know you love me and will want us to marry. I know this is much quicker than you had planned, but we must consider our child. I'll come to you as soon as possible.

"I will be anxiously awaiting your reply to this letter. Does the Army make allowances for situations like this? Surely, they will give us a few hours together. With all the love I have. Laura."

Obie was clenching his jaws, and his expression was one Cassie had never seen before; it was pure pain.

Laura was crying. Obie's response was tortured. "It's true, then. You were pregnant, and I never knew."

"You'd have known if you'd tried harder," Laura said.

"Laura, please," Cassie said. "There's no blame in this for either of you."

"That remains to be seen."

Cassie ignored the remark. Changing a mindset so thoroughly absorbed over decades wasn't easy. "This next letter is also Laura's, written on August nineteenth, five days after the other one. You obviously hadn't received a reply from Obie. It would have been too soon to expect an answer anyway."

"Can you blame me for being impatient?"

"No, Laura, I do understand," Cassie said, not wanting to upset her further.

"Dearest Obie," Cassie read, *"I have waited anxiously for an answer to my letter. Please, please, my love, tell me that everything is all right. Tell me to hurry to you so we can become husband and wife. Why have you not answered my letter? I finally told Mom that you know about my condition. At first, she wanted to take me to Albany to someone we don't know. She says I'm bringing disgrace to the family.*

"Beth is a good friend and will keep our mail system a secret. I have not told Beth about my pregnancy. Besides the doctor, no one knows except Mom and me. I wanted to tell Cassie, and I may yet, but Mom says Cassie and Dad must never know. I don't know how she expects to keep it a secret. They will know, eventually, and by then, you and I will be married.

"Please, Obie, let me know how and when I can come to you. Maybe we can be married in one of the little Army chapels you told me about. I walk down to the park every evening to meet Beth. You can't imagine the disappointment each day I don't hear from you. I await, my Darling. Yours forever, Laura."

Cassie said, "This next one from Laura was written the next day, August twentieth. That's very soon."

"I remember," Laura said. "I talked Mom into being reasonable, or so I thought."

"Dear Obie," Cassie read, *"This is a quick note to give you wonderful news. Mom has agreed that we can marry. I'm not sure why she*

changed her mind, but she has been talking to Pastor Charles. If she told him of my condition, he might have convinced her. She has also seen Doctor Williamson several times to get some medicine for herself. She has been very nervous. Now nothing can stop us from being together. Please call me at home. You have our number. I wait anxiously, Laura."

Obie said, "I called you, Laura. Obviously, I didn't get this letter, but I called anyway. I was worried after not hearing from you. I talked to Cassie. Cassie, didn't you tell her?"

His words sounded too accusatory for Cassie's comfort. "Obie, don't you remember? You asked me not to. You said Laura might think you were checking on her . . . your exact words, I believe."

She watched Obie's face take on his familiar and sometimes frustrating pattern of introspection. Finally, after an uncomfortable length of time, he said, "Yes, I did say that. I made a big mistake, didn't I? It would have foiled Abigail's plan if I had asked you to tell Laura about my call."

"Maybe. Maybe not," was all Cassie could think to say. She opened the next envelope and was distressed after having glanced at it. Laura and Obie were having enough trouble dealing with this avalanche of Abigail's mischief. "You wrote this the same day, Laura. It's something you told me about a few days ago."

"Is it about my phone call?"

"It is. Obie needs to hear this. I'm sorry if it hurts."

"Read it, please."

Cassie read: *"I am devastated and can only imagine some terrible mistake. Right after posting the letter to you, I decided to call you instead. Mom was supportive and made the call herself. I sat next to her this afternoon while she talked to one of your officers and asked him to go and find you. We waited ten minutes while he looked for you. When he finally returned with your message that you didn't wish to speak to me, I thought the world had ended, and for me, I fear it has. Oh, Obie, how could you do this? How can you desert me?"*

Obie interrupted. "I never received any such call, Laura. Believe me . . . I didn't."

"She knows that now, Obie," Cassie said. "Mom made her think they were talking to someone at your Army post. They weren't, of course."

"Keep reading, Cassie," Laura said without looking at either.

Cassie continued, *"Please, Obie, if there has been a mistake, please call me immediately. If there has been no mistake and you really do intend to desert me, I want you to tell me why. Does our pledge to each other mean nothing to you? Oh, Obie, please, please call me. Laura."*

Cassie had made a pot of coffee before their arrival and suggested a break. "No, finish this," Laura said. Obie agreed with a nod.

"Obie wrote a letter on August twenty-first. It's short, but it shows his worry."

Cassie tried not to hurry. *"I have not heard from you for a week and a half. I would not be worried, except you usually write two or three times a week. Are you sick, my love? I love your letters so much. I love you and worry when I don't hear.*

"Only three weeks to go in basic training. We have been overly busy. Dad wrote the other day. He said he sees you occasionally. Please write soon. With love always, Obie."

Cassie went straight to Laura's next correspondence, written on August twenty-third. It had the same information Laura had recently given Cassie about going to Doctor Williamson's office, thinking they would discuss her pregnancy. Near the end, she wrote, *"Ben Williamson wants to marry me. He proposed with my mother sitting right there. I was horrified. I ran from the room. Mom followed and called me all kinds of names. She accused me of ruining the one chance for a good life for the baby and me and for saving the family's honor. I am so very angry at you, Obie. You have turned out to be a coward. How could you do this to me, to us? Never to be yours again, Laura."*

Cassie could see tears in Obie's eyes. "I'm sorry, Laura," he said.

She answered without looking up, "You needn't be. I see now that you weren't to blame."

Obie's next letter was written on August twenty-eighth and contained phrases such as, *"I cannot imagine why you have not written for three weeks"* and *"Did I say something to offend you? I would cut out my tongue or cut off my writing hand before purposely saying anything that would hurt you."* The end of his letter revealed his desperate search for the reason behind her failure to write. *"If you are just busy with preparations for going away to school, it will relieve my mind. If you are sick or something like that, I need to know about it. Please, dear Laura, please write, if only a short note to tell me everything is all right. All my love, forever, Obie."*

There were only a few letters remaining. Cassie had been

standing the whole time and realized her legs were trembling. She took a seat in a chair at the end of the table.

After previewing the next letter, she feared it would upset Obie. Nevertheless, she proceeded. *"September first. Dear Obie, you are probably not interested at all, but I thought it the right thing to write this letter. I have given in and decided to marry Ben Williamson. He has visited the house a few times, and I have gotten to know him better. I don't love him and never could. I've told him that, and he is still willing to marry me. That alone says something about him. He has some strange ways, but it is something I will get used to, I guess."*

Obie's words, quickly spoken, revealed annoyance. "September first? That's only a little over two weeks from when you discovered you were pregnant." He slapped the table. "Do you mean to tell me you gave up on me in two weeks?" he slumped back into his chair.

"That's not fair," Laura said.

Cassie interceded. "She was desperate. Don't get angry at the wrong person, Obie. Keep in mind who caused all this hurt?"

Obie looked contrite. "Yes, you're right. Abigail's to blame. I'm sorry, Laura." Then, to Cassie, he said, "Please read the rest of it."

She read, *"Ben is going to set up a practice in Boston, and the plan is for us to get married next Monday, September sixth. Pastor Charles will marry us at our house without anyone there except my family, and we'll leave for Boston right away. Mom's plan is to give the baby a birth date different from and after the real one."* Cassie paused. "She was protecting the family's precious honor."

Cassie continued reading. *"During all this, Dad and Cassie have been kept from knowing what is really going on. Both are surprised at my choice. Dad takes it in stride and gives us his blessing, but Cassie is fit to be tied. She asks over and over why I'm doing this. I don't explain because I can't. Dad and Cassie will never know the truth unless you tell them, and I doubt you will.*

"I am at a loss to know what to say to you, Obie. Only you can answer why you have chosen to let this happen to us. Your actions are the most unkind and un-Christian actions I've ever seen. I'll say it to you in a language you might understand. You have much to answer for to our Lord and Savior.

"Yet, even now, there is time if you change your mind. If not, I will indeed become the wife of Doctor Benjamin Williamson."

Tension in the dining room was still high, and Cassie felt the need to get through the remaining three letters quickly; she went straight to Laura's September third letter. It was short. *"Obie, my darling, Please call me. Please change your mind and let me come to you. Think of all our dreams, the life together we planned. You said you wanted children. Don't you want your own child to love and protect? Please call me, Obie. It's not yet too late, but it will be soon. In spite of it all, I still love you. Laura."*

Cassie held up an envelope, one of two left. "This is from you, Obie. It's dated September fourth and was the last letter you wrote."

"Let me see it first," he said.

He spent a minute reading silently. "I remember writing it," he said as he handed it back. "Please read it. I want Laura to hear it."

"Dear Laura," Cassie read, *"This will be the busiest week of basic training. It is also the last. I cannot say all I have to say in this letter. Some things I must save for when I see you in person. I will see you, won't I? My mind has been in turmoil. I don't know why you have stopped writing, Laura. I only know I have not wavered in my love for you. It is as strong as it ever was. If you have stopped loving me for whatever reason, I hope you will allow me to redeem myself from whatever wrong I have done.*

"I have a confession. I telephoned your house some time ago and talked to Cassie. If she didn't tell you, please do not blame her because I made her promise not to. I am glad I called because I learned that you have no serious illness or anything like that. Cassie did seem a little concerned about your frame of mind. I have decided that you would have told Cassie if anything serious was the matter.

"I'll go ahead and carry out the plan we agreed on. I will leave on Friday, the 10th, for Northampton. I already have my bus ticket. I'll arrive about noon the next day. It will be on a Saturday, so you should have no classes and can meet me at the bus station. We can be together for a few hours, and if there are any problems between us, we can straighten them out.

"If something is bothering you, we can overcome it. Our love is stronger than any obstacles. I love you so much that sometimes I cannot stand it. Dear Laura, I look forward to seeing your beautiful face at the Northampton bus station. All my Love, Obie."

Laura spoke, and her voice was soft. "I'm sorry too, Obie. You wrote a beautiful letter to me. You didn't go to Northampton, did you?"

"No, I never made it there."

Cassie observed the eye contact between them, chilling her heart. She went quickly to the last letter, one from Laura to Obie, dated September fifth, 1943. "This won't take long she said, holding up a page with only a couple of lines. She read, *"By the time you get this letter I will be married to Ben Williamson. Obie, I hope you burn in Hell."*

Cassie folded that last letter and put it back into its envelope. She could barely see through eyes that threatened to become opened floodgates at any moment. She had watched them as she read and now tried to gauge their feelings. Obie sat with his chair tilted back; his eyes were closed. Laura rocked back and forth, tears coming freely. Her mouth was frozen in a frown. They didn't look at each other.

Cassie said, "I'm not sure why Bernadette saved these letters, but I hope you won't be too angry at her. I believe she's a decent person. I think that, subconsciously, she knew this day would come."

Cassie waited. Obie put his head in his hands with elbows resting on the table. "I don't know what to say." His voice was a scratchy whisper.

Laura rose and walked to the dining room window. The window faced Blackberry Hill, and she stared toward it, although it was dark outside.

Cassie was drained of emotion. After years of wondering, suspecting—all the answers were now revealed in an explosion of evidence. She couldn't imagine how Obie and Laura must feel. She wanted to say something, anything, to start a conversation. "Well, does this finally clear things up?" she asked.

Laura's reaction was unexpected. She whirled from the window. "Why did you do it, Cassie? Why have you brought all this out now?" She sobbed.

"I did it so that the truth would be known."

"For what? To tell us about what we've missed? That nearly thirty years of our lives have been a lie . . . that no matter what we do, we can't get them back? Tell me, Cassie, how would *you* feel?"

Cassie was shocked. "You'd rather not have known?"

Laura returned to the table but didn't sit. "Yes! It would have been better not to have known." She looked down at Obie, who raised his eyes for the first time since Cassie had finished reading. "What about you, Obie," Laura asked. "Is this good news to you?"

"I'm glad you know that I didn't desert you."

"In that, you've been vindicated. Fine. You're blameless. We both are. Cassie's right. It was a big misunderstanding. Mom wronged us. But tell me, how does it help us to know the truth? Does it make us better persons for grieving about what never was?"

"I don't intend to grieve. That's a waste of time."

"Aren't you a little bit angry?"

"Very much so, and I hate all the years I believed the worst of you. However, I'm not going to grieve." Obie stood. "Over the years, I've forgiven you several times, but I still remained angry at you. At Abigail too, but angriest at you. It seems my anger was directed at the wrong person. Now I've gained a clear objective for my hate."

"Our mother?"

"That's right. It's not that I haven't loathed her for something else she did, but this is beyond my comprehension." He swept a hand toward the letters on the table.

"She's an old, misguided individual," Laura said.

Cassie didn't hide her disgust. "Mom is evil, Laura. She deserves contempt."

"She's still our mother."

"Well, I no longer claim her as such."

Laura turned again to Obie. "I'm curious about something. When you left to join the Army, you said you were leaving because you wanted to protect my honor, that if you stayed, people would think ill of me because of us spending time alone together. It wasn't a satisfactory explanation. Was that what you *really* meant?"

"Laura, I never said that. *You* did. You said your mother told you that. I never told you why I left."

"Well, please do.

They listened as Obie told them about the confrontation with their mother in the barnroom after she caught Obie and Laura together and about the threats she made toward him and his father. "She told me she'd have Dad murdered if I didn't leave Stafford Rest."

"I was wondering what you meant by the remark you made a few minutes ago about 'loathing' her," Cassie said. "You have reason for that alone. I'll never speak to her again." Cassie placed her hands on Obie's arm to empathize the sincerity of her declaration. *"Never!"*

Laura said, "Were those her actual words, that she'd have Ken murdered if you didn't leave?"

"It's exactly what she said. I was afraid of her. I thought she meant it. It was, I'm sure, just an idle threat, but when you're seventeen and just been caught . . ."

"I understand," Laura said quickly.

Something occurred to Cassie. "Laura, Dad believes the worst of Obie. Will you talk to him? I guess you don't need to tell him about the letters. That would break his heart. Let him know Obie didn't desert you."

"I'll talk to him," Laura said.

Alternating in the telling, Cassie and Laura informed Obie about how the deception was carried out and of Dan's actual birth date.

"Who knows about all this, that I'm . . . that Dan's my son?"

Laura said, "The people still alive are Mom, Dad, Ben, Cassie, some clerk in Boston who doesn't care, and now you. That's all, and I want it to stay that way."

"What about Charles? Pastor Charles? You said in your letter that your mother went to see him. And he married you and Ben. Is it possible he knew?"

"I don't believe so. I saw him several times. I would have known if he knew."

"Do you really want to keep this from Dan?"

"Yes, he must not know."

"Do you think that's fair to Dan . . . or to me?"

"Fair? I hardly know what the word means at this point. His life, his name, it's all he's ever known. I'm not sure how he'd feel about it. It's better he not know, don't you think?"

Obie didn't answer the question. Instead, he said, "For nearly thirty years I've had a son I knew nothing about. Of course, this tragedy is no fault of ours, but I'd like Dan to know that I'm his father. I believe he can accept it. He might even welcome it."

Laura stomped her foot. "No, no, no! That will never do. Hasn't there been enough pain? Why cause more?"

"What if I chose to tell him, anyway?"

"You'd be, in truth, the insensitive man I believed you were for all these years."

"I'm not. You know that."

She grabbed his arm. He put a hand on hers. Her voice became softer. "I know. I know now. Please, Obie, I beg you. Don't tell him. You loved me then when he was conceived, and I loved you. To honor that, please promise me you'll not tell Dan."

They appeared to have forgotten Cassie's presence, looking at each other for what felt like a full minute. Then, finally, Obie looked away. "All right, Laura, I'll not tell him."

"Thank you, Obie. I truly thank you. I know you'll keep your word."

"I think I deserve to know more about all those missed years. Do you have photographs?"

"I do, all through his growing years and into adulthood. I'll let you take them to look at."

"Can we sit down together? I want you to tell me all about him."

Laura looked at Cassie. The request was reasonable. Why did she feel threatened? Cassie nodded her consent.

Laura said, "You can come to my apartment, or I can go to your house."

Cassie was ready to suggest they return to her house, but Obie said, "My place if you don't mind. I have some photographic equipment I can use to make copies."

"I'd rather you didn't make copies."

"All right, no copies, but bring them all. I want to see everything I've missed."

"Tomorrow afternoon? Will that be all right?"

"Fine."

Laura glanced at Cassie again. Cassie tried making her face expressionless.

CHAPTER THIRTY

July 1970

Obie slept fitfully. Events at Cassie's house were so momentous that he could think of little else. *He had a son. Dan was his son.* They'd spent time together and connected, but he'd not suspected.

In hindsight, he should have seen clues: Their meeting in Vietnam was so unlikely that Obie wondered if it might have been foreordained. Other events in his life had caused him to consider such things. Dreams, too, had been markers.

But there had been no dreams about Dan. So why would he have dreams about other far less significant matters and not about something as important as this?

During the night, he alternated between elation over the turn of events and anger about Abigail's abominable actions. He fought to keep the latter from prevailing; since his arrival in Stafford Rest, he'd controlled his emotions by simply avoiding her. He knew all about the sinkhole of hate, having experienced it in himself and others, but now he seemed unable to move back from its edge. The next time he saw Abigail, he would confront her.

He worked around the house all morning to fill the time before Laura's arrival. Anxiety about her visit intensified. After wolfing down a ham and cheese sandwich at noon, he called Cassie.

"I want you here, too," he said.

"Obie, this is a time for you and Laura to share. I'm not a part of it."

He detected unease. "You *are* a part of it. And you're an amazing woman. You kept digging after the truth until you found it."

"You were both diverted by mistrust, although 'mistrust' is too mild a word in this case. You needed someone to intervene. I should have stepped in a long time ago."

"I'm happy you finally did. Cassie, you're the most important person in my life, and I'd like you here, too. Laura will arrive in about half an hour."

"No, Obie, this time is for the two of you. You must talk. Talk to Laura, and then come back to me."

"Do you think I'm going away somewhere?"

"Sorry, I'm in a mood, I guess. Call me tonight, please." She hung up.

He went to sit on the screened-in front porch to wait. He watched Laura's new white Caddy turn in Cedar Creek Road from Main Street. It was out of sight for half a minute before reappearing over the crest of a rise a hundred yards below his house. He went out to meet her when she pulled in behind his car. She took a cardboard box from the back seat.

Considering all that had transpired, Obie wasn't sure what her frame of mind would be. But nevertheless, he was pleased and a little surprised to see her smile. As he took the box from her, she kissed him on the cheek, then turned away, looking embarrassed. "My, how things have changed here. You've done a marvelous job, Obie."

He regained his composure. "A lot of work, but it's been worth it. I'll show you around later."

"The barn looks pretty much the same, at least from the outside."

"I left it alone, for the most part. Use it as a studio for painting and photography. This spring, I did put electricity and water out there. I also closed off one little corner for a dark room. Otherwise, the barnroom is about the same." He opened a door onto the porch for her. "It's a nice day. Do you mind if we sit out here?"

"Not at all. This is pleasant. This was an open wooden porch, wasn't it? I believe you've made it larger, though. I like the flagstone floor."

After several minutes of small talk about the house and the weather, she withdrew photograph albums from the box. For the next hour, Laura led Obie through significant events in their son's life. After she closed the last album, she said, "I'll leave them with you for a few days if you like."

"Thank you. I want to go through them all again."

"You'll keep them concealed, won't you? I know Dan comes here. He'd wonder why you have them. And please don't copy them, Obie."

"I promised you that I'd not make copies. And I'll put the

albums where he won't see them."

"You liked Dan, didn't you, even before you knew?"

"I did. He's intelligent and sensitive."

She laughed. "I just had a startling thought. We're grandparents."

"No doubt."

There was suddenly sadness in her voice. "A child we'll probably never know. Obie, is there any chance Ly Yen will be found? She's the love of Dan's life. He grieves for her every day."

"I expect you're right about his feelings for her. But Vietnam was, and is, a dangerous place. We may never know what happened to them."

"Do you think they might not have survived?"

"I didn't mean to imply that. I meant that the country is in such turmoil that people are displaced. It's hard to tell where she might be. It's my guess they're all right, and I say that because she's a resourceful young woman. I've given Dan some help. Advice mostly. There are still a few roads we haven't explored."

"I'm sure he'll appreciate it, but please be careful what you say. I don't want him to suspect that . . . ."

"Laura, I'll handle it with care, but there *is* something." The thought had come during the night. "Dad deserves to know he has a grandson, don't you think?"

She appeared to consider. "I don't know, Obie. Would he keep it to himself? He drinks, doesn't he? He hates my mother. He might enjoy hurting her."

"Dad hasn't had a drink for nearly thirty years. There's indeed no love lost between him and Abigail, but he'll keep that secret, as I will."

"He'll tell Angie."

"Yes, he probably will. She's trustworthy, Laura." He wasn't one hundred percent sure about Angie's secret-keeping ability, but he wouldn't tell that to Laura.

"All right, I guess. Just make him understand how important this is. And please tell him how all this came about. I don't want him thinking any less of me than he already does."

They'd been sitting together on the glider. He moved to a chair facing her. She was still beautiful, even with the few streaks of grey hair. She wasn't dyeing it. Worry lines on her forehead and around her mouth showed maturity, but her skin appeared as satin smooth as ever. If she had gained more than a few pounds, it didn't show.

"Would you like to see the rest of the house?" he asked.

The tour didn't take long. "It's lovely," she said after they returned to the porch.

"It's still a small house."

"You don't need much space, do you?"

"No, and I kept it that way for a reason. A simple life is what I've desired. However, it might be too small after Cassie and I are married."

"So, the three of you are going to live here?"

"Yes, I plan to add a couple more rooms. We could get by, but a little more space would help."

"Obie, I want to see the barnroom."

His stomach churned. He'd hoped she wouldn't ask for that. Nevertheless, he couldn't ignore her request. "All right."

"If you'd rather not."

"No, it's okay."

He led the way across the lawn between the house and barn. As soon as they entered, she said, "It still smells the same, like hay and new wood, a nutty smell. Isn't it strange how some things stay with you even after such a long time?"

"It is." He believed it best not to expound on his memories of the youthful intimacy they'd shared in the room.

"I see you've finished several paintings." She examined canvases stacked against the wall. "You're a gifted artist."

"It's only a hobby, and I've found some time to paint recently."

"I'm glad, Obie." She grabbed his hand. "And, I'm glad this has happened . . . that we've learned the truth. What I said last night was just a reaction to the suddenness of everything. I won't grieve, either. I'll always wonder what might have been, but I'll not grieve."

Even aware that he should pull his hand away, he didn't. She turned toward him. "Obie," she said, lifting her face up to him, "Hold me, will you? Hold me close . . . just for a moment."

"Laura, we shouldn't."

"Please, Obie, for a moment."

He held her in his arms and tried to think clearly; he must put her feel and scent out of his mind. Her forehead rested on his chest, and her eyes held tears when she looked up at him again. Then, before he could turn his head, she kissed him. Her lips on his were as familiar as breathing. He lingered a moment instead of breaking away, and she melted farther into his arms.

"Oh, Obie," she whispered, "I never thought that . . ."

He pulled back. "Laura, we can't do this." He was gentle as he pushed her away.

"Yes, you're right," she said, making nervous motions, smoothing her blouse. "I'm sorry, Obie."

"It's just the emotion for what's happened in the past few hours," he said, hoping the explanation would suffice.

He loved Cassie. He was going to marry Cassie. How could he have let himself enjoy that, even if it had been only for a moment?

"Yes, that's it," Laura said. "It's just the emotion."

He needed to be firm. "I'm engaged to Cassie. I love her, Laura. I do."

Laura changed her demeanor. "I know. I'd murder you if you ever hurt her." She turned toward the door. "I should be going. You can leave the photographs at Cassie's, and I'll pick them up there sometime."

"Fine." As they walked out, he said, "Are you going to tell your mother that she's been found out . . . that we know what she did?"

"Oh, she already knows. I called her this morning. I also told her I wouldn't come to her house again. I want nothing more to do with her. It'll upset Dad, but I've made up my mind. She's reprehensible."

"Be careful, Laura. Bitterness can bite you." He remembered an old saying about the pot calling the kettle black and questioned what right he had to give such advice.

She picked up on the inconsistency. "Who are you to talk, anyway? Last night you said you had someone else to hate, implying that Mom is your new target. Shouldn't you follow your own advice?"

"I won't let my feelings for her wreck my life. I'll get her out of my head." But even as he said it, he knew it was a lie; he had no intention of forgetting Abigail's sins against them.

"And I'm simply putting something ugly out of my life," she said as she got in the car and started the engine. He leaned in the window. She placed a hand on his. "Promise me something?" she said.

"It seems like I'm making a lot of promises."

"They're important promises. Please don't tell Cassie about that . . ."

"Lapse of sanity?" Obie interjected.

"Yes, that nails it, I guess."

"Don't worry. I've already decided not to say anything."

* * *

That evening, Obie and Cassie went to Saranac Lake for dinner. He was thankful she asked no specific questions about what transpired during his time with Laura. He wouldn't lie, but if she never asked, he would remain silent. He avoided her eyes while volunteering safe information about their meeting. Nevertheless, keeping something from Cassie made him feel guilty. He wouldn't put himself in such a position again.

They ate a leisurely breakfast following an overnight stay at Saranac Lake. It was after eleven o'clock when Obie dropped Cassie off at her house. On arriving home, he was surprised to find Dan's pickup in his driveway.

Dan sat on the porch, which was never locked. For a moment, Obie panicked. The photograph albums were in the box in a corner. What if Dan had seen them? Laura would never believe it was accidental. He walked close enough to see they were undisturbed. A part of him was relieved. Another part wished Dan had seen them. Did anyone have a right to demand he not tell his son the truth?

Dan sat on the chaise longue, one foot on the floor. His other leg stretched out full length. He was more than six feet tall. Obie saw him in a new way. He had observed Laura's likeness in his eyes and expressions but realized that seeing Dan was like looking in a mirror in many ways. Their hair and complexions were the same. They had essentially the same body build.

"Where have you been?" Dan asked as he put down a book he'd apparently been reading. "I've been here over an hour."

"Where I've been is no business of yours."

"I know, anyway. You and Cassie have been away. Am I correct?"

"I repeat, it's none of your business."

Dan smiled. "I was in the Diamond Inn last night, and

Chuck Hinky told me you two had gone to Saranac Lake. I thought you'd have been back sooner."

"I'm still getting used to everybody knowing my business," Obie said.

"You and me, both," Dan said with a grin.

Obie sat on the glider. "You don't usually come up here this early. What's up?"

"I'd like you to go to Plattsburgh with me. I'm flying there to pick up a professor and his wife from New Jersey. They drove up the Northway. They're looking for a summer place, isolated, something on a lake. I have three or four locations in mind. I want to give them a personal touch. Having you along will ensure that the conversation doesn't lag. Give you a break away from the routine, too."

"I'm in. Sounds like an interesting thing to do." Although nothing could ever make up for the time lost, from this day on he intended to seize every opportunity to be near Dan

Dan said on the way through town, "I forgot to give Grandmother some papers she needs to sign. She's been sick and hasn't been in the office for a couple of days. It'll only take a minute to stop by there."

Obie kept quiet. There was no place in Stafford Rest he would rather avoid. He hoped Dan's 'minute' would be just that.

It was the first time he'd been on Hunt property since he was seventeen.; it made him uncomfortable. Dan went inside through a door that led to the kitchen if he remembered the house layout correctly. The door no sooner closed than the garage door opened and Abigail's car started backing out. With Dan's pickup blocking her way, she had to stop. Obie's fear became a reality when she got out and walked to the driver's side of the truck.

"Danny," she said as she leaned down to peer inside. She saw Obie but didn't display immediate recognition. "Excuse me. I was looking for my grandson." She stopped and said, *"You!* What are *you* doing here?"

He said what felt safest. "Dan's inside looking for you."

"What are you doing with Danny?" She jerked her hands from the door and took a step back. She wagged a finger at him. "I know precisely what you're doing. You're going to tell him, aren't you? And everybody else? You're going to drag our names through the mud so that you can tell him his mother be-haved like a slut and his grandmother acted to protect her? Isn't that it?" Her voice trailed off; she had run out of breath.

Obie tried to remain calm. His anger at her hadn't less-ened, but he wanted to manage it. The last thing he needed was to get into a confrontation with Abigail in Dan's presence; he'd do that at his convenience.

"I don't intend telling anyone outside our families. I've given my word."

"*Your word?* Then, all is lost."

He was surprised at how calmly he could say, "Abigail, you've become so used to disparaging me that you forget it was you and not I who caused all this."

"*I* caused it? Tell me, Obie, who was it that violated my daughter? Who was it who got her pregnant?"

He leaned toward the driver's side window. "I don't deny that some blame falls on me, but there's a bigger issue. You stole from me and from your daughter. You caused us to believe the worst of each other. You caused me to wait thirty years to find out I have a son. And you've tried breaking up Cassie and me. You have no right to talk in such a way." He slid back to the passenger side.

Obie heard her breathing hard as she stood up straight. He couldn't see her face. "Wait until Pinky hears about this, she said."

"Pinky has learned the truth, Abigail."

"Truth? I have truth on my side!"

"Your version of the truth and mine are as far apart as North is from South."

Dan came out the side door of the house at that moment, a puzzled expression on his face. "What's the matter, Grand-mother?" he asked as he approached the truck. "Why are you trembling?"

"This man has insulted me," she said.

"Grandmother, I don't believe Obie would do that. You must be mistaken."

"No, I'm not mistaken. He called me a liar."

Dan put his head in the window. "Obie, what's going on?"

"I'm sorry, Dan, it's a misunderstanding. It's nothing."

Dan looked at Abigail, then back at Obie. "I know you two don't get along. I figure it's something about Mom. Am I right?"

Abigail's horrified face betrayed her fear. Obie felt satisfaction. It now fell to her to steer Dan away from the subject. Obie wasn't going to help her. If she had to make revelations, it would serve her right and maybe pave the way for letting Dan learn the truth. Although he'd promised Laura that he wouldn't tell Dan, that didn't mean he'd not want him to know.

Abigail was no amateur in hiding the truth. "Danny," she said, her voice now mushy, "This involves something else entirely. It's not anything I should have become so upset about. Mister Gainsworthy and I rub each other the wrong way. We'll never agree on anything, it appears. That's just the way it is. So there's no real harm done, is there, Mister Gainsworthy?"

She had paved an easy road out of the situation, one Obie knew he had to take, but he couldn't help saying, "Nevertheless, I'll have to consider what to do with the information I've recently acquired." She could stew about his meaning.

Dan was quiet on the way down the hill to the marina. Later, in the floatplane, while taxiing toward the beach to turn for a takeoff, he said through the intercom, "What was that all about? Why was Grandmother so upset? You evidently said something to her."

"We had words, Dan. We were angry."

"Obie, as good friends as you and I are, I'm damned if I'm going to let you insult her."

"I didn't insult her."

"What's going on? Why all this anger? I believed things would improve when you and Mom started talking. What's the information you said you'd acquired? I'd like to know what happened between you and my family. Will you tell me?"

"Your mother and I are fine, Dan. What happened today with Abigail was just something left over from old hurts. I think it'll be okay." It never would be, and the white lie would not make things easier.

Dan wasn't deterred. "I repeat, will you tell me what it's all about?"

"No, I can't, Dan. I'd like to, but I can't."

"Yes, you can. Just open your mouth and say the words."

Obie grimaced as Dan swung the Cessna around. He wanted to blurt out the truth. Instead, he formed the words in his mind. *"Dan, you're my son, my flesh and blood. I love you."* He said aloud, "I've given my word. I hope you understand."

"Given your word to who?"

"It's best I not say."

Dan pushed the throttle forward and as quickly yanked it back. The engine returned to idle, and they slowed in the water. "Obie, I'm annoyed as hell. You're not even a part of my family, at least not yet, and here you are telling me you know things about them that you're not willing to divulge. Wouldn't that piss you off?"

"It would, but that's how it is, and you're sounding like a spoiled child."

"On the other hand, you're treating me like a child. I'm an adult, and I'm entitled to know what's going on."

"Ask your grandmother. She has all the secrets."

Dan grabbed Obie's forearm. His grip was like iron. "Man-to-man, Obie, what's it all about?"

"I can't say."

"Then you're not my friend."

"That's childish of you, withholding friendship simply because you can't have your way."

"I believe I'm justified in feeling that way."

"You brought up the man-to-man thing. Part of being a man is keeping your word. I've given my word. I consider it an obligation to God and man."

Dan's face was red. "There you go again, hiding behind God. You do it all the time. You use God as an easy out for justifying things Obie Gainsworthy has already decided to do."

"I'm not sure what you mean?"

"You talk about belief and faith as though they were things you shed and pick up again on a whim. You were a Methodist minister, and then you weren't. You were a chaplain, and then you weren't. You believe in God, then you . . ."

"Dan, I believe in God. Firmly. My faith has never wavered in that respect."

"That may be true, but you do have to admit that you change to fit your circumstances. You have no right to hide behind that obligation to God talk."

"Well, I'm still not telling you."

As they drifted back toward the beach, Dan said, "Obie, our friendship seems to mean little to you. So maybe you'd better get out."

Obie hoped Dan wasn't serious. One look at his face told

him otherwise. The younger man clenched and unclenched his jaw.

"Fine," Obie said. "Are you taking me back to the dock, or do I wade ashore?"

"Take your pick."

Obie unhooked his harness, opened the door, and stepped out onto a pontoon. For a moment, wash from the idling propeller took his breath away. Dan's expression was one of surprise. He yelled at Obie over the engine noise, "Don't be silly! I'll take you back. Hang on."

Obie gave him a dismissive wave and stepped into the water. It was warm and came only halfway up his thighs. By the time he had waded onto the beach, the Cessna had lifted into the air and was nearly out of sight.

* * *

Obie walked home. His pants were nearly dry when he got there, although his sneakers still made a sloshing sound. He didn't know whether he should be angry or sad. He wanted to tell Dan the truth and was sure he would welcome the news, yet he was prevented by a promise he'd made to protect "Hunt family honor." *What honor?* The whole idea was beginning to gall.

Cassie called later that afternoon. "I'm coming over," she said, sounding urgent.

"Sweetheart, I'm warning you. I'm not in the best of moods."

"Neither am I. I'll be there in five minutes."

Even from a distance, he saw her anger. She walked toward the house with a resolute stride.

"Am I in trouble with you, too?" he asked as she entered."

She flopped onto the glider. "Obie, I'm disgusted with you and . . . what do you mean, 'me too?'"

"I had a verbal battle, brief but acidic, with your mother. Then Dan and I quarreled about it."

"What were you doing talking to my mother?"

He told her what had happened at Garnet Point and on the lake. She listened, but he could see she still seethed; she had something else on her mind.

"Obie," she said, "I know what happened yesterday between you and Laura. You didn't tell me, but she did."

"Oh!" he managed. He was afraid his face would display his shame. "Cassie, I'm sorry."

"Are you still in love with her?"

He looked into her eyes. They displayed hurt, like a puppy that had been disciplined. "No. No, Cassie. It just happened, a spontaneous act. It won't happen again. Please believe me."

"I'd like to. The thing is, I don't think you know your own mind when it comes to Laura."

"That's not true. I love you. Only you."

"So, tell me, why did you take her into the barnroom when you knew the place held old memories?"

"She asked me to. Cassie. It was an innocent kiss. I pulled away at once."

"Are you saying you're no longer attracted to her?"

He was on shaky ground. She would know if he were anything but truthful. "No," he said, "I can't say that. Memories were revived, but only for a moment. I remembered you, and I stopped."

"Too bad you didn't remember *me* sooner."

"I'm sorry, Cassie." He studied her face for signs of forgiveness. "Why did she tell you, anyway? She asked me not to say anything."

"As if you would. I don't know why she told me. We were having coffee this morning, and she blurted it out as though it was the most natural thing to have happened. I pretended I didn't care, but I did. And I do."

He went to sit beside her. As he put an arm around her shoulders, she drew back. He said, "Please, Cassie, Laura no longer means anything like that to me. I don't know why she told you."

She turned her head away. "Why don't you ask her yourself?" she said.

"I'd better stay away from her."

"No, Obie. That won't do. I think the reason she told me was to give me a warning. I know Laura. I believe she wants you back."

"Cassie, that's preposterous. I have no such interest in Laura, and I'm sure it's the same with her."

She stood and said, "Obie, there are too many questions to give my mind any rest. I don't want you to avoid Laura. On the contrary, I want you to see her. Please get this settled between you. I want us to be together, but it can't happen until you work it out. She'd always be there between us. So get her out of your system, or realize you still love her. After all, you two have more in common than you and I do."

"Sweetheart, please! Our marriage is in two months."

"I'm postponing it, Obie. You have new options now. You're free to take a good hard look at them."

She ran out the door and toward her jeep. He followed. She slid under the steering wheel, started the engine, and was gone in seconds. Obie stood in the middle of the road as the car disappeared over the hill.

CHAPTER THIRTY-ONE

July 1970

Obie worked on several projects, moving with short bursts of energy: He painted; he worked in the garden; he tightened an outline for his new book; he mowed the lawn. But, whatever the activity, his thoughts seldom strayed beyond the bounds of his new and troubling situation.

For three days, he periodically dialed Cassie's telephone number. As soon as he spoke, she hung up. On one call, she told him quickly, "It's too soon." Finally, on the fourth day, he gave up; she could call him. Her driveway wasn't visible from his house, so he couldn't see if her jeep was parked there. He tried watching the road for it to leave. He would follow her and effect a "chance meeting."

After a week of fruitless observation, he decided to go and talk some sense into her. Her jeep was gone. Across the fence, Ken told him that Cassie and Julie had been gone several days.

"Did she say where she was going?"

"Syracuse, to see her aunt who's been hospitalized."

"Did she say when she'd return?"

"Nope."

Angie came outside. "Come on over, Obie. I'm fixing lunch. There's enough."

He hadn't told them about Dan, but this was an opportunity. Anyway, he needed company. While they ate a simple meal of soup, salad, and homemade bread, Obie considered how best to break the news.

Before he could speak, Ken asked, "What's going on this time with you and Cassie?"

Obie decided to disclose the whole jumble of recent events, even if it meant sharing hurtful emotions. After pushing his plate back, he told them everything—even about kissing Laura. His words came so fast that Ken made him slow down. Angie sat at the table with her hands clasped, her terse smile never changing. Ken's expression alternated between anger and amazement as Obie told them about the letters and Dan's parentage. When he finished, he waited for their reaction.

"Well," Angie said, "You'd better have some more mine-strone. You're going to need lots of strength."

Ken shook his head in disbelief. "So Dan's my grandson? *Good!* And to think I saw him around here when he was a kid but never really spoke to him then. Well, well!"

Obie told them about the encounter with Dan in Vietnam and about meeting Ly Yen. "So, Dad, you also have a great-grandchild."

"Which we'll probably never see."

"Ken, you don't know that," Angie said. "Such coincidence? Surely, God has a hand in all this. He'll lead us to this girl and her child. You'll see."

"Maybe," Ken said. He turned to Obie. "So, Laura was innocent in all this? I'll have to revise my opinion of her, I guess. But I still think she's a lot like her mother."

"Laura's a good woman, Dad. You need to get over it."

Ken ignored the rebuke. "The Hunt saga never ends, does it? That old witch sure messed things up for you and Cassie . . . and for Laura, too. But you know what? Except for not knowing about Dan all these years, it may have been a good thing."

"How do you figure?"

"You'd of married Laura and ended up miserable."

"Dad, I don't know how it might have turned out, nor do you. But I do know we can't go back and do anything over. We need to move on."

"And just where is it you're moving on to, Son? Cassie's stepped aside to let you decide which sister you favor, and I figure Laura's scheming about how she's going to win you back. Just what on earth were you thinking, kissing her like that?"

"You were being unfaithful to Cassie," Angie said.

Obie smarted under his aunt's remark. She sometimes criticized, although never in such a direct way. He was tempted to blame Laura, for she'd initiated the kiss, but that wouldn't be fair since he'd willingly participated. "I wasn't thinking at all," he admitted.

"Obviously," Ken said. "So, what're you going to do? You'd better make up your mind, and quick."

"Cassie loves you," Angie said.

"I know, and I love her."

Ken hit the tabletop with a balled-up fist. "Then, tell off the other one, and do it immediately. And, for God's sake, tell Dan the truth."

"I've made a promise not to do that."

"A foolish promise, in my opinion. Well, I've made no such promise. He's a fine young man, even with the influence he's had from his mother and grandmother. I can't wait to tell him I'm his grandfather, the same as Pinky is."

Angie squawked at Ken. "It's not your place! It's up to Obie. You must respect his decision about it."

Obie was convinced that if his father had gears in his head, it would be possible to hear them grinding. "I suppose you're right," the older man finally conceded. "But I don't want to die before Dan knows the truth. You say he hasn't been up to see you since you quarreled?"

"Not once. He used to come at least twice a week."

"He'll get over it. This fall, I'll take him deer hunting. You, too! How long has it been since we did that?"

"Dad, I'm finished with hunting, but I think he'll like going with you."

"So, will you tell Laura to take a hike?"

"It's not that simple. She has her own troubles, sorrows she doesn't deserve. I'll let her know in my own time and in my own way."

"You'd better do it quick, or it's going to spoil what you have with Cassie."

Angie said, "Ken is right, Obie. You don't want to lose Cassie."

Obie had another sleepless night following that discussion. In succeeding days, he delayed, despite the advice from Ken and Angie. He was overwhelmed by events. What had seemed a revelation that would change his life for the better had started a domino effect. One lousy incident had bumped up against another until his hopes and plans seemed ready to topple.

For the first time since his return to Stafford Rest, he had recurring dreams about the war in Italy. One dream, a familiar one, came several different nights and caused him extreme discomfort; a faceless young man in a German uniform rose from a stone wall and pointed an accusing finger at him. Each time, he awakened drenched in sweat. He considered seeing Doctor Osborn for something to help him sleep but delayed, hoping the dreams would stop.

By the time Laura came to him, his nerves were frayed. She came unexpectedly, entering through the side door without knocking. He was sitting at the kitchen table drinking coffee and didn't get up to greet her.

"Good Lord, Obie," she said, "you look terrible. Your eyes are bloodshot, and you look like you've been on a drunk. How long has it been since you shaved?"

"I don't know. It hasn't seemed important."

"Have you been sick?"

"Sick at heart, I think."

"Can I help? What can I do, Obie?"

"Do you know where Cassie is?"

"She's been in Syracuse for two weeks. Aunt Lorena was in the hospital. She died three days ago."

"I'm sorry about that."

"I just returned from the funeral an hour ago. Dad is still there. He's staying longer to take care of some legal matters. I wasn't as close to Aunt Lorena as Cassie was. She lived with her for four years when she was at Syracuse University."

"I remember. When are Cassie and Julie coming back?"

"Today. Maybe late tonight."

"Why did you come up here, Laura?"

"To let you know what's transpired. And I was worried. Dan said he hadn't seen you around town."

"You could have called instead of coming."

She looked away, then back. "I wanted to talk to you, face to face."

"Laura, this isn't the best of times."

"I see that now. Have you and Cassie quarreled?"

"You must know we did. Why did you tell her, Laura? Why would you do that?"

He watched her go to the cupboard, take out a mug and pour coffee from the pot on the stove. He wondered what answer she was concocting. Finally, she sat down at the end of the table opposite him.

"It was a mistake," she said. "I know it now. It was impulsive on my part. I never imagined she'd misunderstand."

"Well, she did. And she blames me. She postponed our marriage."

"Obie, I'm sorry. I really am." She patted his hand. "What

can I do to help fix things?'"

"I don't know. She says that you and I must talk, thrash things out."

"I don't understand. Thrash out what?"

Cassie must have told her; he believed Laura was in self-denial concerning their relationship. *He must make it plain.* "Cassie needs to know how you and I feel about each other."

There was momentary hesitation before Laura said, "Well, Obie, you certainly haven't tried thrashing anything out with me. And you should have called me instead of moping alone up here all this time."

"Yes, I've been slow to act, but since you're here, let's talk this through. Cassie wants assurance that we have no lingering feelings for each other. She said we must clear the air, or it'll always be an obstacle between us."

"Are you saying she won't marry you unless she's assured that you and I aren't still . . ."

"Yes . . . *entangled.*"

When she failed to comment, he added, "You asked if you could help. Well, you can. You can assure Cassie that there's nothing like that still between us. Will you do that, Laura?"

Laura was studying his face. "Maybe," she said.

"Maybe? What the hell do you mean by that?"

"Obie, I do want to help, but stop and think for a minute. This thing that's happened is a bombshell. It's changed everything. Me, you, Cassie. It's turned our lives upside down. I can see Cassie's point of view. She knows we need to work out our feelings."

"I don't have to work anything out. I know what I want."

"Do you, Obie? *Do you really?*" Her hand had never been far away; now, she put it on his forearm. Her voice was hardly above a whisper. "So why did you kiss me? It wasn't a brother-in-law kiss."

He found it difficult to look at her. He wanted to tell her what he was thinking, that she had initiated the kiss. He said, "It was nothing. It was just a weak moment, one I regret."

"Was it that, or was it something more?"

Her dark blue eyes were like whirlpools, drawing him in. He felt seventeen again, caught in a swift current, struggling to escape. Summoning integrity, he blurted out, "Laura, I do often wonder how life with you would have been, and, to be honest, you'll always have a piece of my heart, but I love Cassie. I love her as I've loved no other person on earth. You *must* understand how things are now."

She sighed and removed her hand from his arm. "I do believe you, Obie. Let me ask you one question, though, and this is important to me. What if you were not in love with Cassie?"

"But I am."

"Yes, I know, but what if you weren't? What if you and I had learned the truth somehow, and Cassie was still married to Ed Jackson in San Antonio?"

"Laura, I was in love with Cassie even before she was married. But I was too much of a fool to act on it."

"I suspect so, too. However, my question is, if Cassie were unavailable, for whatever reason, how would you feel about me?"

He knew he was wincing. The question was a loaded gun pointed right at him. How was he going to disarm her? "Laura, I don't know," he said. She was studying his face, seeming to search for meaning. *He had to let her down easily.* "I would only know if it were a fact. It isn't, so I don't know how to answer your question. I can say, however, that I *have* loved you. I loved you when Dan was conceived, and in a different way, I love you still. Do you understand, Laura?"

Tears had appeared in the blue eyes. "Yes, Obie. I do now." She sighed. "At least you didn't tell me you could never love me again. You only said that you didn't know."

"My future is with Cassie."

She sighed again. "I hope you'll not think less of me for putting my heart on my sleeve today."

"I don't, Laura." He smiled. "I have to say, though, it was uncharacteristic of you."

She smiled, too. "Obie, we're not youngsters anymore. Mature adults take chances. That's what I just did. I'll get on with my life now." She looked toward the ceiling. "I'm a little embarrassed, Obie."

"Don't be. We have feelings that are raw right now."

"You're generous, and maybe we can just forget I was ever here today." She got up.

He didn't follow her to her car. As soon as he heard her drive away, he called his father. Angie answered the phone.

"Aunt Angie," he said, "Please call me tonight if you hear Cassie come home."

"Do you have a message for her?"

"Tell her that things have been thrashed out. She'll know what it means. Tell her to call me as soon as possible, even if it's late."

* * *

Cassie hadn't called, and by the following morning Obie had concluded that she wasn't home. As he was wondering what to do next, the phone rang; it was Laura.

"I just wanted to let you know that Cassie's staying in Syracuse longer to help Dad take care of Aunt Lorena's estate matters and secure the house. She'll stay at least another week."

"That's disappointing, but I understand."

"Are you feeling better?"

"I am. At least I was until I learned that it may be several more days before I can square things with Cassie."

"I'm sorry you're experiencing this hurt because of me."

"I'll be okay."

"I could come and keep you company."

Although it might have been an innocent offer, he wouldn't agree to it. "I'll manage, Laura," he said.

He did, in fact, feel better. He had slept well, arisen early, showered and shaved, and devoured a hardy breakfast of sausage and eggs. He'd put Laura in perspective, he believed.

With renewed hope, he could concentrate on restoring his relationship with Cassie. He considered calling her or going to Syracuse but soon discarded the idea; she needed to be alone, unfettered by other family matters.

By noon he'd grown restless and considered going to the high peaks, a personal refuge, but settled for a mid-afternoon climb to the tree-lined ridge above his house. There, he sat on a large stone where he could see the Morass, the town, and most of the lake.

The flat rock near the cliff's edge was a deposit from the last ice age and the one on which he and Laura had shared their first kiss. Cassie saw them there and ran down the hill, crying. Thirty years later, the situation felt similar—Cassie discovering—and running. Was she going to run right out of his life?

The Morass stretched out below under a cloudy sky. Its desolate mass implied something sinister, but he knew there was more life within its boundaries than in any comparable square mile within sight.

His adult life had been a "morass" in the traditional sense, jumbled, devoid of meaning. Yet, despite that, there was always a return of hope—hope resurrected by prayer.

He knelt beside the rock. During his ministerial career, he delivered prayers he'd been told were elegant; some were borrowed, some he had written. He believed they'd been delivered with effect, sometimes within the sound of enemy guns, but more often while cloistered in fine and secure houses of worship. However, elegant prayer on this day did not fit his humble state of mind.

He prayed aloud but softly: "Lord, here I am *again*. I've strayed from your presence many times. Forgive my neglect. I've abandoned the paths I've begun. I've broken all my promises. And because of my weaknesses, I can't help being the wayward servant I've so often been.

"But, I ask, if there's anything left in my grace bank, that I might make a withdrawal. You are aware of all things, and you know how much I love Cassie. You brought her back into my life, a gift I don't deserve but for which I offer my thanks. Also, I'm thankful for the blessing of a son I never knew I had.

"Cassie has lost her trust in me, and I'm not without fault for that. Please bring her back to me, Lord, if it's your will that we be together. And please help her sister to understand the situation.

"Father, I've accumulated many faults, some of my own making and some imposed on me. I have lingering hate residing in my heart for the one who has caused such great pain and misunderstanding. Please help me to cast out that hate.

"It seems there are other obstacles in my life that I can't control, hindering my restoration. I want to be the man you'd have me be. Ghosts of my past loom over me, disturbing my mind and upsetting all my endeavors. You've spoken to me in dreams and even sometimes in subtle whispers. *I know you have.* But, Lord, I need these burdens lifted. I'm desperate. I need your help . . . if you still find me worthy. Jesus was generous about helping those who were hurting. So it is in his name that I ask for your help."

His tears flowed freely. He knelt for a long time, listening. When he finally rose, he saw that some of the overcast had lifted, and a burst of bright sunlight enveloped the full extent of the Morass.

CHAPTER THIRTY-TWO

July–August 1970

It was late afternoon when Obie returned home from the ridge. He was surprised to find Dan there, looking annoyed. "I've been searching all over for you."

"I didn't think you wanted to speak to me again."

Dan didn't acknowledge the comment. "There are people here to see you. I've taken them to my apartment to wait. Where've you been?"

"Up on the ridge straightening out a few things, or so I hope. Who is it?"

"I can't tell you. I promised. I will say that it's a mother and her son, and she's a knockout. Has a little accent. Do you have a son you haven't told me about? He's about my age, the right age to be your war brat."

Obie was stumped. He sat subdued in the pickup cab on the ride down the hill and onto Main Street. Who had come to see him? Only a limited number of people knew where he lived. Adam did; they had continued exchanging letters. But the description didn't fit Adam.

The two visitors sat on Dan's back porch that overlooked the lake. Their backs were to Dan and Obie. The woman rose first and faced him. Dan was right; she was beautiful. She was medium height and willowy with long dark hair flowing over strong white shoulders. Her low-cut dress exposed the tops of her small shapely breasts. Her eyes sparkled. Her face was vaguely familiar.

Dan said, "Obie, this is Mrs. Turmack. She and her son came all the way from Virginia to see you."

Obie held out his hand, knowing he must look confused. "Glad to meet you, Mrs. Turmack. You'll have to excuse me, but how do we know each other?"

"Oh, come on, GI Obie, has it been that long? Say hello to my son, Matthew. Matt, say hello to Obie."

Obie froze; he was seeing a ghost. When he realized Rosa was real, he took her into his arms. The years fled away as he

346

held her, a mature woman where once there had been a thin, emaciated girl in war-torn Naples. She nestled her head on his shoulder. A long sigh escaped her.

When Obie felt composed enough to stand back and observe his visitors, he saw that Matt was a slightly larger duplicate of his father. His grip was firm, and he had the same determined jaw Obie remembered about his progenitor. It was Rosa, however, who was amazing.

"I can't believe it," Obie said. "Rosa, you were a skinny kid who could speak only a few words of English. Now, you're a beautiful . . ."

"Middle-aged woman. Is that what you were going to say?"

"No, you don't look a day over thirty. Matthew . . . Matt, your mother has hardly aged at all. It's wonderful to have you both here. But I have many questions. So let's sit down and get some answers."

Their story unfolded as mother and son alternated in the telling. When Matt was fourteen, they finally came to the United States. They'd remained in the Burroughs household for several years until Rosa married Buford Turmack, an attorney in Richmond. The elder Burroughs were both deceased. Mathew had graduated from the University of Virginia and was in his final year of law school.

"We have a big, big house in Richmond." Rosa's eyes sparkled.

"What about you, Matt? Are you married?"

"Haven't found the right one yet. I'll know when I do, though." His English was perfect.

"Where have I heard that before?" Obie said, remembering that Matt had uttered similar words. Rosa listened, smiling, as Obie told Matt the story of his parents' meeting and how his father had fallen so deeply in love. "He found the right one that very night," Obie said.

"I've heard Mom's side of it, but it's good to hear another viewpoint. I'd like you to tell me other things about my father. Grandma and Grandpa Burroughs told me about his early life. I'd like to know something about him as a man. You must know about that."

"And I will tell you," Obie said, "but first, how did you find me."

Rosa said, "Matt was going through a box of old letters his

father had sent home from Italy to his family. Your name was in nearly all of them. I told him as much as I could remember about you."

"I wanted to know the man who was so close to him in his last days," Matt said. "I was in the library about a month ago and asked a librarian how best to find someone whose name you know but little else. He asked your name and said right away that he thought he knew who you were. Handed me a book with your name on the cover. There was other information inside the jacket, about your roots, about Stafford Rest."

"And you came all this way?"

"We were going to New York City anyway, so Mom and I decided to drive up here. We didn't know it was so far, or even if you lived here. The first person we asked told us that a man standing nearby was his friend. He was pointing at Dan, here."

"I'm certainly glad you came. This is such a pleasant surprise. Yes, I have stories about your father, Matt, but we have all evening. How long are you staying?"

"We'll leave tomorrow morning," Rosa said. "We're meeting Buford in New York tomorrow evening. We'll find a motel somewhere for tonight."

"You'll do nothing of the kind," Obie said. I have lots of room up at my place. And not only that, we'll have dinner this evening to celebrate our reunion."

Mother and son continued their story. Tina, the Burroughs's daughter, had three children and was with her third husband. Mervin had died of a heart attack ten years earlier and Carla of cancer a few years later.

"I will always be glad I came to the United States," Rosa said. "Otherwise, I would not have known how wonderful they were."

"Rosa, what about your father? Did you ever find out what happened?"

"No. I searched for many years, but I know now that the Nazis killed him."

"And the rest of your family?"

"Mother passed away four years ago, but she was able to visit us here several times, and for that I am thankful. My brothers and sisters are alive and well in Italy. So is my cousin Beppe."

Dan, who had been silent, but was obviously listening to every word, said, "It's great to hear these stories. I've read a lot about the Second World War, and hearing about it like this brings it alive. My father wasn't in the war, so I didn't hear such stories from him."

Obie wanted to scream at him that his father *was* in the war and would have told him all about that and more had not the opportunity been taken from him. Rosa stared intently at him, then at Dan. "So, you are not related? I thought you must be. You look a lot alike."

"No," Dan said. "We're good friends, though." He glanced at Obie as though wanting confirmation. "I suggest that we have dinner together at Ernie's?"

Obie said. "It's my treat. And I'll call Dad and Angie."

"Do you mind if I invite my mother?" Dan asked.

"It is like a merry party," Rosa said, heading off Obie's answer. He let it go, as he knew he must.

Obie rode with Rosa and Matt in their Mercedes and directed them to Blackberry Hill. After settling them in, he called his father to tell him about his guests and the dinner. That evening, Obie took Rosa and Matt to Ernie's Restaurant at the marina. Everyone else was already there, sitting at a large table. When the visitors were seated, the only place left for him was beside Laura.

He wished Cassie were there; she would remember his having written about Matt and Rosa from Italy. Obie hadn't had a chance to tell Rosa about Cassie and couldn't remember if he'd even said anything to her about the sisters.

The dinner period went well, with the chat never lagging. The waitresses had started picking up dirty dishes before there was a lull in conversation. Rosa sat across from Obie. He studied her face, trying to make a connection between this beautiful woman whose social skills were impeccable and the emaciated girl he remembered in bombed-out Naples who gulped down her food for fear it would be taken from her.

How could she be so changed? *Had he also changed that much?* Had everyone changed like that? He glanced at others around the table. His father, the drunk, was no longer that person. Aunt Angie, the abrupt and opinionated young woman who had once ridiculed the Adirondack way of life now lived in it with pride. And there was Laura, with elegant maturity but possessed by some unknown melancholy.

"You did not believe me, did you?" Rosa said, smiling at

him.

"What do you mean, Rosa?"

"I told you in Naples, right after the war, before you left to come home. I told you we would see each other again. You did not believe it."

He laughed. "And yet, here we are. We'll not wait so long again, will we? Virginia and New York are not so far apart."

"You are a beautiful man."

Laura stirred beside him. He glanced at her and saw she was annoyed. "Hardly, I think," he said, trying not to let his voice reveal his discomfort.

Rosa saw his embarrassment. "I'm sorry, Obie. It is my Latin temperament."

"Mom gives out compliments with lavish enthusiasm, sometimes," Matt said. "She has embarrassed me often."

Rosa kept her determined look. "We should tell people how we feel about them while we have the opportunity."

"You're right, Rosa," Obie said. She had experienced the pain of losing people she loved. He reached across the table to take her hand. "You are the bravest person I've ever met."

He addressed the whole group. "Rosa walked from Naples to Rome. She walked through German, British, and American lines, through minefields, and through battlefields to look for her father and be with the man she loved. How can anyone beat that?"

Angie wiped away a tear. "You can't," she said. "Rosa, we're adopting you into our family right now."

"Hear! Hear!" was the consensus. Although dinner was over, wine continued to flow. It was late when they returned to Blackberry Hill.

* * *

Matt had retired to one of the bedrooms. Obie would go to the barnroom to sleep, but he and Rosa lingered, continuing to talk, despite the hour. They sat in dim light on the porch.

"She is the one Matt told me about, is she not?"

"Laura? Yes, how did you know?"

"Well, that has an easy answer. She is Dan's mother, and Dan is your son."

"Rosa . . . no! You heard Dan say he's only my friend."

"Lying is not like you." She was smiling. "He does not know, does he?"

"I'm not sure how to respond."

"Just say, 'Yes, Rosa, you are correct.'"

He tried not to laugh. Not only was she a waif turned into a princess, but she was also intelligent and intuitive. He told her about the sisters and the events since his return to Stafford Rest.

Rosa said, "And Cassie . . . she is your true love?"

"Indeed. We were to be married in September. Now, she may not want to marry me at all. What I did was very foolish."

"Yes, you are a foolish man, but she will marry you, Obie. You may be foolish, but you are a *good* man."

"Not so good, Rosa. I've been a broken man, and I'm still a broken man in many ways. But, thanks for lying to me."

"It is no lie."

"Rosa, are you happy? Your marriage, I mean?"

"Yes, Buford is good to me, and Matthew loves and respects him. I do miss Italy. I will go back to visit sometime. I want to see my brothers and sisters again."

"You have the resources, I suspect, to visit Europe as often as you like."

"Yes, I live well. It is almost like a dream. What about you? Is it not an exaggeration when you call yourself a 'broken man?'"

She listened as he poured out his heart, plans he'd made to live a life of service to God, only to let his failures yank it away from him, of a failed marriage, and of the fixes he tried to make for his mistakes.

Her expression showed compassion as he told her about letting Cassie go, of eventually reclaiming her, about the years of hating Laura, and of the recent truth that had surfaced. She grimaced and nodded when he told her of the bad dreams he was still experiencing. Obie was nearly breathless when he finished.

She was quick with a diagnosis. "You must go back," she said. "You must go back to Italy. That may be where you lost your way. If you want to find it again, you must return there."

"I honestly don't know what good it would do."

"I think certain life events stamp us, like a postmaster stamps a letter." She pounded her small fist into the palm of her other hand to demonstrate her meaning. "We carry that mark all our lives. If the event was a bad one, then bad things pop up whenever something reminds us. You saw terrible things there. Matt's death was one."

"The worst," he said. He hadn't told her about the German soldier at the stone wall, nor would he. That memory was too painful. "Rosa, I don't sit around thinking about all those incidents, bad as they were. Hundreds of thousands of war veterans have experienced as bad or worse. Most get on with their lives."

"People react differently, Obie. Some are different than they might have been if they had not been in war."

"So, you're saying that I've been marked by what's happened to me."

"I believe so."

"What good would going back to Italy do? It will have changed, and I'll see no service members who were there with me. I saw my relatives only for a very brief time."

"That is true. You will see that the time and place where the bad things happened are not now the same time and place. The bad things were only for that time. They are gone now. *They are past.* Accepting that will help you see that they are *truly* in the past. I am sorry, Obie. Maybe I am not clear with my words."

"You're being very clear."

"I once had a bad memory. My father worked at a bakery. I saw him one day there and asked him to put aside grain for our hungry family, which was dishonest. When he refused, I became very angry and cursed at him. I told him that I would never speak to him again. That was the last time we spoke before he was taken north by the Germans."

"Rosa, you never told me about that."

"I told no one. I was too ashamed. After the war, and when I had come to believe that my father was dead, I had dreams too . . . like your dreams."

"Do you still have them?"

"No, they are gone. They left after I went to the ruins of the bakery and asked him to forgive me." She did that fist-in-palm stamping movement again and said, "Cancelled! After that, I felt forgiven by both him and God."

They became quiet, but finally, she said, "We have many good experiences. Those are in our memories as well and are good to revive. You could see your relatives again, yes?"

"Yes, Aunt Maria and her family. I haven't kept in touch. Angie is her younger sister. They've written to each other for years, but I haven't talked to Angie about it for a long time."

"You should go back. And you should take Angie with you."

The idea had appeal. "I'll consider it, Rosa."

The following morning, they picked up Dan and went to the diner for breakfast. Rosa cried when they parted. She placed her head on his shoulder. "GI Obie," she said, "you *really* are a good man, but you must live as if you know it."

"I'll try, Rosa. I'll try."

* * *

Rosa's visit had stirred poignant memories, but the pity he'd once felt for her was gone; she had prevailed despite the difficulties in her life. Nevertheless, the recollection of events in war-torn Italy came with new intensity after her departure. He tried to perform routine chores and concentrate on meaningful projects, but Rosa's suggestion kept recurring.

And there was Cassie. The time passed for her expected return. Laura had given him her Syracuse telephone number. For days he was unsure about whether to call until one evening he could resist no longer. "Please don't hang up," he begged. "This is important."

"All right." She sounded harried. "How have you been, Obie?"

"Besides missing you, I'm surviving. When are you coming home?"

"I'm not sure. I may be here for some time."

"I miss you terribly."

"You have something to say, don't you?" Her tone was cool. "What is it?"

He told her about Rosa and Matt's visit, the dinner, and his and Rosa's late-night conversation. "Sweetheart, I want to go back to Italy, and I have an idea. If we get married in September as planned, we can go there for our honeymoon. What do you think?" He held his breath.

Her answer came swiftly. "No, Obie. It won't work. You go ahead if you want to. I agree with Rosa. You need healing. Maybe such a trip will help, but I can't go with you."

"Can't, or won't?"

"Don't play word games with me."

"Cassie, when will you stop being angry at me?"

"That depends."

"What does that mean? I love you. I love *only* you. What else can I do to make you believe it?"

"I asked you to talk to Laura. Have you?"

"I saw her a few nights ago when Dan brought her to the dinner for Rosa and Matt."

"And that's the only time you've seen her?"

"Well, she did come to the house. And we did talk. We talked on the telephone, too. Cassie, there's nothing between us. There won't be. I've told her that. Please believe me. It's you I love."

"Obie, I must say something." He heard her catch her breath. "There was a time in our childhood when you were my best friend. Then you abandoned me for Laura. She had your whole attention. I stayed in the background, waiting and hoping for some miracle that would make you notice me. After she married Ben, my hopes soared again. We wrote to each other all through the war, and I believed you'd return to Stafford Rest. I thought you'd finally see me and love me. You didn't."

"I *did* love you, Cassie, but I was a fool."

"At the urging of your friend Adam, I went to California to see you. You told me you loved me, that you wanted to marry me. I came home expecting to make wedding plans, but it was a wedding that never happened."

"You called *me*, Cassie. *You* picked that fight."

She continued as though she hadn't heard. "We quarreled over Laura."

"And you believed I'd done something terrible to her. As a result, you lost trust in me. Now that you know the truth, it shouldn't be an issue at all."

"You stopped writing. You didn't call."

"Anyone would get tired of writing if there's no answer."

"You could have tried harder."

"I did try!"

"Another man came into my life. I thought he was a good person and consented to marry him. Even then, I went to you again, thinking you'd rescue me from the promise. You didn't. You even broke off our communication in the cruelest way."

"I'm sorry, Cassie."

"We're both sorry, Obie. Me for not respecting the sacredness of marriage by marrying someone I only marginally cared for, and you for being too dumb to know the depth of my feelings for you."

"I'm sorry."

Don't you see, Obie? You've disappointed me every time. So can you blame me for not wanting to face disappointment again?"

He was stunned. "I'm sorry," was all he could think to say.

"You go on to Italy. By the time you return, I'll be back in the classroom. Maybe, and I say it with reservation, maybe we can reevaluate our relationship. Obie, someone here wants to speak to you."

Julie had picked up the phone. "Obie," she said, "are you a good boy?"

"Yes, Julie, I'm being a good boy. And are you taking good care of your mother?"

"Yes, I showed Mommy where we can buy hot dogs and root beer. I could take good care of you, too."

"How would you do that, Julie?"

"I'd let you go to Italy."

"What do you know about Italy, Julie?"

"You should go there and find the parts you lost."

"Julie, were you listening to our conversation, or did your mother tell you that?"

"Mommy didn't tell me. A pretty woman in my dream told me that it's time for Obie to go to Italy."

Obie nearly dropped the phone. "Julie, dear, why do you think the pretty woman told you that?"

"She said you prayed. She said that you are going to Italy."

"Were those her words?"

"Yes. She had white hair. Goodbye, Obie."

Cassie came back on the phone. "Julie comes up with some strange ideas."

"Strange, indeed," he said. "But she might not be far off the mark."

"Obie, I have to go."

He knew she was finding a way to exit. He made one last try. "Cassie, there's nothing between Laura and me. There never will be."

"That's not the impression I got from her recent phone call. She informed me that she asked you straight out if you could ever still have feelings for her, and she said you didn't tell her that you couldn't. Can't you see why I'm still confused? You had a perfect chance, and you let it go by. I question why you did that."

"Cassie, sweetheart. I was just being considerate . . ." Cassie had hung up.

Obie moped several more days before he decided things were out of his control, that unseen forces were at work in his life. The Italy suggestion had hit him from two directions. It gnawed at him until he decided to act. He discussed it with Ken and Angie, then called a travel agent in Albany to explore possibilities.

Things fell into place quickly. Angie would go with him. Ken wanted no part of such a trip. Obie planned to leave his car in a parking lot at the Albany Airport for the two weeks they were gone.

With arrangements made and two days to wait, Obie contemplated what the trip would mean. Seeing Aunt Maria and his other relatives would be a wonderful experience, especially for Angie. She had hurried off a letter to Maria, who responded with equal speed. Both women looked forward to the reunion with great anticipation.

The day before time to leave he sorted through a box holding his mementos from Italy, looking for anything to help orient him to a country that would be greatly changed. He took out the small Bible, the one belonging to the young German prisoner, and wondered why he had kept it, a physical reminder of an event he desperately wanted to forget.

The leather binding wasn't changed. He held the book in his hands, remembering the situation. He'd believed the man was drawing a weapon; this was the weapon. He opened it, something he'd done only once before. The ribbon still marked the page with an underlined passage from Psalm 121. That scripture was probably the last thing the man had ever read.

Before the battle that had taken Matt's life, Obie had underlined nearly the same passage in his own Bible. He had later thought it a strange coincidence, but now it seemed astonishing. From his bookcase, he took down his own small Bible, the one Charles Lansing had given him when he was thirteen years old.

He found the underlined passage and read it aloud.

The Lord is thy keeper: the Lord is thy shade upon thy right hand. The sun shall not smite thee by day, nor the moon by night. The Lord shall preserve thee from all evil: he shall preserve thy soul. The Lord shall preserve thy going out and thy coming in from this time forth, and even for evermore.

The words intensified Obie's misery. Although he had been "preserved," he'd fallen far short of God's will for him. He turned to the front of the German Bible. On the title page was a name, written in pencil—*Günter Erdmann*. Underneath was "Heidelberg – situada a la vall del Neckar."

"Who were you, Günter Erdmann?" Obie said to whoever might hear. "What would you have been had I not taken your life?" He bowed his head. "Forgive me, Father. Forgive me, Günter Erdmann."

He started to put the German Bible back into the box but, on impulse, placed it in the handbag he would take on his trip.

On the morning of their departure, Dan pulled in behind him as he was putting baggage into his station wagon. "Do you know a minister named Charles Lansing?" Dan asked. "Mom sent me up here to catch you before you left."

"Indeed, I do. I've been meaning to go see him. He said in his last letter that he wasn't well."

"I'm sorry, Obie. Reverend Lansing died yesterday."

CHAPTER THIRTY-THREE

August–September 1970

They took a direct flight from New York City to Rome, arriving there early morning. Obie rented a car and drove toward Tarquinia. Angie, although tired, was as animated as Obie ever remembered. Her voice was high with excitement as she looked for places she recognized; she had little trouble communicating. Obie was becoming marginally proficient again in a language long neglected.

Roads had changed, and progress had brought congestion, but they finally arrived at Maria Bertoni's gate. Maria's smile was one he remembered. Another woman stood beside her. It was a tearful reunion. Although Maria walked with a cane, she stood erect with a stately bearing. "I knew you would return one day," his mother's sister said as she held onto his arm.

The other woman was slender. Her dark hair showed only a few streaks of gray. Her eyes were a brilliant blue. "Hello, Teresa," he said to his cousin. "You're still very beautiful."

"And you are little changed," she said, with a smile.

"And how is Anton?"

"He is well. We have three children, a son and two daughters. Anton tends our farm and vineyard here."

Obie inquired of Maria, "And what of your son and your other daughter? How have Gerardo and Sonia fared?"

"Gerardo lives in Rome. He will come here before you leave. He has a good government job. He and his wife, Rachele, have two children. Sonia and her husband, Davida, have three. They live in L'Aquila and will also make a trip to visit with us while you are here."

Early in their visit, Obie told them about Dan and the events leading up to and surrounding that discovery. Teresa laughed heartily, saying, "And I thought mine and Anton's story was interesting," referring to the fact that she had married a German soldier who deserted his army. But then she apologized, saying, "Obie, I can see that you have suffered much because of the wrong someone did to you, but now it will be better.

You have discovered a son, and you will soon have a wife. I am sorry for Laura, but you and Cassie will have great love, just like Anton and I love each other. Cassie will forgive you."

"I pray that she will."

Days flew by as his cousins and their children came and went. Stories were told and retold as the walls of Maria's home reverberated with prolonged conversation and laughter. Obie planned to stay with the family until four days before their departure. Then he would go alone to the site of his regiment's last battle, perhaps to find Julie's "lost parts."

However, when the day came for his side trip, he realized he'd not reserved enough time. So he told Angie, "I'll stay here until the date we planned to leave, then I'll take you to Rome for the flight home, but I need more time in Italy. I need to do more than visit a couple of battlefields. I hope you understand."

Angie hated traveling alone, but she acquiesced, bravely telling him to "do what you need to do."

Their departure from Tarquinia was tearful. Maria told him, "Obadiah, the last time we parted, I knew we would see each other again. But we will not see each other again in this life, so we must say a final goodbye now."

"Aunt Maria, you don't know that." He realized, however, that she was probably right.

After seeing Angie off at the Rome airport, he drove south to Naples. The city had grown, and much there was unrecognizable. He hired a guide, a college graduate student, to accompany him. In a leisurely manner, they retraced his regiment's approximate route in pushing the Germans back toward the Alps. That military campaign had been a slow and torturous march northward.

Amedeo was a history major and a wealth of information concerning ancient and modern battles. Nevertheless, he seemed awed that Obie had "been there" with the Fifth Army. The young man spent lots of time writing in his notebook. Obie took his own notes; they would be helpful in future writing.

Several side trips allowed Obie to soak up the flavor of modern Italy. In a little over a week, they covered territory that had required many months during the war.

The last war site was one he would visit alone. He put Amedeo on a train at Bologna with a substantial bonus in his pocket.

* * *

Obie drove to Busseto, marveling at the changes and the speed with which he covered the terrain. The day was calm under a bright sun. This was the last site he would visit before returning to Rome—but maybe the most important one.

He felt anxious as he parked the car on a side road. From there, he could see the farmhouse where they had captured a platoon of German soldiers in the war's waning days. It was two hundred yards away and surrounded by several newer buildings.

The land between the road and the house was a cultivated vegetable garden. Many varieties of vegetables were ones he recognized. There was no one in sight. He searched until he found the spot where he believed Matt had died. There were melons there, their long vines intertwining. He was surprised that he could smile; Matt would have joked about dying in a melon patch.

He'd often wondered if standing on the spot would be an emotional experience, and it was, although not the ordeal he expected. *Had the years dulled his sensitivity, or did he realize Matt would want no part of such memories?* He took photographs anyway; he would decide later whether to share them with Rosa and Matt's son. Before leaving the location, his prayer was silent, merging peacefully with the surroundings.

He walked toward the house. This was terrain over which he and Adam, mad with rage over Matt's death, had run together, firing their weapons at whatever moved. Today, however, there was no relentless rat-ta-tat-tat of guns nor sandbags stacked to hide enemy positions. Nevertheless, for a few seconds, the sounds of battle and the scent of gunpowder were present, if only in his mind. He looked around; it was warm and still.

When he entered the compound, he saw that the rock wall where he had shot the young German still stood. Obie's knees were suddenly weak. Images from that day were clear in his mind. He half expected to see a pool of blood form on the ground from the head wound the Luger bullet had inflicted.

Who, really, was the young man whose life he had taken? Obie had an urgent need to know. A large stone had been placed near a gate in the wall. He sat on it to try and sort his jumbled thoughts.

A man approached. He was about Obie's age, maybe a little younger. He looked concerned. "What are you doing?" the man asked. "Why are you here? You have no right to be here."

That angered Obie. He rose to his feet. "No right!" he said in English. "I have every right to be here! I fought so you could occupy this space! My friend gave his life a few yards away from where we stand! What do you mean I have no right?"

The man obviously didn't understand, but he could see Obie's anger. "Who are you?" he asked in a more subdued manner.

Obie calmed and said in Italian, "I fought here against the Germans. They were in this house. We stormed them and drove them out."

The man's face went white. "You are one of the Americans, then? I apologize, senior. You are most welcome. I was but a boy. I remember, however. The Germans made my family stay in the cellar. I crept out and hid in the barn. You must come into my home. We will drink wine together."

"I appreciate the offer. However, I must be going. I simply wanted to see this place again. I lost a friend here. Right down there." he pointed.

"My name is Gilberto. It is good wine, three years old. I make it from the grapes of my vineyard. Come . . . please."

Obie relented and followed him. They sat at a broad wooden table in the kitchen, and the man's wife brought them a full bottle and glasses, along with cheese and bread.

"It *is* good," Obie said as he held his glass up in salute.

Gilberto said, "Most things we eat and drink are consumed soon after harvest, but when we make wine, it is for future consumption. It is made with love and is an act of faith. Even during the war, nearly every family here continued to make wine. An act of faith, making wine even when things were so bleak. Wine is a most wonderful thing, is it not?"

Obie smiled, for Gilberto's words had a familiar ring. When he had asked Grandfather Jacob why he had lived so long, Jacob said "I think it's because I make wine." He remembered another thing the old man had said: "When you make wine, you're planning a future." Obie's Grandmother Prissy was his "excellent wine," he'd also said.

In his pensive way, Jacob had added words Obie knew he

could never forget. "You have to have hope, even if you never get to drink the wine. It's the belief you will that counts." Jacob had concluded in his aged and shaky voice. "It's a choice, boy . . . you have to decide whether or not to make wine."

Sitting at the table of this newfound friend, his thoughts turned to Cassie. She was his excellent wine. Without her, his future looked desolate, indeed.

Gilberto's expression indicated he expected an answer to his question. "Yes, indeed, wine is a wonderful thing," Obie said. "Gilberto, I can see you are something of a philosopher, like someone else I knew."

"Oh, no, senior, I am nothing more than a farmer, and a poor one at that. I grow vegetables and have a small vineyard. My wine is not a great production." He paused a moment, and his voice softened to a whisper. "Have you come here looking for peace in your heart?"

The words were disquieting. "Perhaps I have. You are very perceptive?"

"Another man came . . . two years ago. Those were his words, 'looking for peace in my heart.'"

"An American?"

"No, he was German. He was here too when the Americans made them prisoners." He stopped and looked at Obie, obviously waiting for his reaction.

"Was he one of the Germans occupying your house?"

"Yes. He was a high-ranking officer. His name is Julian. He is a rich manufacturer in his country. His younger brother was here too. I assume Julian had requested that his brother be close to him for protection. His brother was killed in the skirmish, and Julian had some guilt. The Americans took the prisoners away, but they left the bodies. They came back later that night and picked up their own dead. They left the Germans, nine of them."

"The dead ones, you mean?"

"Yes. The Germans had treated us badly, but we are civilized people. My father and I buried them in our cemetery down below." He pointed. "Julian could not get it off his mind for many years, grieving at having left his brother behind. Their mother is still alive, and she encouraged him to come back and see what he could find out, maybe even take the body back to Germany. He was amazed that his brother was buried in our cemetery. He visited the grave and shed many tears. He said he would come back again. But he has not as yet."

Obie was touched by the story. "Could I also visit the cemetery?" he asked. The odds were that the young man he had shot was buried there. Obie and Adam Silverman had killed more than one enemy soldier that day. They were probably buried there too.

"Yes, I will take you."

The cemetery was small, not even a quarter-acre. The nine German graves were together in a row. Obie was surprised to see large granite headstones with inscriptions marking each gravesite. "Julian sent the money to have these headstones erected," Gilberto explained.

"How did you know their names?"

They all had identification of some kind, wallets or papers. My family kept them along with a written record. Julian was, at first, going to take his brother's body home, but he was impressed at how serene it is here and reconsidered."

"Which one is his brother?"

Gilberto pointed. Obie read the carved name aloud. "Günter Erdmann." That was the name on the Bible in his travel bag. He placed a hand on the cool headstone. A shiver went up his spine.

Gilberto stared at him. "What is it, senior?" he said.

"I killed this man," Obie whispered.

Gilberto was silent a moment before saying, "It was war."

"I killed others here, as well." He remembered how he and Adam had stormed the house, more in fury than in military duty. "But this man didn't have to die," he said. "He was already a prisoner. I believed he was pulling out a weapon. It was a bible, and I fired too quickly. He was very young."

"Yes, Julian said he was young. He was going to be a priest, a Lutheran minister. He had not been at the front long, and Julian had pulled some strings to have him assigned to his unit. Their family grieved much."

"It has bothered me all this time," Obie said. "I wonder if there is anything I can do to honor him."

"You said he had a Bible. We found no Bible on him."

"I kept it. I have it with me."

"Why do you not return it to his family? They would appreciate that."

"Do you have their address? I can put it in the mail."

"No, senior, you must take it to them. I do have their address, but you must go to Germany and place the Bible in their hands."

"That would be hard."

"Forgive me, Senior Obadiah, for speaking so plainly. I can see that you have carried this pain with you for many years. It will always be so, but seeing this brother and mother can ease the pain. If they forgive you, you will find relief. If they do not forgive, there will still be relief, for you will have sincerely tried."

"Thank you, Gilberto. You *are* a wise man, and you are right. I see that what you suggest is what I must do."

It dawned on Obie that it was probably the most challenging thing he'd ever have to do.

*   *   *

On the flight to Germany, Obie was nervous about the situation. Gilberto had promised to forewarn the Erdmann family of his coming, and Obie had written them a letter explaining the reason for his visit and the details of his arrival. However, that they would even talk to him required a leap of faith.

Obie was surprised to find a car at the Mannheim Airport waiting to pick him up and take him to Heidelberg on the Neckar River. When they stopped before a palatial factory office, Obie worried he might be at a great disadvantage. He spoke no German and didn't know if anyone there spoke English. Moreover, his travel-weary clothing needed pressing. He entered the building with trepidation.

A secretary ushered Obie into Julian Erdmann's office. The man, short and stout, had a manner of assuredness. His English was nearly perfect. "Mr. Gainsworthy, it's my pleasure to meet you." He held out his hand.

"The pleasure is mine," Obie said. "I hope I'm not interfering with your routine."

"Not at all. I consider this a momentous occasion, as does my mother, whom you will meet tonight at dinner. You are welcome to lodge with us for the night."

"I thank you, but I have reservations at a hotel. I'll be leaving for the airport early tomorrow morning and wouldn't want to awaken your household."

They talked of mundane things for several minutes before Erdmann said, "I hope I have put you at ease, Obadiah. I imagine you might feel some nervousness at meeting Günter's family."

"Yes, I confess that I do. It's not easy to talk to people who . . ."

"Whose relative died at your hands?"

"Yes." It seemed unreal, the warm reception this man was offering. "It has haunted me since that day, even though I put it out of my mind as best I could."

"Some events cannot be forgotten."

"It has stayed there always . . . always in the background."

Julian told him in words similar to Gilberto's, "Obadiah, it was war. I took lives, and their families grieved. Now, we have gone back to being civilized again."

"Still . . ."

"You are not responsible for either Günter or me being where we were. The blame belongs to our country and the sickness it brought to the world. That is the way I feel, and it is the way my mother feels. I have discussed it with her. We hold no grudge toward you. On the contrary, we admire your courage in coming. My family has recovered from our loss and is doing well, as you can see." His hand swept out as though taking in things around him.

"Do your other relatives feel the same?"

"I believe they do, although I have not had time to discuss it with everyone. My son is anxious to meet you. My daughter seems to have some reservations, but she will come around."

The chauffeur took him to his hotel and returned later to pick him up for dinner. The family home was a spacious mansion near the river. The extended family members, about twenty in all, were there to meet him.

Most of the family accepted him, it seemed. He was still reeling from the strangeness of it all and was most surprised at not feeling the animosity he might have expected. Julian's wife was gracious. His mother, though cordial, at first exhibited reserve. But, in time, she warmed. When the departure time came, he took out the Bible and, with Julian interpreting, presented it to her. She held it to her cheek and cried.

"She wants to ask you a question," Julian said.

Obie hoped she would not request details of her son's

death. "I'll answer if I can," he said.

Julian repeated her question. "My son says you were once a minister of the Holy Word. Why have you stopped doing that for which God called you?"

Obie formed an answer with difficulty. "My unworthiness," he managed.

She studied his face; he imagined she was searching for some redeeming quality. "If worthiness were a prerequisite," she said, "there would be no one to preach the word. We are all unworthy. My son, the one you . . . the one who died in the war . . . he struggled with the same issues, young as he was. Günter did not want to go to war and take lives. He had no choice. He aspired to be a minister, his great desire. Was that not your desire as well? If you have regrets about Günter, as Julian says, maybe you should do what Günter cannot. You could take up your calling again."

"I will give that consideration," Obie said, humbled. Then, he felt compelled to add, "The word can be preached in other ways, though, ways for which I'm more suited."

"Yes, that is so. But you must serve." A tear ran down her cheek. "Günter was Lutheran, as are we, but he believed the Holy Father embraces all humanity and that love matters more than anything. We have not known each other long, but I sense you share the same sentiment."

Shades of Jacob. "Indeed, I do. However, I have had to grow into that belief."

"You will remember Günter, then?"

"He will be my inspiration."

Despite the evening being emotional, Obie slept well that night. Early the following morning, he was surprised when Erdmann came to pick him up.

"We were warriors together," Erdmann said, "even if we were on different sides. I decided that, as one warrior to another, I would see you off, myself."

* * *

Obie stayed busy on the flight across the Atlantic. He added new entries to the swelling journal that would form the framework for a future book.

The jetliner's engines revved down for the first time in eight hours, and a flight attendant announced their approach into New York. The trip was nearly over, not counting a short hop from New York to Albany and a drive home.

He'd been gone nearly a month, twice as long as planned. Angie had been home for two weeks; frost had already fallen on higher Adirondack towns; Cassie would be teaching a new class. He experienced satisfaction as he placed the journal in his bag and put it under the seat in front of him in preparation for the landing.

Later that evening, on the drive from Albany to Stafford Rest, a clearer picture emerged of what he must do. First, he would repair his relationship with Cassie. How, he was unsure, but it would happen. Next, he must practice forgiveness, especially toward Abigail Hunt, even if she doesn't want it. He must also forgive himself. Last, he would help Dan find his Vietnamese girlfriend and their child. It was possible, he believed, and long overdue.

His mother's face appeared before him, and he remembered the dream in a vineyard in the Russian River Valley of California. Her words, never spoken in life but communicated across God's unfathomable void, had been, "Obie . . . you must turn your belly up to God."

He'd heeded those words then and tried, but circumstances in his life had muted their meaning. Now, there was a new beginning, uncertain but ripe with expectation.

An image of Grandfather Jacob came as he turned onto Cedar Creek Road leading to his house. Jacob's life had influenced his own, not in the formation of religious belief, but in his simplicity of thought—his humility. He'd been a man who indeed turned his belly up to God.

And there was the wine thing, coming from two different directions. *Cassie was his "good wine."*

* * *

Contemplation about Obie's imminent return caused Cassie concern but also relief. During his absence, she had returned home, started a new school year, and cried all day on their canceled wedding date. She was a fool to have let it go on so long. Laura hadn't been shy in confirming that fact.

"We've always been honest with each other, haven't we?"

Laura said.

"About most things. We're still shaking out some truths, but yes, we are generally honest with each other."

"Believe me when I tell you that Obie loves you. He has no interest in me."

"He kissed you."

"That was my fault. I placed myself in his way. I shouldn't have done that, and I'm sorry. We were so excited about learning the truth. Obie's a gentleman. You know that. I put him in a position where not kissing me would have been an affront."

Cassie had reached the same conclusion and was glad Laura wanted to put things right. "Thank you for telling me," she said. "You didn't have to. I couldn't have blamed you if you had wanted to renew what you two had. You know what they say about love and war."

Laura glanced away and sighed. When she looked back, Cassie saw tears in her eyes. "I tried Cassie. Forgive me, but I tried to make him see me again like he used to. I still don't know the extent of my feelings or if I have him fully out of my system, but I do know he loves you. If I thought otherwise, I'd fight you for him, but I know that's pointless."

Obie had sent postcards throughout his trip, and the last one gave details of his return. She stayed up late that night waiting to see lights go on at his house. She'd made plans to meet him there after his arrival but decided against it as soon as she saw the lights go on at the house. It would be presumptuous, considering what had transpired between them.

She hoped he would call or come to her the following morning. He did neither. He would sleep late because of jet lag, she concluded. It was a Sunday morning, and she and Julie went to church. After the service, she could wait no longer. She took Julie home and drove up Blackberry Hill alone.

He was fixing breakfast. "Hungry?" he asked as nonchalantly as though he'd only been gone for a day.

"Don't go to any trouble."

"How hard is it to scramble a couple more eggs and put bread in the toaster?"

"Okay, then."

"You surprise me by being here," Obie said while stirring the eggs. "That's different from what was going on when I left."

She went to him and kissed him. He put the spatula down

and took her in his arms. They held onto each other until she said, "The eggs are burning."

He told her about his travels as they ate. "There's a lot more to tell," he said as he gathered the dirty dishes. "Assuming I'm going to have the opportunity."

"Obie, my Love," she said as she went to him again and leaned on his shoulder, "You're going to have as much of me as you want for as long as you want."

"I can't wait to get started."

CHAPTER THIRTY-FOUR

September 1970

The trip to Europe had prevented Obie from attending Charles Lansing's memorial service. After his return, he grieved because he believed he had neglected their friendship. He might have noticed the extent of Charles' illness if he had been more attentive.

Three days after Obie's return, Pinky Hunt came to visit. He stood in Obie's porch doorway, cap in hand. "I know you and Charles were close," he said, "and I admired and respected him. I attended the memorial at his church. Several hundred people were present." Pinky cleared his throat. "I simply wanted you to know that, Obie." He turned to go.

"Please come in, Pinky." Obie held the door open wider.

High windows on three sides of the enclosed porch let in bright light from the cloudless late September sky. Pinky sat in a rocker after casually identifying it as one made in his factory. Obie filled two mugs from a newly brewed pot of coffee and handed one to Pinky. He remembered that the older man preferred his coffee black and in a cup with a handle "large enough for four fat fingers."

"I wasn't sure you'd talk to me," Pinky said, "considering all that's gone on lately."

Obie was uncertain how much Pinky's daughters had told him. "I'm not blaming anyone for the past," he ventured.

"That's noble of you, but it's what I might have expected. I know the story now, Obie. I think I know the *whole* story, although that's not always a certainty in my family."

Pinky had more to say, and Obie wouldn't discourage him. "Truth has surfaced." He waited.

"Indeed, it has. And I'm happy for this chance to talk."

"Pinky, you can say whatever's on your mind. You were a rock for me when I was growing up."

"Well, first, I apologize for thinking you'd done something terrible to Laura. She told me about the letters and what Abigail did. I have to say that I'm appalled. I've known you all your life, your integrity, and the man you've become. I'm ashamed I doubted you, and I'm truly sorry."

"Apology accepted." For a moment, Obie thought to leave it at that, then quickly decided he had something to get off his own chest. "I had no idea Dan was my son. The truth is, I couldn't be happier about it. Abigail was wrong to do what she did, but I'm not blameless. I understand why she dislikes me. She was angry with Laura, and with me, for what we did. We were young and in love if that's any excuse. But I'm delighted about Dan. He's a fine young man."

"Yes, he is. I'm very proud of him too." Pinky casually placed his mug on the low table in front of him before saying, "Obie, just so there's no further misunderstanding between us, I've known for a while that you're Dan's father. Laura told me several years ago, but neither she nor I knew you were in the dark about everything. I believed as she did . . . forgive me . . . I thought you had deserted her. It was a father's misguided anger."

"I can't fault you. I know about misguided anger. I was angry at Laura for nearly thirty years. I couldn't understand why she suddenly stopped writing to me or why she married Ben Williamson without giving me an explanation."

"You and Laura are okay with it now, aren't you?"

"We are. We're fine."

"Good. I know things are different now, but it's a relief knowing that you're friends again." Pinky sighed. "I've loved Abigail ever since I met her, and I believe I'll continue loving her. But what she did has caused a rift in our marriage. I'm having a difficult time with it." His face took on a stern look, notable for its rarity.

"Pinky, I've forgiven her. I might not have been able to say that a month ago, but now I've finally moved past that frame of mind. You must forgive her too. And so must Laura and Cassie."

"I'll try. I will. Speaking of Cassie, I was surprised when you two postponed your wedding. It's only postponed, isn't it? Do you have a new date?"

Obie was unsure how to answer. Although everything seemed all right between Cassie and himself, there had been no discussion of wedding plans. He was leaving it to her to say something. "We're waiting to make further plans," he said, hoping that would satisfy Pinky's curiosity.

"In the end, it's all turning out well, isn't it?"

* * *

The day after his conversation with Pinky, Obie called Charles' church by Lake Champlain, hoping to find someone who could tell him about Charles' final days. A man answered and identified himself as the Reverend Lambert Williams.

"I'm Obadiah Gainsworthy, a longtime friend."

"Yes, he spoke of you many times. I knew Charles mostly through conferences and committee work, but he became more friend than collogue."

"I'm afraid I let him down in recent years," Obie said. "He told me he was having health problems. I had no idea it was so serious."

Reverend Williams gave him details: Charles had advanced colon cancer; he'd known about it for over a year but told no one except the church secretary. "He drove himself to the hospital in Saratoga Springs one day and died the next. He worked up to the last, one of God's faithful servants."

After talking for several minutes, Obie was ready to hang up when he remembered something. "I had a letter from Charles some time back. In it, he told me he was putting aside a box for me. He said it was in his desk drawer."

Obie could hear Williams shuffling things around. After a moment, the minister said, "Yes, it's here. Your name is on the cardboard box. Will you come for it, or should I mail you the contents?"

"Mail them, I guess. No, on second thought, I'll come for the box on Saturday. Do you mind holding it until then?"

"Not at all. I'll be here all day Saturday."

Cassie had suggested they go somewhere for the weekend. She came to Blackberry Hill that evening, and after he told her of his telephone conversation, they agreed to go to the Champlain Valley. It would give them time together to repair their bruised relationship, and he could get the box.

They sat together on the glider. "You're changed, Obie," Cassie said. "You're more relaxed. Happier."

"I have you back."

"It's more than that. Maybe it's because you've found those

lost parts Julie talked about."

Obie laughed. "That may be a part of it, but the big deal is that I have a much clearer idea of where I'm going."

"What you'll be when you grow up?"

He laughed again. "That, too."

"I didn't mean that, Obie. You've accomplished a lot in your life. Your deeds, your words, they've influenced many people."

Something still nagged at his mind. "Cassie, about the money . . ."

"Annie's money?"

"I hope you don't resent what I'm doing with it. Because we're together, what I do affects you too."

"No, it's your decision. It has nothing to do with me."

"As I told you, I'm setting up substantial trusts for you and Julie. But I'm giving away the rest."

"I'm not surprised. But you're keeping the house in California, aren't you? I want you to keep it. Promise me."

"I'm keeping it. I promise."

"Obie, I think you really have turned a corner. I'm so happy about that."

He grabbed her hand. "My feelings and my frustrations have dragged me down. I'm determined to put it all behind me. And I already have, to a great extent."

"Even after all the things Mom did to you?"

"That's part of what I'm putting behind me."

"I don't care if I never speak to her again. I only see her in church and when she parks by my gate to pick up Julie. We never say anything more than is necessary."

"Cassie, I'm determined to make peace with her."

Her expression was one of skepticism. "You can't mean that?"

"I do. Jesus said to forgive your enemies."

"I don't think he meant it in such a literal way. Jesus didn't know Mom when he said it."

It seemed a critical moment. Obie wanted to make the woman he loved understand his feelings and the change he wanted to undergo. "Sweetheart, for years, I've let people and events influence who I am. I'm putting an end to that. Other people don't control who we are. We do that ourselves."

"I decided that some time ago."

"I let my feelings about Laura linger on my soul like a scab. Then, I'd let something rip it off and start the bleeding again. That's been resolved, and I'll not let my anger transfer to your mother. I forgive her for what she did, and I'll tell her that."

"It won't make a bit of difference to her."

"Doesn't matter. That's up to her. I'll be out from under the burden of hate I've carried for so long. I hope you'll come to see it my way, as well."

"You want *me* to forgive her?"

"Yes."

Cassie was silent a long time before saying, "I don't know if I can."

"I'll help you. I'll make that a priority. And there's something else I'm going to do. I'll make a concerted effort to find Ly Yen and her child, even if I have to go to Asia. I'll do it for Dan and Dan's family, which includes Abigail."

"Do you really think she'd welcome an Asian woman and her child into her WASP family? You're dreaming."

"Maybe she won't, but I'll try . . . for Dan, if for no one else."

"Have you seen him since you've been back?"

"No. He's still a little peeved at me, but he'll get over it."

"He should know the truth, regardless of what Laura wants. It's not fair."

"I've made a promise, Cassie."

"I didn't."

"It would create a rift between you and Laura. We don't need that right now."

"Dan looks beaten down. I hope you'll succeed in finding Ly Yen because she occupies far more of his thoughts than he admits."

"I'll give it my best effort. And, about your mother . . . can you arrange a way I can talk to her?"

"You mean face-to-face?"

"Yes."

"Maybe, but only through Dad. I don't speak to her. What can I give as a reason?"

"If she believed my father would sell her his lake property, it might open the door."

"Yes, it might. It would serve her right, making her believe that. She's schemed to get it for years."

"I don't mean to deceive her, Cassie. I believe Dad would sell it. All I'll have to do is overcome *his* stubborn streak."

She laughed. "That might be an impossible task. But I'll talk to Dad and let him figure out how to proceed. I'll have to tell him what you're up to, though."

* * *

On Saturday, they drove to the Champlain Valley by a roundabout way. The fall colors were brilliant. After eating a late breakfast in the village of Lake George, they proceeded up the scenic west side of the lake to Ticonderoga. From there, the rolling hills and apple orchards beside Lake Champlain spread out before them. Not long into the afternoon, they stood in the church office introducing themselves to the Reverend Lambert Williams.

The box was small. Obie removed the rubber band to look inside, then quickly decided to examine the contents when they had more privacy.

They were headed for an overnight stay in Plattsburgh but stopped at a roadside park to eat sandwiches Cassie had packed in a picnic basket. She stretched out her long legs in front of their bench. "You haven't looked in the box Pastor Charles left for you," she said.

He retrieved it from the car, removed the rubber band, and opened the box. Cassie sat beside him, looking like a cat watching a mouse hole. The contents consisted of three envelopes. One was sealed and addressed to him, obviously from Charles. The other two were addressed to Charles and had been opened. One had a Vietnamese return address; the other had come from San Francisco. Obie took the letter from the Vietnam envelope because it had the oldest date. The childish handwriting was hard to read. He stared at the signature.

"It's a letter from Ly Yen," he said.

"A letter from Ly Yen to Pastor Charles? That's strange."

"Maybe it's not so strange. When I met Dan in Vietnam he asked me to find his girlfriend. I did find her . . . in a little village a nun in Saigon had told me about. I think the name on this envelope is the name of that village."

"But, why would she write to Charles? I'm not aware that Dan knew Pastor Charles. He was gone from Stafford Rest

375

before Dan was old enough to remember."

"I believe there's an explanation. Ly Yen told me she wanted to contact someone in Dan's family to get his address. I didn't have Laura's address or yours, and knowing your mother as I do, I thought the best way was through a third party. Charles was the most responsible person I could think of, so I gave her his address. This must be her letter to him."

"Well, read it."

"It's hard to make out her handwriting."

"Let me try." She took the letter and studied it. "I can read it," she announced.

"Read it aloud."

"I'll read it the way I'm sure she meant it," Cassie said. "This is quite interesting."

She read, *"Dear Reverend Lansing, March 7, 1966. My name is Ly Yen. Please excuse my writing. I can speak in English well, but not so well with writing. I have taught it to myself and I have much to learn. American GI Dan Williamson is the one I must find. A man gave me your address. He was an Army man of Jesus with a cross on his collar."*

Cassie stopped. "That was you?"

"It seems so."

She continued reading, *"He said you are a good man. He said you will tell me where I can find Dan. He said you know how to talk to the mother of Dan or to his grandmother and grandfather. Please talk to them so they will tell you where I can find Dan, my dear one."*

Cassie stopped again to dab at her eyes with a napkin taken from the picnic basket. She continued reading. *"We love each other and wish to be married. The man of Jesus told me to write a letter to you. Yes? Dan knows I am going to have a baby. That will be in two months. He is the father. He will send for me to come to him. He told me that. He will be surprised because I told him I would not marry him because my parents are ill. They are better and say I should marry Dan. They said I would do it for them, that my baby and I would be safe. The Army man of Jesus says you love Jesus. I love Jesus too. I thank you."*

Cassie added, "Her signature is on the bottom."

"The letter was written more than four years ago," Obie observed.

"The other letter has a return address from San Francisco,"

Cassie said as she held it up. "Could it also be from Ly Yen, from San Francisco? Obie, she might be there. Wouldn't that be something?"

"I'll read the letter Charles' wrote to me next. Maybe it'll clear things up." Obie slid his thumb under the envelope's flap. "It's a long letter," he said.

"Please read it aloud. I'm dying of curiosity."

"Let's read it together." He laid it on the table between them. "It's easier this way."

The date indicated the letter was more than a year old.

Dear Obadiah,

When you read this letter I will be with my Maker. You and I have had a grand correspondence following a warm friendship during your youth. Finally, though, one of us has had to go on to the place prepared for us in God's Kingdom. Do not be either sad or envious that it was I. You will have your turn, though not for a while yet, I hope. Accordingly, these are my last earthly words to you, Obadiah. Some will surprise you, but when you have read the entire contents of this letter and the others in the box you will have a better understanding.

First, I apologize to you, for in the midst of our letter writing, I have kept a secret from you that I should not have. I have prayed to God often that He will forgive me for it because it changed the course of your life. I hope you will also forgive me. My sin was born from selfishness but continued because of a promise I was forced to make to cover the sin.

Here it is: When you went into the Army in 1943, you left behind your girlfriend, Laura Hunt. What you did not know, and no one told you, including me, was that Laura was pregnant with your child. Daniel Williamson is your son, in case you have not already discovered that fact. Abigail Hunt came to me desperate for help in finding a way to save Laura's reputation. At first, she was considering abortion and was looking for my help in justifying it in terms of her spiritual beliefs. I gave her no comfort in that respect. I told her that I wanted no part of it. Laura didn't either, I found out later. Abigail asked me to speak to Dr. Williamson, the younger one. She thought Ben might think enough of Laura to marry her. I was to be discreet and use skillful and persuasive language. Those were her words. As it turned out, I found Ben was quite

377

willing.

In the beginning, I asked Abigail why she was not contacting you. She told me she considered you too young and immature to marry her daughter. I agreed with that assessment. Before I talked to Ben, I told her I would write to you because you had a right to know what was going on. She became very angry with me.

And that was where I went wrong, Obadiah. She hit me where she knew my weakness lay. You know how I had struggled to get money for the new education wing. I knew I would not serve at Stafford Rest Methodist forever. It was a dream of mine that my legacy to that church would be the much-needed renovation. She told me she would provide the money for the entire project if I would help her keep secret the fact that Ben Williamson was not Daniel's father. The other side of that pact with the devil was that if I did not agree to her terms, she would see that I never had another church in the conference, maybe anywhere. I was afraid of her power. I was weak. I gave in.

All those years, I carried the secret, and it was a burden, indeed. I regret it with all my heart, Obadiah. I have wanted to tell you the truth, but I had given my sacred word. And, of course, I feared Abigail.

At this point, you may be wondering why I am telling you this now. I might not have, except for the contact I had with a young lady by the name of Ly Yen. I suspect you know what I am talking about. I am sure it was you who gave her my name and address. She informed me of her situation. She was looking for Daniel to bring her to the United States and marry her.

I thought much about it. Was God at work in the situation? Here you were meeting Daniel in Vietnam and also the woman who was carrying his child ... your grandchild. What are the chances? I took the easy way. I called Abigail and asked her to pass along the information to Daniel. I should have found a way to do it myself. I should have known she would not tell Daniel.

However, I did something else on impulse. I answered Ly Yen's letter and told her of Daniel's true parentage. In my heart, I didn't think she would ever see Daniel again, and she deserved to know at least that much. Did I break my word? I probably did, and I may have to answer to my Maker for that, but I cannot say that I am sorry.

Recently, I received a phone call from Ly Yen telling me she was in San Francisco and had been trying to find Daniel. That was when Daniel was planning to marry a woman from Ohio. When I told her about that, she made me promise not to tell Daniel about her. I was reluctant but agreed. Recently, I heard that Daniel had broken his engagement. I tried, in vain, to find Ly Yen to tell her. She must have moved. I believe, from what she told me, that she will stay in the Bay Area of California. If she is found, that is the most likely place.

Now, to the last part of this narrative that is fast becoming a saga. Ly Yen has *two* children, twins, a boy and a girl. Daniel is the father, and you, Obadiah, are the grandfather of twins.

As to why I am telling you all this, I have come to believe it is God's will. It was me, not He, who made that stupid promise, and I figure He can reveal what He wishes. Anyway, I believe my promises end at my death. The truth will probably all come out, anyway.

I say that because Ly Yen wrote a letter to me that arrived right after I spoke to her on the telephone. She revealed some information that will bring out the truth immediately if she and her children ever meet the Hunt family, which I believe will eventually happen. I will not tell you here but will let you discover it yourself in the letter I have put in the box if you have not already read it. In any event, you will see what I mean.

Obadiah, you are still young, and your mother was right. I believe you have been anointed as one of God's special servants, regardless of the curved path you may have taken. You will soon settle into your preordained calling, whether from a pulpit or through your writings. I will not attempt a guess as to which that will be. In fact, your destiny could be something else entirely. My prayers are with you and will be with you from this side, if that is possible. (God's mysteries are so far beyond us that we cannot begin to comprehend, only accept. I learned that from your Grandfather Jacob, bless his soul.)

Take care, Obadiah. God loves you. I love you.

Charles

Cassie said, "Twins. How wonderful. Obie, you're the grandfather of twins."

"I'm amazed about that . . . and pleased."

"I'm surprised that Charles had those secrets."

"I can't help being annoyed about that."

"Obie, that was my mother's doing. He was under her influence. She contaminates everything she touches. Don't hold it against Charles."

"I don't . . . and I won't."

He removed the last letter from its envelope. It was dated July 14, 1969. "This is easier to read. It appears Ly Yen has learned a lot. I can read this."

He read aloud: *"Dear Pastor Charles, this letter will tell you of my recent events. I am now live in San Francisco and I greet you from there. I am healthy and happy as I can be without Dan with me. I am hoping you can help me make that happiness still more. Much has taken place with me and my children. This letter will tell you of my recent events."*

In the rest of the letter, Ly Yen wrote about her parents' deaths, her struggle to get herself and her children out of Vietnam, and her arrival in San Francisco. She had found a distant relative there who helped her find work and was willing to help care for the children. She also told of her unsuccessful attempts to find Dan.

Cassie interrupted. "This was written before she learned of Dan's engagement."

"It'll be a pleasure to update her about that."

When Obie came to the last paragraph, one expressing her gratitude for what Charles had done for her and her children, he paused and looked again at the words that seemed to bounce from the page.

"What is it?" Cassie asked.

Obie couldn't help laughing. "Look at this," he said. "You won't believe it."

She laughed, too, after looking where he pointed on the page. "No more secrets!" she said. "This will derail Mom's scheme to save our family's honor. It'll also serve Laura right for making you keep quiet."

"I'm not out for revenge, Cassie, but people are going to figure out the truth if I take Ly Len and the children to Stafford Rest . . . which is what I intend to do."

"Why do you keep saying, 'I?' I'm in this, too, Obie. I want to help."

"Good! I'm going to San Francisco. How about you going with me?"

"Yes! Yes! When?"

"You'll have four days off at Thanksgiving. We can go then. Maybe we can even extend it a few days."

"That's a month and a half away."

"It'll give me some time for preliminary work, get some search teams in place. Don't forget that I know many people around the Bay. They'll help."

"Obie, will we have time to stop in Berkeley?"

"Why?"

"I feel like it's where some things went wrong for us. It's not that anything is wrong now. It isn't. But isn't there some symbolic significance in us being there again?"

"Okay. And we can visit Hershel and Virginia."

For the first time in a long time, everything seemed right.

* * *

Cassie did her part to aid Obie's reconciliation efforts. She talked to Pinky, who spoke to Abigail. Cassie called early in the day to say her mother would meet him later that morning at the coffee shop on Main Street.

"She's meeting you because she expects to buy Ken's farm," Cassie warned. "And, as you know, she drives a hard bargain."

Ken's farmland, passed to him after Abner's death, consisted of one hundred acres between the road and the lake with some acreage, including the cemetery, extending above the road. It was a well-known fact that the farm was prime land.

"What are your intentions for the property, Dad?" Obie asked as they sat at Ken and Angie's dining room table one evening. "No one has lived there for a while. The barns are starting to decay, and both houses will deteriorate with no one living in them."

"I've had no luck finding a tenant, someone who'll work the farm," Ken said. "Why don't I just deed it over to you? You'll get it when I die, anyway."

"No, Dad. It would go to Angie. She's younger than you and will probably outlive you. You must provide for her."

"I have insurance and savings."

"She might need more. The way inflation's soaring these days is scary."

"You think I should sell it?"

Obie had hoped Ken would ask his opinion. "Look at it this way, Dad, if it were passed on to either Angie or me, it would be sold, anyway. Angie couldn't take care of it, would probably need the money from it, and I don't have the time nor inclination to own a farm."

"I'd like to see it remain farmland, or at least not sold off in house lots like the Epps place was."

"So would I, but it's not realistic. Farming in the Adirondacks is hard. Abner nearly killed himself keeping up. Your farm on the lake, and the smaller ones on the town edges, are anomalies."

"If I put it up for sale I'd probably have to deal with Abigail Hunt. I won't do that. So how could I make sure it went to someone else?"

"Dad, you asked my opinion." He'd rehearsed the words several times. "I suggest you consider selling to Abigail."

"You're out of your mind. After all she's done to us?"

"Maybe you can make her pay."

That caught his father's attention. "How?" he said.

"She wants the property. She *really* wants it. I say you sell it to her . . . at your price. What's it worth, Dad."

"I don't know. A lot, I guess."

"Give me a figure."

Ken stated a number. His smug expression indicated he thought it ridiculously high.

"Good," Obie said. "Double it. That's what you should ask."

Ken laughed. "She'd never go for it."

"Maybe not that amount, but I'd bet close to it. Like I said, she wants it. She's been thwarted in her efforts to buy it for years. But, if she has the chance, I believe she'll go for it. It's worth a try, and it'd be a little payback, wouldn't it?" Obie experienced a tinge of guilt speaking about payback while at the same time preaching to Cassie about forgiveness.

After more debate, Ken agreed, provided he would end up with no less than ten percent below his asking price and on the provision that he'd not have to deal personally with Abigail.

"Another thing," Ken said. "I don't want it broken up."

"Now, that's hard. Once it's hers, she can do what she wants with it."

"Well, try!"

Obie assured Ken that he would handle any negotiations with Abigail. With that hurdle cleared, he said, "I have some news for you, Dad. Two things, actually. I have some letters I want you to read. No one except Cassie and me know about this yet."

Obie sat back and waited for his father to finish the letters handed to him one by one. As Ken finished the last letter, he laughed, as Obie knew he would. "Sure as hell serves them right," he said with a smile of satisfaction. Ken read the end of the last letter aloud to Angie, who clapped her hands in appreciation.

"The other news is that Cassie and I are visiting the Bay Area two days before Thanksgiving. We're going to find Ly Yen and her children. If we're successful, we'll bring them back here. After that, everything is up to Dan."

"You're not telling him about it?"

"No, it'll be a complete surprise if everything works as planned. It's up to Ly Yen, too. A lot could have happened in two years. She could even have married."

"Well, good luck with it. It could change a lot of things."

"Oh, there's something else, too," Obie raised his voice so Angie, who had gone back into the kitchen, could hear. "I want you to hear this from me."

"Well, what?" Ken said, sounding impatient. "What would top what you've already told us?"

"Remember the church I served there, the one in San Francisco?"

"We remember," Angie said.

"Cassie and I have made arrangements to be married at Greenleaf Methodist the day after Thanksgiving, and we'll stay in the Bay Area for a week after that."

Angie clapped. "About time," she said.

CHAPTER THIRTY–FIVE

October 1970

Abigail arrived ten minutes late at Ward's Coffee Shop on Main Street. She hardly looked at Obie as she hung her coat on a rack by the door. "I'm given to understand your father wishes to sell the Ashdown place," she said as she seated herself across from him.

"He's considering it, provided he can get what it's worth and be assured that it won't be broken up."

"What's he asking?"

When he told her, she emitted an audible puff of indignation and replied, "Ridiculous! No property around her goes for that price. I may as well leave." However, she made no move to go.

"All right, I guess that is a little on the high side, and I fully understand. I'm sure Dad will find a buyer who isn't as real estate savvy as you."

"Well, I do have experience in this sort of thing. Maybe I can . . ."

He wasn't going to lose sight of his reason for being there. "You know, Abigail, since we're together and aren't making any progress with real estate, maybe we could discuss something else that's been on my mind. And maybe yours, as well."

The words she spat at him were colder than the winds on Mount Marcy. "What could you and I possibly have to talk about?" Then, after a moment, she said in a softer tone, "Let's keep to the business at hand."

He ignored the request. "We do have common interests. My son is your grandson, and . . ."

"Keep your voice down. You promised Laura."

He wanted to avoid confrontation. However, she had taken his bait, and he would reel her in. "As I said, my son is your grandson, and I'll soon be your son-in-law. Really, this time. You must have heard by now that Cassie and I have set a new date for our marriage?"

"Yes, I have heard and want no part of it. Cassie can marry

whomever she wishes, but *you* wouldn't have been my choice."

He wanted to keep her off balance. "Abigail, I owe you an apology."

"*What?* What do you mean?"

"Not that either of us is guiltless. Nevertheless, what I did, my relationship with Laura back then was wrong, and you were right for being angry with me. I can understand how you felt and why you did what you did." He must not let her off too easily. "But your actions changed our lives, mine and your daughters' lives. But I've forgiven you for it, and I'd like you to forgive me for what I did."

Her expression, whether shock or bewilderment, was hard to decipher, and it was fleeting. "*Never,*" she said. "I'll never forgive you for that."

"Abigail, I was seventeen years old and terribly in love with Laura, as she was with me. You'd forbidden her to even talk to me. Can't you see how such a situation might play out? And there's Dan. You love Dan. I know you do. If what happened hadn't happened, we'd have no Dan." She offered no answer, and her expression was inscrutable.

He continued. "You've wanted revenge, and I understand that, too. But, Abigail, haven't you had your revenge? Look what was taken from me. Isn't that enough? I want it to end and for there to be peace between us." He paused.

She waited a moment before answering. "You've turned my daughters away from me. Neither will speak to me. Pinky hates me too. I'm an old woman who needs to have my family around me. You say you want peace between us. If that's true, why did you turn my family against me? Tell me!"

"Abigail, I didn't do that, and you know it." He was purposely gentle with his words. "You and Cassie have been at odds about many things, and not only about me. With Laura, it's all about the letters, *our* letters that you had Bernadette Simon remove from the mail."

"She betrayed me, that woman."

"Don't hold it against Bernadette. Think about what you asked her to do . . . something against all her instincts. She did it for you, and there came a time when she couldn't stand keeping such a secret any longer. None of us can hold on to guilty secrets forever if we expect to have peace in our souls." He waited until she looked at him. "However, we were talking about your daughters. They're very angry at you. But that can be fixed."

"*Fixed?* How? I'd love to have my daughters back. Back the way things were."

Was she asking for his help? "You'd have to give a little, Abigail."

"I'd give anything . . ." She stopped short. "What would I have to do?"

"You'd have to tell Laura that you're sorry for taking our letters. Then, you might have to beg her for . . ."

"Forgiveness?"

"Yes. You'd have to tell her everything."

"All of it?"

"Yes, all."

"She already knows."

"Yes, but it's not the same as hearing it from your lips."

"What about Cassie? How do I make her love me again?"

"You can't make anyone love you, Abigail. But it would go a long way toward reconciliation if you gave your blessing to our marriage."

She glared at him. "That would be giving my blessing to you."

"Yes, it would. Is that so impossible?"

"I wouldn't like to do that."

"Why?" The question needed to be asked, even if it derailed progress. "Am I so bad? Really?" He paused a moment. She didn't answer. "I've questioned something else too, and what you tell me will just be between you and me. Why did you think I was *beneath* you?"

She looked uncomfortable to an extreme. The waitress had brought coffee right after Abigail's arrival, and neither had touched their cups. Abigail opened a sugar packet, emptied it, and stirred her coffee. She was delaying an answer; he wanted to elicit one. "Well," he said.

"Did I say that?"

"I was told you did."

"I don't remember."

"Was it a social thing, a class or economic divide between your family and mine? I believe you liked my mother."

"I loved your mother, Obie." The soft edge of her words left no doubt that she meant it.

"So, what was it?"

She cleared her throat. "I suppose it *was* a social thing, as you call it, a concern of mine then, but not so much anymore." She hesitated. "This is hard for me."

"I know, Abigail . . . I know. I'm a good listener, though."

"You have to understand my background. My family, the Beachtons, were semi-upper-crust. We had servants, powerful contacts, that sort of thing."

"Money?"

"Not as much as you might think. My father lost a lot of it through bad investments. I think Pinky's family had more, although I never told him that. I developed a mentality early on for making and keeping wealth."

"You're good at it, too. There's nothing wrong with that. You've done a world of good here in Stafford Rest."

She smiled briefly. "In my background, there was a sharp distinction in class, a wide difference between haves and have-nots. Here in the Adirondacks, the hardest thing to get used to was the blurring of classes."

"Not much here to blur. Nearly everyone's poor."

"Pinky treated everyone the same. But, frankly, I've had trouble doing that."

"So, you loved my mother but wouldn't have invited her to dinner with you in a restaurant?" He wondered if he might have gone too far.

She was having trouble looking at him. "I've mingled with all sorts over the years. Just look at how many church committees I've chaired. Our church has well-educated people, and a few who can barely read and write. Some are poor, and some are well-to-do. And I get on well enough with them all."

"I know, Abigail. You hold a position of respect at Stafford Rest Methodist."

"I've learned to get along with people here, to please Pinky." She paused. "I also wanted the very best for my daughters. I wanted them to marry well, to have money and social contacts, or at least good prospects for those advantages. To answer your question more fully, your family and your situation never fit my template for success. There, is that what you wanted to hear?"

"It explains a lot of things. Nevertheless, you said it was no longer a concern. What do you mean? Have my circumstances changed so much?"

"You've gained power and respect."

He laughed. "I have little of either."

"You've held some important positions, and you have the ear of influential people whether you know it or not. I've read your books, but don't tell anyone that. I admit you're a gifted communicator, although I'm afraid I disagree with much of what you say."

"I have little money by your standards. Is that where I still fall short?"

"You're a fool when it comes to money, Obie. There's even a rumor that you're giving away money you inherited."

He was surprised. Only Cassie and his father knew anything about it, and Ken knew little details. Maybe she was guessing. "Where did you hear that?"

"I overheard Pinky talking to your father on the phone. Pinky was trying to get him to admit that a very large gift to that Love Fund project came from you. Your father denied it, but from what I could discern, I think it *did* come from you. I know of the O'Shane family and their textile factory. And your wife was their only child."

"You've been checking up on me, have you?" He was sure she would detect his annoyance.

"I have my ways of getting information. But, of course, that doesn't surprise you, does it?"

"Not at all, and since this seems like a time for disclosure, the truth is that I did inherit some money." He wasn't going to tell her how much. "And yes, I'm giving most of it away. Not many people know about this, Abigail. I trust you'll keep it confidential." He added the last, hoping such a shared secret might help forge a bond.

"If you wish. Does Cassie know about your inheriting that money?"

"Yes, she shares all my secrets."

He anticipated the next question. "How much did you inherit?"

"Enough to make some charities extremely happy." She might not believe him even if he told her.

"I can guess that it's a large amount. Don't you think it would be wise to take care of your family members first?"

"Abigail, if you're referring to Cassie and Julie, I've

arranged for them in case something happens to me." She had a right to know at least that much.

"You had so much in your hands, and you're giving it all away."

"Yes, almost all."

"That's outrageous. Simply foolish!"

"Does it make me unworthy of Cassie?"

"It's not only about the money. It's also about your bad personal decisions. Such irresponsibility! You could ruin Cassie and Julie's lives. That's my objection to you, Obie."

"At least I'm not the barbarian I was." He smiled, hoping the irony might further soften her rigid heart.

She wasn't so easily cornered. "There's still plenty about you that I don't like."

Although he wanted to reply in kind, he said, "If I make an effort to work on my decision-making, do you think you might give our marriage your blessing?"

Her smile, a slight curvature at the corners of her mouth, surprised him. "I doubt I could, Obie. I've always needed to save face, and I wouldn't want my family thinking I'm wishy-washy in my thinking."

The absurdity of her admission left him speechless, but only for a moment. "You're ashamed to admit you were wrong about something?"

"I've never admitted to being wrong about anything."

He made a sword thrust. "You'll have to do that if you want your daughters back."

After toying with her cup for a while, she surprised him again. "How can I go about it?"

It was strange that a person so adept at manipulating others needed help deciding how to perform one of the most basic human interactions. He said, "You simply pick up a telephone and tell them you want to come and talk."

"I wouldn't have to *go* talk to them. I could tell them over the phone."

"Abigail, you and I have accomplished some important things today."

"Perhaps."

"Do you think we could have accomplished as much if we were talking on the telephone?"

She seemed to consider. "Probably not."

"So, you've answered your own question. There *is* something else, however. You need to apologize for things you've done, but you must also *listen* to Cassie and Laura, not talk *at* them. I mean, *really* listen. They're mature women with their own ideas and likes and dislikes. They need respect for who they are. Do you know what I mean?"

She was so quiet that he feared he might have overstepped. Abigail was a proud woman. For once, she met his eyes. "Maybe I do understand. Pinky has told me much the same thing. I suppose there's room for improvement. Maybe I should try."

"If you like, I'll talk to them first, pave the way for your call. Would you like me to do that?"

"I suppose so."

"I'm sure they'll agree to talk to you." He hoped that was true. "They'll forgive you if you ask them to."

"Do you think so?"

"I do."

"Forgiveness is hard, isn't it?"

She had asked his opinion; that was progress. "Yes, Abigail, it is. Sometimes we need to work at it. Take you and I. We've each been wronged by the other, and we had reasons for anger. Nevertheless, I forgive you, and I hope you'll forgive me. It'll make our lives so much better."

Obie said a silent prayer for her reciprocation. If she didn't bend now, it was unlikely she ever would. His conscience was clear. His concern, now, was for her.

She seemed to struggle for words. "I guess so."

"You forgive me, then?"

"Well, all right, I guess. I doubt we can ever be close friends, but to have peace in the family . . ." She paused as if she had no more to say.

Obie was satisfied. Considering with whom he was dealing, it was about as much as he could expect, at least for the present.

"Abigail, there's something I want to tell you. It's only fair that you should know. You're aware that Cassie and I are going to California to be married, but there's also another reason for going there. We'll look for Dan's girlfriend, Ly Yen. We've recently discovered that she lives there. As you know, she bore Dan's . . ." He stopped. He'd nearly said 'children.' It wasn't the right time for her to learn that truth.

"Dan couldn't find her."

"Yes, I know. And we know that Ly Yen was in touch with Charles Lansing. You know it too since he called you about it once." He stopped to gauge her reaction. She didn't flinch, and he hesitated at the manipulation of truth he was about to perform; it was for a good reason. "We believe she was in touch with Charles even later, after the birth."

Abigail sat up straighter. "Charles knew something of her whereabouts?"

"It seems so. He left word in a letter to me about Ly Yen going to San Francisco, and he said she may still be there."

"Did he know of her child?"

He ignored the question. "Cassie and I think we're on the verge of finding her. We think she still lives in San Francisco."

Abigail had a pained expression. "Do you think that's wise? Isn't it better for Dan to let it lie? Why upset his life? Have you asked him about this?"

"No, we haven't. He deserves to know, eventually, but Cassie and I will check it out first to save him from disappointment. She might even be married. I'm sure he'd want to see his offspring. I know I do. What about you, Abigail? Don't you want that pleasure?"

"No, I don't," she said quickly. "The last thing I'd want is a little Asian bastard running around my living room."

The meeting had brought progress, Obie believed, but there was still a long road to travel in affecting the moral rescue of Abigail Hunt. Were it not so sad, he might have laughed.

"It's only fair to tell you," Obie said, "that Cassie and I plan on bringing them to Stafford Rest if she wants to come. Dan will welcome it. We'd like your approval, as well."

"You do what you feel is best. I'll have no part in it."

"We'd like you not to tell Dan."

"I have no intention of talking to him about that. I don't think you'll find her, anyway. My grandson has had enough disappointment on that front. Does Laura know of your plans?"

"Not yet."

"Good. I'm not about to mention it to Danny, nor Laura either."

He nudged his chair back a few inches. "Abigail, I'm delighted we've had this discussion. I'll talk to Cassie and Laura so they know you'll call them. I'll do it tonight. You should call tomorrow. This is going to work out."

He was pleased to see the corners of her mouth turn up again—just slightly. He rose to leave.

"Wait," she said. "About the land?"

"Yes?"

"You said he didn't want it broken up. My plans for it would fit his wishes. The stone house will make a great lodge and restaurant with a lakefront for boaters. We can keep the rest of the grounds as they are, better even, with professional grooming."

"There's a place on the farm my grandparents loved dearly, a circle of woods in the pastureland, in the center. Dad wants it undisturbed but available for folks to visit."

"I know the spot. That's an easy fix. It can be made into a little park with benches."

"You understand, too, that there's a right-of-way to the cemetery above the road?"

"Yes, I know, and I'll honor that."

"Are you seriously interested in buying the farm, Abigail?"

"Do you think Ken would take less than that ridiculous asking price?"

Obie pretended to consider. "Maybe . . . some."

"Twenty percent less?"

"I don't know . . ."

"All right, ten percent? That's my best offer!"

"I can ask him." He tried, unsuccessfully, to hide his smile.

CHAPTER THIRTY-SIX

December 1970

"This cold drizzle started yesterday afternoon and has kept up ever since," Ernie Boswell complained as he escorted Obie and Cassie across the dining room and through a maze of already arranged tables. The warmth of Cassie's hand erased any negative thoughts about the day's gloom.

"Well, it *is* early December," Cassie said as they stood by the fireplace. "We're lucky it's not snow."

"It made for a dreary ride up from Albany last night," Obie said to Ernie. "We'd hoped our guests would wake up this morning able to appreciate the beauty of our Adirondack town. But I guess they'll have to wait a day or two for the full effects."

"Does this setup look okay?" Ernie asked. "There are fifty-three place settings with name tags. Why didn't you just go ahead and invite the whole town?"

Cassie laughed. "This is for our families and selected friends. That includes you, Ernie. You will join us, won't you?"

"Not for dinner, although I appreciate the invite."

"Is it because Abigail will be here?"

"I guess you didn't hear the news yet. She dropped the lawsuit against me last week right out of the blue. It could've knocked me down with a feather duster. I'd eat with you if I could, only I'm too busy. I'll join you for after-dinner drinks, though."

"You might want to look in on the before-dinner program as well," Obie said. "You'll find it interesting."

"Okay, I can do that."

"The arrangement looks good," Cassie said.

"I want to make sure I've got this right," Ernie said. "When everybody else is here and seated, we'll wait exactly ten minutes before ushering in your Asian lady and her children?"

"Yes, that's right." Obie pointed to three chairs. "They'll be seated here by Dan."

"They're his girlfriend and children, aren't they?"

"Can you keep that a secret, Ernie?"

393

"Sure. You know that." Ernie grinned.

"Well, you've got it right, but Dan doesn't know they're in town, and we want it to remain that way until they're brought into this room. He's not the only one who'll be surprised."

Ernie laughed. "I get the picture," he said. "Who's bringing them?"

"Dad and Angie. They'll pick them up at my house and bring them in through the kitchen door. They'll stay in the little back room you showed me until they're brought in. After that, we can all enjoy the reunion."

"All right. It'll work. People are going to start arriving in about half an hour."

Obie took Cassie's hand again. "Well, Mrs. Gainsworthy, here we are, standing on a pinnacle of suspense."

She snuggled up to him. "*Mrs. Gainsworthy!* I love it!"

"It took much too long to make it so. I love you, Cassie, so much."

Their ten days in California had been eventful. George Dulany, now semi-retired, invited them for Thanksgiving dinner. George took the time to goad Obie.

"You're a fine minister. Get back in the saddle."

"George, I have other irons in the fire." He told his friend about the new book on which he'd begun serious work and about his ideas for future ones."

"Yes, I sometimes forget you are an accomplished writer. That's an excellent way to serve, although I know you'd be a great pastor."

"I have to do what I feel called to do. My inclinations are toward writing, but I must remain open to whatever God puts before me."

George said, "Obie, you do seem at peace with yourself. That's a change from the last time we talked."

"It's Cassie. She's reshaping my life. There have been other events as well." He told George about his trip to Europe, including the visits to battle sites. On impulse, he revealed his dialogue with Abigail.

George listened, nodding occasionally before saying, "Forgiveness is a wonderful thing. God patterned it with his grace. When we learn to forgive ourselves and others, our lives change. I'm most happy for you."

George married them the following day at Greenleaf

Methodist Church in a simple ceremony in the Sweetwater Chapel. Obie had chosen the church sanctuary, but Cassie convinced him the chapel was more suitable. Only later did it occur to him that she might have insisted on that because Obie and Annie had been married in the sanctuary.

There were only a few at their wedding, mostly churchmen from the area whom Obie had known while he served at Greenleaf and a few members with whom George could get in touch. To Obie and Cassie's delight, Hershel and Virginia Silverman attended. The dynamic couple seemed unchanged, except that Hershel now used a cane.

A minister friend, who served as an impromptu best man, told Obie, "We've been looking for your Vietnamese lady. She's actually a member of one of our churches. Here's her address," he said as he slipped a piece of paper into Obie's hand.

Finding her at the San Francisco address had been simple. Ly Yen held onto Obie and sobbed when she remembered who he was.

It took little time to make travel arrangements for her and the twins. Obie called Ernie to make reservations for a "celebration." He didn't explain everything over the phone; he would do it later. Cassie called Laura to help contact everyone on the list she read over the phone. Laura assumed, and Cassie didn't enlighten her, that it was a dinner for Obie and Cassie.

After two days in Berkeley, they went to the Napa house, which Cassie loved as much as he did. Then, coming home, Ly Yen and the children were on the same flight, simplifying matters.

Now, they were minutes away from reuniting Dan with his lost love and the children he knew nothing about. "We're doing the right thing, aren't we?" Obie asked Cassie.

"Yes, we are. Indeed, we are."

"Some of your family will be uncomfortable."

"That's their problem."

People started arriving, greeting Cassie and Obie and wishing them well. Tom Matthews said he was surprised to see them there so early. "I thought you'd make an entrance after everyone was here."

The Reverent Carl Enslow was chatting with other clusters of people but edging his way toward Obie; he would avoid Carl if he could, for he knew the direction their conversation would take. Obie would tell him soon that there was little chance he would ever apply to the conference. His resolute decision was driven by the conviction that he could reach far more people through his writing than from a pulpit. Nevertheless, he mustn't be smug; he must always listen to the Spirit's direction.

Laura arrived with Dan. She chatted with them before going to the bar for a glass of wine. Cassie had talked to her earlier that day and told Obie she felt guilty. "Laura worked to help set this up," she said. We should have told her what we were doing. She'll be surprised."

"I think it's a good surprise. She'll love her grandchildren. She's wanted Dan to find Ly Yen."

Pinky and Abigail arrived after nearly all the seats were filled. Pinky shook Obie's hand. "Welcome to the family, son," he said, "although you'll find it a dysfunctional one. But you already know that."

"Pinky, keep your voice down," Abigail said. "The whole world doesn't need to know our business." Obie imagined he saw the hint of a smile. But probably not, he concluded.

Abigail extended her cheek for Cassie to kiss. She'd made a tenuous peace with her daughters; a start, Obie believed.

When Ken, Angie, and Julie entered the room, Obie and Cassie took their places at the head table. Ken raised a thumb for Obie to see.

Obie stood and clinked the side of his water glass. Dan, next to him, said, "There are three empty chairs here. Shouldn't we wait?"

Obie couldn't resist saying, "They'll have occupants soon enough."

Someone else clinked their glass, and the room became silent. "Speech, speech!" Chuck Hinky called out.

"No speeches," Obie said. "I simply want to thank you all for coming on such short notice. Cassie and I appreciate it. There aren't many secrets in Stafford Rest, are there?" Scattered laughter came from around the room. "You must know that we've been in love for some time. Now, it's official." A cheer went up, and people clapped. "As soon as drinks are served, I'll have a few more words to say." There were good-natured boos and some laughter.

"Who's still to come?" Dan asked, indicating the empty chairs.

Cassie looked ready to say something, but Obie cut her off. "Surprise guests. Wait, you'll see."

A few minutes later, Obie again called for quiet. He spoke as clearly as he could. "Ladies and gentlemen, we have some out-of-town guests joining us tonight." He nodded to Gertrude Buress, one of their waitresses. Gertrude disappeared into the kitchen. "They'll come out in a moment. While we're waiting, I want to tell a story some of you may not have heard. You know I was a minister for a time and served my country as a chaplain. While in Vietnam, I ran across Dan Williamson here. He was in a hospital, banged up, and feeling sorry for himself. He asked me to look for a girl he'd become rather attached to. He told me that her name was Ly Yen."

Dan tugged Obie's sleeve and whispered, "What are you doing? Are you trying to embarrass me?"

Obie ignored him and continued. "I did find her, and I could see why he liked her so much. She was a real sweetheart. The only thing was, they lost touch with each other. Dan has tried for years to locate her but without success."

"Obie, what's going on?" Dan demanded.

Obie said, "Dan, I want you to know that while Cassie and I were in San Francisco, we located Ly Yen . . . and she's here tonight."

Obie signaled, and Ly Yen emerged from the kitchen holding the twins' hands. She wore a long black dress cut low in front. Her dark hair was held back with a red ribbon. Obie gasped at her elegant beauty. The children were immaculate, the boy in a blue suit with a white tie and the girl in a red dress with her hair held back like her mother's.

"What beautiful children," someone said.

Dan's countenance was one of disbelief. Seconds went by before he found his voice.

"Oh, dear God! Ly Yen . . . it's really you!" He jumped to his feet so fast that his chair toppled backward.

As the two embraced, there was applause from around the room. "How wonderful," someone said. Obie stole a glance at Abigail. Her face showed alarm. Laura was smiling and had risen.

Ly Yen was crying. "Oh, Dan," she said several times. "Oh, my dear one, it has taken so long. Do you still love me?"

"I do! I do! I will forever."

The whole room was animated. People stood, trying to get a better view. Laura hurried to stand behind them. She placed a hand on each child; her expression alternated between confusion and joy; her eyes were filled with tears.

Obie said loud enough for everyone to hear, "Ly Yen, would you like to introduce your children?"

"Yes, I would," she said, and the room quickly grew silent. "First though, I must say to my Dan, here are your children you gave me by our love."

Laura now had an arm around each child. Obie had never doubted her acceptance of her grandchildren. Nevertheless, the secret about to be revealed might cause her discomfort.

Dan knelt beside the children, tears on his cheeks. "Two children, twins . . . a boy and a girl. I can't believe this." He stood and said to Obie, "Thank you. Thank you, my friend. Thank you both, Obie and Cassie." He knelt so his face was on the same level as the children's. "What are your names?" he asked.

Cassie told Ly Yen, "Go ahead and introduce your children to all these people."

"I would be pleased," Ly Yen said. "Come here, children. Dan, you come, too, and stand beside us."

There was more applause. People were enjoying it; nearly everyone. Obie could see Abigail edging her way toward the door. Her face was red. Pinky gripped her arm and held her back.

"Everybody," Ly Yen said as though she were used to doing it every day, "I want you to meet the children of your good friend, Dan Williamson, and myself."

Dan said, loud enough for everyone to hear, "And I want you all to know that Ly Yen and I will be married before the week is out . . . if she'll have me."

"Oh yes, she will." Ly Yen said, laughing.

"Shut up, Dan, and let your woman talk," Chet Boswell said.

Ly Yen stood up straight. "Here are our children, *Laura and Obadiah*. Dan has honored me with them, and I have honored their grandparents with their names." She stopped and waited. The room had grown hushed.

Dan whispered just loud enough that Obie could hear, "Ly Yen, sweetheart, it's a nice gesture, but my father is . . ."

Dan turned to look at Obie, a question in his eyes. He swung back toward his mother. Obie could see that her Mona Lisa countenance was going to reveal little. Dan turned once more toward Obie. This time, the dawn of understanding lit his face, and he smiled. "Oh! I see!"

It was the easiest thing in the world to return Dan's smile.

The End

A LAST WORD

All characters in this book are works of the imagination and are not meant to resemble any person or persons, living or dead. A few prominent people mentioned have no interaction with the fictional characters.

My imaginary characters move through this time in our history (1952–1970) against the backdrop of real-world events. They deal with human fears, joys, and anxieties; they experience love, hate, betrayal, loss of faith, and sometimes redemption.

Except for the imaginary villages of Stafford Rest and Evergreen, both set in the real Adirondack Park of New York State, the book is true to geography and topography. A few unnamed settings throughout are composites of real places.

This book is the sequel to *Wine for Tomorrow*, the novel that took Obadiah (Obie) Gainsworthy from his hometown of Stafford Rest to the war in Italy and finally to the Bay Area of California. In this volume, he has regained lost faith and intends to allow God to use him as he wishes.

But Obie suffers not only from the bitter disappointments of his love life but also from the scars of war. And two factors cast a shadow over his peace of mind and his ability to follow his duel "callings" of writing career and pastoral ministry: He still harbors hate for Laura Hunt and her mother over their betrayal; his guilt for having killed an innocent German prisoner in Italy is never far from his mind. It's a love story, too; Obie's love for Cassie is the glue that holds things together.

Of course, these situations are fictional, and I hope my creative solutions are believable. I have tried to be true to the theme I established in *Wine for Tomorrow:* "Love and hate cannot exist side by side."

Before *Wine for Tomorrow*, I published two non-fiction books, each winning a *Silver Medal for Biography* from the *Military Writers Society of America.*

Rupert Pratt
2023

ABOUT THE AUTHOR

Rupert Pratt grew up on a small farm in Salt Rock, West Virginia. He graduated from Barboursville High School in 1951, and after an enlistment in the United Air Force, earned a BA degree from Marshall College (now Marshall University) in 1957 and a MA degree in 1959. He married Mildred Mereness from Schenectady, New York, and taught in the Schenectady City School District for thirty-six years. Rupert and Millie have two sons, Gregory and Jonathan, and three grandchildren, Elizabeth, Nathan, and Andrew. Millie passed away in 2013.

In addition to *Touching the Ancient One: A True Story of Tragedy and Reunion* (2006, 2021), he is the author of *Tri-State Heroes of '45: Together With a Year in the Life of a West Virginia Farm Family* (2020). Information about Rupert Pratt's books and other related subjects is available on his website: https://www.touchingancientone.com.

Touching the Ancient One—A True Story of Tragedy and Reunion is my story of a 1954 Air Force C-47 crash on Kesugi Ridge in South-Central Alaska that took the lives of ten military service members; I was one of six survivors. It's also the story of a reunion forty-two years later bringing together crash survivors, their families, families of the victims, and civilian and Air Force personnel from that time. There followed other reunions, the erection of plaques honoring the men who perished, a high military honor for rescuer Cliff Hudson, and a 1998 return to the mountain crash site.

This is a reprint of the 2006 edition with some updated information.

Touching the Ancient One
was awarded a Silver Medal from
Military Writers Society of America.

https://www.amazon.com/Rupert-Pratt/e/B002BMD2DM

Independent Review:

Tri-State Heroes of '45: Together With a Year in the Life of a West Virginia Farm Family resurrects selected local, national, and world events of 1945, but hangs on a framework of diary entries of Pratt's mother, who was thirty-seven that year, while Pratt himself was only twelve. The daily life on their little farm in

Salt Rock, West Virginia, presents a unique mosaic that tells an unforgettable tale of faith, family, and hope on the home front. Pratt honors military service members of the Tri-State area of West Virginia, Ohio, and Kentucky with 'mini-stories' from Huntington, West Virginia newspapers of that year [1945 Huntington Herald Dispatch and Huntington Herald Advertiser]."

There are over 8,000 personal names in the imdex.

Tri-State Heroes of '45 was awarded a 2021 *Military Writers Society of America* Silver Medal in Memoirs/Biography.

Tri-State Heroes of '45 can be ordered on Amazon:

https://www.amazon.com/Rupert-Pratt/e/B002BMD2D

Love and hate battle for control between two Adirondack families: One family enjoys wealth; the other struggles for survival. Obie, a child of the Depression, loves two sisters: Cassie is his best friend and confidant; Laura is the one he's determined to marry. Abigail, the girls' mother, will do anything to prevent that. Suffering bitter betrayal, Obie is cast into a world ravaged by war. This story plays out over the diverse areas of the New York Adirondacks, the boot of Italy, and the Bay Area of California. Above all, it's a story about a young man's loss of faith and his convoluted journey to reclaim it.

Wine for Tomorrow can be ordered on Amazon:

https://www.amazon.com/Rupert-Pratt/e/B002BMD2DM

Or in bookstores.